SCARS FROM
A MEMOIR

Marni Mann

Booktrope Editions
Seattle WA 2012

Cover Design by Greg Simanson

Edited by Dawn Higham

This is a work of fiction. Names, characters, places, brands, media, and incidents are either the product of the author's imagination or are used fictitiously. Any resemblance to similarly named places or to persons living or deceased is unintentional.

ISBN 978-1-935961-64-2

For further information regarding permissions, please contact info@booktrope.com.

Library of Congress Control Number: 2012912541

DEDICATION

To Brian, my everything,
my dreams are all possible because of you.

ACKNOWLEDGMENTS

From the very first word I typed of *Memoirs Aren't Fairytales* to the last sentence of *Scars from a Memoir*, you've never left my side, Mom. You gave me more than just your shoulder, your time, and your advice. You gave me everything I needed. Dad, your smile was my fuel. James Watson, my voice of reasoning, you turned ugly into brilliance, panic into excitement; you supported every step I took. Melissa Roske, once again you made my words sparkle; you encouraged me to find what was buried within and helped me bring it to the surface so my best would be revealed. Matthew Merrick, you treated this novel like family, loving, nourishing, and coddling every page, and that will never be forgotten. Jody Ruth and Jo Hall, lots of X's for everything you both have done for me. Jesse Freeman, Steven Luna, Tracey Hansen, Gale Martin, and Tess Hardwick, your words wrap around me and squeeze me like a hug. Katherine Sears, Ken Shear, and Heather Ludviksson, thank you for believing in me. And finally, to my team Krista Basham, Dawn Higham, and Greg Simanson, you gave this novel everything it needed—a life, a face, a voice, a clear direction—and I couldn't have done this without you.

SILHOUETTE OF ADDICTION

Addicted, sleepwalking through life, a wasted youth imprisoned
   by the mind.

Once my soul was incarcerated,
no sun, no wind, just a steel breeze.

My first taste of freedom,
the sun hints at light,
the rays dance along the jagged edge of scars.

The moment after the storm,
emotions no longer blue,
my skyline, a gray silhouette.

Will I dream again,
learn to live again?

Too many ghosts,
too few enjoyed breaths,
but one sings the loudest,
one inhalation, the deepest.

Am I a runaway train,
or am I the track?

Sunlight plays with dark skies,
a tortured soul, an addict, or the silhouette of addiction.

—*James Watson*

CHAPTER ONE

I had been running to the toilet every few minutes. If I didn't leave the bathroom soon, I'd miss Dr. Cohen calling my name. The ceremony had started twenty minutes ago, and a lump filled my throat. My chest fluttered. Something held me back.

With my hands on each side of the sink, I leaned forward, my nose inches from the mirror. The acne and blemishes had cleared. My tangled mess of hair had been chopped to my chin. Blue eyes stared back with unpinned pupils. Most of the signs were gone.

"Are you ready, Nicole?" Allison asked. The bathroom door was open, and her head poked through.

"I'll be there in a second."

She smiled. "I'll see you out there."

For the first time in the eight years I'd lived in Boston, there was a glimpse of the old me. The girl I'd been before getting raped and dropping out of college. I looked…normal. That word was as foreign as pretty, but there was some of that, too. The change was more than skin deep, though. Energy pulsed in my veins. My head was clear; my limbs felt attached.

My hand itched, and as I scratched, my eyes followed. In the middle of my palm, I pictured a mound of dope. I wanted to kiss every grain, craving the numbness.

I shook my head, pushing the hunger away.

Looking in the mirror again, I straightened my collar and smoothed the stray hairs that had curled from the humidity. The speech I'd written was in my pocket. I took it out, tucking it under my fingers.

The hallway was empty; the only noises were my clicking heels and my breathing. Allison had told me to breathe in through my nose and out through my mouth when I was feeling anxious. My gag reflex set in during the exhale. She hadn't told me how to breathe when I was nauseous.

The back door of the rec room was locked, so I went around to the front and through the open doorway. Rows of folding metal chairs ran like bars around the aisle that coursed through the middle. There were a hundred seats, and they were all full.

The counselors sat to the right of the podium, facing the crowd; the other graduates to the left—they'd already completed their speeches. Their skin ranged from dark to light, wrinkled to smooth. Like cancer, addiction could affect anyone. I wasn't the oldest. I felt ancient.

Dr. Cohen, the head counselor, announced my name and then took a seat next to Allison, who gave me a wink.

To keep my brain busy, I counted each step down the aisle. I didn't look at the people who turned in my direction. I forced my lips to smile and tried to keep my feet steady by focusing on what was in front of me. I knew how an athlete felt when she won a gold medal; tomorrow would be another race.

"Hello," I said into the microphone. My hands shook as I unfolded the piece of paper. The light blue lines on the page turned to waves; my handwritten words, swirls of black. Everything was spinning. An older man uncrossed his legs, then crossed them again. A woman coughed. In my head, a clock ticked.

I held each side of the podium. "My name is Nicole Brown," I said. "And today, I'm ninety-three days sober."

Once everyone stopped clapping, I spoke about moving from Bangor to Boston. How Eric, my best friend, and I had become addicted to coke; weed and alcohol weren't strong enough. Blow led to heroin. The tingles, sparks, and melting were my love, and I'd fallen for the needle too. I told them how I'd spent the next five years: tricking and stealing for drug money, getting shot in the chest, and having a miscarriage. My arrest had made front-page news, but I told them about it anyway.

Cold, hard truth poured from my mouth. I bared my heart, and that was something I never thought I'd do. The faces in the crowd weren't judging my honesty; they were filled with trust and kindness. My chest relaxed, and my hands stopped shaking. This was the release I needed. As I glanced around the room at the wives, husbands, parents, grandparents, and friends of the addicted, I crumpled up the piece of paper. They deserved my eye contact and emotion.

I ended my speech with the last night I'd spent on the streets before serving two-and-a-half years in jail. Michael, my brother, had found me on the corner and tried to stop my pimp from beating me. The sound of the gun going off, how I held Michael in my arms while his blood pooled over me. And the doctor's final words, "Michael didn't survive."

Tissues wiped noses, and sniffles echoed. The eyes looking back at me dripped with tears, but the eyes didn't belong to addicts. They belonged to victims. People who watched, helplessly, as those they loved were swallowed by addiction. They knew this story all too well.

Dr. Cohen hugged me and whispered, "I'm so proud of you." In my hand, he placed a coin with an engraved triangle. On one side of the triangle was *sobriety*, on the other side, *anniversary*, and in the middle, *90*.

The coin felt cool against my sweaty skin, and the color matched the ring I wore on my right hand. It was from Henry, the son of my best friend Claire—he'd given it to me right after Claire died in the hotel fire. Told me to wear the ring when I got sober; I'd just put it on this morning.

After Dr. Cohen thanked all the guests for coming and invited them for lunch, my parents walked over to me. They had visited twice while I was in prison, but I hadn't seen them on the outside since the night Michael was murdered. Their brown hair was heavily mixed with gray. Wrinkles flowed from their forehead to their cheeks, and puffy, dark bags hung under their eyes.

Allison had explained how parents were affected by their children's addiction: sleepless nights, worrying about the health and whereabouts of their child, and constant fear of them dying. My parents were grieving Michael's death too. It showed.

Mom hugged me first, filling my nose with her vanilla and fabric softener scents; aftershave and mouthwash for Dad. Their smells were the one thing that hadn't changed.

"Are you hungry?" I asked.

They shrugged.

I brought them to the cafeteria. I didn't know what else to do with them and placed a sandwich and chips on my tray. My parents grabbed fruit cups, and we found seats at the end of a long table.

"We didn't know..." Mom said. Her fruit sat untouched. Dad's too. A quarter of my sandwich was already eaten.

When I'd gotten to Step Nine—make direct amends with the people I'd harmed—I'd sent my parents a letter telling them about my past with heroin. The only thing I'd left out was my miscarriage.

"I'd already hurt you enough," I said. "I didn't know how to tell you this too."

The way I had killed my baby, a shot of dope too strong for her little body, was as sick as sticking a clothes hanger up my crotch. But I was asking them to trust me again. With truth came trust.

Dad covered my hand with his. "If you don't learn how to forgive yourself, you'll never stay sober."

My parents were seeing a therapist and attending Nar-Anon meetings. Dad's words matched Allison's. But were they going to learn how to forgive me?

"What are your plans?" Mom asked.

"Tomorrow morning, I'm moving into sober living."

Dad studied me. "Is that nearby?"

"It's an apartment in the North End," I said, wiping my mouth with my sleeve. My lip gloss smeared onto the cotton. It was deep red, the color of blood. My mind wandered, the same question repeating in my head: Would I ever be able to forgive?

"Cole?"

My eyes met Dad's.

"We lost you there for a second. Are you OK?" he asked.

I cleared my throat. "What was your question again?"

"Will you have roommates?"

I told them I'd have a housemother and three other roommates, and I was required to get a job, keep curfew, and test clean. Sober living was a six-month program. When it was over, I'd have to find my own apartment.

"With everything that's happened here," Dad said, "do you really think Boston is the right place for you?"

"Until I finish out my probation, Boston's home."

It didn't matter where I lived; the memories would follow me everywhere. But I wanted to stay not only because of my probation. I had so many questions about my brother, and none of them had been answered.

"You're always welcome to come live with us," Dad said.

Mom stared at her fruit cup. She didn't say anything. She didn't have to. Her raised eyebrows and pursed lips were enough.

Jail had been my punishment for getting busted with heroin, and while I was in there, I did a ninety-day substance abuse program. I fucked up again, trading cigs, food, and sex for whatever pills or powder I could get in the prison yard. It was a lonely place.

A few weeks before my release date, I'd asked my social worker to get me into rehab. I wanted to face my other crime—living in Boston without Michael—with clean eyes. The memories and nightmares weren't a big enough sentence for getting my brother killed. Neither was the look on my mother's face.

It was going to take a lot more than jail and rehab for my parents to forgive me...if they ever did. They'd heard my apologies, but my words had only proven to be lies. I had to show them what I'd learned from being in the dark, that I was never going back there again.

"Thanks for the offer, Dad," I said. "But I don't think Bangor is the right place for me."

He nodded. "Your cheeks have filled out," he said. "And your color is coming back."

I'd gained only a few pounds while I was in prison. The food was so bad. In the last three months, I'd put on fifteen, but I was still underweight.

"You guys look good, too," I said.

Mom glanced over at Dad; her forehead creased as she raised her eyebrows again. Then her eyes moved to me. "How are you going to get a job? If they run a background check—"

"I don't know," I said.

Dad told me I should go back to school. If I could show an employer that I'd gotten my shit straight and finished my bachelor's degree, they might overlook my criminal record. Mom asked if I could apply at the rehab center. They weren't hiring, but even if they had been, I'd need a year of sobriety before they'd consider me.

I munched on the rest of my sandwich.

* * *

After lunch, my parents had to leave. Dad had work in the morning, and Bangor was a four-hour drive. I walked them to their car and handed them a piece of paper with my new address and phone number. Mom put the paper in her purse, and they both hugged me. Dad squeezed tighter than Mom.

When I got back inside, I asked Allison if we could talk. She took me into her office, and I told her about the conversation I'd had with my parents. She asked how I felt. That was the way she started and ended all our therapy sessions.

"I thought they'd tell me they were proud of me."

"They are," she said. "Trust me, they are."

I didn't know if that was true, but I was proud of myself. Ninety-three days was the longest I'd ever gone without using. In rehab, we were told to take one day at a time.

Today I was sober, but tomorrow wasn't here yet.

CHAPTER TWO

I didn't have much to pack. I'd left prison wearing the same sweatshirt and sweatpants I'd gotten at the hospital the night Michael died. In rehab, I was given two pairs of jeans and three shirts because I didn't have any other clothes. I threw it all in a trash bag along with my soap and toothbrush. When I'd lived on the streets, a thin, white plastic bag used to hold everything I owned.

After I said good-bye to the staff, Diem and I went to the parking lot and got in the van. She was an ex-junkie, too, and looked no older than twelve, standing less than five feet tall, with a flat chest and acne. She was twenty-five. She had also been honored in yesterday's ceremony and was going to be my roomie in sober living.

Because I'd gone straight from prison to rehab, I hadn't seen the city in almost three years. But every night I'd looked at the skyline tattooed on my foot. I'd gotten the tattoo not too long after Eric and I had moved to Boston. It represented how well I'd been doing since the rape and how free I'd felt since leaving Bangor. Drugs had already owned me by then. The inked buildings on my foot were marred with tracks that hadn't healed. Heroin had a hold of me. It wasn't ever going to let go.

In rehab, I wondered if I'd feel the tiniest taste of freedom when I saw the real skyline. I didn't. Fog covered most of the high-rises. It was an overcast day.

Stan, the rehab tech, double-parked outside our apartment. It was a six-story brick building, snuggled between a dry cleaners and nail salon, and a meat market was on the first floor. Slabs of beef hung in the window, and men in white jackets worked behind the counter. As I got out of the van, I was hit with the scent of spaghetti sauce and garlic—one of my favorite smells. The North End was the Italian section of Boston, and restaurants boarded both sides of the street. As long as I didn't get kicked out of sober living, I'd be back to a healthy weight soon.

Tiffany, our housemother, met us on the second-floor landing. She was a little bigger than me but fit, with long, blonde hair that curled at the ends and makeup that looked like it had been done at the beauty counter of a department store. She showed us her bedroom, the bathroom, and then the room Diem and I would be sharing. Diem placed her suitcases on the bed by the door. I dumped my trash bag on the twin by the window and fit all my clothes in the top drawer of the dresser. I gave Diem the other five.

Once Diem unpacked, Tiffany called us into the living room. We took a seat on the couch, and Tiffany sat on the floor in front of us. She was twenty-eight and told us she'd been addicted to coke for five years. After two interventions and four attempts at rehab, she'd been sober for three years.

"Remember, I know what you're going through, so I want you to feel comfortable coming to me for anything," Tiffany said.

When she talked, her eyes went wide as though she'd popped an E pill. They were the same color green as Karam's, one of my old Johns.

"Now about the rules," Tiffany said. "They're simple. Attend three meetings a week, pass my random drug tests, keep the apartment clean, get a job, and be in by your midnight curfew."

"Midnight?" Diem asked.

Tiffany raised her eyebrows. "Is that a problem?"

If I had friends or a place to go, the curfew might have been a problem. I didn't have either.

"What happens if we break the rules?" Diem asked.

"You'll be kicked out," Tiffany said. "Rent and groceries are a hundred a week. You have three weeks until your first payment is due, and if it's late, you'll be kicked out for that too."

Diem said she was going to our room to search for jobs on her parents' laptop. Tiffany's cell phone rang, and she left the room to answer it.

There was nothing in my room that was going to get me a job. Since living in Boston, I'd worked at two different places. I waitressed at Mark's bar and smoked dope in the bathroom until he busted me and took my stash. I tried to steal it back, but he caught me and cornered me in the hallway. Eric found us while Mark's hands and lips were all over me, and he beat Mark's ass. I was also a maid at the hotel we lived in, but when Eric OD'd and died in our room, the owner threw me out. Everyone else I knew who could hook me up with a job was either dead or in jail.

"Need help?" Tiffany asked. She stood beside the couch, holding a glass of water.

"I need a résumé, right?"

She nodded.

I didn't have one. I didn't have a cell phone either, and until a few weeks ago I didn't even have a driver's license. I'd left it at my first rehab center. What was I going to write? College dropout, junkie, and ex-con still on probation? Even a drug dealer wouldn't hire me.

In the corner of the living room was a desk with a computer and printer, and Tiffany sat in front of it. "Let's see what we can find."

By the time I brought over a chair, she had already pulled up an employment site.

"Do any of these categories sound interesting?" she asked.

The first one was administration. Working in an office where I'd have to answer phones, do filing, and use techy gadgets wasn't my thing. "Are any coffee shops hiring?"

I'd worked at a coffee shop in college and made sure the carafes were full at rehab. Serving caffeine would be safer than waitressing at a restaurant. Alcohol wasn't my drug of choice, but being around it every day would be too tempting.

Tiffany found eight ads. Each said to email a résumé and that they'd contact me if they were interested. I didn't have email, so she helped me set up an account. Instead of putting together a résumé, I wrote a paragraph explaining my job at Mark's bar and the coffee shop, and then clicked send.

"Seven more to go," she said.

I pecked at the keyboard; I was supposed to meet with my parole officer in a few hours. "This is going to take all day." I didn't have all day.

"No, it won't; I'll teach you how to copy and paste."

Her words were another reminder of how much I'd forgotten.

She took control of the mouse, copying the email addresses from the ads and the paragraph I'd written. When all eight emails were sent, she asked if I wanted to practice interviewing.

I moved over to the couch, leaned back into the pillows, and curled my toes around the edge of the table.

"Is that how you're going to sit?"

I put my feet on the floor.

"Why do you want this job?"

Staying busy would help keep my mind off heroin. If I didn't get a job, I'd be kicked out of sober living. I couldn't say either of those. "Next question."

"Nicole—"

"We'll come back to that one."

"OK, then tell me what makes you a good candidate for this job?"

"I have the experience. I'm a hard worker."

I could cook up a shot of dope in less than thirty seconds. Finding a vein took a little longer because most of them had collapsed, but I would keep poking or stick muscle if I had to.

My mouth began to water.

"What are your skills?" she asked.

Seeing the flash—when my blood crept into the chamber— would boost my adrenaline, and my heart would beat really fast. The tingles and rush would start as soon as the needle was empty.

"I know you must have some, Nicole, so what are they?"

My palms were sweating.

I slid to the edge of the couch and rubbed my hands over the fabric. My heels tapped the carpet. I felt my body sway back and forth.

"Where's your head at?"

I looked up at her. Slowly. "I want to use."

"But you want to stay clean?"

"Yes—"

"And you want a job?"

"I need a job," I said.

"Tell me why."

"I'll end up back in jail if I don't start working soon. And my brother...I need to stay sober for him."

"So your brother is behind you, supporting—"

"My brother's dead." I took a deep breath. "My pimp shot him, but he should have shot me instead."

She came over to the couch and put her arm around me. "I know this is a lot, but you're doing great."

The lump in my throat was choking me.

"Your brother is looking down at you right now, and I know he's so proud." She wrapped her other arm around me, and I squeezed back as hard as I could. When she released me, she took my hand and led me to the front door. "We're going to a meeting."

"But I have—"

"Meeting first; then we'll go see your parole officer together."

* * *

The other girls trickled in while Tiffany and I were making dinner. At some point during the afternoon, Diem had gone to hand deliver résumés and landed a job at a boutique. Another roommate, Ashley—a meth addict—worked at a music store; Kathy—an alcoholic—was an assistant baker at a café. The three of them were at the kitchen table, comparing their jobs and hourly wages. The only good thing that had happened to me was that after the NA meeting, Tiffany had offered to be my sponsor and I accepted. I wasn't sure at first if living with my sponsor was the best thing. But I wouldn't have to worry about finding her—she'd always be available to talk at midnight, and maybe having her so close would keep me track free.

I stood at the stove with my back to them and stirred the rice.

"I think you can stop mixing," Tiffany said from behind me.

The rice had formed into a big clump, glued to the middle of the pan. I lifted the pan off the burner, and when I turned around, Tiffany was still standing close.

"Don't get discouraged; your time will come too," she whispered.

Time was something I didn't have. Every hour that passed, I was that much closer to getting kicked out of sober living. The street would become my home again. Then I'd end up back in jail because I'd be too high to meet with my parole officer.

Diem had left rehab only ten hours ago and already found a job. Ashley and Kathy found theirs on their first day out, too. They all had it so easy. It was as though their addiction had merely been a pause in their real life, and now they were back living again. Not me. Eight years of using wasn't a pause; it was almost a third of my life. And heroin was going to stay with me forever. If the coffee shop owners ran a background check, it would take me more than two weeks to find work.

* * *

I went to bed before everyone else. I really wanted to go for a walk, but I knew I'd end up in Roxbury, buying dope from some street pusher. Sober living wasn't much different from jail except that my desire to stay clean was what kept me locked inside. Not just for Michael—for me too.

When I closed my eyes, mounds of powder filled the darkness. We didn't have a TV in our room or any pictures; except for the poster of the Twelve Steps above the dresser, there was nothing to look at. I'd memorized all the Steps. I'd rehearsed them at the NA meeting today. What I wanted to read was the emblem stamped on a wax-paper packet of junk that would tell me what brand it was and how strong the hit should be.

My roommates laughed at the TV in the living room. Cars swished by and honked. Doors slammed.

I got out of bed; the lights from the buildings sparkled against the window glass. Clickety-click. The pedestrians on the sidewalk rhythmically sped by. Maybe I was just used to everything moving so slow in prison. And when I'd been high...

I shivered.

My bedroom was as cold as the air outside. It was lonely. My sweatpants and T-shirt weren't warm enough. But I'd always been so warm. Even when I'd been naked, a toasty feeling was in my veins.

I put on a sweatshirt.

I was still freezing.

The flood of memories should have been enough to put me to sleep. My body was the only thing that was exhausted.

* * *

When I came out of my bedroom the next morning, everyone had left for work except Tiffany. She was in her pajamas making coffee. I grumbled a good morning and logged onto the computer, where two new emails were waiting in my inbox. Both were replies from coffee shops, saying they'd like me to call them to schedule an interview.

I gulped down a mug of coffee and brushed my teeth, hoping my voice wouldn't sound like I'd just woken up. Tiffany sat next to me on the couch and watched me dial the first number. I was told to come in at four and bring a résumé.

I hung up with the second manager and put the phone on the table. "He wants me there at two."

"What's with the frown?" she asked. "You've got two interviews lined up."

"I'm just nervous and…"

"I'll help you get ready. If you need clothes, you can borrow mine."

I didn't ask how she knew. I just nodded my head and smiled, but it quickly faded when we got to work on my résumé. Tiffany's fingers hovered over the keyboard, waiting for me to give her something to type. I told her the name of the college coffee shop and Mark's bar and the dates I'd worked there. Everything about the hotel was too fuzzy—the name and how long I'd been a maid—so I decided not to mention it.

"What were your responsibilities at the coffee shop?"

"I poured coffee."

"And at the bar?"

"I smoked a lot of heroin and was too high to work, so the other waitresses delivered my food for me."

She glanced toward me. Her lips were rubbing together, and the corners of her eyes pointed down. "Go hop in the shower."

"But—"

Her lips changed to a smile. "I'll take care of this; don't worry about it."

I silently thanked her and went into the bathroom.

* * *

After Tiffany dressed me in her clothes, painted my face with her makeup, and straightened my hair with her flattening iron, she hugged me good-bye and wished me luck. Once I stepped outside, the cold March air ransacked my body and I tied the strings of her coat around me. The coffee shop was on the other side of the North End. I didn't have money to take the train; I walked. Her black boots rubbed just enough to give me blisters on the back of my feet. The pinching gave me something to focus on. I could handle pain better than nerves.

When I got to the counter, I asked one of the girls if I could speak to the manager. I couldn't remember his name. I should have written it down.

"He's out sick today," she said. "Can someone else help you?"

"I just talked to him this morning, and he asked me to come in for an interview."

"You must mean Al, the owner, not the manager," she said and picked up the phone by the register. She hit a few buttons and spoke into the receiver. "Your two o'clock is here."

After twenty-two deep breaths, a middle-aged man appeared at the counter. He introduced himself, and I followed him through the kitchen and down a long hallway. Just as I stepped inside his office, the door shut behind me and the man sitting at the desk turned toward me.

The heels of the boots wobbled, and I gasped. What the hell was Mark, my old boss from the bar, doing here? I glanced over my shoulder. Al was standing next to the door with his arms crossed.

"What do you want?" I asked.

"You look good," Mark said. "I was hoping jail would have that effect on you."

Al moved across the room and unfolded two chairs that were resting against the wall. He offered me a seat before he sat down.

"To answer your question, my brother called for a reference," Mark said, nodding in Al's direction. "And I told him I'd like to sit in on the interview."

Before becoming an addict, I would have been surprised that Mark's brother owned this coffee shop. Nothing really shocked me anymore.

My eyes shifted between the two men. "Why?"

"Nicole, please take a seat," Al said.

In case I needed to bolt, I slid the chair closer to the door and sat on the edge of the seat.

"I wanted to see how you are doing since you've been released," Mark said. He looked at his hands, which were intertwined on his lap, and then his eyes closed. When they reopened, he said, "I care about you."

"But you fired me."

"You didn't give me much of a choice, did you?"

Before he'd canned me, I thought I was holding it together. But Mark was right. I was a mess. I barely made it through my shifts, used the other servers to wait on my tables, and nodded out in the bathroom during my breaks.

"Are you clean?" Al asked.

"Ninety-five days," I said.

"In that case, I need someone to work the counter," Al said. "And to serve the seated customers at their tables."

I shook my head. "You're offering me a job?"

"Mark said you were one of the best servers he's ever had. You were a fast learner and great with the customers."

"You could hire anyone for this job. Why me?"

Al was the one who was supposed to be asking all the questions. At least that was what Tiffany had told me when she'd prepped me for this interview. But this situation was...different.

"I know what you're going through." Al reached into his pocket and pulled out a coin. "Ten years clean." He held the coin up in the air.

When Mark had busted me smoking dope in the bathroom, he wasn't even mad. He took me into his office, stayed with me while I nodded out, then sent me home to rest. Now it all made sense.

Al described the responsibilities of the job, the pay, and how after three months he would give me benefits. "So what do you say?"

The pay was more than I was expecting.

"Can I let you know in the morning?" I asked.

"Of course," Al said. He moved over to me and shook my hand. "It was a pleasure."

I thanked Mark, and we walked out of the office together. His pace matched mine. He followed me to the door, opening it, but he stopped in the doorway.

"I'd love for you to come work for me again."

"The bar wouldn't be good for my sobriety."

"That's why I didn't ask. I hope you'll consider what Al's offering. It's a great opportunity."

"I will."

His expression was so inviting, his lips slightly parted in a soft smile and his eyes flirting with their slow blinks. "I appreciate you helping me out, Mark," I said, stepping out onto the sidewalk.

The compassion Mark had showed during the interview was because of Al's addiction. But I still had questions about why he'd tried to fuck me in the hallway before Eric had found us. I needed to ask him, but today wasn't the right time.

During my walk home, I thought about what my dad had said at the graduation ceremony. Too many things had happened here. Because I'd taken a plea and ratted everyone out, both of my drug dealers and their gangs were in jail. But they had friends who could be looking for me. Although Mark wasn't involved in that mess, he was someone I had mistreated and used, too. He had forgiven me. That didn't mean the next person would.

I unlocked the door to our apartment, and just as I touched the knob to the bathroom, it was yanked from my hand and opened from the other side. I lost my balance. Before I hit the ground, Tiffany pulled me upright and walked me over to the couch. She sat next to me. "What happened? You don't look right."

Even though I wasn't proud of what I'd done to Mark, my counselor—Allison—had told me not to keep anything in. That was what NA meetings and a sponsor were for. I didn't want to burden Tiffany with any more of my drama, but she was my sponsor and it sounded like she wanted to hear it. I told her the whole story. Not just that Al had offered me a job but that I knew Mark and what had happened between us.

"I'm really proud of you," Tiffany said.

"I got the job because of Mark, not because I earned it."

"That's not why I'm proud." She pulled my fingers into her hand and squeezed. "Mark was in your life when you first started using heroin. Those memories of being high at his bar and nodding out in his bathroom could have easily triggered you to use, Nicole. But you didn't."

Heroin's voice woke me in the middle of every night and early in the morning. It was the silence between my breaths.

"Dope will always be there," she said. "But maybe not in the forefront of your thoughts."

"This is the first time it hasn't been."

"It won't be the last."

CHAPTER THREE

During my second interview, the manager held my résumé up to his face, the paper clamped between his hairy fingers like a cigarette. Without putting it down, he asked why I'd been unemployed for so long. Tiffany had told me to say I'd been out of work due to health problems because she didn't think an employer was allowed to ask specifics. He didn't, but he moved the page a little, eyeing me. He started at my forehead, and when he got to my lips, he asked if I'd ever been convicted of a felony. He paused at my chest. The meeting ended when he finally noticed I was nodding my head. Before I left the coffee shop, he said he'd be in touch, but judging by the expression on his face, a blowjob was the only thing he had in mind.

What Al was offering would cover my rent and give me some extra to save. It also meant that I would still be connected to Mark, and I was trying to move on from my past. But I hadn't heard back from any of the other coffee shops. Tiffany said Al would be influential in my sobriety; he'd completed a rehab program, worked the Steps, and still attended meetings. Mark had showed he was just as supportive. Even if the job was temporary and I looked for others in the meantime, at least I'd be making money.

After my first week, I stopped checking the Internet for employment ads. I wasn't making as much money as I had at Mark's bar, but I didn't have an addiction to feed. Al let me float, helping out the pastry chef and busboy when the shop wasn't busy, and told me I could work overtime. He was impressed with all the hours I put in and said he wished his other employees were as committed. I didn't tell him he was actually doing me a favor by letting me work so much.

I hated being home. Ashley and Kathy went to bed after they ate, and the sounds coming out of their room told me they were doing more than just sleeping. Diem watched TV or talked on the phone. Tiffany was finishing her bachelor's degree and was taking fifteen credits this semester. We'd go to meetings and cook together, and before she hit the books, she'd ask about my day. Eventually, the stories about our customers got repetitious and weren't funny anymore.

Heroin talked to me when no one else did.

Jami and Sada, the girls who worked the counter with me, were chattier than my roommates. Jami, a single mom of two, looked like she'd been run through a press. Her body was long and thin, and she wore gloves because she chewed her nails so short they bled. Sada was a junior at Northeastern University. This week, her long, black hair was streaked with hot pink highlights, matching her feather earrings and eyeliner. Her personality didn't demand attention; her looks just attracted it. Neither knew about my heroin addiction or that I'd spent time in jail. The only time we hung out was at work, so there wasn't a reason to bring it up. That was, until Sada invited me out on a Saturday night. She said it wasn't a party—just some friends hanging out at an apartment. She wrote down her address, said to be at her place at eight and then we'd walk to her friend's together. I told her I'd be there.

I'd been in sober living for three weeks, and I left our apartment only to go to work or NA meetings and to see my parole officer. I didn't want to spend another Saturday night alone in my room, and there was no reason I should. Alcohol wasn't tempting. Sada's friends wouldn't be doing heroin, so I was going to be just fine.

My roommates were sitting around the kitchen table when I got home from work. Other than some gravy and a few mashed carrots, their plates were empty. Tiffany must have made pot roast.

"We saved you a plate," Kathy said. "You just need to stick it in the microwave."

"No need, but thanks," I said. Tiffany was sitting closest to the door, and I stood next to her. "Can I talk to you?"

"You OK?" she asked.

"Yeah, I just want to ask you something."

She pushed out her chair and followed me to her bedroom. I took a seat on her bed, crossed my legs, and pulled one of her pillows into my arms. Her sheets were much softer than mine. They were teal and matched her comforter.

She closed the door and sat in front of me. "What's up?"

"Do you mind if I borrow some clothes?"

I'd gotten only two paychecks. The first went toward a whole month of rent, which was my parents' idea. I bought a cell phone and work clothes with the second and put the rest into savings. Opening a checking and savings account was another of Mom and Dad's suggestions.

Tiffany moved over to her closet and flipped through her hanging clothes. "Dressy or casual?"

"Jeans, and maybe something tight but cute for on top."

She pulled out a pair of dark blue jeans and a black-and-pink sleeveless shirt that tied at the waist and set both on the bed. A pair of knee-high boots came next. "For Josiah's sake, you better wear a sweater during the meeting." She placed a black cardigan by the shirt.

Tiffany thought Josiah, a recovered tweaker who attended our meetings, had a thing for me. She wasn't very observant. Josiah had flirted during the first week, but that had long since ended. He'd asked me out for coffee, saying he could use someone to talk to, and then I found out what he really wanted. I kicked him in the balls before the night was over. He'd known I was a hooker; I had discussed it during a meeting.

After my toe hit his sack, he'd yelled, "You'll always be a fucking whore, you used-up bitch." I hated him. I'd never forget the burning of my face, the silence that seemed to stretch each second into an hour. He had seemed like such a nice guy. But so had Dave, a man I met in rehab, who stuck his fingers up my shorts in the smoking lounge. So far, the men who came on to me didn't think I deserved any respect.

"I'm not going to the meeting tonight," I said. "Sada invited me out."

"Where is she taking you?"

"Just to her friend's apartment."

"Will there be drinking?"

"I don't know."

Her hands went to her hips. "You've only been out of rehab for less than—"

"Aren't you going to test me when I get home?"

"That's not the point." She broke our eye contact and took a deep breath. When she looked at me again, her arms dropped. "I just don't want you to be triggered to use."

"I'll be fine."

Her eyes inspected my face as if she didn't recognize me.

I passed all her random drug tests. We were required to attend three NA meetings a week, and I went to at least five. I paid my rent and was tearing it up at my job. Didn't that prove I could be trusted?

"If I feel like I want to use, I'll call you." I got up from the bed and stood in front of her, putting my hands on her shoulders. "I can't spend the rest of my life hiding from everything that might tempt me."

"It's just too soon."

I reminded her of my good behavior over the past three weeks, but no matter how much I tried to reassure her, she continued to shake her head. Staying home was the only thing that was going to make her happy, so I told her I'd wear my work clothes and turned to walk out of her room.

She called me back, took the clothes off the bed, scooped up the heels, and handed everything to me. "Just be careful."

I got ready in the bathroom, using the little makeup I owned and some eye shadow from Diem's cosmetic bag. When I came out, the girls were still sitting in the kitchen. The dishes had been cleared, and the flowerpot had been put back in the center of the table. If Ashley and Kathy weren't in bed yet, something had to be up.

I felt their eyes on me as I went to the fridge and tipped my head back to take a sip from a can of soda. "What's with the looks?" I asked.

"We're silently praying for you," Ashley said.

"Is there anything we can say to stop you from going?" Kathy asked.

The soda began to slosh inside the can.

I glanced at Diem, but she didn't say anything. She couldn't. She'd gone out when her family came to visit and had met friends for dinner a few times. No one had said anything to her, so why was I different? If I started asking questions, I'd be late. With my hand on the knob of the door, I turned around. "I'm going to prove you all wrong."

"You have no idea how overwhelming the pull can be until it's too late," Tiffany said.

I knew. I'd been fighting it for weeks.

"I'll be back by midnight," I said.

I hoofed it to work every day to save money, and my NA meetings were only a few blocks from our apartment, so I hadn't taken the train since before I'd gone to jail. But Sada lived in the Back Bay, which was a long walk, and it was almost eight. There weren't any empty seats on the Orange Line. There was barely enough room to stand. I leaned against the door, and when it opened, I stepped onto the platform to let the passengers on and off.

I'd forgotten what it was like to be this close to anyone. Strangers pressed against each side of me, inhaling my scent, their eyes bearing down on my body. For April, it was an unusually warm night, and I'd pushed the sleeves of the cardigan up past my elbows. With my hands gripping the rim around the door, my track marks weren't hidden at my sides. The cyst that had formed on my arm, which had to be lanced in prison, had left behind something nasty.

I could make up a story to cover the last eight years, but the scars on my arms told the truth. So did my ankles, the skin between my toes, even the veins that had burst on my breasts. I was like that board my dad used to tack papers to in his office. Eventually, the cork fell apart because it had too many holes, and my dad got a new one. Did my battle wounds really prove I was a survivor? Or was I too damaged to be glued back together?

I got off at Massachusetts Avenue. A few blocks to the right was where my old hotel used to be before it'd burned down. I'd lived there with Sunshine, the prostitute who taught me how to turn tricks, and Claire was our neighbor. Claire, my best friend, died in the hotel fire with the broken heart that I'd given her when I wouldn't stay sober. After my first attempt at rehab, I moved back in with my boyfriend, Dustin, and empty packets of heroin and dull syringes had covered the floor of our room.

I turned left and focused on my feet, the sound they made as they hit the pavement, and the different colors of shoes I shared the sidewalk with. After a few blocks, something made me look up: Michael's old apartment building. The scene from the last time I'd been here flashed in my head.

*   *   *

Michael didn't say anything when he came outside. He stood against the building with his arms crossed. But his scent filled the air. He smelled so clean, like the hospital room.

"I need help," I said. "I'm starving."

His eyes didn't move from mine. His posture didn't shift; his expression didn't soften. He still didn't say anything.

"Please, Michael, I need your help."

"I'll only help you if you're willing to help yourself."

Help myself? Did he mean tell the cops the truth about how I'd gotten busted with a van full of heroin and take the plea bargain, go to jail and get sober? If he thought I was going to do that, he was fucking crazy.

"Can I have some food?" I asked.

He covered his face with his hands. "As much as I want to feed you," he said from behind his fingers, "I can't until you get clean."

"All I need is some food, and I promise I won't ask for anything else ever again."

He shook his head and reached for the door.

"You can't leave me like this," I shouted. "I'm starving."

The door slammed in my face. I banged on the glass, leaving smudge marks and prints. "I'm your sister," I yelled.

He got into the elevator.

"Please," I screamed. My foot slipped and I fell hard, my ass hitting the pavement.

*   *   *

My eyes opened and I reached behind my back, spreading my fingers and pushing against the same glass I had left my prints on. Michael had asked for only one thing. If I had accepted his offer and turned myself in, would things have gone differently?

There wasn't an answer to that question. Standing in front of his building wasn't going to bring him back; what I'd done had forever changed his destiny. What I *could* do was prove to Michael, my parents, and my roommates that I was strong enough to stay sober. I glanced over my shoulder, taking one final look at the lobby before I walked the three blocks to Sada's place.

I called her from the box outside her building. When Sada met me at the door, she was out of breath. She led me up two long flights of stairs and down a long hallway. Once we got inside her apartment, she left me in the living room and told me she had to finish getting ready. I guess it didn't matter that I was fifteen minutes late.

Everything in the apartment was so girly, and pink. Furry lampshades, shaggy rugs, and jewelry used as decorations. I'd never seen a plant with earrings, but Sada's had pierced leaves.

"There's wine in the fridge," she said.

"I'm good, thanks."

She poked her head out from the bathroom. "Not a wino?"

"Not a drinker."

"You're a straightedge?"

A straightedge was a person who didn't smoke, drink, or do drugs. But, according to Sada, that term now included people who didn't eat or wear anything that came from an animal. She had said a lot of her friends were straight, and they had some weird symbol tattooed on their wrists to prove their loyalty.

I'd found an *out* for tonight.

"I guess you could say that, but I'm not a vegetarian."

"Don't tell Cutter that," she said. "He'll give you a lecture on animal cruelty."

"Who's Cutter?"

She walked by me and yanked down the collar of her shirt so that it hung past one of her shoulders. Her bra strap was leopard print. "You'll meet him tonight. He's a straightey too."

Her purse was hooked to the corner of a painting; she grabbed it, along with her keys, and we left.

At work, Sada did most of the talking. She was an art major from Chicago who didn't know whether she wanted to be an artist or jewelry designer—maybe create a business out of the hairclips she made. She'd broken up with her boyfriend last week after he'd carved her name into his leg. I guess she wasn't into body modification, even though she had a full sleeve of tattoos.

She didn't know much about me, other than that I was from Maine, had lived in Boston for a while, and used the same brand of tampons as her. She wasn't one for questions, and I liked that about her. She also didn't like silence. There was never a moment of it at work, so during the walk, she told me about everyone I'd meet tonight. There was a melody to her voice; her words were like lyrics, flowing as if she read them off a page. I was so entertained by her expressions that I almost ran into her when we got to the doorstep of the apartment.

After we were buzzed in, I followed her down the hall to the back of the building. Nobody seemed to mind when she entered without knocking. They all stopped their conversations, turned toward us, and yelled her name.

"Loves, I have someone for you to meet." She looped her arm through mine and led me into the living room.

Like Sada's place, this wasn't your typical college apartment. At least not the ones I'd been to at the University of Maine. There were framed canvases on the walls and matching leather furniture. There was even an herb garden on the kitchen pass-through window.

The apartment belonged to Nadal and Asher. They were identical twins, and the only way to tell them apart was by the freckle between Asher's eyebrows. Sada told me that Tyme, Nadal's girlfriend, wanted to be with Asher instead. I wondered what was so special about the freckled one. Tyme was at work, so I wasn't going to get a chance to ask her.

Someone came out of the kitchen holding a tray of shot glasses, each filled with a dark green liquid. It looked like the slime that came in those plastic eggs from the nickel machines at the grocery store.

"Cutter, this is Nicole. She's a straightey too," Sada said.

Cutter was colorful. The only part of his body that wasn't tattooed was the whites of his eyes. His earlobes were so stretched they would have fit around my wrists.

"You'll enjoy this then," Cutter said, handing me a shot glass and passing out the rest of them.

I smelled it. "What is it?"

"If you like it, I'll show you how to make it," he said.

A half circle had formed around the three of us. As I glanced at each staring face, I felt myself turn red.

"Is there alcohol in it?" I asked.

"No, love, he's a straightey too, remember?" Sada said.

Cutter made some kind of toast—about spread legs and hard dicks—and I tipped my head back. And then I waited. The mixture was so thick I had to scoop it with my tongue.

Something got stuck between my teeth, and I used my nails to dig it out. "Was there grass in there?"

"It didn't come from a lawn," Cutter said. "I grow my own."

Sada, her arm still looped through mine, pulled me into the kitchen. Soda was the only nonalcoholic drink in the fridge, so I grabbed a can and handed her a bottle of wine. I was hoping that after I chugged down a few gulps, the Coke would peel off the flavor in my mouth like it did to the paint on cars. It didn't.

When we returned to the living room, more weird names were thrown at me from the people who had just arrived. All the girls were dressed like pin-ups; different colors streaked their hair, thick makeup covered their eyes and faces, and art was inked all over their skin. Maybe Sada needed more Nicoles in her life. Maybe that was why she liked me.

"I'll be right back," she said, disappearing down the hallway.

With Sada gone, the energy instantly changed in the room and everyone left the dining area. A few people went to the kitchen. Some sat on the couch, so I joined them, squeezing in by the armrest. I couldn't remember the last time I'd been alone and sober with people who knew nothing about me. In rehab, we all had something in common. In jail, too.

"Sada told me you guys work together?"

Asher stood next to the armrest, the lamp shining on his freckle. "We do," I said. "How did you two meet?"

"I had a class with her last year. She's a hard one to miss. The professor didn't call on anyone but her."

"We have customers who will only let Sada make their coffee."

I waited for him to say something, but he didn't. He crossed one arm over the other and rested his chin on his palm. Then he smiled. The hair on top of his head was spiked, the tips slanted forward like there was a breeze from behind him. The rest of his head was shaved, and he had a swirl of piercings on the left side of his skull. Except for the ruby in the middle, they were all black diamonds.

"What's with the red one?" I asked, blurting out the first thing that came to me. "It looks a little lonely surrounded by all black."

He traced his lips with his pointer finger. "It's the eye. It allows me to see *everything*."

Asher did have an intense stare. It was as though he could see my hard nipples through the padding of my bra. I suddenly felt like I wasn't wearing any clothes.

"Has it ever let you down?"

He shook his head. "Never." His lips parted, and he bit the end of his tongue. He stayed like that with his eyes focused on mine.

I was the first to blink. "Do you mind if I use your bathroom?"

His face didn't move, but his hand pointed to the hallway.

I stood from the couch and headed for the hallway. I knew if I turned around, I'd see him still looking at me. His eyes bored through my clothes.

There were four doors, all of them closed. The first one was locked, so I tried the second and got it halfway open before I realized it was a bedroom. Sada and Nadal were sitting on the bed. There was a mirror between them.

"I'm sorry," I said. "I... I should have knocked."

"No, love, you're fine." Her jaw was swinging. "Is everything OK?"

There was white powder on the mirror, chopped and separated into lines.

"I thought..." I stopped, trying to remember why I'd left the living room. "I thought this was the bathroom."

She wiped her nose. "It's across the hall."

I could feel the burst of energy that ran through her veins the second the coke hit her brain. The urge to never stop talking. The drip, from her nose to the back of her throat, that filled her mouth with a bitter taste. I hadn't done coke in years. It felt like I'd done it moments ago.

Sada was never on coke at work. I would have known; no one could hide their high from me. She had to be a recreational user—a term thrown around by the addicts in rehab. Some believed recreational use was possible. The term never existed in my life, even before I'd turned into a junkie. It never could, regardless of how long I was clean.

And how many days was that? There was a coin in my pocket, but I couldn't remember the number that was engraved on it. I would have known that answer before I saw the lines on the mirror. I didn't have to go to the bathroom anymore. I didn't care that Sada thought I was a straightey, which was probably why she wasn't offering me any. I didn't care that I would be drug tested by Tiffany as soon as I got home.

Or did I?

I'd be kicked out of the apartment tonight, and I'd have to rent a hotel room. I'd be craving more coke as soon as the high wore off. I'd go through my entire savings account to re-up, and Al would fire me because he knew all the signs. Blow would lead to heroin.

I had to get the fuck out of here.

Sada was rubbing powder on her gums, and Nadal was bending over the mirror with a straw up his nose. I shut the door quietly and walked to the living room. No one looked at me when I left.

The outside air wasn't much of a relief. There wasn't a breeze, and the humidity was thick, as though it had just rained, but the ground was dry. There was a train station just a few blocks away. The token I'd purchased for the return trip was in my pocket. I could get on the train and go straight to the North End. But would I? The same train would take me to the streets of Roxbury, where dope pushers were selling packets of junk.

"Where are you going?" Asher asked.

Without turning around, I knew he was on the front steps of his building. I was a few feet away but could almost feel his breath on my back.

"The eye saw me leave?"

"No, I saw you leave," he said. "Now why don't you come back in?"

There was no way I could go back inside. If Sada used, even recreationally, I didn't know if I could hang out with her again. If I did, I'd have to tell her about my addiction.

"I—"

Asher came closer. His hands touched my shoulders and swung me around. The movement filled my nose with his scent. It wasn't cologne or alcohol, laundry detergent or smoke. It was the scent of sun baking the sand on a beach.

"You were bothered by what you saw, weren't you?"

The ruby really did see *everything*.

I didn't know whether a straightedge just didn't use any substances or was scared and bothered to be around them too. It didn't matter.

I nodded.

"You feel like going for a walk?"

I knew nothing about him, but I didn't get the impression he would disappear during our walk. If he did, I knew these streets well. I also didn't think he'd try to stick his dick down my throat.

I looked at my phone; it was a little past ten. "I have to be home by midnight."

A wrinkle formed between his eyebrows.

"I've got to get up early for work."

His hands dropped from my shoulders, and he moved past me. When he got to the neighbor's steps, he stopped and turned around. "Are you going to make me walk alone?"

CHAPTER FOUR

When I got home, Tiffany was sitting at the table with a breathalyzer and pee test in front of her. Without saying a word, I stuck the breathalyzer in my mouth and blew. When it read zero, she followed me to the bathroom and watched me pee in a cup. I didn't bother to wait for the result; I went to my room and got in bed.

I heard the floor creak beneath Tiffany's feet and then the flush of the toilet. The next noise was her bedroom door closing. I'd proved them all wrong, but it was close. Too close. If Sada had been doing heroin, or if Asher hadn't come outside, I might have used. I was still powerless.

Asher hadn't asked a lot of questions, but he made me forget about how much I wanted a line of Sada's coke. Not just one line. I wanted a whole bag. When I commented on something he talked about, like the classes I'd taken at UMaine or my hometown, he didn't push for more. He was open with me, telling me how he'd traveled in Europe for a year after high school. When he was ready to go to college, his father wanted him to go to Dartmouth, so he'd applied to Northeastern for early enrollment. He was getting a degree in English literature and recently had a collection of short stories published.

While we walked, he'd looked at me instead of at the pavement. And he looked me in the eyes. He didn't try to keep me out when I told him it was time for me to go home, and he didn't ask for my phone number. He hailed me a cab and closed the door behind me. Before the driver took off, he knocked on the window.

I rolled it down.

"If you ever want to go for a walk again, call me," he said, and he gave me his number.

Asher didn't rip my clothes off, promise to take care of me, and shoot me up with heroin like the guys from my past had. I didn't need him to. The hunger inside me that those men had once satisfied was gone.

Asher must have told Sada we'd gone for a walk, because for the next few days at work, she brought his name up constantly. She tried to tell me everything he was into and the girls he'd been with. I told her to stop. It wasn't her place to air his business.

According to Tiffany, if I was committed to staying clean, my main priority shouldn't be what I wanted. The question I had to ask myself was who was good for my sobriety. It wasn't that I didn't have time to call Asher. As with Sada, I just didn't know if he could have a place in my life. But the only way I'd know would be to spend more time with him. It took me a week to give him that chance. I was hoping he wouldn't answer and I could leave a message, but he did.

"It's Nicole."

After a brief pause, he said, "It's nice to hear your voice."

"I was thinking maybe we could go for that walk."

"How's tonight?"

Sada watched me from inside the café. She mouthed "Asher" and waved her hand for me to come closer.

I turned my back to her. "Tonight?" I asked Asher.

"Do you already have plans?"

I should have sent him a text instead so that I could have more time to think before answering. "I get off work at seven."

"I'll pick you up; where do you live?" he asked.

"Why don't you come to the café? Do you need the address?"

"I'll see you there at seven," he said, and we both hung up.

That was only two hours away. I had no idea how much I was going to tell him about my past—if anything at all—but I knew that if he was going to be my friend, I had to be honest with him.

* * *

The clock showed it was ten minutes to seven, and everything on our list of closing duties was checked off except taking out the trash. I went to the backroom; six bags were waiting by the door. I propped the door open with a brick and carried the first three into the alley. The dumpster was in the narrow path between the buildings. The last three were much heavier—liquid sloshed and banged against the metal inside—and I was winded by the time I got to the dumpster. Just as I got the bags in, I heard someone behind me. Asher must have seen me when he'd passed the alley on his way to the front entrance.

"I just have to punch out," I said, closing the lid. I turned around. "Then I—"

A man was standing only inches away.

"I have a message for you," he said.

"Who are you?"

He moved closer.

I tried to sneak to the right, but he shifted his stance.

"Who are—?"

He cornered me; my back was against the dumpster. "Don't scream, I'm not going to hurt you."

He was so close that I could feel the air that he exhaled through his nose.

"Dustin says he misses you."

Dustin? My ex-boyfriend? How did he know him?

I thought Dustin fucking hated me. When I'd ratted him out to the DA after we'd been arrested with a van full of dope, he'd received a twenty-five-year sentence. Melissa, my attorney, had notified me while I was in jail that he was appealing his case. If I was called into court for the appeal, I'd have to give my testimony again.

His eyes devoured my body, as though he were choosing which dessert he wanted to taste first. His stare settled on my chest; he bit the corner of his lower lip.

"I can see why Dustin says you're so beautiful, why he misses you so much. He wishes he had made different choices so that you wouldn't be on these streets alone. He's always telling me how he craves you, that you were the best part of his life."

There wasn't any part of me that belonged to Dustin anymore. He was in jail, and that was where he belonged.

"You know Dustin always gets what he wants, don't you? And what will happen to you if you mess up his appeal?"

Didn't he know that if I didn't cooperate with the court and district attorney I would be put back in jail? Of course he did; he just didn't care.

"Why don't you be a good girl and nod your head so I can tell Dustin—"

"Get away from her. Now," Asher said.

I hadn't heard Asher come into the alley. I hadn't heard anything except the messenger's voice. I couldn't smell anything besides the weed on his breath.

"If you know what's good for you, you'll get the fuck out of here," the guy said, looking over his shoulder.

Asher appeared at my side.

The last time someone had tried to save me, he was shot and killed. I knew my eyes were failing me, but Asher's face looked so much like Michael's.

I shook my head, trying to signal him to leave.

"I don't think you heard me," Asher said through gritted teeth. "I said get away from her."

Everything happened so quickly. There was a swish of clothes and arms before the man was on the ground. Asher stood over him, his foot on the guy's throat. "I'll kill you if you come near her again. Understood?"

"Yes," the guy said. "But Dustin's got more friends."

"Let them try to come near her." Asher pulled his foot away. "Nothing is going to happen to her."

The guy stood. "After Dustin hears this, his other friends won't be as nice as I was." He took a long look at Asher before he ran toward the main street.

Asher reached for my hand and intertwined his fingers through mine. "Are you OK?"

I nodded.

"Let me get you out of here."

I nodded again.

His arm went around my waist and he brought me to the curb. When a cab pulled over, he picked me up and placed me in the backseat. He climbed in next to me and closed the door. "Back Bay, between Tremont and—"

"No, not your apartment," I said.

"Then tell me where."

His place wasn't safe. Not if Nadal was there with coke in his bedroom. And we weren't allowed to bring men to our apartment. There was only one place to go.

CHAPTER FIVE

Asher didn't say anything when I told the cab driver to take us to the corner of Boylston and Arlington. When I walked through the entrance of the park and to my favorite spot, the bench right in front of the duck pond, he didn't question why we had to sit here.

This bench had been in my life for as long as heroin had. Maybe longer. I came here when I needed air. I came here to escape the cops. I'd even slept here. There was something about being under a sky full of stars, having the trees whistle as the wind rustled through their leaves, and the twinkling lights from the surrounding buildings that made me feel at ease.

I took a deep breath. "Do you want to know what that was about?"

"Only if you feel comfortable telling me."

He kept his hands on his lap, but his eyes were focused on my profile. Mine were on the pond. The water was still; not even a ripple broke the surface. "I'm a heroin addict."

I focused on the water. I didn't want to see an expression full of disgust and judgment in his eyes or repulsion on his lips.

"I know," he said.

"What?" I turned my head toward him. "How?" And then I remembered the outfit I'd worn to his apartment that night. I just couldn't remember if I had rolled up my sleeves. "Because you saw the scars on my arms?"

"There's that, yeah, but—"

"I was on dope for five years, Asher, and…"

The grass was easier to look at than his face. It just stood there, waiting to be stepped on and mowed. It turned greener in the summer and got covered with snow in the winter. Why couldn't I be a blade of grass?

One of his hands covered mine, and he placed the other on my cheek, moving it so I faced him. "Don't be afraid."

How could I not be? Josiah and Dave, the only two men who'd shown a little bit of interest lately, treated me like I was still a whore as soon as I was honest with them. Once the truth came out, every time Asher looked at me he'd see my scars. Not just the ones on my skin. The ones I buried inside.

"I did some shit, shit that would make you sick."

"We all have regrets."

"Not like I do." I shook my head and looked down. "I hurt innocent people; people died because of me. If the cops hadn't busted me, I'd still be fucked up. I spent two-and-a-half years in jail, then three months in rehab, and now I'm in sober living."

"But you're clean, right?"

"Yeah, I'm clean, but you don't get it." I stood and walked over to the water, taking a seat at the edge of the pond. I wrapped my arms around my legs and begged for rain. Not a drop fell from the sky.

"You're right," he said from behind me. "I'm not an addict, so I don't understand what you went through." He sat next to me and pulled my legs, turning me toward him. Once I was settled, he put his hands on the tops of my sneakers. "Make me understand."

A light from one of the buildings was shining on his face. It made his eyes glow. They were gray with swirls of brown on the outer edge.

"I thought the time I served and being sober would be enough to pay for my mistakes, but my past is still haunting me."

"Did you know that guy?"

Dustin and his messenger weren't the only people who haunted me. Asher wouldn't know that, though. I hadn't told him who had died because of me.

"No, my ex sent him to woo me," I said. "He wants me to help him win his appeal."

"Are you going to?"

"He was guiltier than me. I was just an accomplice."

He ran his fingers through the hair that hung by the side of my face. After a few strokes, he tucked the strands behind my ear. "He can send whoever he wants. I won't let anyone hurt you."

"I don't understand why you want to help me. You barely know me."

His gaze softened, and he pulled my hands into his lap, covering them with his. "I know you better than you think."

"But I haven't told Sada anything about me. She—"

"Sada didn't tell me anything."

"Did you read the articles about me in the paper?"

The expression on his face was the same one he'd had when he found me outside his apartment. He was holding something in. What could he be hiding?

"Nadal isn't my only brother. I have another one—an older one."

Was his older brother one of my Johns? I didn't want to ask, just in case it wasn't true. He probably assumed I was a prostitute, but saying that word would solidify it.

"His name is Jesse," he said.

A giant lump formed in the back of my throat.

"Not the same Jesse who was dating my brother?" I asked.

He nodded, and when I tried to stand, his hands flew to my shoulders and stopped me. "I was going to tell you at the party, but the timing wasn't right."

Jesse and Michael had been together for over a year by the time I found out Michael was gay. Michael had tried to tell me about him before, but I was too strung out to listen. They were still dating when my pimp killed him.

"How well did you know Michael?"

"We were good friends."

It suddenly all made sense. Sada must have told Asher she was bringing me to his apartment, and when I showed up, he matched my name with the pictures he'd seen of me at Michael's. He followed me outside because he wanted to make sure I wouldn't leave his place and score some dope. That's what Michael would have wanted. He was honoring my brother, so he'd given me his phone number. The reason he wanted to go for a walk with me wasn't that he liked me. He hated me as much as Jesse did.

I threw his hands off my shoulders. "I have to go."

"Nicole, this doesn't change how I feel."

I'd already passed the bench, but I turned around and took a step closer. "The way you feel? I know exactly how you feel."

"Tell me, then."

I put my hands on the back of the bench, grinding my palms against the wood. They were wet and slid over the surface. "When you look at me, all you see is Michael's killer."

"That's not true." He kneeled on the bench. Our eyes were level. His had beamed with strength when his foot was on that guy's throat, but now they showed sadness. "I knew of you then, and I'm beginning to see who you are now. There's a truth in you that proves you could be different. You didn't lie, and that's what I had expected."

"What do you want from me?"

He didn't smile or move his mouth, but the corners of his eyes pointed down and his eyebrows rose. "I just want to take you for a walk."

A laugh escaped from my lips. Nothing he said was funny, but laughing hid the quivers that rattled my body and the tears that filled my eyes.

"Just a walk?"

He nodded. "For now."

CHAPTER SIX

There were thousands of students enrolled at Northeastern, and Sada just happened to be friends with Asher. She could have chosen to take me anywhere that night she'd brought me to his apartment. I had to believe that was more than a coincidence. But was it to punish me, or was I supposed to fall in love with him? Maybe both.

My past had collided with my future in the most fucked-up way.

If I had met Jesse like Michael had wanted me to, I might have met the twins. I'd at least have heard their names or seen their pictures. Instead, I chose to abandon my brother when he was struggling with coming out. Heroin entered, and Michael exited.

My father shut down whenever I mentioned Michael, and my mother just sobbed. Asher was my only solid connection. Whether he used drugs and whether I was ready for a relationship weren't important. I couldn't lose what we had.

What I didn't understand was why, after everything he knew about me, I'd caught his interest. People didn't visit the murderer of their loved ones on death row. They sighed with relief when execution day came. But Asher wanted to take me for another walk instead. I couldn't let my questions keep me from finding him a place in my life. Being near Asher meant I was closer to Michael, so I called him the next morning. He got out of class an hour before my shift ended and came to the café. He sat at one of the tables, with a large coffee and a soft, covered notebook and wrote. Even if it was just short glances between sentences, I knew he was watching me. I could feel his stare throughout my whole body.

When I finished my closing duties, I walked over to his table. "Are you ready?"

He got up, folded his notebook in half, and put it in his back pocket. Once we got to the sidewalk, he asked how I was feeling. I hated that question. Until I'd gone to rehab and was forced to spill, I'd never been good at sharing my feelings. Practice hadn't made me any better. "Confused," I said.

"I'm sure you have a lot of questions," he replied.

I'd gone from one all-night coke binge to snorting it every day. I never wasted time touching my Johns or kissing them. I was impatient and would do whatever it took—sucking their dick or riding them—to make them bust the quickest. Asher didn't act as though we were on a deadline, but I wanted all the answers before we reached the next street.

"Nadal knows we've been hanging out, so if you ever want to come to our apartment, he'll make sure there aren't any drugs there. Jesse knows too."

The sidewalk was so busy that we had to weave through hoards of people. Asher reached for my hand, making sure we didn't get separated, and led me into an alley. He sat against the side of the building. I joined him.

"What do they think about...us?" I asked.

"Nadal and I may look alike, but he's like my father—quick to judge and only willing to hear one side. His side, usually. Jesse's like me. We think with our hearts."

"I can see why Tyme wants to date the freckled one."

That was the first time I heard him laugh. It was deep and honest. Asher had a funky haircut and a pierced skull but underneath was something soft.

"Tyme isn't my type," he said. "I like women who aren't afraid of their darkness. There's a little bit in all of us; some just choose not to embrace it."

"What if it's not just a little bit? What if it's all of me?"

He looked at me for a few seconds and then pulled me to my feet. With my back against the brick, I just stood there, silent. He placed one hand beside my face and leaned down. "You don't see me running, do you?"

I gazed up into his eyes and shook my head.

"I'm not scared of what I know," he said.

"You should be."

He laughed again. This time his tone was lighter, but his smile was just as wide. "Your past only makes you more beautiful." His hands went to my cheeks, and his lips hovered over mine. "Tell me you want this."

No one had ever asked before.

"I want—"

He gently parted my lips, surrounding the top one and then the bottom, his tongue teasing both. His hands never left my face, pulling it closer, though there was hardly any space between us.

To stop his hands from moving, I gripped his forearms. I didn't want him to ever let me go. His lips became hungrier. His body grew and pressed against me. But when his thumbs pushed into my skin, like he was trying to squeeze out all my emotions, I felt something inside me grind to a halt.

Both rapes had left me with scars: a horseshoe-shaped mark under my chin from when I was in college, and memories from the night Richard—my old drug dealer—had forced himself inside me. My body had already been taken and abused, so it was the only thing I'd been willing to give to men. But that wasn't how I felt anymore. The attraction to Asher was more than physical. I wanted to make sure those feelings were real before I let him peel off my layers.

As I was about to pull away, he moved his face back and stared into my eyes. "I'll never hurt you," he whispered.

I wanted to believe him. A part of me did.

"I'm a mess."

"A beautiful mess." He ran his thumb over my bottom lip. "We'll take it slow."

* * *

Tiffany looked awful. She'd been studying for a week straight and pulling all-nighters. Besides coffee and cigarettes, I didn't think she'd eaten in days. I made her a sandwich, but when I got out of the shower, the plate still sat in front of her. Untouched.

"Let's go to a meeting," I said.

She wasn't required to go, but that didn't mean she should skip them as she'd done for the past week. Without looking up from her textbook, she said she couldn't take a break. This was her hardest semester, and she needed to ace her finals next week; otherwise she wouldn't get accepted into her core classes.

I stood in front of her with my arms crossed. "You're powerless over your addiction." When she didn't respond, I yanked the book off the table. "Get dressed."

The addicts at our meetings were at various stages of sobriety. The rookies, who had just graduated from their first shot at rehab, would initially share their story. Then they'd mostly just listen. Eventually they'd start showing up late and would leave once the meeting was over. After a few weeks, maybe a month, they'd stop coming altogether. For most addicts, at least the ones I knew, it took more than one attempt at rehab to get sober. I was on my third.

The vets were hardcore followers of the Twelve Steps, the mentors of the group. They believed silence was a sign of relapse and encouraged the newbies to express their feelings. Before we swarmed around the coffee and cookies, the vets would ask us to join hands and pray for God's will and the power to carry it out.

During the first year of sobriety, relationships weren't encouraged. With a twelve-month foundation, we would learn how to add sex and love into our lives instead of using them to replace drugs. I didn't mention Asher when one of the vets called on me and asked how I was doing. He was my little secret. Lying was also a sign of relapse, but I was only hiding our kiss. Until that kiss turned into something more, no one needed to know.

Tiffany, with three years of sobriety, was considered one of the vets. But during the meeting, she stayed silent and even fell asleep when one of the newbies shared her story. She said she hadn't been sleeping because of finals next week and apologized to the group. She got some stern looks from the other vets; they said she needed to put her sobriety first and stop skipping meetings. She nodded and then went over to the table to pour a cup of coffee while the rest of us recited the prayer.

Once we got outside, I asked her why she didn't say the prayer. Instead of answering, she told me about her psychology professor.

They'd been emailing and talking on the phone, but they were waiting until the end of the semester to hang out. She said if the faculty busted him dating one of his students, he could get in a lot of trouble.

Tiffany hadn't been in a serious relationship since getting sober. She'd gone out with a few addicts, but all of them had relapsed. Her professor was the first nonaddict to understand her addiction and still show an interest after she'd told him about her past.

"It takes someone special to love us, Nicole."

Josiah and Dave had both been addicts, but even junkies despised me for what I'd done to earn my drug money. Asher accepted my addiction—as well as my role in Michael's death and everything Michael had told him about me—and the things I'd shared so far. Did that make him amazing or totally insane?

"That's why when you find him," she said, "you don't let him go."

"Do you think..." The woman up ahead caught my attention. She was sitting in a doorway with a blanket underneath her and a bag at her side. She held a cardboard sign. Panhandling had once paid for my drugs. I had stuffed my belly with socks or toilet paper and hoped the people passing by would feel sympathy for my baby bump.

I grabbed a dollar out of my wallet, and when I bent down to place it in front of her, I read the sign. It said, "6 Months Pregeanat, Plaese Help." I had written the same thing on my sign, but I think I had spelled the words correctly.

I held the dollar out in my hand. "Here, take this." She was wearing a hood that covered most of her face, and her head was slumped forward. I couldn't tell if she was nodding out or just sleeping. If she had overdosed, her chest wouldn't be rising and falling. When she didn't respond, I wiggled her foot, and she finally picked her head up. Her face was covered in dirt, her left eye was swollen shut, and her lips were cracked and flaky. "Sunshine?" I asked.

I'd lived with her, worked the streets with her; we'd gone through withdrawal together. I'd recognize her anywhere. The only time I'd seen her look worse was when Richard, our old dealer and the fucker who raped me, had beaten the shit out of her and put her in the hospital.

"Who's askin'?"

"It's me." She didn't say anything. "It's Nicole."

"What the hell do you want?"

When Dustin and I had left rehab, we'd moved into Sunshine's hotel and he'd supplied her with dope and needles. But that ended as soon as he and I moved to Dorchester, and I hadn't run into her since.

"You look a little out of it," I said. "You OK?"

"I'd be a whole lot better if you'd stop talking and give me some dope."

Tiffany kneeled down next to me and put her hand on Sunshine's leg. "Why don't you let us take you to the shelter so you don't have to sleep on the street?"

"Who the hell is she?" Sunshine asked.

"You can trust her; she's one of us," I said.

Sunshine looked me over, from my hair to my shoes, and then snatched my hand. "Look at you all clean and mighty now." She stared at my fingernails. They were cut short and painted in light pink polish; they had once been dirty and broken like hers. "Don't matter, though, you still ain't no better than me."

There was nothing else we could do. The shelter would probably be full at this hour, and I couldn't bring a user to our apartment. The dollar I'd given her was resting on top of her sign. I would never give her money for drugs, but it was enough to buy her a cheeseburger.

"Let's go," I said to Tiffany.

Just as I was pulling my hand out of Sunshine's grip, she latched onto my arm and yanked me into her lap. "I need heroin," she cried, dragging out the *n*'s. "Nicole, I need a nod. Help me get a fucking fix."

I knew exactly how she felt. Her stomach was churning, wanting to spill. Her muscles ached like she had the flu. The visions in her head were so real she could close her eyes and taste the powder on her tongue.

There was a moment in my life when I had actually felt thankful I'd met this woman. She had helped me out when I'd run out of money and had given me a place to live.

I wrapped my arms around her and cradled her against my chest.

"It hurts," she sobbed.

Her tears leaked through my shirt. They were hot, but her skin was cold and clammy.

"I know it does."

"You remember when we were shittin' all over my room from being dope sick? And you were telling me how you wanted to die?" she asked. "That's gonna happen to me real soon if you don't give me enough money for a taste."

"Nicole, don't fall for it," Tiffany said.

I gave her frail body a squeeze and kissed her forehead. "Take care of yourself, Sunshine."

"Fuck you, then," Sunshine yelled as we walked away. "Think you're better than me now that you're clean? You'll fucking fall, Nicole. You'll be here soon, and don't come askin' for my help."

When we got to the end of the block, waiting for the cross signal, Tiffany put her hand on my shoulder. "There was nothing you could have done to help her."

I nodded.

"Doesn't make you feel any better, though, does it?" she asked.

"If I relapsed, I'd be sharing a doorway with her."

Tiffany stayed completely silent.

* * *

I called Asher when I got home and told him what happened—how I'd met Sunshine all those years ago and worked the streets with her. He never interrupted me, but when I finished, he was still quiet on the other end. Had I said too much?

"You're incredible."

"Why do you say that?" I asked.

"Sunshine could have been a trigger, but you were strong and you didn't enable her. You did the right thing, and it must feel so good."

I'd just told him I'd lived in a crack house hotel with Sunshine and prostituted to pay for my heroin. I wasn't the one who was incredible. But I couldn't get Sunshine's look—the spit that flew from her toothless mouth and her pleading eyes when she begged for dope—out of my head. "It never feels good to see someone you care about in that much pain," I said. "But I know I did the right thing. Even if I tried to get her help, she wouldn't take it."

"It's hard to believe someone would turn down a chance at getting sober."

"Believe it; I turned it down so many times."

"Why are you sober now?" he asked.

I got off my bed and went over to the window. The sky was clear and full of stars. I didn't know where people went when they died, but I hoped Michael was one of those little bursts of white. "Sobriety feels better than heroin," I said.

CHAPTER SEVEN

Asher and I met almost every night for a walk. He'd pick me up either at work or at my apartment after a meeting. Tiffany hadn't said anything to me about going out since the night of Asher's party. I wanted to believe that was because she thought I could handle it, but in reality, Tiffany was too busy with her summer term and Professor Allen to care. They'd been dating for a few weeks, and when I saw her at curfew—the only time we were both home—he was all she talked about.

Being outside with Asher meant fewer distractions. No TV, no stereo; all we had were our own words. And Asher had lots of them. He would read me short stories he'd written for school, some he'd gotten published. He was working on a book, but he didn't talk about it much. He wanted me to be surprised when I read it. Since his graduation a few weeks ago, he'd been debating whether to take a semester off to finish the book or go to one of the grad schools he'd been accepted to. I never told him what I thought he should do. His passion was writing, and he was good at it. A master's degree would only make him better, but all the schools were on the west coast. I knew it was selfish of me to want him to stay in Boston. I didn't care.

I still hadn't been back to his apartment, and he never pressured me to. But there was so much more I wanted to know about Asher: the walls he stared at when we talked on the phone, the color of his sheets. And was his smell from an aftershave he kept in the medicine cabinet or cologne on his dresser?

Asher told me Nadal spent the weekends at Tyme's, so I sent him a text during my lunch break and asked if he wanted to hang at his place tonight. His reply said to come hungry.

"Texting your boy, huh?" Sada asked, smiling over my shoulder. I laughed. "Get out of here."

It was better to keep things light with Sada. She never asked a lot of questions, but I didn't want her to start. My feelings for Asher weren't to be shared. She had been nagging us to go on a double date with her and Roger, her new boyfriend. I changed the subject whenever she brought it up. I didn't need to hear her voice outside of work; she talked enough during our eight-hour shifts.

"You and Asher," she said, pulling out her lip gloss to apply another layer, "are totally scrumptious together."

"We're just friends."

"Does Asher know that? The only time I see that boy anymore is when he's picking you up."

"You should talk; Roger's been keeping you pretty tied up."

"Oh, love, he has." She closed her eyes and smiled. "With handcuffs and scarves, and—"

"I get the point."

She puckered her lips and strutted to the counter.

* * *

I went home after work to shower, but none of my roommates were there. Each of us had changed so much since my first week at sober living. Kathy and Ashley had finally come out and told us they were together. They weren't hiding anymore, so I had to wear earplugs to bed. Diem hung out with the girls she worked with and was doing a summer term at Boston University. The only time I saw any of my roomies was at meetings and curfew. We would always be there for each other whenever it was needed, but in our own way, we had learned how to live again.

I put on a strapless sundress and belt that I'd gotten at Diem's boutique. Asher never commented on what I was wearing, which was usually my work clothes, but tonight I wanted to feel pretty. The dress showed off my waist, and Tiffany's cardigan hid my arms. I didn't want to appear too overdone, so I covered my lashes with a thin layer of mascara and swiped gloss across my lips.

While I was walking through the kitchen, the phone rang, and I stopped to answer it. "Hello?" When no one replied, I checked the caller ID and "Unknown" showed across the screen. "Hello?" I repeated.

"Have you missed me?"

Dustin?

I hadn't heard his voice in so long; it caused my skin to prickle. His breathing filled the silence. I closed my eyes and could almost feel it on my neck—his smell, the chunk of flesh missing from his nose. It was all too clear.

"How did you get my phone number?"

I also wanted to know where he'd gotten the money for a cell with an unlisted number. Cell phones were smuggled into prison the same way drugs were, but it was really expensive to get a number that couldn't be traced. But Dustin was never one to answer questions—and plus, I knew he had ways of getting money.

He let out a tiny moan. "I need to hear you say you miss me."

"Is that why you called?"

"My friend, who paid you a visit, said you became breathless when he mentioned my name."

"Did he tell you he got his ass kicked, too?"

"Baby, tell me you love me. Tell me you dream about my tongue licking—"

"I'm going to hang up if you don't tell me what you want."

Dustin's friend hadn't delivered a strong enough message to get me to help him out. Reminding me of his tongue wasn't going to persuade me either. The only thing I missed was his heroin.

"I need you to disappear if you're asked to testify."

"I'm the state's main witness; if I don't show up and give my testimony, you'll probably get out of jail."

"Exactly."

"Why would I want to do that for you?"

"Don't you want to be with me again?"

"I have to go," I said, my finger hovering over the button.

"Do this for me, baby. I don't deserve twenty-five years in jail."

"Good-bye, Dustin."

"What the fuck is wrong with you? You're not taking me seriously. You should be."

"There's nothing I need from you, so I don't have to listen to you anymore."

He was silent for a minute. "When you close your eyes, you can still feel me touching your body. No one has made you moan like I have. Baby, let me make you moan again."

"I...I'm done listening to this."

As I was hanging up, he said, "Just think about it."

There was nothing to think about; I was done with that life. I wasn't going to help him get out of jail by failing to appear in court. I could get in serious trouble for that. He deserved to be in there— even more than I had. For the five years I'd been a junkie, I hadn't made any right decisions. I wasn't that girl anymore, and nothing Dustin said was going to bring her back.

* * *

On the way to the train station, a pair of ratty sneakers stuck out of the storefront where Sunshine had been. As I got closer, the gray blanket came into view, and then her cardboard sign.

I reached for my wallet and handed her a dollar.

"I need a hell of a lot more than that," she said.

She was more awake than before, and her eye looked a little better. It was no longer swollen, and there was only a small line of black under her lid.

"That's all you're getting; just enough for a cheeseburger," I said.

"You know I ain't gonna buy no cheeseburger."

"You look like you could use one."

"I could use a bundle of dope and a new rig. You got that for me in that little purse of yours?"

"The contents of my purse are much different than they were when I lived with you." I paused. "You be careful out here."

"Nicole," she yelled, and I turned around. "Is it hard? You know, not being on the needle anymore?"

"It's harder than being on the needle."

She swiped the air with her hand. "Fuck that."

"But I know you don't want to keep living like this. I didn't."

She answered with her eyes.

"I can help you," I said.

"I ain't going to no rehab."

"You know how bad I was, and I did it. You can do it, too." She didn't respond. "Let me know if you change your mind."

Sunshine had been in the game for so long that heroin had made her stop believing she deserved any better. I'd been out of the game for months, and I still wasn't sure I did, either. Was sobriety my savior? That answer wasn't clear yet. What I did know was that dope teased and begged, asking Sunshine to chase its high. The one she got when she injected for the first time, the one that gave her body the most intense feeling it'd ever had. But no matter how much dope she shot after that, she'd never get that high again. At least not from drugs. I just hoped I could convince her to chase life before she took the shot that killed her.

* * *

Asher buzzed me in and met me in the hallway. His hands gripped my waist and he went to kiss my cheek, but I moved my face so he landed on my mouth. The peck was soft like his lips.

"You look beautiful," he said.

Asher's words were so different from Dustin's. But Dustin was right: no one made me moan like he had. Sometimes all it had taken was a glance in my direction or his hand on my thigh, and my legs would spread. Wide.

He led me into his apartment; the lights were dimmed and the table was set.

"Do I smell lasagna?" I asked.

He pulled out a chair for me. "Didn't you say it was your favorite?"

I noticed a bowl of salad and a plate of garlic bread on the table. "Did you make all this?"

He disappeared into the kitchen and came back with a pan of lasagna. He wasn't using potholders and almost dropped it on the way to the table. "I got the recipe from the Internet," he said. He cut a piece and put it on my plate. The sauce was watery, and the top noodle slid off the stack.

Other than my father and Michael, no guy had ever cooked for me. None of them would have known my favorite foods either. Dustin didn't need to; his heroin filled me.

Asher tried to fix the noodle, but the cheese fell off too. "Nadal usually does the cooking." He grinned bashfully.

I put my hand on his arm. "It's perfect." I waited for him to plop a piece on his plate and take a seat. "I really appreciate you doing this for me."

His face turned a little red, and he took a sip of the light brown liquid.

I pointed at my glass, which was filled with the same. "Iced tea?"

"That's always what's in your to-go cup when you leave the café."

I scooped the first bite into my mouth. "This might be the best lasagna I've ever had."

"You're being kind," he said. "I know it's missing something."

It was missing more than one thing. The sauce tasted like watery tomatoes.

"It's a hell of a lot better than what I could make. I should have brought dessert from the café."

"Got it covered."

"You made dessert, too?"

"I know how much you love chocolate, so I made something with fruit." He winked.

The knob on the front door rattled as it unlocked, and Nadal came in with his arm around a girl I assumed was Tyme.

"Shit, I forgot you said you were going to be home tonight," Nadal said with a smirk.

Asher shook his head. "You didn't forget."

Tyme walked over and stuck her hand out. "You must be Cole."

I felt all the color drain from my face. That was the nickname my family had given to me when I was kid. No one called me Cole except them.

"Nicole..." I took a deep breath. "My name is Nicole."

"Oh, I thought Nadal said—"

"Her brother used to call her Cole." Nadal glared at me as though I were a mosquito. "That was, until she got him killed."

The lasagna and garlic bread rose in my throat.

"That was fucking low, Nadal," Asher said.

"Michael was my friend, and he died because of her. What else did you expect from me?"

I pushed my chair away from the table and moved for my purse on the back of the couch. When I turned around, Asher was in front of me.

"Please don't go."

If I opened my mouth, something other than words was going to come out. I shook my head and tried to move around him.

He put his hands on my sides and shielded me with his back. "You're an asshole," he told his brother. "She's suffered enough."

"No, she hasn't. And I don't understand you."

"What's going on?" Tyme asked.

"You don't have to understand me, but you have to respect her," Asher said.

"Respect her?" Nadal laughed. "She's nothing but a junkie and a murderer."

I wiggled out of Asher's hold, yanked the door open, and ran until I got to the end of the block. My chest was so tight I could hardly breathe.

I was sober, but life wasn't suddenly all better. I was still in Boston, the city I'd fucked for drugs. And Dustin, whose dick I'd sucked for almost a year, was threatening me. In the past, he'd killed people for hurting me. What would he do to someone who was hurting him?

My knees felt weak. I reached for the stop sign, but my fingers missed the pole. My ass hit the pavement, and the movement sent all the food to my throat. I dug my nails into the ground and leaned over, throwing up Asher's dinner and the coffee I'd had for breakfast.

"I'm sorry," Asher said. He was out of breath and kneeled beside me. "Nicole, I'm so sorry."

I didn't want him to see my tears, the mascara that was probably streaking down my cheeks, and the bile on my lips. I covered my face with my hands and rested my forehead on the pole.

"You didn't deserve that."

My hands dropped, revealing the mess underneath.

"I deserved everything he said. Nadal's not the only one who doesn't understand you. I don't either. I'm—"

"Do you feel this?" He took my hands and placed them on his chest. His heart was beating so fast. "This is the way I feel whenever

I'm with you. I felt it the first night we met, and I've been feeling it ever since."

"But—"

"You need to stop blaming yourself. You didn't kill Michael."

"Yes, I did! He fought my pimp because he was trying to save me. I didn't pull the trigger, but I might as well have."

"Stop." He stood and helped me to my feet. "I—"

"Nadal's right. I'm nothing but a junkie and a murderer."

"Don't ever say that. You deserve better."

"Don't you see my scars?" I tore off my sweater and threw it to the ground. "They're all over my fucking body!"

He held one of his hands up in front of my face. "Do you see this?" There was a thick white line that ran across his wrist. "I have them too. Every day they remind me of the place I was in. I'm not there anymore, but that doesn't mean I've forgotten."

I pulled his hand toward me and pressed my lips against his skin, kissing the length of the scar.

"The person I care about is the one standing in front of me," he said.

I fell into his arms. My fingers clutched the back of his shirt, and he gripped my hair.

"The past is behind you," he said. "It doesn't change the way I feel about you. Nothing will, especially not Nadal."

The past was supposed to be behind you. Mine wasn't. It was swirling around me and closing in. I wasn't sure if it would ever be behind me.

CHAPTER EIGHT

The way Asher had stood up for me in front of Nadal was a lot to process. So was the dinner he cooked, the way he had paid close attention to everything I liked, and the fact that my heart wasn't the only thing that throbbed when I was around him. He was slowly peeling back my layers, getting to know what made me tick and how to make me smile. For some reason, I wasn't stopping him.

I thought I'd memorized every part of his body that wasn't hidden behind clothes, but I had missed his scar. He might have seen more of mine if Nadal and Tyme hadn't busted in. That wouldn't happen now. I wasn't going over to his apartment again. After that night, things weren't the same between the twins. I told Asher I didn't want him to fight with his brother; if he had to choose a side, he should choose Nadal's. He wouldn't listen. He didn't care that Nadal didn't agree with him; he was pissed at the way he'd treated me.

Because Nadal had voiced his opinion in front of Tyme, Sada now knew about my past. I could tell by the look on her face when she came through the door and the way she walked toward me. It was a march, unlike her usual prance, and she grabbed my arm on her way to the backroom.

Fucking Nadal. I was a junkie and a murderer, but did he have to say that in front of Tyme—who couldn't wait to tell Sada? Knowing Sada, she would probably run her mouth to everyone who worked here. This had been a place where no one knew anything about my past, besides Al. Once Jami, the girl I worked the counter with, and the guys in the kitchen found out, that would all change. Their looks alone would make me want to quit.

Once we reached the back, Sada blurted out, "Why didn't you tell me you were a junkie?"

"Would it have made a difference?"

Her stare hardened and her lip curled.

"I didn't tell you because I didn't want to see that look on your face—the one you're showing right now." I stood up straight and clenched my fists in a ball. "Plus, it's none of your business."

"It isn't my business? I invited you over to my apartment and brought you around my friends. I trusted that you were normal. That you wouldn't...you know, steal from them like all you junkies do."

I couldn't believe what I was hearing. My ears literally burned from her stupidity.

"Have I ever done anything to make you believe I'm not trustworthy? I'm dating one of your friends, and he thinks I'm good enough."

"Asher's an idiot to be dating someone like you. I thought he was better than that. I guess I was wrong."

"Better than what? You? I saw you snorting coke that night at his apartment, you fucking hypocrite. How dare you stand here and judge me."

She grabbed my arm and pushed up my sleeve. I could have pulled away. I didn't. I wasn't proud of my scars, but I sure as hell wasn't going to let her make me feel bad about them.

Her stare traveled over my forearm, up my chest, and penetrated my eyes. "Just like I thought. Track marks everywhere. With all the men you've fucked for drugs, you're probably loaded with diseases. Stay the hell away from me, you junkie whore."

I wasn't going to fight with her or bother separating the lies she said from the truth. I didn't trust my voice. I knew if I opened my mouth, my tone would turn high-pitched and my lips would quiver.

She tied her apron around her waist and pushed up her padded bra. "Don't worry, I won't tell all our coworkers that you're a slut. I'll just tell them you're a heroin addict who got your brother murdered." She pranced down the hallway toward the front.

I went into Al's office and asked if we could talk. He was going to find out soon enough; he might as well hear it from me. Mark had already told him about my brother and how he'd died, so I filled him in on what he didn't know: how Sada had introduced me to the twins, their connection to Michael, and the fight I'd just had with her. "I'm sure Sada's telling everyone right now," I said. "I don't want them to look down on you for hiring me."

He leaned forward in his chair, closing the space between us. "I met Jami at AA, and the guys who work in the kitchen were in rehab with me. Trust me, none of them will look down on either of us."

The knot in my stomach started to settle.

"If she says a word to anyone, she'll be gone," he said.

"I didn't come in here to get her fired," I said, gripping the edge of his desk.

"I know you didn't, but she's constantly late and always has an attitude. When she starts talking about other people's business, that's the final straw." He briefly checked his watch. "There's an AA meeting going on just a few blocks up the street. If you leave right now, you'll have time to share. I don't want you to come back until your head is clear."

He gave me the address, and just as I got to the door, he said my name. I turned around.

"All of us here have worked too damn hard to stay sober; we don't deserve to be judged."

*　　*　　*

When I got back to the café, Jami ran out from behind the counter and pulled me into her arms. She was even taller than Asher, so I had to turn my head so my face wouldn't land in her chest.

"That bitch is gone," she said. "She started talking shit about you, so I went into Al's office and had her taken care of."

Jami must not have known I'd spoken to Al. I was sure her push had helped, but he'd sounded like he was looking for any reason to get rid of Sada.

"Welcome to the family, girl," she said. "I know we go to different meetings, me being in AA and all, but if you ever want to come with me, you just tell me, OK?"

I squeezed her a little tighter.

"I will."

"Don't you let girls like Sada get to you. We here understand you." She kissed the top of my head and went back to the counter.

On my way to the backroom, I thought about what Jami had said. Al and his employees weren't the only ones who understood me. There were new people attending my NA meetings every day. I'd graduated from rehab with over thirty addicts, and more had come in to take our beds. There were so many other rehab centers around Boston, and NA groups in various parts of the city. In my world, Sada and Nadal were minorities. Despite what they thought about me, I would never be alone.

Support came in many forms—Ashley and Kathy worrying about me relapsing, Tiffany giving me a hug before bed, my parents calling a few times a week, Asher cooking my favorite dinner, or the people at my job sharing a similar past. Everyone in my life was there for a reason.

* * *

I'd already gone to a meeting in the morning, so I sent Asher a text to let him know I could meet earlier. I went into the kitchen to say good-bye to the guys, and the baker and busboy stopped to give me a hug. They were just as sweet as Jami, inviting me to their meetings and out for coffee if I ever needed to talk.

"That goes both ways," I said.

"I appreciate that," they replied.

I grabbed my purse and stopped by Al's office. He was on the phone, so I waved and headed outside. Sada and her boyfriend, Roger, were standing on the sidewalk between the café and alley. They looked like they were waiting for me. As I walked toward them, Sada looked down and reached for a piece of her hair. Roger stood like a bodyguard: arms crossed, back straight, feet grounded.

"Nicole," someone said from behind me.

It was Mark. I didn't know what he was doing here, but I let him catch up.

"Al told me what happened. Are you all right?"

"He made me go to a meeting, and I feel much better."

"What's she still doing here?" he asked, using his head to point to the alley.

I shrugged.

"Let's go find out."

"You don't have to—"

He put his arm around my shoulders. "You're crazy if you think I'm going to let you deal with this on your own."

Mark led me to the corner, and we stopped just in front of them. Roger was the size of a professional wrestler, with lots of tats and long hair.

"Who the hell are you?" Roger said to Mark.

"What the fuck are you two still doing here?" Mark asked.

I suddenly had a flashback of when I'd worked at Mark's bar. A college boy was being too flirty and grabbed my ass. When Mark told him to apologize, the guy called me a whore. Mark punched him in the face. Roger was bigger than the college boy, but Mark didn't seem like a guy who got intimidated by size.

"He's my boss' brother," Sada said. "My old boss, anyway."

"What's the problem here?" Mark asked.

Roger pointed at me. "That junkie bitch got my girl fired."

"She got herself fired," Mark said. "She should have kept her mouth shut instead of gossiping about business that wasn't hers to tell."

Sada finally looked up. A bruise had formed around her left eye. It was swollen and she could hardly open it, but she tried to cover it with her hair. She had mentioned that Roger got a little rough sometimes. He must have punished her for losing her job.

"So fucking what." Roger took a step forward. "Gossiping ain't a reason to fire someone."

"No, but decreasing employee morale, breaking the dress code, and being consistently late for every shift are," Mark said. His hand tightened on my shoulder. "You got anything else to say?"

"I'm going to convince Asher to break up with you," Sada said, "and when he does, Nadal and I are going to laugh behind your back."

"You're a stupid bitch," I said.

Mark looked at me. "We done here?"

"We are now."

Roger pointed at me. "You better watch your back!" Sada wrapped her hands around his arm and pulled him away.

"I'm parked around the corner," Mark said. "I'll give you a lift home."

I thanked him as soon as he put the key in the ignition. Not just for giving me a ride home but for helping me out with Sada and Roger. I'd been hesitant to take Al's job with Mark being a link to my past. I had just wanted to move on, but every night when I got in bed and closed my eyes, I remembered what happened the night my brother got killed. I realized my future would always be intertwined with my past. I couldn't fight it. I wasn't going to anymore.

"Who's that guy Sada was talking about? What was his name... Asher?"

"He's just someone I've been hanging out with."

"Aren't you supposed to wait a year before you start dating?"

"That's what they teach us in rehab, but Asher and I aren't dating."

"But Sada said—"

"Sada has no idea what she's talking about."

"Is Asher an addict too?"

I shook my head. "There's something I need to ask you," I said.

"You know you can talk to me about anything."

I looked at him. His eyes seemed so genuine, like he was really trying to help. How could I ruin that by asking him why he'd tried to take advantage of me at the bar that night, all those years ago? No, it had been worse than that. Even understanding my addiction, Mark had used it against me, offering to give me my dope back for a quick fuck. I hadn't forgotten. I needed to talk to him about it, but was this really the right time?

We were only a few blocks from my apartment when Sunshine's sign caught my attention. She was sitting in front of an apartment building rather than her usual doorway, with her sign resting in her lap. Her head wasn't slumped forward, but her face didn't look right. As Mark's car came to a complete stop, I said, "I'll be right back."

I jumped out of the car and ran to Sunshine as fast as I could. When I got to her side, foam was coming out of her mouth. Her lips were blue.

"Sunshine?" I slapped her face. "Sunshine, wake up!"

I remembered someone telling me not to let an addict slip further into their nod. You had to get them up and move them around to increase their pulse, or blood pressure, or some shit like that.

I put her arm around my shoulder and lifted her to her feet. The people passing by didn't stop or volunteer to help. I was on my own. She was dead weight but couldn't have been more than eighty pounds. Her toes dragged as I hauled her down the sidewalk, and I shook her face and hands. She started to slowly come back, opening her eyes and talking gibberish. Her feet began to move, and she took small steps.

"Who is she? And is she OK?" Mark asked, out of breath.

"Nicole?" Sunshine's question sounded more like a moan.

"Help me get her to the blanket," I said.

Mark took her arm off my shoulder and picked her up, setting her down on her gray blanket.

Sunshine's eyes fully opened, and she glanced between Mark and me. "What the hell happened?"

I sat in front of her and took a deep breath. "You OD'd. You probably would have died if we hadn't been driving by."

"Isn't that something," she said, drool slipping out of her mouth.

"That's all you have to say?" Mark said

"You should've let me die."

Before placing her arm in my lap, I flipped it over. It was covered with track marks, some so deep they looked infected. My scars weren't any prettier, but she could overcome hers, too. "You deserve more than this."

"It's too late for me."

"It's never too late," Mark said.

"Do you want me to get you some help?" I asked.

"I can't do it," she said. "I won't make it in rehab."

"Do you want help?" I asked.

She rested her elbows on her knees and covered her face with her fingers. She sat like that for a few minutes and then her hands dropped. "I want it."

"Stay here," I said to the both of them. I walked to the end of the block and called Tiffany. As an employee of the rehab center, she'd know who to talk to about getting Sunshine admitted. After I told Tiffany the whole story, she said she'd call me right back.

Sunshine and Mark were smoking cigarettes when I returned. He handed me the pack and I lit one up. Just as I fired up my second one, the phone rang. Tiffany said they had a bed, but it wasn't in the detox wing. Sunshine would have to detox in one of the main wings, which meant they would assign her a nurse to help her get through withdrawal. And her being dope sick would really piss off her roommate. I told her that didn't matter as long as they could admit her tonight. She said to get there as fast as we could.

I hung up the phone and looked at Mark. "Can you drive us?"

"Right now?" Sunshine asked. "I need one more hit first."

I reached for her hand. "Your last one almost killed you."

"Then I'm not going," she said, yanking her fingers out of my grip.

"You're going," I said.

"Not unless I can shoot up. I need to say good-bye."

I couldn't get needles in prison, so I'd snorted a bag of dope the night before I was released and then went to rehab in the morning. It was a final good-bye, like Sunshine said.

"Fine. One last nod."

"Wait, what? You can't be serious," Mark said.

"If that's what it takes to get her to come with us, I'm dead fucking serious. It's better than the alternative." I acknowledged Sunshine. Her head was drooping, and white foam had dried on her dirty cheeks.

Mark's eyes told me he wanted to argue, but he nodded and said, "You're right."

"Do you have some, or do we need to stop?" I asked.

She tapped her bag. "Got just enough."

My hands started to feel numb; I squeezed my fingers into fists. My mouth watered.

"I can't..." I swallowed. "Mark, I can't be with her when she does it."

Mark helped Sunshine to her feet. He folded up her blanket and slung her bag over his shoulder. "What's your phone number?" I gave it to him, and he put it in his phone. "I'll call you when she's done." They both walked to his car.

I leaned against the apartment building and pictured Sunshine in the backseat. I'd shot up with her so many times that I knew her routine. She'd take the packets of dope from her purse and then a bottle of water, spoon, needle, cotton ball, and lighter, and put it all on the seat next to her. She'd dump the packets onto the spoon and add in a little water. The lighter would heat it, and she'd drop in the cotton ball once the mixture was hot. The tip of the needle would suck up the liquid, and while she looked for a vein, she'd put the chamber between her lips. Her fingers would tap different spots on her arm. When she found one, she'd slide the tip into her skin and pull back on the plunger to make sure she'd hit a vein, and blood would trickle into the chamber. The rush would set in as soon as the needle was empty.

The packets of powder, the nod, and the rush were all so close. Its flavor was on my tongue; its euphoria was in my veins. I turned in the opposite direction Mark had taken Sunshine, and my feet began to move. I couldn't stop them. I didn't want to.

As I got to the corner, only a block from the train station, Claire's voice echoed in my head. She was telling me to turn around. *Fuck*, I thought. I was so close. The best high of my life was waiting for me in Roxbury. I hadn't used in so long that the rush would blow my mind. I wanted to cross the street, but there were too many cars. I reached up and pushed the button on the light post, again and again, as if pushing it repeatedly would make the light change faster.

The light turned yellow, and as I stepped onto the crosswalk, a glimmer caught my eye: the ring Claire's son had given to me when she died. It fit perfectly on my finger, just like it had on hers. Her comforting voice kept repeating, "Turn around."

Claire had been my invisible roommate while I was in prison. I had never spoken to her—I only listened—but I was talking to her now. I asked her to keep me strong and to help me fight the urges. She told me I was sober, and that's all she had ever wanted. That I had fought too hard to relapse. Horns honked, and reality came rushing back to me. My heart was thumping in my chest. Angry drivers flipped me off as I stepped back onto the sidewalk. Claire's voice had turned me around. When I'd put another block between the train station and me, Claire's voice told me she was proud.

My phone rang.

"I'm on the corner of Commercial and Hanover Street," Mark said.

My feet began to move again. "I'll be there in a second."

"Are you OK?"

"I think so," I said. "Thanks…you know, for doing that for me…and for everything today."

"I'm always here for you."

Just as I climbed in the backseat, Sunshine's chin was beginning to droop. "Come here," I said, guiding her head onto my lap. She curled her knees up to her chest and wrapped her arms around them.

I ran my fingers through her blonde hair. Her locks smelled like smoke and felt like they'd been soaked in olive oil. Her jeans were full of holes, and her brown, sleeveless shirt was stained. When she had to throw up, I grabbed a plastic grocery bag off the floor and held it for her. She wasn't dope sick; the rush was just too much sometimes.

I could smell heroin in her bile. The scent was a mix of kid vitamins and vinegar, and it used to be the only fragrance my nose craved. The taste trumped that of all my favorite foods. The feeling was like a fleece blanket and a campfire on the coldest night. It wrapped me in a cocoon and wouldn't let anything else inside. I was free to explore the depths of each dream, the tingling of my muscles, and the sparks shooting from each nerve.

"Where do I turn?" Mark asked.

I blinked a few times to clear my vision. "At the next light."

He pulled down the street and into the front parking lot. I slid out from under Sunshine's head and knocked on the front door. The secretary smiled and held up a finger. By the time Mark had pulled her out of the backseat, a tech was coming out with a wheelchair. He set her on the seat and put her feet on the pads.

"I'll come see you when they allow visitors," I said.

Her pupils were the size of sand, and the whites of her eyes were bloodshot. Her lids were getting heavy; her hands gripped the side rails.

"Hang in there," I said. "I know you can do it."

Mark and I watched the tech's back as he wheeled Sunshine into the building. He moved past the front and turned down the hallway.

"I'll pray for her," Mark said.

"That's all we can do."

CHAPTER NINE

My cell phone rang just as Mark and I crossed the Tobin Bridge to the city. The clock on the dashboard showed seven. I'd forgotten that I'd sent Asher a text to meet me an hour early. When I answered, I told him I was running late and would be there soon.

"Was that Asher?" Mark asked.

I nodded.

"You guys hanging out tonight?"

I didn't want to be rude and turn up the radio, but I didn't feel like talking. This was the first time I'd had any quiet all day, and I really needed the silence. With everything that had happened with Sunshine, the fight with Roger and Sada seemed like days ago. Sunshine shooting up in the seat behind me, however, was fresh in my mind. I could still hear Claire's voice echoing in my head, stopping me from relapsing. And it made me shudder.

"Nicole?"

I sighed. "Yes, we're hanging out."

I needed to go to another meeting. Asher could walk me there and hang out at a coffee shop until it was over.

"He was friends with your brother?"

"His older brother dated mine, so yes."

"Does he have good intentions?"

"Does it matter? I told you; we're not even dating."

Was that true? I didn't know what was true anymore. I wasn't strong enough to fight off heroin on my own. If I wasn't at work or at a meeting, I was with Asher. I used to spend as much time with Eric, until he died from an overdose. But Eric was just my best friend; we never kissed. Things with Asher were different.

As I directed Mark to my apartment, he stayed silent, staring out the windshield. His lips were pursed. He must not have liked my answer. But what did he want from me? He had tried to take advantage of me, and if Asher hadn't been sitting on the front steps of my building with his arms crossed and heels tapping the pavement, I'd have confronted Mark about it.

"Is it all right if I call you tomorrow?" Mark asked.

"I guess that's fine." I shut the door and turned toward Asher. Mark's car pulled away from the curb, but Asher didn't move.

"So that's Mark?" Asher asked.

"How do you know—"

"Sada told me you got her fired and gave her a black eye. Why would you do that?"

"*What?*" I remembered the bruise around Sada's eye. She really was trying to get him to break up with me. "I didn't touch her, and I definitely didn't give her—"

"So you and Mark weren't hanging all over each other when you left the café?"

"We did leave the café together, but it's not what you think."

"I'm thinking a lot of things right now. None of them are good."

I stood in front of him, but he wouldn't look at me. "Let me explain." I crouched down and put my hands on his knees. "Sada doesn't want us together. Once she found out I was a junkie, I wasn't good enough. She has it out for me."

He stepped over me. "Maybe you have it out for her."

"You believe her?"

"She's never lied to me."

"And I have?" I stood and pushed past him, looking over my shoulder. "After everything I've told you, I sure as hell wouldn't start lying now."

"Where are you going?"

"To a meeting," I shouted.

I didn't stop walking until I got to the small basement where our meetings were held. I was twenty minutes late, but no one cared. I had come.

Everyone sat in a circle, and I found a space between Ashley and Diem. I slid over a chair and squeezed between them, listening until it was my turn to speak. When one of the vets called on me, I took a deep breath and explained how I'd run into Sunshine twice over the last month. How I'd found her today, overdosing in front of an apartment building, and how I took her to rehab.

"How do you feel now?" someone asked.

I closed my eyes and replayed the scene in my head. I was leaning against the building, picturing Sunshine prepare the dope, and then I was walking toward the needle. "I can still feel it in my veins."

"What stopped you?" someone else asked.

I hadn't told them about Claire. I didn't want them to think I was crazy; hearing voices inside your head was never a good thing. I already had one disease, and I didn't need another

"I don't want to go back there," I said.

"Back to what?"

"Living on the street, fucking Johns to get my next fix," I said.

"As a junkie, that's part of the lifestyle. Neither matters much when you're high," one of the vets said. "What really stopped you from using?"

I closed my eyes again. "My best friend's voice was in my head, telling me to turn around."

"What if you hadn't heard her voice?" Ashley asked.

"I wouldn't be at this meeting."

"Eventually, that voice will be replaced with yours," the vet said.

I hoped that was true.

"I'm proud of you, Nicole," Kathy said. "We all are."

Were they? I know I wasn't proud of myself.

One of the vets asked me to lead the prayer, and we all joined hands in a circle. I spoke the lines we recited at the beginning and end of each meeting, and we all moved over to the coffee station. While I waited in line, some of the people gave me a hug and patted my shoulder. Kathy offered to pour me a cup, but I asked for a donut instead. I didn't need caffeine to keep me awake; it was going to be hard enough to sleep already.

My roommates and I walked up the stairs. Just as I got through the door, I noticed Asher. He was standing by the building, his head pressed against the wall. Nonaddicts weren't allowed at our meetings, so I signaled him to move into the alley. I didn't want Asher to make anyone uncomfortable, and I didn't want to answer questions—like I'd have to do if we were seen together.

"What's wrong, Nicole?" Ashley asked.

I hovered on the edge of the street as they began to cross. "I have something I need to do. I'll see you all at the apartment, OK?"

"We'll come with you," Kathy said.

"No, I have to do this alone."

"Are you sure? You've had a long day," Kathy said.

I gave her a hug and then wrapped my arms around Diem and Ashley. "Don't worry, I'll be fine."

Once everyone had cleared away from the entrance, I met Asher in the alley. "What are you doing here? You know you can't come to my meetings—"

"You just left me on the sidewalk."

"What else was I supposed to do? After the day I've had, I didn't need to come home to Sada's lies and your accusations."

He gripped the spikes of his hair. "My brother's got me all fucked up, and then Sada..." His shoulders drooped, and his hands fell to his sides. "I overheard you in the meeting, talking about what happened with Sunshine. I didn't know..."

"That's because you didn't let me explain."

This was a lot, even for me. Addiction was new to Asher, and so was I; I couldn't expect him to understand it all, or to trust me either. Not when our relationship was still so new.

"I know, and I'm sorry," he said.

"Will you listen now?"

He reached for my fingers. "Tell me everything."

I pulled his hands up to my face and kissed them.

"But before you do," he said. "I want you to know I'm proud of you."

"Can we just get out of here?"

He put his arm around my waist and hailed a cab at the end of the alley.

* * *

I called the rehab center in the morning to check on Sunshine. I knew I wouldn't be able to talk to her, at least not for the first thirty days, but I was hoping my old counselor would give me an update. The secretary told me she'd page Allison and put me on hold.

"Nicole," Allison said, "it's so nice to hear from you. Tiffany tells me you're doing so well."

"I'm one hundred and eighty-nine days clean."

"I couldn't be more proud of you."

There was that word again: proud. With everyone so proud of me, why did I feel so horrible? I went into the kitchen and sat down next to Tiffany. "Thank you, but I'm actually calling to check on a patient. Her name is Sunshine."

"Would this be the same Sunshine we spoke about in our sessions?"

"Yes, I brought her in last night," I said.

"I'm sorry to say that Frances is no longer with us. It happened early this morning."

"Frances? Who's that?"

"Frances Nelson is Sunshine's real name."

I'd known Sunshine for six years and never knew her real name? A knot formed in my throat as I repeated, "Frances is no longer with us?"

Tiffany looked up from her textbook.

"Unfortunately, no. She discharged herself early this morning," Allison said.

"What's going on?" Tiffany whispered. "Is Sunshine OK?"

I put my finger up. "So she's not dead?"

"Oh no, honey, not that I know of. I didn't mean to scare you. I just meant she's not in our facility anymore."

I pictured Sunshine on the side of some suburban road, dope sick and starving. The rehab center was at least a twenty-minute drive from the city. Without any money, she'd have to hitchhike her way back to Boston.

"I really thought she wanted to get sober," I said.

"You should discuss these feelings at your next meeting. I hope you will be attending one today?" Allison asked.

"The group I usually go to meets at night."

"Is Tiffany with you?"

I handed the phone to Tiffany and went into the bathroom. While I scrubbed my hair with shampoo, I thought about all those nights Sunshine and I had worked the track together. Johns would slowly drive up and down the street, looking for a cheap girl to get them off. Sunshine would steal my clients. She'd offer to give them head for five bucks when I charged twenty. She also had me running to Richard, the man who had raped and beaten her, to re-up on our supply. The entire time I had been going to his house, she never told me he was the one who had done that to her. We gave up everything for our addiction—including the truth—even with other junkies. Sunshine had two children and lost them to the state. The only things she owned were a bag for her clothes, a purse, and a blanket. She didn't care, and I hadn't either.

Sobriety was a decision; we had to fight our disease and take away its power. Using was the easier choice. But if I was tempted to relapse again and Claire's voice wasn't inside my head, the image of Sunshine's face would be. I could never forget the foam that dripped from her mouth, the desperation in her eyes, or her blue lips. Heroin's high was magical, but life was starting to taste a whole lot better.

* * *

When I came out of the bathroom, Tiffany stopped reading and asked me if I wanted to talk about Sunshine.

"Why is that everyone's answer for everything?" I asked. "Talking isn't going to make it better."

"Allison is afraid you're going to be triggered to use."

"I don't want to use. I want to find Sunshine and bring her back to rehab."

"You know you can't do that, right?"

I sat down at the table and rested my chin on my palms. "What do you think I should do?"

"I think you should stop worrying about Sunshine and start worrying about yourself."

Tiffany should take her own advice. She hadn't been to one of our meetings in weeks. She said she'd been going to a group by Professor Allen's apartment. I didn't know if I believed her. She was getting skinnier, and her forehead was covered in acne. Even if she wasn't using, neither of those things was a good sign.

I got up from the table and hugged her from behind. She felt even bonier than she looked. "The five of us haven't done dinner in a while. How about this week?"

"I can't. I have study group."

"Every night?"

"This week and next," she said. "We'll do it soon, I promise."

I grabbed my purse and said good-bye. She didn't respond. With a lit cigarette in one hand and a can of Red Bull in the other, she'd gone back to her textbook.

My phone rang while I was walking to work. Mark's name appeared on the screen. "Have you heard anything?" he asked.

"Sunshine left rehab this morning."

"Oh…how are you holding up?"

"I'm bummed out. We did a lot to try to help her." But I knew the other side all too well. The side that yanked Sunshine from rehab and made her run back to heroin, just like I'd done with Dustin. The feeling in my stomach had been stronger than a craving or an urge. Like the starving who hadn't eaten in weeks, I would have done anything to get a hit. And I did. With my fingers intertwined with Dustin's, I'd walked out of rehab and had gone straight to Richard's. The debate in my head lasted only seconds before I'd glided the needle into my arm.

"Maybe she'll realize the opportunity she lost and ask you for help again," he said.

"I hope so."

"Hope is all we have."

CHAPTER TEN

A week had passed since Sunshine had left rehab, and I still couldn't shut off my brain. I lay in bed, and heroin drifted in and out of my mind. Faces from my past lingered behind my lids, words replayed in my ears, and my eyes would shoot open.

My fingers took me over the peak; my body would shudder, and I'd try to relax so that sleep would come easier. It never did. Even after two, sometimes three orgasms, I still didn't feel fulfilled. I craved Asher's touch. We'd been teasing each other for more than a month, and with nowhere for us to be alone, I ached. I'd been fucked against a dumpster in an alley and in the backseat of a car; I didn't want that again. I'd spent years living in hotels around Boston, and none of those memories were good, so hotels were not an option. Neither was Asher's apartment. I wasn't taking the chance of running into Nadal again.

I was lying awake in bed waiting for the alarm to go off when Al called to ask if I'd come to work a few hours before my shift. The assistant baker was on vacation and he needed someone to fill in. I was relieved; the overtime would help. I had only three months before I had to find a place to live. Ashley and Kathy were getting a place together, and Diem was moving to Florida with some of the girls she worked with. No one at work or at my NA meetings was looking for a roommate. I could afford a studio apartment on my own; I just needed to save enough to furnish it.

While I was mixing a batch of biscotti, Jami came into the kitchen and told me Asher was here. I was only halfway through my shift; something must have happened.

Asher was sitting by the window, his head down and his hands folded on the table.

"Are you OK? What's wrong?" I slid into the chair across from him.

He looked up. Slowly. Something was off, and it took me only a second to realize what it was. "*Nadal?*" I asked.

He nodded. "Can we talk?"

My hands started to shake. My legs, too. The three shots of espresso on an empty stomach weren't helping. I didn't want to say anything until I knew where the conversation was headed, so I nodded. If he was here to reprimand me or make me feel bad, I wasn't going to listen.

"I owe you an apology," he said. "I never gave you a chance, and I'm sorry."

"Does Asher know you're here?"

"He hasn't spoken to me since I interrupted your dinner."

That was a funny way to put it. He'd done more than just interrupt.

"Is Asher the only reason you're apologizing?"

He looked at his hands and took a deep breath. "I miss my brother." His eyes moved back to mine, and he shook his head. "I judged you because of your past, and I didn't think you were good enough for him."

I missed my brother, too. Nadal had said some harsh words to me; they had caused me to flee his apartment and throw up all over the sidewalk. He couldn't take those words back, but I could eventually forgive him. I knew all about forgiveness. It was exactly what I was asking my family to do.

"I'm not the same girl Michael told you about, but I'm not asking you to forget her. I'm asking you to give me a chance. Can you do that?"

He stuck out his hand. "Can you give me another chance? Maybe in time, we can even be friends."

"I would like that," I said, shaking his hand.

"Nicole, I know you're not the same girl you once were. If you were, Asher never would have fallen in love with you."

My jaw dropped.

Love. Was that what it was? We'd shown our feelings through actions instead of words. Maybe that was because once we discussed how we felt, I would have to make a decision. The counselors in rehab said we needed to spend our first year getting to know ourselves as people and not addicts. They said it was common to replace drugs with love, which could give us the same kind of high, and it increased our chance of relapsing. Heroin was a body and mind high. Asher's attention was an emotional high, but it spread to each limb, and he made me smile more than I had in years. I knew I shouldn't be with him at this stage of my sobriety, but was doing the right thing always the best thing?

"I care about him, too," I said.

"He understands pain; he's been through it. Don't make him feel that kind of pain again."

I thought of the marks on Asher's wrist. He hadn't been as open about his scars as I had been about mine.

"Isn't that something Asher and I have in common?" I asked.

He nodded.

I smiled, silently thanking him for coming to talk to me, and he returned the expression. It wasn't just the freckle that made their appearances different. Their smiles weren't alike; Asher's was warm and inviting, but Nadal's looked forced, like he was trying to please.

Suddenly, I heard my name; Mark was pulling a chair over to our table.

"I'm sorry to interrupt," Mark said, "but I have to show you something." He took out his phone, tapped the screen, and handed it to me. It was an article that had been printed this morning in the *Boston Globe*.

"What is—"

"Just read it," Mark said.

Mark introduced himself to Nadal while I began reading the article. A woman had been found in a dumpster in Dorchester, ruled a homicide. The victim didn't have any identification on her, and dental records couldn't be cross-referenced because she didn't have any teeth. She appeared to be in her late forties with fair skin, blonde hair, and blue eyes. Her approximate height and weight were listed, and it said signs of drug use were evident on her body. She was wearing blue jeans and a brown, sleeveless shirt. The police were asking anyone with information to come forward.

I looked at Mark, my eyes wide and my mouth open.

"Sunshine was wearing blue jeans and a brown shirt, and everything else matches up," Mark said. "Do you think it's her?"

CHAPTER ELEVEN

The last time I'd been at a police station, I was wearing handcuffs. My fingerprints were taken, and I was booked and then thrown behind bars for two-and-a-half years. This time was different. Mark and I sat in front of Officer Hunt's desk, giving Sunshine's description and the last place we'd seen her. Hunt took notes as we spoke, probably comparing our statement to the one we'd told personnel just an hour earlier. After we answered all of his questions, Hunt told us he'd be back in a few minutes.

"Do you think it's Sunshine?" I asked.

"I hope not, but he's not giving us any information."

All the desks were filled with uniforms who were either typing on their computers or reading from files. For the first time in a while, I wasn't guilty of anything, but that didn't mean I wanted to hang out here. The few run-ins I'd had with cops weren't good ones.

I cracked each of my knuckles, and when they wouldn't pop anymore, I bit the skin around my nails. "I can't wait to get out of here."

"It shouldn't be much longer," Mark said. He put his hands on my shoulders and massaged, finding a knot behind my blade. "I don't like being here either."

Hunt returned with a man who had a thin gray mustache and wore a black suit. "This is Detective Raymond," Hunt said.

Raymond shook both our hands. "I'd like you to come to the city morgue," he said. "Your description of the victim is almost identical to the medical examiner's evaluation, but unless you identify the body, we won't know whether it's Frances Nelson."

I looked at Mark.

"Are you up for this?" Mark asked.

"Do I have a choice? If I don't go, we won't know."

We followed Raymond through the station and out toward the parking lot. The unmarked car he led us to was the same color as his suit. As Mark and I got in the backseat, I wished Raymond would put on the siren to get us there faster. He didn't. We waited through the traffic and stopped at all the red lights.

He pulled into a spot marked for law enforcement, and we went in through the main door, taking the elevator to the medical examiner's office. He flashed his badge to the woman in the front, and we were escorted down a long hallway and into a private room. There was a table along the far wall. The outline of a body could be seen through the white sheet.

My teeth chattered despite the long-sleeved shirt and jeans I wore. The room felt like the walk-in fridge at the café. The smell, decayed meat and rancid lobster, reminded me of when I was a maid at the hotel and found a dead man naked on top of a bed. The smell had made me throw up. I put my sleeve over my nose and mouth and breathed in the scent of laundry detergent.

Mark held my other hand, and when Raymond moved next to the body and asked us to join him, Mark's got as sweaty as mine.

Raymond's fingers gripped the top of the sheet; he pulled it back, revealing blonde locks, a fair forehead, a nose, lips, and finally a neck. He stopped and released the sheet.

Goose bumps covered my whole body.

"Ms. Brown," Raymond said, "is this Ms. Frances Nelson, or Sunshine, as you refer to her?"

Not too long ago, I'd been as addicted as Sunshine. I bought my drugs from the same dealer and walked the streets of Dorchester where all the gangs hung out. I'd heard stories of what happened to girls like me who were out late at night: shootings, stabbings, muggings. I hadn't cared. Sunshine hadn't either. The skin on her neck was turning purple, her complexion was gray, and her eyes were closed. But it was her. My friend had taken her last shot and ended up in a dumpster with probably a whole lot more than just dope inside her.

"Yes," I said, and my voice cracked. I cleared my throat. "It's her."
Raymond looked at Mark.

"That's her," Mark said, shaking his head.

"I'll take you back to the station so you can fill out some paperwork and get your car," Raymond said.

I glanced at Mark. Based on his expression, we were thinking the same thing: it could have easily been me on that table.

* * *

Mark took me out to lunch even though neither of us was hungry. We couldn't have a drink to celebrate Sunshine's life, so we had iced tea and forced down a bowl of soup. He didn't know much about her except that we were roommates. I shared some of our stories…the good times we'd had together, like when Claire had cooked us Thanksgiving dinner and made cakes for our birthdays.

"Not all of it was bad," Mark said.

I tried to think of other times we'd hung out when we weren't working the track, getting high, or going through withdrawal. I couldn't come up with anything. "Most of it was, but she shouldn't have been beaten to death and left in a dumpster."

"I hope they find whoever killed her and that he rots in prison…" He put his hand on mine. "I'm sorry, I didn't mean to offend you."

"You didn't. I deserved the time I spent in jail. If I hadn't gone there, I probably would've ended up like her."

"As awful as this sounds, I'm glad you went there too."

There was something about Mark that was comforting. Maybe it was that he knew the old me. He knew how far I'd come, and somehow, he showed up whenever I needed help. He'd changed a lot, too; he didn't smell like stale beer and cigarettes anymore. His hair was cut short, he'd taken out his earring, and—even though they looked vintage—I could tell his clothes were expensive.

"I owe you an apology," he said, cutting off my thoughts.

"For what?"

"We've come a long way, Nicole, and I'm glad you're back in my life. But that doesn't excuse what I tried to do to you."

"I was going to talk to you about that."

He took a sip of his drink. "I was so in the wrong. You were high and vulnerable, and I took advantage of that."

"I was—"

"No, this is all on me. I never should have touched you. I'm so sorry."

He apologized, and there was sincerity in his eyes. There was no point in dragging it out. I had agreed to fuck him to get my heroin back. It wasn't like I'd been in the right, either.

I put my hand on his. "Me too."

"I better get you back to work. If Al wasn't short staffed this week, I'd take you to the aquarium."

I laughed. "The aquarium? Really?"

"Haven't you ever been there?"

"Junkies don't hustle to buy tickets to see fish."

Mark smiled. "You don't know what you're missing. We'll go next week, and I'll introduce you to Myrtle the Turtle."

The waitress dropped off the leather receipt holder, and Mark put his credit card back in his wallet.

"Sounds like fun," I said.

After he signed his name, he looked up and smiled. "You're going to be with me; of course it will be fun."

There had been an awkward silence when we'd driven back to the city after dropping Sunshine at rehab, but that was gone. Mark told me about the townhouse he had just closed on, a three-bedroom place in the South End, and how the bar was doing so well that he was opening a second one in the Back Bay. The new bar was more upscale: no framed posters of AC/DC and Kid Rock, no beer and wings on Sundays. He was catering to the professional crowd and was turning into one of them himself.

When we got to the café, Mark double-parked and asked, "You going to be OK?"

"I'll be fine."

"So we're on for next week?"

"You know where to find me," I said and got out of the car.

I walked inside the café; Nadal was still at the same table, but now Asher was with him. I rushed into his arms.

"How did it go?" Asher asked.

I pushed my face into his chest. "She's dead."

"I'm so sorry," he said. His arms tightened around me.

I closed my eyes and took in his scent. "Me too."

Nadal moved to my side and put his hand on my shoulder. "I'm sorry about your friend."

"Thanks for calling Asher and for sticking around."

He squeezed tighter. "I'm glad I can be here for you."

"Why don't you come over?" Asher asked. "We'll watch some movies and get your mind off everything."

Jami was managing the counter by herself, and there was a long line of customers. Through the window pass, I could see that Al was mixing something in a big bowl.

"My boss really needs me here." My eyes shifted between the twins. "Can I come over tonight?"

"I'll cook us dinner," Nadal said. "I promise it will be better than that shit Asher called lasagna."

Asher punched Nadal's arm. "Hey, Nicole said she liked my cooking."

"She lied," Nadal said, and they both looked at me.

I shook my head. I wasn't getting in the middle, at least not today. "Can we make it a late dinner? I want to go to a meeting first."

"We'll see you at eight," Asher said. He kissed me on the cheek and moved toward the door.

CHAPTER TWELVE

Something delicious wafted into the hallway when Asher opened the door. Nadal's cooking smelled a hell of a lot better than his, but I would never say that to either of them. I held the box of cupcakes off to the side, brushed my lips against Asher's, and snuggled into his chest. "What did Nadal make?"

"I don't know; he won't let me in the kitchen."

Nadal poked his head out of the pass through. "Nicole, come in here, I need a taste tester."

"He wants my opinion?"

"You better do what he says." Asher laughed and winked. "He takes his cooking very seriously." He took the box out of my hand and shut the door.

The TV was off, and Coldplay came out of the speakers. The table was set for three, with candles in the middle and ice tea in all the glasses. Nadal stood in front of the stove, stirring a pan of sauce. He held the spoon up to my lips. "Blow first, and then tell me what it needs."

"I'm not going to know if it's missing something," I said.

"He doesn't actually think it needs anything," Asher said. "He just wants you to tell him it's amazing."

It tasted like garlic and seasoning, with a hint of mushrooms. "It's incredible, whatever it is."

"Go sit down; I'll bring your plates out," Nadal said to both of us.

Four trips later, Nadal finally joined us at the table.

"All right, we have green beans with toasted pine nuts, roasted potatoes with rosemary, and chicken with a mock marsala sauce." He smiled.

This was the first time I'd seen the twins interact. They fed off each other; when one started telling a story, the other inserted random details. At times, they only had to look at one another to have a conversation without words. By their tones and expressions, they had missed each other. This dinner wasn't just about Nadal getting to know me or about me showing him I wasn't going to take his brother away. They were reconnecting.

"Before the summer is over, why don't we take the girls to the Cape?" Nadal asked.

Asher looked at me. "Can you get off work?"

"Would it just be a weekend trip?"

"A long weekend," Nadal said. "Mom and Dad are going to be in Italy for Labor Day, so we should go then."

"What do you think?" Asher asked me.

Jami would take my weekend shift, and if I gave my parole officer enough notice, he'd probably reschedule my visits as long as I came in before and after the trip. I didn't know how I would be able to afford splitting the hotel room with Asher, though. I'd only been to the Cape once, when Eric and I had first moved to Boston. His boss threw a party there, and our room was over three hundred a night.

"I'll just be moving into my own place, and I'm going to need to buy furniture—but I'll try."

"Our parents have a house there, so you won't have to pay for a thing," Asher said.

Nadal brought his plate to the kitchen but didn't sit back down. "I'll call Stacey in the morning to confirm that Mom and Dad will be out of town. Once you get the OK from your boss, I'll have her make sure the house is ready."

I helped Asher bring the rest of the dishes into the kitchen. Nadal was an excellent cook, but a messy one. Sauce had splattered all over the stovetop, and specks of green seasoning were sprinkled on the counter and floor. Asher wiped down the tile while I washed the dishes.

"Who's Stacey?" I asked, handing him a clean pan.

"She's my parents' assistant."

"At their office?"

"No, their personal assistant."

Asher rarely spoke about his parents and hadn't mentioned what they did for a living, but a house in the Cape didn't come cheap.

Once the kitchen was clean, we moved into the living room. I slid out of my flip-flops, put my feet under me, and leaned into Asher. This was a lot more comfortable than the park bench.

Nadal walked toward the couch with a bag over his shoulder. "I'm glad you came over."

"Me too," I said.

"Where are you going?" Asher asked.

"Tyme just got out of work." He looked at me. "I hope I'll be seeing more of you."

"You will be," Asher said before I had a chance to respond.

We were alone. Finally. And by the way Asher's eyes followed Nadal to the door and then traveled slowly back to me, I knew he realized it too. His face was so close to my neck that the air he exhaled hit my skin, sending tingles all the way down my chest. I could see the light from the TV, but I had no idea what was on or how the lamp had suddenly turned off. My eyes were closed. Asher's hand held the back of my head, and his lips were by my ear, moving down my jawline. I felt his warm breath roll over my neck, and something tightened low in my body.

He turned my chin toward him, and his heat vanished. When I opened my eyes, there was hesitation in his expression.

"Are you ready for this?" he asked.

After a month of teasing, there was too much space between us. I reached forward and pulled his lips to mine. His kisses were too soft for the way I'd answered his question, and after a few pecks, he pulled away.

"Tell me," he said.

"I'm ready." I pulled his hands to my waist and bunched my shirt under his fingers. "I want you, Asher."

The passion in his eyes devoured me. I could feel the tips of his fingers rubbing against my hips, and he leaned forward. I welcomed his tongue into my mouth. His lips were soft but hungry, and my fingers dug into his shoulders, pulling him against me. There was a fire inside him that hadn't been there a moment ago, and I wanted more.

Asher pulled at my tank top, lifting it over my head, and with it came my cardigan. He threw them both on the floor, and his lips found my neck. His tongue, hot and wet, slid over my skin, moving lower down my chest. His thumbs pulled at the waist of my shorts, stopping halfway down my thigh.

"Tell me again," he demanded.

"I want you," I said, but it came out in a whisper.

He kneeled on the floor, my legs wrapped around his back, and his mouth warmed my stomach. His tongue traced my curves, sending goose bumps across my body. His lips moved up my body, and my head fell back onto the couch as he went between the cups of my bra, stopping at my neck.

His arms slid underneath me, scooping me up and pulling me against his chest. He kissed me while he carried me down the hallway and into his room, his lips moving away only when he placed me on the edge of his bed. The blinds were cracked enough that the streetlights cast a glow on his skin, and the piercings in his skull sparkled.

I pulled off his shirt, and my fingers climbed down his chest. My breath hit his stomach, and I unclasped his belt and the button of his jeans, using my feet to slide them to his ankles. Boxer briefs were all that remained, and his scent—sun baking the sand on a beach—was as strong on his lower half as it was by his neck.

My lips touched his stomach, and I felt the muscles beneath clench. He was hot against my mouth, and as my tongue dipped below the elastic waist, his palms moved to my cheeks. I looked up, and his dark eyes met mine. They showed his desire; I wanted to give him exactly what he wanted.

I pulled the briefs down his hips and let them fall to the floor. I ran both of my hands slowly up the sides of his legs, over his hips, and across his stomach. I dragged my nails down his body, and when I wrapped my fingers around him, the moan he let out vibrated the air. I squeezed softly, moving my hand back and forth. He let out a deep breath, and his gaze met mine. I didn't pull my eyes away as I leaned forward, letting my lips part as I got closer. Just as my mouth met the tip of him, he pushed me against the bed, undoing the button of my shorts. He removed my panties, and my bra was the last thing to come off. My eyes were closed, waiting for his touch—his hands, his mouth, all of him, but it never came. I sat up, searching his face for an answer.

"You're just as beautiful as I imagined." His voice was deep, almost raspy, and it made me tingle.

He lifted one of my legs in the air, kissing the inside of my ankle. His mouth moved all the way to my knee before he picked up my other leg and did the same. The touch of his lips and tongue, traveling higher up my leg, made me breathe deeper.

Asher grabbed my arm, and I gasped when his tongue touched my wrist. I tried to pull it away, but he held me tightly, his hand covering the crevice behind my elbow.

My eyes opened wide with fear. "Please, Asher, don't…"

He didn't stop. His stare locked with mine, and his lips wrapped around my skin. Even though my body had tensed, the look in his eyes sent sparks of warmth through me.

"Share your scars with me."

"I can't. The memories are—"

"Let me love them."

He kissed around my wrist, up and down my forearms, but always came back to the biggest scar, where my skin had been lanced. As my body started to relax, he moved to my other arm, covering every inch before he straddled my waist.

I gripped his knees; the spikes on his head tickled my chin, and I moaned when his lips moved down my chest and around my nipple. He flicked the other with the pad of his finger before pulling it into his mouth and between his teeth.

The springs in the bed creaked, and he disappeared in the darkness, pulling me closer to the edge of the mattress. My knees bent, and my toes scrunched into the blanket. It was as though he were speaking without any sound, blowing short bursts of air over the inside of my leg. His tongue moved over my skin, up my thigh, and then higher until he was right where I wanted him.

He was gentle at first, spreading and licking, pressing his tongue against me. His finger slid in and out of my wetness. He pulled me into his mouth and began flicking his tongue over my clit. I grabbed the blanket, squeezing it into my palms, and my hips rocked back and forth.

His tongue built a heat between my legs that moved low in my stomach and sent vibrations through my body. I felt it grow. My back arched, and I reached for his head, wrapping my hands around it, pulling his mouth against me. A scream came from my lips as I shuddered. All my muscles relaxed; heavy breaths escaped my mouth, and everything around me went in and out of focus.

I heard the crinkle of a wrapper, and my legs opened as he came between them. His arms went to each side of my head, holding my face while he brushed kisses over my cheeks. At first, he teased my wetness with his tip. I lifted my hips, trying to take him inside me, but he pulled away. When I finally lowered myself, he pushed forward, giving me a little more.

I dug my nails into his shoulders, and his mouth dipped to my chest, nibbling my nipples. My fingers moved through his hair and pulled him closer. When I took a breath, soft grunts filled the air. He still wasn't giving me enough.

I looked him in the eyes and bit my lip. "I want you."

He slowly gave in, pushing himself deeper—and I gasped. My hips moved back and forth to greet him. His fingers were never far, covering the parts of my body that his mouth couldn't reach. And mine couldn't get enough of his skin, running down his arms and chest and the sides of his stomach.

When I'd been a junkie, sex was for dope money and nothing more. I faked moans and orgasms just to get the Johns to bust quicker, and without the lubricated condom, my insides would have ripped. With Asher it was different; the wetness wasn't just what his tongue left behind. There was passion in his thrusts—I could taste the desire on his lips and feel the genuine emotion in the way he held me—and my body responded to all of it.

He flipped over to his back, pulling me on top, and I used his chest as leverage. He didn't stay flat. He sat up and leaned against the headboard, his eyes moving over my body as quickly as his hands did. The grinding made me louder, and my hands gripped the headboard as his mouth found my nipples, rubbing and sucking. The buildup was back.

I gently bit his lower lip. He gripped my face, and our bodies rocked in the same rhythm. I pushed against him, taking all of him inside me, and I felt him throb, reaching places his fingers hadn't. My orgasm came hard and fast, and when my muscles clenched, Asher moaned and our bodies shuddered together.

I fell against his chest, and heavy breathing filled the air around us.

"I don't ever want to move," he said, his face pressed into my chest. "This is exactly where I want to be."

I squeezed his head even tighter.

"Kiss me," he said.

There was still hunger in his movements, sending tingles to my stomach again, but his lips were tender. I couldn't get my body any closer, yet I tried. His hands crawled up my sides, but when he got to my breasts, he pulled away. "Before this goes any further, let me take care of something." His eyes traveled down, stopping below his waist, and I realized why he had to leave. He covered me with the blanket before he went to the bathroom.

I'd been too busy before to notice his room, but now that he was gone, I sat up and looked around. His stuff was so organized; everything seemed to have its own place. Dark wooden furniture filled the open spaces, hardcovers were packed into both bookshelves, a silver laptop and desktop sat on his desk. Above the bed was a painting done in red-and-black swirls. It looked just like the piercings he had on the side of his head.

An unemployed, recent college graduate couldn't afford two computers, a full library of books, or the rent in this neighborhood. Neither Asher nor Nadal had jobs, so their parents had to be paying for everything.

When Asher joined me under the covers, his hand went to my face, and I shivered from its dampness. He immediately pulled it away.

"No," I said, putting it back where it was.

"I don't want to make you cold."

I put my fingers over his to warm them up.

He pecked my lips, taking my top one within his and holding it for just a second between his teeth. "Do you know what time it is?"

I knew it had to be close to eleven, if not later.

"Don't tell me," I said.

He pulled me onto his chest and ran his fingers through my hair. His heart quickened when my fingers dipped below his belly button and slowed when they stayed around his neck. He was thin, but his muscles were tight and defined from running. It was a hobby he'd picked up when his writing became serious. He said it helped him when he couldn't work out a scene in one of his stories.

"Are you sleeping with anyone else?" he asked.

His question forced me to sit up. There hadn't been a need to discuss this before, but I'd figured the answer was obvious. I spent all my free time with him.

"Are you?" I snapped.

"What just happened was…different."

I covered my chest with the blanket. "Yeah, that's an interesting way to put it."

Asher reached forward to tuck a chunk of hair behind my ear, and I pulled away.

"That's not what I meant. It was amazing, but for me, it was more than just sex. What you gave me…is that what you've given everyone else you've slept with? Or just the ones you've cared about?"

He didn't know that when I'd fucked Johns, there had been no emotion behind my moans or grunts. Or that the only part of their bodies I touched with my fingers was their dicks when I slid on the condom, or that I wouldn't kiss them unless they forced me to.

"I'm not having sex with anyone else." I paused, thinking how to answer his other question. "What you felt came from here." I dropped the blanket, and my hand went to my chest. "That's not something I can fake."

He sat up. "I'm sorry. I…"

"Your timing couldn't have been worse."

"I know. I lost myself for a second."

"So you doubted my feelings?"

"I wanted to make sure yours were as real as mine." He pulled my hand off my chest and stared at my fingers, tracing the wrinkles on my knuckles. Then he leaned down and rested his face on my palm. He turned his head, kissing each of my fingers, slowly looking up after my pinkie. "Do you want me?"

I knew what he was asking, and it wasn't if I wanted to have sex again.

I didn't want anyone else to touch me. When I wasn't with him, I was thinking about him. He was a connection to Michael, someone to vent to, someone to rely on when I needed help. His feelings mattered. He was my friend, but I wanted him to be more.

I nodded. "All of you."

"Are you sure you're ready for this?"

Everything everyone said about having a relationship during the first year of sobriety didn't matter anymore. Asher was an addition to my recovery, not a substitution for my addiction.

"I'm sure."

He pulled me on top of him. His thumbs pushed against my cheeks, and his lips found mine. The first time we'd kissed in the alley, his thumbs had done the same, as though he were trying to squeeze out all my emotions. That time, something inside me had come to a halt...but here, my tongue danced around his; my mouth reached to be closer. Our passion matched. The intensity behind our kissing grew, and my palms pressed into his chest, trying to reveal everything inside.

Sleeping over or staying past midnight would get me kicked out of sober living. I didn't have to look at the clock on his nightstand to know that time was approaching.

"I have to go," I whispered, slowing my kisses down to pecks. I could feel that it was just as difficult for him to stop.

He turned toward the clock. "I'll get your shirt from the living room."

Just as I finished buttoning my shorts, I noticed him standing in the doorway. He was leaning against the frame, smiling and still naked. I slid my arms through the bra straps and clasped the hook behind my back.

"I'll never understand why you came into my life, but there has to be a reason," he said.

He was still hard, but he wasn't looking at me as though I were a porn star or a centerfold in some magazine. He was admiring what was beneath my skin.

I closed my eyes for just a second, and my brother's face appeared. He wasn't speaking and I couldn't tell where he was, but he showed up behind my lids for a reason. Michael had led me to

Asher. Not to punish me for my mistakes or to remind me of what I'd lost. He wanted me to fall in love with him.

I opened my eyes. "Michael sent you to me."

"I'm so glad he did." He reached forward but stopped right before he got to my waist. "Put your shirt on; I've got to take you home." He slipped on a pair of shorts and a T-shirt and grabbed my hand on our way out of his bedroom.

The streetlights swished by the windows of the taxi. So did the trees that lined the road and the passing cars. The cab driver talked on his phone in a language I didn't understand, and when I shut my eyes, everything around me faded except for Asher. His arms tightened around my stomach, and his chin rested on my head. The tingling hadn't stopped, and his warm breath on my ears made the urge more intense.

After what seemed like only seconds, I heard the door open. Asher reached for my hand. We stood outside my building, and he held my fingers up to his face, kissing each of my knuckles. "I don't want you to leave."

"Pretty soon, I won't have to."

I brushed my lips over his, knowing that if I didn't go now, I never would, and I unlocked the door. When I got halfway through, I glanced over my shoulder. He hadn't moved. The only thing that had changed was that his smile was gone.

CHAPTER THIRTEEN

Mark sent me a text message the next day asking how I'd been doing since Sunshine's death. My reply said I was fine. I was still pretty shaken up from seeing her lifeless body, but Asher was much more present in my mind. Mark didn't need to hear those details, and I didn't share them, but he continued to send me a text every day. After about a week, he showed up at the café. I was helping a customer, so Jami asked if he wanted his usual.

"No coffee for me today; I've come to kidnap her," he said, pointing at me.

"Miss Nicole, you're getting kidnapped for the...*day*?" Jami said "day" a little too loudly, in the same teasing tone she used when Asher came to pick me up.

I finished helping my customer and wiped my hands on my apron. "What's up?" I asked, leaning over the counter to give Mark a hug.

"You free after work?"

My shift ended in five minutes, but I had a feeling he already knew that.

"For what?" I asked.

"I promised I'd take you to the aquarium."

The aquarium would take hours, and it was already three. I was going to a meeting with my roommates and then having dinner with Asher, and I didn't want to cancel either.

"You could have called," I said with a smile. "It would have saved you a trip."

"How about a late lunch?"

"A snack?"

"Go get your stuff; I'm starving for a snack."

He ducked under the counter and walked with me to the back, stopping outside Al's office. I grabbed my purse from my locker, and as I returned to the counter, a man standing in front of Jami asked for me. He was dressed in a gray suit, with a gold clip around his tie and a briefcase in his hands. He didn't look familiar.

"Who wants to know?" Jami asked.

My eyes shifted between them; I was unsure whether I should stay by the register or come out from under the counter.

He handed Jami his card. "My name is Martin Bellows."

She read his card, looked over at me, and shrugged.

"I'm Nicole Brown."

He turned and extended his hand. After I shook it, he gave me his card. The card was simple and white; it didn't state his title or the company he worked for. Just his name and phone number were listed.

"I'd like to talk to you for a minute. Is there somewhere quiet we can go?" he asked.

I wasn't going anywhere with him outside of the dining room. He followed me toward the front of the café and took the seat across from me. I glanced back at the counter; Mark was standing next to Jami, reading the business card she had handed him.

Martin set his briefcase on the table, opened it just slightly, and removed an envelope. He handed it to me. "Look inside."

The envelope was thick and padded. I unsealed the top; the inside was filled with money. My breath got caught in my throat. I didn't know how much was in there, but it looked like a lot. My shaking hands dropped the envelope on the table. "Why did you give this to me?" I searched his eyes; I didn't recognize him. "Who are you?"

"I'm someone who collects information and passes on messages. And I'm passing you this message: you can take the money and disappear and not show up when there's a trial. Or you can do what you've done your whole life, making everyone else pay for your mistakes again."

He pushed the briefcase toward me and nodded, signaling me to open it. Since there was money in the envelope, I couldn't imagine what was in the case. Once I peeked inside, it wasn't just my hands that shook.

"You can have this and more; just make the right decision," he said.

Inside the case, there had to be at least ten wax-paper packets of heroin that were stamped with a skull and crossbones and several syringes. I knew the brand. I could almost feel the tip of the rig kissing my skin. My body practically shuddered as I imagined the heroin launching into my arm and flowing through my veins.

"Is everything all right over here?" Mark asked, surveying our table.

"Move along," Martin said. "The lady and I aren't finished talking yet."

"I'm not going anywhere unless *the lady* tells me to."

I glanced up slowly, biting my lip so hard I could taste blood. Mark's eyes scanned my face. Then he snatched the envelope off the table.

Martin reached forward. "I don't recommend you doing that—"

"What the hell is this?" Mark asked, backing away from Martin's reach.

Martin's jaw tightened as he glanced over to me. "I need an answer. Now."

"Nicole, do you want me to call the police?" Mark asked.

This was the first time I had seen heroin since prison. I knew its darkness. I also knew its beauty, and I smiled for my old friend.

"Nicole," Mark said in a much deeper tone, "should I call the police?"

My teeth had already nipped my bottom lip, but now they were about to break through my skin. I just wanted a taste.

I closed my eyes and immediately heard Michael's voice. I didn't need him to tell me what I'd be sacrificing, how I'd be accepting Dustin's offer and all the trouble I would be in if I didn't show up to court. I already knew. My decision still wasn't an easy one to make.

I opened my eyes, shifting my stare between the two men. Then I glared at Martin. "You want an answer? Tell Dustin to go fuck himself."

Mark tossed the envelope, and it landed right in front of Martin. He put it in the briefcase and stood. "I'll be seeing you again, Nicole. That's if you don't contact me first."

Mark and I stayed at the table as Martin moved around us, and we watched him walk through the door. As I took deep breaths, I ran my thumb over the sharp edges of his business card. My mind needed to be grounded, and the pain seemed to help with that.

"Nicole, what just happened? Who was that guy?"

Everything began to spill from my lips. Not just Martin's offer, but how Dustin's friend had cornered me in the alley and how Dustin had called from prison.

"I think you should tell the police."

I shook my head. "No police; no way. I don't want witness protection or to be sequestered, or any shit like that. I lost my freedom once and...no, it can't happen again. Those were...two-and-a-half years that I'd like to forget."

"I understand, but why aren't you taking Dustin's threats seriously?"

"I've survived much harder things than being threatened by my ex-boyfriend. I refuse to run from him."

"Nicole—"

"Mark, don't you get it? If I did go into hiding and Dustin couldn't find me, he'd go after everyone I love. I'd rather him hurt me than them."

He sighed.

I could tell by his expression that he didn't agree with me. But the one I gave him in return showed there was nothing he could say to change my mind.

"Will you at least speak to your attorney?" he asked. "You have one, don't you?"

"Yes, the one the court appointed when I got arrested."

"Call her," he said, and reached into his pocket for his keys. "If she's in, I'll take you to her office."

If a date for the trial had been set, Melissa would have contacted me. Still, it wouldn't hurt to ask her a few questions. And going to see her would at least settle Mark down a little. He hadn't stopped running his hands through his hair and shifting his weight between his feet.

When I phoned Melissa's office, her assistant said she was in a meeting but that she'd be out soon and would have a few minutes to speak with me. I told her I was on my way and directed Mark to the building on Federal Street.

The last time I'd been to Melissa's was the night Michael died. I remembered it so clearly; I'd come here after stopping at the police station to give my statement. Knowing it would be a while before I saw the city again, I'd walked to her office instead of taking the train. My hands shook when I pressed the number to Melissa's floor. I could barely speak when her assistant asked if she could help me. There was a trash can next to the copy machine in the hallway, and I threw up in it. I wasn't just dope sick; I was scared. I told Melissa I wanted to take the plea, and she set up a meeting with the DA. I went to jail the next day.

As I stepped off the elevator, Mark put his arm around my shoulder and whispered, "Everything is going to be OK." If he thought I was nervous about Martin, Dustin, or my meeting with Melissa, he was wrong. It felt as though I'd been here only moments ago.

My breakfast was splashing around in my stomach, and my mouth started to water. I told him I'd be right back. I already knew where the bathroom was and made it there just in time. Three cups of coffee, a bagel with cream cheese, and some of last night's dinner came out. There wasn't anything left in me. I washed my face, then found Mark standing in the same place I'd left him. The splashing in my stomach was gone, but I didn't feel any better.

Melissa's office was off the sitting room, and her assistant pointed to the closed door. "She's expecting you; go on in."

Mark knocked but didn't wait for a response before opening it. Melissa was typing on her computer, and we took a seat in front of her. Her assistant brought in two bottles of water; I unscrewed the cap, downing half of mine.

"How can I help you, Nicole?" Melissa asked.

The first time I'd met Melissa was right after Dustin and I had been arrested. A cop took me out of my holding cell and into a room where she was waiting. She wouldn't look at me. When she finally did, her eyes had been thin slits, the color of mud, and cold like snow. She had given me the same stare I'd given to Richard after he'd raped me. I hadn't had money to hire a different attorney. I still didn't. And she wasn't any warmer.

"Has a date been set for Dustin's appeal?"

"I haven't been notified of a trial date. I do expect to hear something within the next few months."

"Do you think I'll be subpoenaed to testify?"

"You're the state's leading witness. With your statement, I believe Dustin's appeal will be denied. So, yes, I think you'll be subpoenaed."

Melissa was only confirming everything Dustin and I already knew. He was smart for not wanting me to appear at his trial.

"So what will happen? The state will contact me?"

Melissa glanced at Mark and then back at me. "If you're subpoenaed by the state, we'll meet with the district attorney and review your statement a week before the trial." She walked over to her door and opened it. "Do you have any more questions?"

Mark gave me a pleading look. We had discussed it again during the car ride; he knew I wasn't going to tell Melissa anything about Dustin, his threats, or the messengers.

I thanked her for her help, and she said she'd be in touch if she heard any news. Mark's arm went around my waist, and he led me outside to his car, waiting for me to get in the passenger seat before he shut the door.

"Thank you," I said as he put on his seatbelt.

"For what?"

"Dealing with my drama so well. I shouldn't have dragged you into it, but I seem to do that every time we hang out. And for not saying anything to Melissa—I know you wanted to."

He looked at me when we got to the stop sign. "I did want to say something, but this is your decision, and I have to support you. And it's not drama; it's life."

If that was true, my life was still fucked up. And it wasn't just because of Dustin and all his bullshit. There was my addiction... there wasn't any medicine to cure it—only opioid blockers like Suboxone and methadone. I wasn't on either. Dr. Cohen, the head doctor at the rehab facility, didn't want me on them because when it was time to taper off, the withdrawal could be as bad as heroin. There was no way to stop my mistakes from haunting me. Dope would wipe away my memories of the past: the two times I'd been raped, the hurt I'd caused my family, the night Michael had died, and the two-and-a-half years I'd spent behind bars. But as soon as the high wore off, all those thoughts would come flooding back in. Still, I understood why Sunshine didn't want to get sober.

But then there was Asher, Mark, my roommates, and my parents—who weren't crying as much when we talked on the phone. I didn't know which side weighed more, but the middle didn't feel like a good place.

Mark parked, and we both got out. I looked up and down the street and there weren't any coffee shops or restaurants; nothing looked familiar. "Where are we?"

"I didn't think you'd be hungry, and I have coffee at my place. I hope that's OK…"

I'd forgotten that Mark had come to the café to take me out for a snack. He was right; I wasn't hungry.

"Coffee sounds good," I said.

I had been to the South End only a few times, but that was years ago and I'd been high. Unlike other parts of the city, where shops and restaurants were on the first floor of each apartment building, this area was all residential. Flowerpots hung in the windows, and trees were planted in front of the sidewalk. There wasn't any graffiti or litter on the ground. Mark had picked a nice neighborhood to live in.

Once I got inside, there was a large staircase and a living room off to the right. Most townhouses were divided, an apartment on each floor, with locked doors separating each unit. Mark's was completely open.

"Is all of this yours?"

He nodded. "Along with the three bedrooms upstairs."

When I had worked for him, some days he had been too hungover to come out of his office. I had thought his place would match his appearance: tattered couches, beer spilled all over the table, and a slimy fish tank he'd never cleaned. But Mark had changed. The bloat in his neck and stomach were gone, his skin no longer had a red tone to it, and he said he didn't drink much anymore. Because of how together he appeared, I wasn't surprised his apartment was spotless, but I was impressed with how decorated it was. The couches looked like they were made of suede, and there were plants in the corners of the room and a tropical arrangement on the coffee table. Everything was coordinated, from the throw pillows to the window coverings.

"What do you take in your coffee?"

"Cream and sugar," I said, following him into the kitchen. There was a big island in the center of the room with a basket of lemons on top. Everything glowed under the lights—the stainless steel appliances and the glitter in the stone counters, even the handles on the chocolate brown cabinets.

He told me to take a seat at the table and brought over a plate of cookies.

"These look familiar," I said, holding one up in the air.

"Al gives me a box of sweets every week. I usually bring them to the bar, but I save the chocolate chip ones. They're my favorite."

I took a bite. "Mine too."

He didn't make coffee like we did at the café. He put a little plastic cup inside a machine and placed a mug underneath. Then a steaming stream poured out. When both mugs were filled, he set them on the table and took a seat across from me. "How much longer do you have in sober living?"

"Only two more months."

"And then what?"

"I have to find an apartment to rent."

"If you want to stay here, you know, to save some money, you can."

Most of the men from my past had given me a place to live, clothes, food, and drugs. If I was going to stay sober, I couldn't be anyone's child anymore. I had to learn how to pay bills, budget my money, and be held accountable for my responsibilities.

"I really appreciate your offer, but I have to do this on my own."

"I understand."

I glanced at him out of the corner of my eye. When Mark and I were together, it was always all about me. No one wanted a one-sided friend; he deserved more than that.

"So are you dating anyone? Are the employees giving you any trouble? How's the new bar coming along?"

He wrapped his hands around the mug and laughed. "I'm single. No one has given me as much trouble as you." He winked. "And the grand opening is next week."

"Then why are you here with me? Don't you have a ton of stuff to do?"

"Nothing that can't wait."

Saying "thank you" again for putting me before his work just didn't seem like enough. I had to show Mark how much I appreciated his friendship, and I knew just how to do that. But first, I had to talk to Tiffany to make sure she was down with the idea.

Neither of us had broken eye contact, but his stare turned intense. His eyes, light brown with a touch of tan around the edges, went wide, and then he sighed. "I'm going to talk to Al. He'll start driving you home after work—"

"No, I can't be protected from everyone and everything. Bad shit is going to happen, one way or another, and I'm going to have to deal with it."

He looked at his hands, grinding his teeth together so the lines in his jaw moved. "Nicole, I know all about triggers and how they can cause a relapse. I don't want that to happen to you."

"I don't want that to happen to me either, but I'm taking it one day at a time. That's all I can do."

"But—"

"Why don't you show me around your house?"

His lips parted and stayed open for a few seconds until he finally said, "Follow me."

He took me through the dining room, and we passed a small bathroom before going upstairs. After showing me the guest rooms and bathroom, he stepped inside the only remaining door and watched me look around. The four-poster bed was covered in a black, silky comforter with lots of pillows, and above the headboard was a design made of little glass tiles. The room was painted light gray, and instead of lamps, tiny bulbs were inside the ceiling. When I squinted, they looked like stars. I moved into the short hallway; there was a big closet with lots of wooden shelves and drawers, and the bathroom had a tub with jets.

"Your bedroom is sexy," I said, rejoining him by the bed. His house wasn't too decorated; it was masculine and comfortable. But sexy was the only way to describe his bedroom.

"You think so?"

"Why are you single?"

He tipped his head back and laughed, returning with a huge smile on his face. "None of the women I've been with have made me want to stay."

I'd worked with some of the girls Mark had dated. The waitresses were really pretty, but their personalities were flat. Then there was Renee, my old roommate, who was a heroin addict; she had lied to him, saying he was the father of her child. He needed someone who would challenge him and hold his attention, and none of those girls were capable.

"You just pick the wrong women."

"You're one to talk."

I laughed. "Good point."

My phone vibrated, showing a text from Asher, asking if I wanted to order pizza instead of going out. I sent a quick reply, telling him pepperoni sounded great, and noticed the time. Mark's smile was gone when I looked up.

"You've got to go?" he asked.

"I'm sorry, I don't want to be late to NA."

"I'll give you a ride; come on."

He put his arm around my shoulders and walked me out to the hallway. His hold felt protective, and part of me didn't want him to let go.

CHAPTER FOURTEEN

A week had passed since the first time Asher and I had sex, and we couldn't get enough of each other. If we went out to dinner, his hands would be down my pants during the taxi ride home. When we stayed in, his fingers would find my nipples, and mine would rub the outside of his pants; then we'd leave our plates half full to go into his bedroom. But tonight was different.

When I slid my foot up his thigh at the table, he held it in place so I couldn't move it any higher. As we were washing and wiping the dishes, he didn't respond when I nuzzled his neck. Instead of leading me to his room, he sat down on the couch and turned on the TV. Even with his arm around me, there was a distance between us. I hadn't even told him about Martin's visit or my meeting with Melissa. He spent our entire meal talking about Nadal and Tyme and how they'd hit a rough spot in their relationship. He seemed too full for my drama.

As he flipped through the channels, I asked him what was wrong. He said his editor had given him a deadline and he had only a few weeks to finish his book. His parents were pressing him about graduate school; classes started in a month, giving him a week to decide. Telling him my thoughts on graduate school would only add to his stress. My probation would prevent me from leaving the state for another year. A long-distance relationship, only seeing each other over holiday breaks, would never work.

Something else was bothering him; both his editor and parents had been on him for a while, and it wasn't like him not to look at me when he spoke. But he wasn't saying any more, and I couldn't help with either. I leaned over and placed my lips at the collar of his shirt, kissing around his neck and up his jaw. His eyes closed. I took his lobe between my teeth, gently licking around his ear, and my fingers crawled under his shirt. Just as I got to the button of his pants, he stopped me from going any further. His eyes were open, staring at our hands.

I could feel his rejection rushing through my body. My face turned red, and I pulled away, grabbing my purse from the back of the couch.

"Where are you going?"

"I have to open the café in the morning."

"I'll walk you home."

Asher knew it wasn't like me to leave three hours before my curfew. But he wasn't asking me to stay, and he didn't seem bothered that I wanted to go. Something was off; he wasn't opening up or trying to fix it.

"Don't worry about it, I'm just going to take the train."

He followed me to the door. Before I opened it, I turned and faced him. Maybe he thought we were having too much sex and that's all I wanted. "Let's go to the harbor tomorrow when I get out of work or—"

"I'm going to write all weekend."

There was emotion in his eyes, but I couldn't tell what it was, and the rest of his face was blank. I waited a few seconds, hoping he'd change his mind. Instead, he reached forward and pecked my lips.

"I'll see you on Monday," he said and shut the door behind me.

In the past, heroin had kept me clouded. I wouldn't have noticed if Dustin was acting strange, or cared if he took off for a weekend-long drug run. But Asher's emptiness flowed directly through me. Sure, he was overwhelmed with choices and deadlines, but he didn't have an ex-boyfriend who wanted him to disappear or a friend found dead in a dumpster. He had an editor who wanted to shop his book to publishers and an acceptance letter from every graduate school he'd applied to. His parents' nagging hadn't mattered when he chose Northeastern instead of Dartmouth, so it shouldn't make a difference now.

* * *

Kathy and Ashley were the only ones home when I got back from Asher's. They'd completed their six months at sober living and were in their room, packing up their belongings. In a few days they'd be moving into a one-bedroom in Beacon Hill. I asked if they'd go apartment hunting with me tomorrow; they'd already been through the process. I had less than two months left, and my parents said I shouldn't wait much longer to find somewhere to live. Ashley said she had to work, but Kathy agreed to come.

I called some of the ads I found in the newspaper, scheduling showings at three places. Kathy picked me up after work. The landlord was waiting for us outside the building in Chinatown and led us up the four flights of stairs. When Eric and I had moved to Boston, we'd lived in an apartment only a few blocks away, and this room was almost identical. I could touch both of the bathroom walls when I spread my arms out. The barred window faced an alley. And the smell would be something I'd have to get used to—this apartment and most in this area were above Chinese restaurants. Other than its tiny kitchen, this place wasn't much different from my jail cell.

The air was hot and stale, and I pushed up my sleeves to cool down my body. "How much do I need to move in?" I asked the landlord.

"First, last, security," he said. "No late on rent or I evict you."

"We'll think about it; thanks for showing us the unit," Kathy said. She headed into the hallway, but I looked around one last time.

The landlord followed me. I could feel his stare traveling over my body, and it made me uncomfortable.

"You cook?" he asked.

"Do I cook? A little bit, but not much."

Hi eyes moved down and stopped at my arms. "You no cook for a living?"

"Oh, no, I'm not a cook."

Judging by his expression, I had a feeling I knew where this was going, and I was right.

"Those not burn marks, then. Those drug marks." He put his finger in the air and pointed at me. "I don't want your kind here. No drug users in my apartment."

"Excuse me," Kathy said, raising her voice, "you have no right to talk to her like that, and you're completely out of line. She's not a drug user."

"I call police if you no get out."

"Kathy, it's fine. I think we should go."

"It's not fine," she yelled. "He's making assumptions, and he has no right to do that."

The landlord pulled out his cell phone. "Calling police right now."

"Kathy, we need to go."

I pulled her out the door, and as soon as we got outside, she put her hand up, swishing air into her face. "If you had lived there, you would have smelled like an egg roll."

"What?"

"That's right; that place was a dump, and you would have stunk like egg rolls. Screw him and his horrendous apartment. There are much better places out there."

I knew the majority couldn't identify with my struggles. People from my past had reminded me of that, slapping me with their harsh words and assumptions; I'd wish each time they'd just keep their mouths shut. I didn't look like a junkie anymore; I didn't act like one. I treated people with respect, and I deserved the same in return.

"An egg roll would have been an improvement over how I smelled back then. I used to go weeks without showering," I said. "What a fucker; I can't believe he threatened to call the police because I have scars on my arms."

Her hands went to my cheeks. "Don't let that asshole get to you. Don't even think twice about what he said. You're not a junkie anymore." She tilted her head into my neck and sniffed. Her nose brushed against my skin, tickling one of my most sensitive areas and making me blush. "You definitely don't smell like one; you smell—"

"Get out of here," I teased, wiggling away. My face turned serious. "Thank you."

"I've got you. Always." She grinned and squeezed my arm even tighter.

We were a few minutes early, so we leaned against the building, waiting for the next landlord to show.

"This block doesn't look any nicer. Why the hell did you pick Chinatown?"

"It's halfway between Asher's and work, and I can't afford to live in the Back Bay."

The night after Asher and I had slept together for the first time, I came out to all my roommates, telling them the truth about our relationship. Tiffany was supposed to enforce the rehab's preference on dating, but even she was happy for me. I still hadn't shared the news at a meeting. I wasn't ready to take that step yet.

"Why don't you move in with Asher?"

"He didn't offer."

She opened her mouth to say something but then closed it.

"I think I need to live on my own for a while and learn how to do things for myself," I said.

"You know I don't mind, but why am I here instead of him?"

I broke eye contact, staring straight ahead. "He had a lot of work to do this weekend."

"Is everything OK?"

"I don't know…"

The door to the Chinese restaurant opened, and a man came out, asking if I was Nicole. I nodded, and he took us upstairs, showing us an apartment that was exactly the same as the last. The third apartment we looked at wasn't much different. The sink and toilet were stained orange, and instead of Chinese food, it smelled like bad breath in the room. Kathy wouldn't move past the doorway and yanked my arm into the hallway as soon as I got within her reach.

"Did you see the cockroaches in the kitchen?" she asked as we hurried down the stairs. "You're not living in a place like that; you'll sleep on my couch before I let that happen."

"This is all I can afford."

"Did you check the Internet?"

"Just the newspaper."

"I'm going to find you something better."

When we got home, Kathy and I sat at the kitchen table. She asked me questions, like how many bedrooms I wanted, if I needed to be close to a train station, and how much I could afford. I watched her type my answers into her laptop.

"There are over two hundred apartments that fit your criteria," she said. "We need to narrow down the list. What part of the city do you want to live in?"

I'd lived in a lot of places when I was on heroin: Chinatown and downtown, the border of Roxbury, and Dorchester. My dream had always been to live in a loft in the South End with a Boston terrier named Pork Chop and to teach first grade. But once I got arrested and charged with a felony, I lost the opportunity to ever teach. I couldn't afford a dog and an apartment, and the South End was even farther away from my job than the Back Bay.

Michael had lived in the Back Bay, and so did Asher. It had an artsy vibe, unlike other parts of the city, and even though I saw Michael when I closed my eyes, I felt closer to him whenever I was near his old building.

"The Back Bay," I said.

She tilted her computer screen. "Read this ad."

The listing described a Back Bay loft between Columbus and Dartmouth, close to the train station, with exposed brick and lots of character. The pictures showed the bathroom, tiled in black and white, and bright yellow appliances in the kitchen. I didn't know the building, but I knew the intersection; it was only about ten blocks from Asher's apartment.

"What do you think?" she asked.

"It looks perfect."

Kathy took out her cell phone and called the number on the ad. The landlord said the apartment would be available to rent in two months. He could show it to us tomorrow, and if I wanted to sign the lease, I needed the first month's rent, a security deposit, and a list of references. I had all three.

CHAPTER FIFTEEN

At Saturday's meeting, one of the vets asked if I had anything to share. Diem had to poke me to get my attention. I told him I wasn't feeling well, and he moved on to the next person. My mind was stuck on Asher; why hadn't he called or taken a break from his writing to see me for a few hours? Guiltily, I pulled my mind back to the meeting. I should have told the group about the lease I'd signed, how it was a loft like I'd always dreamed of living in. And I was 236 days sober. Couldn't I have shared that?

Asher was affecting all my decisions, and I was putting him before my sobriety. I couldn't let that happen if I wanted to stay clean, so at Sunday's meeting, I told everyone the truth about our relationship. Some said I should break up with him and stay single until I could take care of myself. Others said I showed maturity by facing my lie. They thought I could handle having a boyfriend as long as I put my well-being first. But I wasn't looking for advice. I knew what was best for me; it was Asher, I believed. Besides, could I really say good-bye even if I wanted to?

I came home from work Monday afternoon to change my clothes for Kathy and Ashley's moving-out party. There was a note on the table from Tiffany saying she would meet us at the restaurant. Diem didn't get out of work until six, and the other girls were probably settling into their new apartment.

I passed their old room on the way to mine, and something made me stop and turn around. Yesterday, plants had filled the shelves, fake trees were in the corners of the room, paintings rested on top of end tables, and new bedding and towels were in bags that covered the floor. Now, the only things left were the two twin beds and a dresser. I missed them already.

Kathy had been promoted to head baker at her pastry shop. Ashley was taking her three children to counseling, trying to repair their relationship after her meth addiction. She had even brought Kathy to a session a few weeks ago. At first, her kids didn't understand how their mom could be a lesbian if she had ever been in love with their father. With help from their counselor, they were slowly embracing Kathy as their mom's girlfriend and letting her find a place in their family.

Neither Kathy nor Ashley let their relationship get in the way of their sobriety; they attended meetings every day and called their sponsors when they needed to talk instead of enabling one another. They were independent women who didn't rely on each other but worked as a team. They were my inspiration.

My phone beeped, snapping me out of my daze. On the screen was a text from Asher, asking if I wanted to come over tonight. I knew I shouldn't just run to him; I should let him know how much he had hurt me. I had acknowledged that my sobriety needed to come first—that was an important step. I wrote back, telling him I was going to dinner with the girls and that I'd be over after. I moved away from the doorway and went to my room to get ready.

* * *

Tiffany was silent all through dinner, her eyes fixed on her plate. She slid around pieces of lettuce and piled the tomatoes in a corner with her fork. Her body was lost in a loose sweatshirt and jeans. Her blonde hair looked crispy, and her black roots were more than an inch long.

I wasn't the only one who noticed. The girls had been staring at her, baiting her to join the conversation, but she didn't. When the waitress took our plates, Tiffany got up to use the bathroom. We all looked at one another.

"Do you think she's relapsed?" Kathy asked.

Diem looked at me and raised her brows. We'd often discussed the same thing in our room after curfew. She thought I knew more than I was letting on because Tiffany was closer to me than to the other girls.

"We'd know if she was high," I said.

"Not necessarily," Kathy said. "She could be taking small bumps while we're at work, but not enough to make her look high."

"Could any one of us just take a small bump?" I asked.

"She could be anorexic," Diem said. "I never see her eat."

"Do you think we should confront her?" Ashley asked.

"Do you remember what happened when someone confronted you?" Diem asked. She glanced around the table when she spoke. "It made *me* want to use more."

"So what do we do?" Ashley asked.

"We can rat her out to the rehab center, but I don't see the point," Diem said. "She's doing her job; what more can we ask for?"

Tiffany was at the apartment every night at curfew, she tested us like she was supposed to, and she was there in the morning when we all left for work. But what was wrong with these girls? If Tiffany had relapsed and we continued to ignore all the signs, we were enabling her. Maybe she needed our help in a different way and didn't know how to ask. I had to get through to her without calling her out or getting her in trouble with the rehab center. I just didn't know how.

"Diem is right," Kathy said. Tiffany was slowly approaching the table, so her voice turned to a whisper. "Until she stops doing her job, I don't think calling the rehab center is the right thing to do."

Tiffany's cheeks were flushed. She was moving her tongue over the front of her teeth, and her eyes darted around the table. When I had snorted coke, I used to wipe the leftover specks on my gums so I wouldn't waste any of it. The powder turned my mouth numb, and I would run my tongue across my teeth, enjoying the feeling.

There was a concerned expression on each girl's face as we made eye contact with one another. No one spoke, and the silence wasn't broken until the waitress delivered our checks.

When we got outside, Ashley and Kathy hugged Diem. I heard them tell her to have a safe move to Florida, and tell Tiffany something about taking care of herself. They both wrapped their arms around me and said they would be over as soon as I moved into my apartment. And they made me promise I would come over to theirs next week for dinner. Once we all said good-bye, we went in different directions. Mine was to the train station.

* * *

I tried to read Asher's eyes as he opened the door, but I didn't have a chance. He grabbed my waist and pulled me against him, cradling the back of my head with his hands. With my ear on his chest, I could feel his heart pounding. He had missed me.

"Fuck you," Nadal shouted, and something smashed to the floor.

We rushed inside and found a broken vase on the carpet. Nadal was sitting in the chair watching TV with a beer bottle in his hand.

"What the hell is wrong with you?" Asher asked.

Nadal turned his head, and his movements were slow. His eyes were glossy and red, but they weren't swollen or teary. Something had to really be bothering him for him to have gotten high before I came over.

"Don't start with me, Asher," Nadal said.

Asher opened his mouth, and I put my hand on his chest to quiet him. "Let me," I whispered, and moved over to Nadal, crouching on the floor in front of him.

I still wouldn't call him my friend, but something had changed between us when we'd talked at the café and during the time we'd spent together since. Asher's shouting wasn't going to make Nadal's pain go away, and neither was Nadal's attempt to bury his feelings under a high. I knew that better than anyone. But I also knew there was something I could do to help.

"What happened?" I asked.

He took a sip of his beer. "Tyme, that's what fucking happened."

"Do you want to talk about it?"

"She got wasted and made a fool of herself, and then my mother called her a stripper."

"Nadal, don't—"

He turned to face Asher, and my eyes followed. When he looked back at me, his expression was soft. "I'm sorry, Brother." He stood and stepped over me, glancing between Asher and me. "I didn't mean to start shit."

"That's exactly what you wanted to do."

Nadal looked between Asher and me and shook his head. "Whatever," he said, disappearing from the room.

"What was that all about?" I asked. Asher wouldn't look at me, so I moved over to the couch and kneeled on the cushions, putting my hands on his shoulders. "Asher, talk to me."

When he finally glanced up, there was hesitation in his eyes. "My parents were in town for the weekend. Nadal brought Tyme to dinner, and it didn't go well..."

"You said you were writing all weekend. You lied to me?"

"I didn't lie; I wrote this weekend."

Asher had finally told me a little bit more about his parents. The doctor and his charity-running wife wouldn't be excited to hear that their son was dating a recovered addict with a criminal record. He said he and his brother were already too dark for their parents' taste, with their pierced skulls and Goth clothes. But if Asher's mom thought Tyme looked like a stripper, I could only imagine what she'd think of my track marks. He was too ashamed to introduce me to his parents. That was the only explanation.

My hands dropped from his shoulders, and I walked toward the door.

"Where are you going?"

"Home."

His fingers gripped my stomach. "Don't go."

"So you typed a few words? I don't consider that writing all weekend. If Nadal hadn't said anything, I never would have found out your parents had been here."

"No, I—"

"I've been a fucking mess for the last three days, wondering why you didn't call or want to see me. Now I know why."

"No you don't," he whispered.

He tried to turn me around, but my feet wouldn't move.

"I told my parents about us, and that didn't go so well either." His lips touched my ear. "I didn't tell you because I didn't want to hurt you."

"They know I'm Michael's sister? I was a heroin addict? I sold my body—"

"They know everything, even how I feel about you."

My whole body started to shake. "Your parents don't want us to be together, do they?"

"I don't care what my parents think."

"I do! If they never accept me, how can we be together?"

"My parents' opinion has never stopped me from doing what I want."

I glanced around the living room. "But you need their support, don't you? What if they threatened to take everything away?"

"Have you told your parents about me?"

He didn't answer my question. Maybe that was because he knew I was right and he didn't want to admit the truth. Not only had he lied, but I was never going to be welcomed by his family. Was Asher really right for me? I searched his face. Had I secretly known this was coming all along?

"They don't know about your connection to Michael," I said. "But yes, I told them."

"It seems like a rather important detail to leave out." His hands went to my stomach. "Come here, I need —"

I pushed his hands off my stomach and turned around. "You don't understand."

He moved closer, and I took a step back. "Make me understand."

"Every time Michael's name comes up, my parents completely shut down. So, yes, I had to leave out that detail. But if I did tell them, would they even know who Jesse is?"

"Would they know who Jesse is? What are you talking about?"

I felt my eyes fill with tears, and I caught them just before they dripped off my chin.

"There's so many things I don't know. So much I don't understand." My chest tightened, and I had to fight through the lump in my throat.

"Like what?"

"Did he tell my parents he was gay? Did they meet Jesse? The letter my parents sent me in prison said the funeral was beautiful, but I don't know who was there or any of the details."

Asher reached for my hands, but I pulled away.

"I don't know what Michael loved about Jesse, if he liked hanging out with you and Nadal, how much he shared with my parents, or how he found me on the street the night he died."

"Do you want those answers?"

"Of course I do. I lost so much because of heroin...I missed so much...I'd do anything to have a little of it back."

"Then Jesse should be the one to give those answers to you."

"But he would never—"

"He's ready to meet you, Nicole. Are you ready to meet him?"

CHAPTER SIXTEEN

Tiffany was making coffee as I came out of the bathroom. I thought I'd smelled it when I'd gotten out of bed, so this must be her second pot. Today, unlike most mornings, she was dressed and her makeup was done. On the table were two packets—like the ones she'd given to Diem and me when we first moved in—listing the Twelve Steps, a cleaning schedule, the rules, address and phone number to our apartment, and our meeting spot.

"When are the new girls coming?" I asked.

She had taken the seat across from me and was reading her textbook. "Anytime now."

"What are they in for?"

"Coke and crystal."

With everything that had been going on with Asher, I'd forgotten about Mark and the idea I'd come up with to show how much I appreciated his friendship. It would also give me a chance to spend more time with Tiffany and possibly find out what was going on with her.

"Do you have plans for Saturday night?"

She let out a long sigh and closed her book. "Why?"

"The grand opening of Mark's new bar is on Saturday, and I want to go and support him."

"Are you telling me this because you want my approval?"

"No, I want you to come with me."

Nothing in our rulebook said we couldn't go to a bar. But as our housemother, Tiffany might have a separate set of rules.

"The rehab center wouldn't be impressed."

"Who's going to tell them?"

She took a sip of her coffee and swished it around in her mouth before she swallowed. "An hour, no more—and you better not say a word to anyone about it."

I grinned and squeezed her shoulder on my way out the door.

*   *   *

Diem had to work, so Tiffany and I took the new girls to their first meeting. While we walked, Chastity, the crystal meth addict, asked how they were run. I told her they were just like group meetings in rehab, where everyone had a chance to speak and share what happened during their day.

"Have you gotten in trouble for being late for curfew?" she asked.

"I've never been late. I wouldn't recommend it; she'll kick you out."

"But midnight? That's bullshit."

"You'll get used to it."

"How do you pass your drug tests?"

I glanced over my shoulder. Tiffany and our other new roommate, Mona, the coke addict, were too far behind to hear us. "What do you mean?"

"Do you use someone else's pee or what?"

"I've been sober for two hundred and thirty-seven days."

"Junkie? Tweaker? Coke head?"

"Junkie."

"So you switched to alcohol so it doesn't show up in your pee?"

"It's not just a pee test; she uses a breathalyzer too."

"How do you get around it?"

We stopped at the crosswalk and I looked into her eyes. They were lost. "I don't."

"Whatever. I'll get it out of you eventually. A girl's got to learn the tricks to every new pad; it's just a matter of time before I figure out yours."

In rehab, we were told at least one of our roommates in sober living would relapse. I guess the four of us had been a rare bunch.

Chastity hadn't been out for a day; she was probably only going to last a few more. I wasn't a goody-goody or about to preach all the wrongs and rights of living a clean life, but fuck, I hadn't been this hungry the day I'd gotten out. Or maybe I had been; I just knew the consequences if I used.

* * *

Asher's lips met mine as soon as he opened the door. His hands grabbed my ass, lifting me in the air, and my legs wrapped around him. He set me on the kitchen table. My fingers fumbled with his belt and button, and I slid his pants down with the heels of my feet. He picked me up again, just briefly, to slip off my shorts.

Last night was still fresh in my mind. I had left his place right after he'd asked if I would meet Jesse. I needed to process everything: the potential meeting of Michael's ex, Asher lying about his parents' visit, and the fact that they weren't willing to accept me. I still didn't know how I felt about any of it, and I'd hit the ignore button the two times he'd called today, sending him a text that I'd be over later. Sometime throughout my day, the confusion I felt was replaced with a need. A tingling between my legs. A jitter in my stomach that floated all the way to my chest.

I spread my legs, curling my toes around the table's edge, and guided him into me. My moans filled the silence; his breathing matched his pace. I dug my nails into his back, forcing him even closer. And deeper.

My shoulders slammed against the wood when he pushed in, rubbing its surface when he pulled out.

He gripped my thighs, pressing so hard that my skin stung. The pain turned me on. It intensified the other feelings that were spreading through my lower body. The louder I got, the harder and faster his hips grinded.

I wasn't in control of what was happening inside of me. I'd lost myself in his movements; I couldn't pause the build, couldn't stop myself from screaming when the peak came. My back arched; my hands reached behind my head, and as I clutched the table, my body shuddered in spasms.

He put my legs on his shoulders and increased his pace, filling me with deep thrusts. His eyes turned fierce. Being held with such strength made me even wetter. My eyes closed when the feeling returned, and my fingers clawed his skin, showing him how hard I needed it. His lips parted, and we moaned at the same time until we both stopped moving completely.

I sat up with the help of his hand, and he gently set me on the floor, keeping me steady while I slid on my shorts. Once they were zipped and buttoned, he brought me over to the couch. There was an open can of soda on the table, and he handed it to me. It was still cold.

"I'm sorry I lied to you."

There weren't any lights on, but the TV lit up his face. I'd always been able to read a man by his eyes. Yesterday, his were sharp and cold. Now they were filled with honesty.

"I accept your apology, but don't ever lie to me again."

He didn't say anything. He didn't need to; his response could be felt in his touch.

"If you want to be a part of my life, you need to understand that my sobriety comes first. I can't be constantly worried that you're hiding things from me to protect my feelings."

"I don't want to be the cause of your pain; I want to be the reason you smile."

"That doesn't make it right."

He nodded. "I know."

I couldn't change the way his parents felt about me. My past wasn't going anywhere, and it was their choice not to accept it. I didn't know how that was going to affect my relationship with Asher, but that didn't matter. What mattered was that there was one thing I could do to heal. For years, questions had haunted me, and those answers were finally within my reach. Fear shouldn't stop me from finding out the truth. "It's time I confront my brother's death. I'm ready to meet Jesse."

CHAPTER SEVENTEEN

Chastity didn't last even a week. On her second night, she tested positive for meth and Tiffany booted her. She didn't go easily. Tiffany had to call the police and have her escorted out of the building. But with her gone, Diem hanging out with friends, and Mona working the night shift at her new job, Tiffany and I didn't have to explain why we were getting ready together or where we were going for the night.

When I'd first met Tiffany, I was envious of her body; she had toned legs and arms, the perfect pinkish complexion, and breasts that were just a little too big for her frame. But now when she took off her T-shirt to slide on a tank top, her collarbone and ribs stuck out. Instead of muscular arms and legs, there was skin tightly wrapped around her bones. Her face was gray, as though she had moisturized with cigarette ash. Her strapless bra pushed up a chest that looked like a teenager's going through puberty.

I chose a pair of dressy, black shorts and a tube top, with heeled sandals to make me average height. Tiffany didn't have to use concealer on my face—there was nothing to hide anymore—but she painted my eyes in sparkly black shadow and traced my lids with liner. My hair had grown out so much since it had been cut in prison, and she straightened the shoulder-length locks and curled the ends.

It was drizzling and chilly; neither of us wanted to get wet, so we took a cab. Tiffany reached into her purse to pay half the fare, and something rattled inside. The noise sounded like pill bottles, but it was too dark to see inside her bag. And when the bouncer at the door asked for her ID, she closed her purse too fast for me to get a glimpse.

Frosted glass chandeliers hung over each of the black high-tops. Sheer silver panels draped over the walls and dangled between the booths to give privacy. The same lighting from Mark's bedroom—tiny, star-like bulbs—were scattered between the chandeliers. The waiters, walking around with trays of champagne, were dressed in all black with white ties. I was underdressed compared to the people around me.

"Thanks for coming," I told Tiffany. With all the chatter and the background music that sounded like rain, I could barely hear myself.

"Should we get a drink?" Tiffany said in my ear.

I nodded, and she reached for my hand, pulling me further into the room. We squeezed into a spot near the end and leaned against the bar's marble edge.

"What can I get you?" a bartender finally asked.

"Orange juice," Tiffany said.

"A screwdriver?"

"Just juice; hold the vodka," she said.

He looked at me.

"I'll have the same."

As I watched the bartender fill our tumblers with ice, I smiled on the inside. This was what normal people did on the weekends, and I fit in. I wasn't tempted to order anything stronger, and from what I could tell, neither was Tiffany. She was still holding my hand, and it wasn't sweaty or shaky. There was no uncertainty or waver in her tone. I glanced at her, noted the weight loss, remembered the quiet behavior and missed meetings. She hadn't relapsed on booze, but something was going on with her.

After the bartender handed us our drinks, we moved back, letting a couple take our place. I scanned the room, but there were too many people to locate Mark. Clusters hung out at the high-tops and tables, a crowd danced in the center, and others moved through the open pathways.

"He'll be working the room, so it's better if we stay in one place and watch for him," she said.

We moved over to the far wall where it was less crowded, and when a group got up, we took their booth. Setting my glass on the shiny, black table, I leaned into the cushions and glanced around. Women's skirts were kicked up to the top of their thighs, their chests spilled out of low-cut tops, and they flirted with their lips. The men weren't looking at their eyes when they spoke. But what really stood out was the sloppiness. People tripping over their own feet and drinks sloshed on clothes. I knew the headache they were going to feel in the morning. I didn't miss that or the regret of waking up next to someone I didn't recognize. But I envied the high, falling into a womb of warmth and giving up the control of my body.

"What are you thinking about?" Tiffany asked.

"I'm so sober."

"Feels weird when you're one of the only sober ones in the room, doesn't it?" She patted my leg, and when she pulled her hand away, I stopped her.

"What's going on with you?"

She held my stare for a few seconds. Makeup covered the tiredness around her eyes, but sadness filled them. Her lips rubbed together; she blinked hard and looked away. "Is that Mark? He's walking straight toward us."

He was dressed in a black suit with a matching shirt and tie, and his shoes sparkled from the pin lighting.

"You didn't tell me he was so good-looking," she whispered.

His dark hair complimented his olive complexion. When he smiled, his white teeth gleamed, and the scruff along his jawline was more defined. I'd never seen him in anything but jeans. He'd never looked this sexy before. Or maybe I just hadn't noticed.

"What are you doing here?" he asked, pulling me against him and kissing me on the cheek.

"This is Tiffany," I said, after leaving his arms.

He leaned over to her side and kissed her cheek as well, but his hand still held the small of my back. "It's so nice to meet you."

"Likewise," she said. "The bar is beautiful. Congratulations."

He thanked her, and his eyes moved back to me. They were intense and full of questions.

"I came to support you," I said.

His smile grew, but his grip on my back didn't loosen. "You look gorgeous."

In all the years I'd known him, he hadn't seen me in anything other than my work clothes, with mascara and a ponytail. He didn't break eye contact, yet his stare covered my whole body.

I grabbed the glass off the table, and just as I got the straw to my lips, he yanked it away from me and took a sip.

"It's orange juice," I said.

"I was just making sure," he replied. "If you came here and rel--"

"I know," I told him, putting my hand on his chest. "Don't let us keep you; I'm sure everyone wants a piece of your attention tonight."

His fingers traced circles on my back, sending my lips into a smile, and he shook his head and sighed. I wrapped my arms around him, and his spicy cologne filled my nose. The scent was delicious. His scruff brushed over my shoulder, and the air he exhaled hit my chest. I felt like I was being tickled on the inside.

"You'll never know how much this means to me," he whispered. His breath warmed my skin. "Please don't take this the wrong way, but I don't want you to stay."

"We're going to leave after we finish our juice." I suddenly felt like a child, wearing Tiffany's clothes and drinking a nonalcoholic beverage. The only thing missing was a sippy cup.

"Tiffany, it was a pleasure," he said.

"Same here."

Mark squeezed my hand before walking away. As I watched him disappear into the crowd, I asked Tiffany, "Do you want to go?"

"I think that's probably a good idea."

There were cabs waiting along the sidewalk, and we picked the first one in line. Tiffany climbed inside and I got in after her, giving the driver the address to our apartment. She rolled down the window, despite the rain trickling in, and used her purse to fan her face.

A thin cardigan covered my arms and I was still shivering, yet there were beads of sweat on Tiffany's forehead. "Are you OK?" I asked.

"Pull over," she shouted to the driver.

He mumbled something in a language I didn't understand and stayed in the middle lane.

"If you don't pull over, I'm going to throw up in your backseat."

The driver weaved into the right lane and came to a stop. Tiffany pulled herself across the seat but didn't make it out in time, throwing up all over the curb. I held her hair and rubbed her back, trying not to get a whiff of the bile that was splattering by my feet.

The rain had turned from a drizzle to a pour, and I was soaked. My hair stuck to the sides of my face, and I was standing in a puddle. Tiffany heaved again; now I heard laughter from behind me. Two girls were pointing and cheering Tiffany on. I gave them the finger and told them to keep walking.

"I'm done. You can let go," Tiffany said. The wetness on her lips gleamed from the streetlights. Mascara and liner ran from her eyes.

She kept the window down, resting her head on the edge, and raindrops sprinkled over her face. Her eyes closed. She hugged her purse against her chest, her rounded shoulders causing her collarbone to stick out even more.

I paid the driver, and when I got on the curb, I held out my hand for her. She didn't take it. She followed me upstairs, and once we got inside our apartment, she went straight to her room. Diem and Mona still weren't home. Curfew wasn't for another hour and I didn't know when we'd be alone again, so I knocked on her door. When she didn't answer, I knocked a second time and waited a few moments before I walked in. None of the doors in our apartment had locks. This was the first time I appreciated that.

Tiffany was standing in front of her full-length mirror. Naked. When she noticed me come in, she didn't cover up. She turned and looked at herself from the side angle. She stretched her hands across her flat stomach. What caught my attention wasn't her frailness, although that was hard to look at; it was the way she rubbed her tummy.

"How far along are you?" I asked.

She closed her eyes and her chin dropped down. "Ten weeks."

"Does the professor know?"

Tiffany was allergic to birth control medicine. It was a conversation we'd had about a month ago when I'd told her I was going on the pill. She said she and the professor used condoms and complained how inconvenient they were. Something else was going on, though—pregnancy alone couldn't explain all the signs—but this was a start.

"He doesn't need to know because I'm having an abortion."

She took one last glance in the mirror before slipping on a bathrobe and getting into bed. Her arms wrapped around one of the decorative pillows, and she held it against her chest.

"I'll go with you."

She shook her head. "I don't need anyone."

"I know what you're going through." I sat down next to her and put my hands on her knees. "Trust me, you need someone there."

"Did it hurt?"

*   *   *

I'd left the clinic right before the doctor had started the procedure, deciding the baby was going to be my reason to quit dope. How I'd sat in the hotel room that I'd shared with Sunshine, my hands rubbing my belly, knowing that little bean-shaped blob was going to grow into something special. There were five wax-paper packets on the table that I'd gotten that morning, and they were going in my vein. Then I'd get clean. During my nod, I dreamed of my little girl. She was on my lap in the park, pointing to different parts on my body and saying their name. That was until I noticed the blood on her diaper. When I woke up from my nod, I went to the bathroom; clots of blood with something tissue-like filled the toilet.

*   *   *

My eyes opened, meeting Tiffany's. "I went to the clinic, but I couldn't do it. I should have—it would have been a better death than the miscarriage I caused from using."

"I can't have this baby."

"Why?"

"I just can't."

I reached for her hand. "I wish someone had been there with me." I took a deep breath. "I'm going to be there for you."

"My appointment is on Monday."

I nodded and pulled her into my lap. She rested her head on my leg, and I ran my fingers through her hair. Her tears fell onto my shorts that were already wet from the rain.

"I'm so fucked up, Nicole."

I rocked back and forth, swaying to the rhythm of the droplets that were hitting the window. When she finally stopped crying, I asked her what was so fucked up. She didn't answer. She pretended to be asleep.

CHAPTER EIGHTEEN

When I woke up the next morning, snuggling one of Tiffany's decorative pillows, she was gone. Last night's clothes were still on the floor, and the kitchen didn't smell like coffee. I sent her a text asking if she was OK and got into the shower. I didn't have much time. Asher was picking me up in an hour, and it was going to take me that long to get ready. I had no idea what a person was supposed to wear when meeting the ex-boyfriend of her dead brother. Maybe he'd kick me out before I even got inside.

I hadn't said anything to my parents about Jesse yet, or that Asher was related to him. I wanted to hear Jesse's side first—how much my parents knew about him, and Michael's last few months before he died—and then my parents and I would have that discussion. I wanted to repair things, not make my parents retell their nightmare.

The only full-length mirror was in Tiffany's room, and I stood in front of it like she had last night, looking at myself from different angles. I'd borrowed one of her dresses, a light pink maxi with vines of dark flowers going up one side, and a pair of flat sandals. I wore my hair down and straight and put on a light coat of mascara and lip gloss. I was sure Jesse had an image of me in his head. I wanted to show him how much I'd changed, not hide behind a layer of makeup.

Asher called when he was outside. I took one last spin, grabbed my purse, and replayed Mark's words as I walked down the stairs. While I was getting ready, he had phoned to thank me again for coming to his bar opening, and I'd told him about Jesse. "You both have pain, but this isn't just about Michael; it's about you and Jesse too," Mark said. "Seeing how far you've come and what you've accomplished will help him heal. Let his words heal you."

I got inside the taxi; Asher pulled me close, rubbed his nose over my cheek, and gave me a kiss. "You look beautiful."

The cars on the other side of the street were idle in traffic, but we passed through each intersection without having to stop. Where were the red lights and the bumper-to-bumper pace?

Until I met Asher, I never thought I'd get the chance to speak with Jesse. Talking to my parents wouldn't be the same; knowing Michael, he probably kept things from them. He wouldn't have done that with Jesse. The truth was only minutes away.

My limbs were numb, my head cloudy. I could barely feel Asher's breath, which hit the side of my face, and his hands resting over my chest. I was floating above my body, watching everything from the outside looking in. Maybe that was the best place for me to be.

I hadn't rehearsed what I was going to say. I didn't know how I'd handle his words. Would I run out of his apartment and take the train to Roxbury to buy dope, or would I feel relief?

The cab double-parked in front of a tall building that had glass windows covering the front and a doorman standing outside. I didn't know what part of the city we were in or what roads we'd taken to get here. It didn't matter. Maybe it did if I had to catch a train to Roxbury.

The doorman opened the door to the backseat, and Asher climbed out. He reached for my hand; my feet touched the ground. He didn't let go when we moved through the lobby, when he signed in at the desk, or when we stepped into the elevator. His finger touched the PH button, and it lit up. Music played softly. There weren't any words, just the sound of a piano. The back wall held all my weight and supported my neck as I watched the numbers change, quickly passing each floor.

Seven. Eight. Nine.

Underneath the button that closed the elevator doors was a red knob. *Stop*, was written on it.

Eleven. Twelve.

The numbers stopped after fifteen.

I yanked my hand out of Asher's and pulled the knob. The elevator jerked and halted between the fourteenth and fifteenth floors. My arms went over my head, my face pressing against the cold metal of the steel elevator door. My lungs felt like they were closed, but I still took deep breaths.

Asher's fingers went to my stomach. His chin nuzzled my neck. "You can do this."

"I can't."

"He's just as nervous about meeting you."

"I'm not ready. I thought I was, but this is...this is all too real."

He moved to my shoulders and spun me around. "You've been waiting years for these answers. Don't you think it's time you finally got them?"

Only one thing could settle my stomach, take away the nausea, and calm my nerves. My arms were healed, so it would be easy to find a vein. It had been so long since I'd shot up that one bag would get me so fucking rocked that this whole day would melt into something beautiful.

"Nicole?"

I shook my head, focusing on Asher's face again.

"Don't go to that place," he said.

"It's so much easier."

"No, you're going to stay here with me and think about Michael."

I nodded.

"Remember what you said; there was a reason Michael brought us together." His hands went to my cheeks. "This is one of the reasons."

"I know."

"Jesse is going to give you the closure you need. The closure both of you need."

We both had pain, but I was the cause of his. My own, too. Maybe the closure Jesse needed was to tell me what he thought of me, that I'd ruined everyone's life. I deserved that, but would hearing about the last moments of my brother's life, how he had found me on the street, and how much my parents knew be enough to help me move on?

"I'm going to push the button now. Are you OK with that?" he asked.

I looked into his eyes.

After today, I didn't know if things would ever be the same between Asher and me. Digging up the past meant Asher would see the hurt and pain in Jesse's face again, and he could resent me for what I'd put his family through. I was sacrificing my relationship for the truth. Was that putting my sobriety first? I didn't know. I didn't know anything anymore.

"Nicole, are you OK with that?" Asher's voice echoed around me, coming from every direction.

My stomach churned, my mouth watered, and my body began to shake. I was about to meet my brother's lover, his soul mate, and all I could think about was nodding out. I didn't have to face this. Heroin could take these nerves away; it could swallow my memories and fill me with warmth. I could have that again. I could make all this pain disappear.

But I needed to stay sober. Not just for me—for Claire, my parents, and Michael, too.

"Cole?"

"Just give me a second!" I snapped. I hadn't meant for it to come out so harsh. My pulse raced through my veins, and sweat ran down the sides of my body. I pushed off the elevator doors and paced the small space. My reflection appeared in the mirrored wall behind us; unpinned pupils stared back at me. I could hear Michael's voice; he was urging me forward. I closed my eyes, and his face came into view. But the warmth I knew heroin could give me was louder, and it caused my veins to ache. Michael shouted so that I could hear him above everything else, telling me I was strong enough. Even dead, his faith in me was endless. His words brought comfort; the love in his eyes gave me strength. He was right. I could do this.

"I'm ready," I said.

The elevator shook for a brief second before it climbed the remaining flight. I watched the PH light up; brightness filled the elevator as the door swung open. As with Michael's old place, the elevator led directly into Jesse's apartment without a hallway or a door to walk through. My eyes adjusted to the sunlight. There was a sitting area, with couches, tables, and lamps right in front of the wall that had floor-to-ceiling windows. The kitchen was to the left. Everything was white and looked clean.

Jesse sat on one of the couches with a book in his hands. He had glanced over when the elevator chimed and opened, but I pretended not to notice. This was where Michael had spent so much time, and I was taking it all in.

Asher held my hand, and we moved into the entryway. The soles of my sandals clicked on the hardwood floors. The heat between our skin caused mine to sweat.

Jesse's strides were long, but he appeared to be moving in slow motion. Everything about his pace was exaggerated: his steps, his arms swinging at his sides, his eyebrows rising as he got closer. He stopped a few feet away. "You look so much like him," he said.

I'd heard that a lot when I was a kid, from Michael's old teachers and from a few of his friends when I had visited him in college. After I'd moved to Boston, I was too much of a mess for there to be any resemblance.

"It's nice to finally meet you, Cole."

"Cole?" I said.

He opened his arms.

Asher released my hand.

I felt my feet move forward and stop right in front of him. My arms wrapped around his stomach. My head fell against his chest. My eyes closed.

CHAPTER NINETEEN

There had been moments in my life that felt like a dream. My body would move and words would come from my mouth, but I wasn't controlling any of it. The first time it happened was when Michael got shot, and then when I turned myself in to the police. It happened again as I walked down the aisle, preparing to say my speech at the rehab's graduation ceremony. And it was happening now.

Jesse was the same height and build as Michael, and his arms hugged me tight. I never wanted him to let go. My eyes welled and my nose ran, soaking his shirt. He pulled me even closer. "It's OK to cry," he said, making the tears come faster.

"You feel just like him," I said between sniffles.

"We were a lot alike," he said. "But from what Asher tells me, you and your brother share many of the same qualities as well."

"We do?"

"Let me get you a tissue, and we can talk."

My mascara had left a stain on his shirt. "I'm sorry, I didn't mean--"

"Don't worry about it; it's just a shirt."

When Jesse went into the kitchen, Asher grabbed my hand and took me over to one of the couches. Jesse returned with a box of tissues and three bottles of water, placing them on the table in front of me. He sat in the chair across from us.

The couch was stiff, and the pillows were for show, not comfort. There wasn't a speck of dust in the air or on the table, and nothing was out of place. But there was a homey feel to his apartment. The décor in the living room was contemporary and bold; it blended so well with Jesse's masculinity and bright blue eyes. His features were sharp, with a strong jawline, defined nose, and hair that was spiked and messy. I could tell why Michael had been attracted to him.

I didn't know where to start, but I wanted to ease into the conversation. His apartment seemed like a good way to do that. "Have you always lived here?"

"If you mean while I was dating Michael, then yes, we spent a lot of time here. I spent a lot of time at his place too."

I glanced over at the kitchen. I pictured Michael making dinner, like he had done for me so many times, and setting the dining room table. I could see him on the couch, his legs resting on the ottoman and a glass of wine in his hand. "What happened to all his stuff?"

"Now that you've almost completed sober living, your parents are hoping you'll take it out of storage and move it into your new apartment."

"They want *me* to have it?"

"That's why we didn't include it in the sale of his condo."

"So you keep in touch with my mom and dad?"

He smiled and nodded. "They've been wonderful. You're lucky to have them as parents."

Did they feel the same way about me? My parents would always love me, but I didn't know if they were proud of what I'd accomplished. Didn't know if they even knew what I'd gone through and how far I'd come.

"When did you meet them?"

"Not too long after you threatened to show them the picture of Michael and me kissing."

I had found that picture during one of my attempts to score money. I'd told Michael I was going to show it to our parents if he didn't help me. He must have taken me seriously. Heroin had turned me into such a monster.

I reached for a tissue. "I'm sorry—"

"You don't have to be sorry. You've already paid for those mistakes. Your past is your past. I don't hold it against you."

"You should."

And I meant that. If I were Jesse, I wouldn't have let me in. I never would have agreed to meet me. He was a better person than I was.

"It wasn't your fault. Michael knew what kind of people hung out on the streets and what they were capable of." He pulled one of the pillows onto his lap and gripped the edge. "He took a risk every time he went to find you and on the night he got *himself* killed."

"How did he find me?"

"The track, where you worked, is how he originally found you."

"But I never told him I was a prostitute." I did tell Michael that I sold my body to whoever was willing to buy it, but I'd never used the word prostitute.

"You didn't have to tell him. He went to Nar-Anon meetings and learned everything he needed to know about your way of life. Once he found you on the track, he followed you to the hotel and paid the owner for information."

"Frankie helped him out?"

Frankie, that scumbag hotel owner, had really scored. He got money off my brother and sex from me because I couldn't afford to pay my rent.

Jesse took the last sip from his bottle of water. "Michael went to Frankie at least once a week, paying him to find out whether you were at the hotel or on the streets, and he'd tell Michael what he knew."

"But Michael never came to my room or tried to stop me from working."

"Would it have mattered?"

I didn't have to think about his question. I already knew the answer and shook my head.

"Knowing where you were, that you weren't dead, gave him some sort of peace," Jesse said. "I didn't understand it, but I guess that was his way of making sure you were still alive."

There was a knot in my throat, a bigger one than I'd ever felt before. I couldn't stop the tears from streaming down my cheeks, my bottom lip from quivering, or my body from shaking. I couldn't get my next question out.

"Frankie called Michael when you and Dustin left rehab and moved back into the hotel. But after the hotel burned down, Michael hired a private investigator." He put up his finger and then disappeared down the hallway.

Asher took his arm off my shoulder and rubbed circles on my back. "Are you feeling any better?"

His expression hadn't changed since we'd sat down. It was intense and serious, and his eyes had moved back and forth, following whoever was talking.

"This is a lot," I said.

"But you're getting the answers you've wanted."

"I'm surprised by all of them."

Jesse returned with a folder and handed it to me. "Open it."

On the first sheet of paper, with the PI's information printed at the top, was a report of the places I'd gone that day, the number of times, and whether I was with anyone or alone. There had to be at least fifty more sheets behind it. Underneath the papers was an envelope with a stack of pictures. I took off the rubber band and flipped through each one. They showed me all over the city— wandering down sidewalks, coming out of the hotel, digging through the trash, and going into stores. They were dated and in chronological order; I looked worse in each one. Near the end of the pile was a close-up in which I was staring right at the camera. I dropped the rest of the photos and held the picture up to my face. My skin was grayish, brown smudges were under my eyes, boils and scabs covered my forehead and cheeks. Sections of my hair were dreaded. My lips were dry and cracked. But my eyes stood out the most. They were lost.

"After you were released on bail, Michael hired the PI again and found out you were working for a pimp," Jesse said. "He hoped that if he showed up on the street and offered to help you find an attorney and negotiate a deal in lieu of jail, you would go with him."

My mouth opened, but no words came out.

"I don't have to tell you what happened next."

I didn't recognize the girl in the close-up shot. She was a shell, with no conscience, no life in her veins, no light in her soul. The only thing living in her body was heroin.

Why did that girl have to be me?

"Cole?"

I shook my head and looked into Jesse's eyes.

"Your brother never stopped fighting for you. He knew what you were capable of, and that's what gave him hope."

"I miss him so much," I whispered.

"So do I," Jesse said. "But he's watching us right now, and so proud of what you've accomplished."

"I won't let him down."

Jesse walked over to me. I grabbed his hand, letting him lift me to my feet.

"I hope you don't," he said, wrapping his arms around me. "I really hope you don't."

CHAPTER TWENTY

As soon as Jesse released me, Asher's hand clasped mine and he walked me into the elevator. Once again, the back wall held my weight, but this time I watched the numbers in reverse. It felt like years had passed since I'd last been here. Three, to be exact, because that's how long Michael had been dead.

When we got outside, Asher pulled me into his arms. "I'm so proud of you."

My nose was stuffed up, my eyes puffy and sore, and him holding me only made them worse. "Everyone keeps saying that. Look at my life; how can anybody be proud of this?"

"What's behind you doesn't matter. Right now, this moment is what matters, and you just faced your biggest demon."

"I..." But I didn't have any words. All I had were Jesse's echoing in my head, "Michael knew the kind of people who hung out on the streets and what they were capable of. He took a risk every time he went to find you, including the night he got *himself* killed." My brother knew he couldn't help me or make me go to rehab, and all I had done was hurt him. And yet, he never stopped putting me first. "I know he's looking down on us right now. And I know he's thankful it's him up there and not you," Jesse had said right before we left. How selfless could Michael be?

I leaned against Asher's chest, my arms on his shoulders, and my body went limp. I wanted to fast-forward to a time when I'd be able to think of Michael without blaming myself for his death, when my parents' voices no longer trembled at the mention of his name, and when heroin wasn't the only thing I thought could take my pain away. When...

Asher pulled away, but his hands went to my face. Suddenly the weight of something stronger than my conscience pushed on my back. There was blackness behind my lids with swirls of white. Sweat seeped out of my pores, but I was freezing. My eyes closed for what seemed like seconds, but when I opened them, I was on a bench. My legs were spread across his lap, and he was rubbing my toes.

I hadn't thought about Asher. How he was feeling or his reaction to everything that had been dug up. He was still with me; that was a good sign.

"Are you OK?" I asked.

A weird look crept over his face, one I'd never seen before.

"Asher?"

His thumb moved to my bottom lip, silencing me. "You just passed out and you're worried about *me*?"

I nodded.

"You shouldn't be; I'm fine." He turned his wrist, and the sun lit up the thick white line. I pressed my lips against the scar we'd never discussed, kissing his memories as he had done to mine.

He tried to pull away.

"Let me love it," I said, holding his wrist firmly. "They're part of you, and they're beautiful."

"It's time I told you, but today is about you."

"No, today is about us."

He closed his eyes and rested against the bench, holding my toes as though I were going to yank them from his grip. "I couldn't take it anymore." He took a deep breath and exhaled through his mouth. "The pressure of my parents wanting me to be perfect, everyone comparing me to Nadal and Jesse. I didn't have my own identity. I was seventeen and I was...lost." His eyes opened and met mine. "I came home after school and threw one of mom's vases against the wall. I wanted the nagging to stop. My hand picked up one of the shards, and I dragged it over my wrist. Again. And again."

I waited for him to say more, and when he didn't, I said, "But you're here."

"Only because of Nadal. He saved me. You've saved me too."

"From what?"

"When the time is right, I'll show you." His voice had changed, and so did his expression. The heaviness was gone. If there was more, he wasn't going to share it with me today.

"But, Asher—"

"Just try to be patient with me." He kissed me, but his lips turned into a grin. "I can tell you this right now, though; I've decided not to go to grad school."

I shouldn't have been happy. Graduate school was going to help better his writing. But I wasn't. We had just started, and I didn't want us to end. It was too soon. Until I could leave the state, which was ten months away, it would always be too soon.

"Why?"

"I think we both know the answer."

"*That's* the only reason?"

He smiled. "I submitted my manuscript to my editor, and from what he's read so far, he's thinks this novel could turn me into a published author. So no, you're not the only reason."

"You're already published, though."

"Just my short stories. This would be my first novel, and that's what counts."

I wrapped my arms around his neck and pulled him against me. "I guess I should tell you I signed the lease."

"A lease to what? An apartment? Why didn't you tell me?"

I had told Mark all about my apartment. I must have forgotten to share the news with Asher.

"We haven't really had a chance to talk," I said.

"That's going to change, right now." He took my hand and led me to the curb, hailing a taxi.

"Are we going to your apartment?"

He winked, and I felt my pulse quicken.

"I think it's better if we go to the park," he said. "We don't get much talking done at my place."

*   *   *

I lay on my bed, cuddled beneath the covers, one hand gripping the blanket and the other holding my cell phone to my ear. My parents had just finished dinner, and Mom was telling me about a cooking club she'd joined and how they were learning to prepare different cuisines. Tonight she had tried Chinese. My father was on the line, too, and said it was almost as good as Panda Garden, the restaurant we'd always gone to when Michael and I were kids. I could picture my father sitting with the cordless phone in the recliner in the family room, the Red Sox playing on the TV. Mom would still be in the kitchen, the phone's spiral cord stretched out from the wall as she wiped down the counters.

Jesse hadn't said anything to my parents about us meeting or that I was dating his brother. He thought my parents should hear it from me. I agreed—I just didn't know how to tell them. During my taxi ride home from the park, I'd rehearsed various ways to approach it. Nothing I came up with seemed right.

"I'm dating Jesse's brother," I suddenly said, interrupting my mom, who had begun telling me why she chose low sodium soy sauce over high. There was silence. My father turned off the baseball game. "You already know that I've been seeing someone, but I thought you should know it's Asher."

"How..." Dad said. "How did you meet him? Through Jesse?"

I told them about the night I'd gone out with Sada, skipping the part about her and Nadal doing coke in his bedroom, and how Asher and I started going for walks. After I explained how Asher had told me that Jesse was his brother, there was silence. "I know you weren't excited when I told you I was dating someone. Do you still feel the same?"

Because my parents were going to Nar-Anon meetings, they knew all about the one-year dating preference. When I'd first told them there was a guy in my life, they were disappointed. They said they were worried that he would enable me and I'd relapse. I tried to assure them he wasn't an addict and was good for my sobriety, but it didn't matter. They wanted what was best for me, and a man wasn't it.

"I still don't think you're ready to date," Mom said.

"I agree with your mother," Dad said. "But since you're not going to listen to us, I feel better knowing it's Asher. Michael always said that he and Nadal were real gentlemen."

It was strange hearing Jesse's name, along with Asher's and Nadal's, come out of my father's mouth. My two worlds were finally merging, but I hadn't told them the most important part.

"I met Jesse today." I waited for them to say something, but they didn't. My mother's breathing just got heavier. "Asher took me to his apartment, and we finally got the chance to talk."

I heard a click, and Dad said, "Hun, wait."

"Dad?"

"Your mother went upstairs. She's getting there, but she's still fragile."

My dad was the stronger of the two, but his pain showed in his voice rather than through tears. I didn't think Mom hanging up had anything to do with Asher or that I'd met Jesse. It was being reminded of what she'd lost, of what I took from her. Her son was gone, and my parents would never be the same. Neither would I.

"I know, Dad, but I wanted to be honest with you."

"You know we're coming to Boston when you move into your new apartment. We had planned on seeing Jesse, but now that you two have met, he should come to dinner. Asher, too."

"You want Asher to be there?"

"He's important to you, isn't he?"

I didn't answer his question. If Asher weren't important to me, I wouldn't have said anything to my parents.

"Before you set anything up, let me run it by your mother."

I told him it was a little over a month away, and he said he'd let me know. Before he hung up, he thanked me for being honest. When an addict was commended for *being honest*, the phrase wasn't just a common statement. I knew my father was thanking me not only for telling them about Asher and Jesse but also for not lying. That was new for me, and he recognized that.

Just as I turned the phone off, I heard a scream from Tiffany's room and jumped out of bed. I hadn't realized anyone was home besides me. Tiffany was in front of her closet, pulling pants and shirts off their hangers and throwing them on the floor. Her mouth was open, her lips in a snarl, and spit was flying out as she grunted.

"What's wrong?" I asked, stepping between her and the remaining clothes.

"I can't find anything to wear."

I put my hands on her shoulders, trying to pull her into a hug, but she wouldn't move. "I'll help you, OK? What do you need an outfit for?"

"Tomorrow."

"For school?"

"Get out of my way!" She pushed my hands off her and reached into her closet, tugging the rest of her clothes off the rod and tossing them across her room. She grabbed her comforter and ripped it off the bed. I ducked as pillows flew toward me.

"Tiffany, stop." I gripped her waist and held her down on the mattress. She was so light that I needed only my arms, but I straddled her waist too. "What's wrong with you?"

Tears and lines of mascara streamed down her pimpled cheeks. Her head rolled from side to side as though she were fighting something that wanted to come out. "I don't know what to wear," she yelled.

"I'm going to help you find something, but you have to tell me what you need an outfit for."

"My baby," she whispered, her head no longer moving. "For when I kill my baby."

I had been so consumed with Asher, Jesse, and my parents that I'd forgotten Tiffany's abortion was scheduled for tomorrow. When I had gone in for mine, I hadn't acted like this. But I'd known what I wanted until I got on the doctor's table. "Are you sure this is what you want? No one is making you have an abortion; you can—"

"Yes!" She shouted the word over and over again, banging her head against the bed. I held her face to stop her, and her expression turned blank. Her lids were covered in black makeup, and the whites of her eyes were red from crying—but her pupils were the right size. Her mouth wasn't dry, and there was no powder on the inside of her nose. Still, something wasn't right.

"Why does it matter what you wear?"

"It's a funeral, Nicole," she said, drawing out the last part of my name. "I'm never going to forget this day."

"It doesn't have to be a funeral. You don't have to do this—"

"I have to; the doctor said I should."

I released her face and moved next to her. "What doctor?"

"The doctor I've been seeing."

"For what?" I asked.

"The cancer."

"You have cancer?"

Her eyes welled again, and her lip quivered. She reached for my hand and rubbed my fingers along her cheek. "I'm going to be joining my baby soon."

CHAPTER
TWENTY-ONE

Tiffany had a brain tumor? Did that cause weight loss and lack of appetite? I needed to do some research. Before my grandmother died, her skin had turned a strange color and her hair thinned and fell out after she went through chemo and took all the medications. I didn't know if brain tumors would cause the same side effects, but Tiffany had symptoms similar to the ones my grandmother had. When I asked where in her brain the tumor was located, how the doctor was treating her, and what medications she was on, she wouldn't answer. She said it was inoperable and terminal and then rolled on her side and sucked the tips of her fingers. She was twenty-eight and in love with the professor...and she knew she was going to die. I couldn't blame her for acting this way.

Tiffany needed someone to talk to...a professional who wouldn't cry and show fear. I wasn't that person. My eyes welled when I heard her diagnosis. But a therapist would have the right words and know how to balance her meds with her addiction. With a death sentence, I wasn't sure whether controlling her medication was even important at this stage.

I stayed in her room for the night, curling up on the bottom half of her bed. I lit her cigarette when her hands fumbled with the lighter, rubbed her back when she thrashed under the covers. My eyes wouldn't leave her. I thought that if I looked away for a second, something might happen, like she'd stop breathing. Or maybe if I stared at her body long enough, my gaze would destroy the tumor that was killing her.

I hadn't envied only Tiffany's body when I'd first moved into sober living; I'd also yearned for her strength. She had it together—finishing her college degree, staying sober after an intense coke addiction, and mentoring the women she lived with. I had been so weak, unsure how I was going to stay clean or get a job with a criminal record, and she'd held my hand through all my insecurities. She brought me to meetings, encouraged me to share my emotions with the group, and made sure I was on time to meet with my parole officer. Our situations were different, but I was going to do the same for her.

The blanket jerked; Tiffany leaned over the bed, throwing up in the wastebasket I'd placed on the floor. I tried to hold her hair, but between heaves, she asked for some privacy. We had only an hour before her appointment, so I left her room to get ready. We passed each other when I came out of the bathroom; her head hung low, and her feet dragged on the ground.

I knocked on her bedroom door. "Do you need help picking out an outfit?" Finding something to wear to her appointment had been really important to her last night, and her room was still a mess. The clothes from her closet were all over the floor; she was never going to find an outfit with everything mixed and piled together, and I didn't want her to be late.

She opened the door dressed in sweatpants and a sweatshirt, her wet hair in a knot on top of her head and wearing no makeup. "Nope, let's go."

"That's what you're going to wear?"

"Do you have a problem with my outfit?"

"No, it's just that last night…" I didn't need to make her relive what had happened. "You're probably going to have some cramps, so something loose around your stomach is perfect."

She scowled.

Nothing I said was right. That's why she needed to talk to a professional. No one had come with me when I'd gone in for my abortion, and I'd wished I had a hand to hold. At least Tiffany wasn't going alone.

We got in a taxi, and when the driver asked for the address, she told him to wait and searched her purse.

"Commonwealth, between Naples and Babcock," I said, and the driver pulled into traffic. Tiffany looked at me. "I've been there before, remember?"

She closed her purse and stared out the window, drawing shapes on the glass. There was a noise coming from her mouth, a combination of humming and groaning. I touched her arm to calm her, but she threw my hand off and continued tracing circles on the window. Heather, one of the squatters who'd hung out at my old dealer's house, had acted the same way as Tiffany: drawing things in the air with her fingers, making weird sounds, and behaving like a child. But Heather was on meth, so being beyond fucking strange was normal for her. People dealt with stress and pain in different ways; cancer meds were probably some heavy shit, but would they make her act this crazy?

Once inside the clinic, Tiffany collected the paperwork from the receptionist and handed it to me, telling me to fill it out and make up what I didn't know. I did the best I could, leaving her list of medications and medical conditions blank, and handed back the clipboard.

Tiffany was gone when I turned around; she had taken a seat at the kids' table, helping a little girl with a puzzle. I sat behind her in one of the adult-sized chairs. There were toys scattered throughout the room and kids playing, reading books, and racing cars around the miniature train track. The clinic didn't only perform abortions. For the women who were here getting one, the children were a horrible reminder of the procedure they were about to have done and the emotions that would follow.

A nurse appeared in the doorway and called out Tiffany's name. Tiffany didn't respond. She didn't even stand up.

I moved to her side. "They're ready for you."

She looked up as though she didn't recognize me and continued trying to fit a corner puzzle piece into the center of the picture.

"Tiffany, we have to go." I put my hand on her elbow and lightly pulled.

"Get off me," she said a little too loudly.

The girl she shared the table with left to sit on her mom's lap, and the other kids stared.

Tiffany pushed off the table, sending the plastic chair toppling over, and joined the nurse. At the end of the hallway, the nurse took her height and weight before escorting us into a private room. I remembered walking down the same hall, the scale showing ninety-six pounds. Tiffany weighed less than that.

She changed into the cloth gown and got up on the table. Her legs swung into it, causing the paper to crackle and her feet to thump against the side. She danced to her humming, dipping her shoulders and wiggling her waist. She obviously didn't want me to touch her, so I didn't get too close.

There was a knock on the door, and the doctor walked in. She introduced herself and briefly explained the procedure. "Do you have any questions?" the doctor asked.

Tiffany hadn't made eye contact when the doctor spoke. She doodled on the paper that covered the table, and her humming turned into a nursery rhyme. The doctor looked at me and I shrugged.

"Are you sure you're ready for this?" the doctor asked.

"Yesssss," Tiffany said.

"Well, then, if you don't have any questions," the doctor said, "why don't you lean back, and we'll get started."

Tiffany put her feet in the stirrups. "Burr-y, cold-y." Her butt went to the end of the table and she flopped back, bouncing because she had hit it so hard.

Resting against the wall, I had a view of Tiffany's leg, the doctor's tray filled with instruments, and her hands moving between Tiffany's thighs.

"This is going to feel a little cold, too," the doctor said.

I could almost feel the hard stirrups pressing into her feet, the doctor's gloves brushing over her skin, the coolness of the tongs she used to open her up. This was all too familiar. I closed my eyes, and a flashback of the last time I'd been at this exact clinic began to appear behind my lids.

* * *

After I filled out the paperwork, I sat in the waiting room and pictured myself coming back here to take the baby class with Claire in three months, with a big belly and swollen ankles. She would come to the hospital when I was ready to give birth, and she'd wipe cold washcloths over my face. She'd cut the umbilical cord.

"Change into this." *The nurse had handed me a gown as she brought me into the exam room.* "The doctor will be in shortly."

The doctor walked in and took a seat on the stool in front of me. She had a little teddy bear clipped to her stethoscope and a gold band around her ring finger. She was probably someone's mom, too.

"Are you ready?" *she asked.*

I had lain back on the table as the doctor moved around the room, getting the tools she needed.

"This is going to feel a little cold," *she said.*

There were posters all over the walls, but the one by the bed stood out the most. It showed a mom at a park, sitting on a bench, and her daughter playing in a sandbox. The park looked like the one I had always gone to with Eric. The mom was reading a magazine but kept it low on her lap so she could watch her daughter at the same time.

This was my chance, I'd suddenly thought. A chance to change my life and live like a normal twenty-four-year-old girl. A chance to get heroin out of my life.

But could I do it—raise a child, be a mother, and be responsible for something other than myself?

The voice in my head kept saying, "You're not alone." *I had Claire, my parents, and Michael. I had people who loved me and would help me raise my baby. I could do this. And I could stop using. Not for me, but for my baby.*

"Stop," *I shouted.*

I sat up on the table and pulled my feet out of the stirrups. "I've changed my mind."

"Are you sure?"

I was sure—I wasn't going to kill for heroin. Everything else, I'd figure out.

* * *

My eyes opened, and I looked around, trying to remember where I was.

"Nicole?" Tiffany said.

The images in my head were gone, but the questions weren't. What if those bags of dope hadn't been waiting for me on Sunshine's coffee table and I hadn't shot them into my arm? Would I have gone to my dealer's place to re-up, or would I have gotten clean? For my baby? And if I had stayed sober, would Michael and Claire still be alive?

"Nicole!" Tiffany yelled.

I shook my head. Both Tiffany and the doctor were staring at me.

"Hand," Tiffany said. She was reaching out toward me. "Ouchies."

I slowly walked to her and clasped her fingers within mine.

*   *   *

I kept my arm around Tiffany's waist while we climbed up the stairs to our apartment. Once we were inside, she pushed me away and rushed into her bedroom, slamming the door behind her. I soaked a washcloth in warm water, made a cup of tea and toast, and brought the items into her bedroom. She was under the covers, her back to me, cuddling a pillow.

"You should eat something," I said, sitting on the edge of the bed.

She tossed the plate as though it were a Frisbee. The glass smashed as it hit the wall, and the buttered toast left a streak as it traveled down to the floor. "I'm not fucking hungry."

"The food would have made you feel better."

"I don't want to feel better." She sat up. Her eyes bulged out of their sockets, and her teeth pressed together like she was going to snarl. "I feel just fine."

"I want to help you."

"I don't want your fucking help."

"You need to talk to someone. If that person isn't me, at least agree to speak to a professional."

She laughed, but it was more of a cackle. "You're a joke. You're all a fucking joke."

"Who is...?" But I stopped. She wasn't making sense, and her answer wouldn't either. She had just killed her baby; I had to remember that. "The way you're feeling is normal; you're grieving—"

"Get the hell out."

"Tiffany, I'm sorry, I just—"

She stood and bumped her body against me. Her eyes bore into mine. "We're not friends. We were never friends. So why don't you get the fuck out of my room before I hurt you."

"You don't mean that." I took a step back. "This is your pain talking."

Her fingers clenched into fists. "I've never been more serious. One call to the rehab center, and they'll send your ass out of here. Stay away from me, or I promise you'll be on the street by morning."

Tiffany had that kind of power. She could call Dr. Cohen, the head of the rehab center; even though I'd always tested clean, a confrontation with my housemother would get me kicked out. I had only about a month left; I wasn't going to ruin that.

The Tiffany I knew wasn't the woman standing in front of me, and nothing I said would bring her back. I didn't bother saying anything else, and I didn't make eye contact before I left her room.

The fresh air outside didn't stop my heart from pounding. Neither did the deep breaths I took while sitting on the front steps of our apartment. There was something building inside me, and I needed to let it out. I called Asher, but it went straight to voicemail. I remembered him saying he had a meeting with his editor that would last most of the day. My NA group wasn't the right place to discuss my feelings. They all knew Tiffany, and it wasn't right to talk behind her back. I dialed Mark's number, and he answered after the second ring.

"I was just thinking about you." His voice was deep and a little scratchy. It wasn't even ten yet, and Mark worked nights. He'd probably just gotten out of bed or was in someone else's.

"Are you home?" I asked.

"Come over; you don't sound good."

I told him I'd be there soon and started walking to the train.

I couldn't imagine what Tiffany was going through—the emotions running through her body while having a sentence of death weighing on her. If that were me, I would want everyone I loved close by so I could spend my remaining time in their presence. I wasn't her. I had beaten my addiction, and according to my doctor,

I was a healthy twenty-eight year old. But now I knew how fast that could change.

Mark came to the door in a pair of holey jeans and a wifebeater; his hair was flat, and he hadn't shaved since the bar opening. He looked like the morning after a hot night of sex. And it looked good on him.

I followed him into the kitchen and took a seat on one of the barstools. After he handed me a cup of coffee, I told him about my morning. While I spoke, he moved between the stovetop and fridge, filling one of the frying pans with beaten eggs and the other with vegetables. I didn't think I'd be eating for a while, not after witnessing Tiffany's procedure, but my stomach growled for the sautéed mushrooms.

"Do you think she meant everything she said to me?" I asked.

"A diagnosis like hers can change a person. The abortion made her even more emotional. Just get through the next month, and speak to her only at curfew."

"So you don't think I should try to fix things?"

"You've done enough. It's now on her to respond. She should thank you for all your support and apologize for the way she acted."

"I don't want her to go through this alone."

He slid one of the omelets on a plate and stuck it in front of me with a fork and napkin. Once he was done cooking, he joined me on the other side of the island. But he didn't sit down. He stood next to me, and his hand touched my arm. "You can't heal everyone, Nicole. Not Sunshine, Tiffany, or anyone else who comes your way."

He was right, which was usually the case, and that was why I'd called him. Mark wasn't that much older than I was, but he had so much wisdom. I had been so focused on Sunshine and Tiffany that I'd forgotten about my own healing.

"Eat your breakfast because we're going to do something fun today," he said.

"I'm not really in the mood—"

"Whether you're hungry or not, you need to eat up. My eggs don't taste as good when they're cold. And you need to get your mind off what happened, so you better get in the mood."

I had taken the day off from work so I could be with Tiffany, but she didn't want me. Mark did, and he had the biggest grin on his face. I never wanted his smile to disappear.

"So what do you think?" he asked.

I picked up the fork and took a mouthful. "These are the best eggs I've ever had."

"I wasn't asking about the eggs."

"Are you giving me a choice?"

He picked up his plate and gave me a quick kiss on the cheek. "Give me fifteen minutes. I promise you're going to have a blast."

CHAPTER
TWENTY-TWO

When Mark pulled into the parking lot of the aquarium, I thought we were going whale watching. How could he think spending the day with a bunch of fish was going to be fun? He'd mentioned taking me here before, but he'd been joking. He had to be.

"You're going to love this," he said.

"I hope you brought Dramamine."

"You only need Dramamine if you're going on a boat."

"Isn't that what we're doing?"

"Will you just trust me?"

It was sunny and humid outside, but once we got inside the aquarium, that all changed. The only light came from the fish tanks that lined the walls, and the temperature was as cold as the ocean.

"We're going to start with the rays," he said, grabbing my hand and leading me through the long hallway.

I checked out each of the tanks as we passed them; there were sharks with hammer-like noses and seals with long whiskers. The little penguins stood on boulders, their eyes following me before they dove into the water.

We stopped in front of a shallow tank, completely open on the top with just a short edge separating us from the pool. The sign said Cownose rays and Bonnethead sharks, and there were lots of them. They were swimming around in a circle, weaving between rocks, stirring up the sand on the bottom. Mark leaned over the ledge and dipped his hand in the water.

I rushed up behind him and pulled his arm. "What are you doing? Are you crazy?"

"This is a touch tank," he said, "so you're allowed to touch them."

"What if they sting you? Isn't that how they got their name?"

I was a huge fan of dogs; you could train them, and they cuddled and licked your face. But these weren't Boston terriers or bulldogs who snorted when you petted them. These were giant fish that ate things probably the size of me, and they had massive stingers coming out of their asses. There was nothing safe about petting them.

He took my hand, but when it got close to the water, I tried to pull away. "No way! I'm not touching those things."

"Do you really think I'm going to let anything hurt you?" He shook my arm, trying to relax the tension in my wrist. "Don't be scared; it's going to be fine."

The water was only at my fingertips, but a chill ran though me. I slid closer to him, feeling his warmth through his clothes. It was his smile that was holding my attention. As I watched his lips spread, I felt the water up to my knuckles.

A few seconds passed, and nothing bit me. He sank my hand in a little deeper, and the rays swam by, grazing under my nails. They didn't stop, sniff my fingers, or attempt to eat them. Mark's grip didn't soften; he continued to move me in until the water was up to my elbow. Their skin was slimy and almost like rubber. The spongy wetness tickled, causing me to laugh.

Mark released me, and my hand bounced under the waves. Almost like being in the middle of the ocean, I was floating in the free water. It felt dangerous. I didn't know whether my fingers were suddenly going to piss them off or they would feel the urge to feed. The unknown was like a high. Not a heroin high—a high with no threshold.

Mark's hand was no longer in the water. He had turned sideways on the ledge, facing me with the same look he'd had over breakfast: a protective and caring expression. "It's movie time."

"We're going to watch a movie? Here?"

"It's not just any movie." He pulled me to my feet, and we walked to the back of the aquarium, where he purchased tickets for the shark show. We took a seat in the middle of the theater, wearing our 3D glasses, and I leaned back and rested my feet against the chair in front of me.

"Have you seen a 3D movie before?" he asked as the lights dimmed.

I shook my head. "But I think I can handle it."

He laughed when, seconds later, I jumped in my chair. A giant shark was inches from my face, teeth the length of my hands, with a stare that penetrated my whole body. I knew it was just a movie, but I felt like I was in the ocean wearing scuba gear and getting whipped by his splashing tail. From the corner of my eye, I saw an orange fish swim toward us; the shark turned, opening his mouth and snapping his teeth down on the fish. I wrapped around Mark's arm, clinging to it as the shark moved around me and acted as though I were going to be his next catch.

Mark's fingers covered mine, and he leaned into my ear. "Wait until you meet the whale shark."

"Meet him?" I whispered. The shark was still eyeing me. I couldn't drag my gaze away. "He's scarier than this guy?"

"He's twice the size."

I laughed, not just because these animated fish were scaring the hell out of me but also because Mark had seen this movie before. There was something really cute about that.

*   *   *

After the movie was over, I was still shaking a little from the crunching of the whale shark's teeth as he devoured an entire school of tiger-striped fish. Mark took me to his favorite exhibit. Unlike the other tanks we'd passed with bright coral, rocks, and fish twice the size of me, this one was simple. But the more I admired the tank, the more I realized there was nothing simple at all about these fish. They looked like parachutes; they were completely clear, and their bellies were shaped like four-leaf clovers and lit up the dark water.

I pressed my face against the glass; the parachutes expanded and tightened as they bounced higher and fell lower in the water.

There had to be hundreds of them, but they all moved so slowly and in unison. Mark read me the card on the wall: "They don't have any bones, brains, or hearts, and they've been around since before dinosaurs."

"They're that old?"

"They're survivors, Nicole, like you."

When I was a junkie, I could have been described the same way as these fish: I hadn't used my brain, and I was heartless. And because of everything I'd gone through, I felt as old as these jellyfish. Today wasn't just about getting my mind off Tiffany. Mark had showed me what I'd been missing. There was plenty of fun to be had out there without sticking a needle in my arm; beauty existed beyond the visions I'd had in my nods. There were smiles and laughter that weren't from the warmth and orgasm-like ripples that ran through my body.

He was only a few feet away, but even that was too far. I rushed over to him and threw my arms around his neck. "Thank you."

"It's true; you survived something that was stronger than you."

"No, thank you for bringing me here."

He pulled away just slightly to look into my eyes.

There was so much comfort with Mark. His arms held me as though nothing could break through. His lips, full and soft, were just above eye-level, and they were inviting me in. Something was pulling me toward him, and I couldn't fight it. I didn't want to. But when I got within inches of his mouth, his hands went to my face and he held me in place.

"Do you feel better?"

His question startled me, bringing me back from wherever I had gone. He wasn't smiling. His expression was intense, and from the way his pupils shifted between my eyes and lips, it appeared that he was fighting something too.

"I didn't think about Tiffany once," I said.

"You haven't met Myrtle yet."

"Who?"

"The turtle."

We both laughed, but his fingers stayed firmly on my face.

"Maybe you should introduce me to her?"

He slowly bridged the gap between us, and I felt my throat tighten. And just when I thought I was going to taste his lips, he pressed them against my cheek. My eyes closed. As he moved away, his hand grabbed mine, and I followed him back through the aquarium, my smile matching the one that he'd been wearing most of the day.

CHAPTER
TWENTY-THREE

My trip with Mark to the aquarium had made me forget what had happened with Tiffany, but I was reminded as soon as I got home. She had ransacked my closet and dresser for the clothes I'd borrowed and had taken all of them. My room now looked like hers. Clothes weren't important, but was she serious about not considering me a friend? I didn't think she'd really push me out of her life for good. It was surely temporary; she'd been diagnosed with a malignant tumor, and her emotions were wrecked from the abortion. She was just taking her pain out on me.

Wasn't she?

When I met her for curfew the following night, she didn't say anything. She handed me a cup and stood in the bathroom while I peed, a smirk plastered across her face. The next night was the same. My roommates weren't getting tested; she made that clear when she told them all to have sweet dreams. She wasn't close to the other girls like she had been with me, which meant the pee test was a punishment for trying to help her. It also meant she didn't consider me as a friend anymore, and if she hadn't threatened to kick me out, I would have confronted her. I didn't deserve to be treated this way, not after all the help and support I'd offered her. But I stayed silent. At my NA meetings, which she'd stopped attending, I didn't mention our fight or her recent news, and I didn't say anything to Diem. I even lied to Allison, my old counselor at the rehab center, during my monthly call-in when she asked how things were going. This was Tiffany's news to tell, not mine.

My roommates didn't notice the tension between Tiffany and me. Probably because except for the hours when I was trying to sleep, I was never home. Al had me on day shifts, and after work I went to Asher's. Nadal and Tyme had broken up; he went to the bar almost every night, so we usually had the apartment to ourselves. Asher hadn't mentioned his parents since our argument, and I didn't bring them up. Some things I was better off not knowing, including the conversations they had about me. When we peeled ourselves out of his bed, he helped me get ready for my move, making lists of everything I needed and going shopping with me. The bags of stuff I bought quickly filled my side of the room, then Diem's.

Tiffany had organized a going-away dinner for Kathy and Ashley, but as Diem and I got closer to move-out day, it appeared she wasn't going to do the same for us. Diem decided to coordinate it instead. Unfortunately, Mona worked night shifts and couldn't find anyone to cover for her. Allie, our newest roommate, had a GED class, and Tiffany said she already had plans. I knew that was a lie; she just didn't want to go out with me.

On our last night, Diem and I met at a diner not too far from our apartment and sat in a corner booth. The restaurant was mostly empty, so we didn't have to speak quietly or shout over the noise. Diem was driving down to Florida in the morning with two friends. She'd never been to Tampa before, but she was excited to live somewhere sunny. She said Boston weather made her depressed.

When I was a junkie, I'd hated the winter. Some days it was too cold to panhandle, making me short on cash. And even just a few inches of snow caused the trains to run slower. Then there was the time when Boston was hit with an ice blizzard, forcing the city to shut down. Sunshine and I had to detox in her hotel room.

But I didn't feel that way about winter anymore. Before the snow hardened or got covered in sand, it looked beautiful. Clean flakes filled the air and sparkled when the light touched them.

"Will you keep in touch with Tiffany?" Diem asked.

During the beginning of the meal, I'd done a good job of avoiding any roommate talk, but I had asked all the questions. I should have known it would go there eventually—and been prepared with an answer for when it did.

"We all have to move on, you know?"

"She keeps getting weirder."

I could probably tell Diem everything I knew about Tiffany, and the news wouldn't get back to her or anyone at the rehab center. But something told me to keep my mouth shut.

I took a bite of my sandwich and nodded. "So what does your place in Tampa look like?"

"You want to see pictures?"

While I finished the rest of my Reuben and a bowl of French onion soup, I looked at the photos on her phone. I made little comments about the palm trees outside her building and how big the kitchen was, but I wasn't really paying attention. No matter how hard I tried, I couldn't get Tiffany out of my head. After tomorrow, two new girls would take our beds. Tiffany would continue to get sicker, and I'd probably never see her again. The only way I'd know she died would be from reading the rehab's newsletter or checking the obituaries. It shouldn't have to be that way.

Diem and I paid our bills, and once we got outside, she asked if I wanted to watch a movie at the apartment. I did, but I didn't want to take the chance of running into Tiffany. I couldn't think of a good enough lie, so I told her I had plans that I couldn't break.

"I understand," she said, but her face told otherwise. "Will you be back before curfew?"

"Probably not."

"I'm leaving at four in the morning. I don't want to wake you, so I guess this is good-bye."

I wrapped my arms around her. "Travel safe, OK? And call me when you get there."

Diem was only three years younger than I was, but because she looked like a teenager, I felt old enough to be her mother. She had been a great roommate, and I hoped we would keep in touch. She was good for my sobriety; she worked the Steps and attended every meeting. That could change once she moved to Florida, though, and I hoped she remained strong. More addicts—even those who had recovered—died from drug overdoses than from anything else. That was the sad truth about addiction.

Asher rented a truck and picked me up in the morning. My building had no elevator, and men weren't allowed in sober living, so he met me on the second floor and I handed off my bags. Four trips later, with the last few bags in hand, I looked around to make sure I hadn't left anything behind. The door to Mona and Allie's room was shut, and I didn't bother to knock. I wasn't close to either of them.

I thought about whether I should say something to Tiffany before I left. As soon as I moved out, I would no longer be attached to the rehab center, and my monthly call-ins with my counselor would end. I'd have no connection to Tiffany, no more opportunities to work things out. But with her being so sick, I didn't want to cause more conflict, so I left a note on her bed. It was a just a few sentences, thanking her for all her help and telling her she was in my thoughts. Once I placed it on her bed, I shut the front door behind me. And I didn't look back.

Asher and I emptied the truck at my new apartment and carried the bags to the third floor. The door was open, and the landlord was waiting in the kitchen. I'd been here once before with Kathy when I signed the lease, but the place had been filled with the tenants' stuff then. Now that they had moved out, the room appeared much larger. The second-floor bedroom, overlooking the living room and kitchen, reminded me of a tree house, with beams of wood across the ceiling. The rest of the apartment looked antique, with vintage appliances and an outdated tub. It was perfect. Time had aged this loft just as heroin had done to me.

I handed the landlord a check for the first month's rent, and he placed the keys on the counter. The door squeaked when he shut it behind him. This was my place now. A room that wasn't closed in by bars, checked by nurses throughout the night, or full of rules and a curfew.

"You did good. This place is perfect for you," Asher said, moving into the kitchen after he'd explored the bedroom. He smiled. "I know you're limber, but I hope you're strong."

"Why do you say that?"

"Carrying Michael's furniture up those stairs is going to be a bitch."

I kissed his cheek. "I think you, Nadal, and Jesse will do just fine."

He laughed and took my hand, leading me back down to the truck. We drove only a few blocks before we reached the storage facility; Asher parked in front of the unit, unhooking the padlock and lifting the door. Michael's belongings were packed from floor to ceiling. I stopped in front of the first piece of furniture, pulling the sheet to reveal a corner of his living room couch. I ran my fingers over the armrest before taking a seat, pressing my face against the back cushion. It was faint, but his smell still lingered. Michael had always sat in this spot. This was where we'd cuddled and he'd placed his arm around me the morning before I'd gone to rehab. The memories didn't stop there, though. The guest room headboard, where I'd slept with my mom, was carried into the truck. Michael's desk, where I drank a half bottle of vodka and threw up in my mom's arms, was right next to me.

"Do you feel him?" Jesse stood a few feet behind me.

"I smell him, too," I replied.

Jesse sat down. Our knees touched. "I came here a lot after we sold his apartment. Being around all his things made me feel close to him."

A tear dropped from my eye; Jesse caught it before it hit my chin. "Today isn't about being sad, Cole," he said. "It's about moving on."

"He should be here."

"I know." His lids closed, and he swallowed hard, as though there were a knot in his throat. "He should be, and I would do anything to bring him back."

Whenever Michael had hugged me, something about the way he breathed and squeezed my body gave me comfort. Jesse's embrace did the same. Nothing could take away the loss of my brother, but Jesse's love made it hurt a little less.

* * *

I stood in the middle of the living room, glancing around the apartment. With Jesse and Nadal's help, all the furniture was moved in. Michael's artwork hung on the walls, the bed was made with new sheets, and pots and pans were in the cabinets. The only thing I hadn't unpacked was my clothes. I was too tired to find a home for them just yet.

I turned off the TV; silence filled the air. This was the first time it had been quiet all day. Nadal had blasted music from Michael's stereo, and someone's cell phone was constantly ringing. Asher had gone to pick up Chinese, but even with him gone, I didn't feel alone. Michael was here. Maybe it was just his stuff filling my apartment or knowing how close I was to his old place. But I could feel him.

Sobriety was going to be a fight. I'd have to attend meetings for the rest of my life and continue to work the program. Heroin's voice would always be there, but with Michael's presence and his old life surrounding me, maybe relapse would be less tempting.

The front door opened. Keys jingled in Asher's hand as he carried the bags of food over to the counter. It all looked so right: him walking into my home with dinner and his own set of keys. I hadn't forgotten how I'd wanted Mark to kiss me at the aquarium; I just tried to block it out of my memory. I was devastated by the way Tiffany had treated me, and Mark just felt right. He was familiar and comforting—and incredibly sexy. But nothing like that would ever happen again. Asher was perfect for me.

"You got a delivery," he said, moving back into the hall. When he came in again, a bouquet of flowers was in his arms. "Do you know who these are from?" The flowers were so tall they hid his face.

He set the arrangement on the coffee table, and I reached for the card. "Congratulations, Nicole. I hope your apartment is everything you've always wanted and more. Love, Mark."

CHAPTER
TWENTY-FOUR

Asher held my hand, but my fingers kept sliding away. Wiping them on my pants didn't help; the sweat reappeared in seconds. The clamminess would stick around until dinner was over. Maybe even throughout the weekend. I hadn't had the opportunity to spend this much time—sober—with my parents in nine years. My glands were responding to their presence. The next three days would tell a lot; this would be either their last trip to Boston for a while or their first of many.

My phone showed seven o'clock, but Asher and I were the last to arrive at the restaurant. Jesse and my dad sat on either side of my mom, both supporting her. They all stood as we approached the table, and I hugged my parents first and then Jesse. I needed his strength to get me through this dinner.

Once Jesse released me, I squeezed in between Asher and my father. "Mom, Dad, meet Asher."

"Mr. and Mrs. Brown, I've heard a lot about you," Asher said.

"Likewise, *Son*," Dad shook his hand.

My father had used that expression in the past when speaking to Eric and some of my other guy friends. I always thought *son* was his way of not having to remember their names. That could have been true, but he knew Asher's. The word meant a lot more now.

We sat around the table, and a waitress took our drink orders. I requested a Diet Coke. When she looked at the others, no one said anything; their eyes were on me.

"Do you mind, Cole, if we order some wine?" Dad asked.

"Order anything you want," I said. It didn't seem appropriate to tell my parents that alcohol wasn't my drug of choice. Plus, this was a great opportunity to really *show* them how well I was doing.

My parents ordered two bottles, a red and a white, to share with Jesse. Asher got a beer, which surprised me. Except on the night I'd met him, he never drank in front of me, even though I'd told him he could. My parents weren't big drinkers either, but there was tension in the air. If I weren't an addict, I'd want a few drinks to take the edge off too.

Over the last month, I'd spoken to my parents about my meeting with Jesse: what we'd talked about, how warm and welcoming he had been. My parents told me they stayed in contact with him, so I assumed they'd heard his take on our meet-up. I wasn't sure whether my parents had an agenda or just wanted to see how well I'd been doing since graduating from rehab. I sure as hell wasn't going to ask. I was having a hard enough time swallowing my spit.

"I hear you've decided to defer graduate school and pursue your writing," Dad said to Asher.

"I have, for the time being." The waitress delivered our drinks, and Asher took a sip of his beer. "My book is being edited right now."

"Fiction? Nonfiction?" Dad asked.

"It's a novel."

"What it is about?" Mom asked.

"It's a family saga."

This was the first time Asher had ever mentioned the topic of his book. Whenever I asked, he always said I'd be able to read it soon.

"I look forward to reading it," Dad said.

"Thank you," Asher said. "I appreciate your interest in my work."

"That's an interesting design you have on your head," Mom said, referring to Asher's piercings. "Is it symbolic?"

"Nadal has the same piercings. He and I are fans of Egyptian art. The middle symbol is commonly found on their artifacts. We liked the design more than its meaning."

"The twins are braver than I," Jesse said. "I pass out at the sight of blood."

Mom placed her hand on Jesse's. "So do I, dear." She had already refilled her glass once, and the *dear* was a little dragged out.

"Mom, you should tell Jesse about the time you took Michael and me to the ER after he fell off his bike."

"Yes, honey, you should," Dad said. He looked at me, and we both smiled.

Mom's face turned even redder. "Thanks, you two, but passing out at the hospital and getting a concussion is a memory I'd like to forget. Just like the time Michael pierced Cole's ears."

"Oh, good lord," Dad chuckled. "That was a much easier fix than when Michael cut Cole's hair."

I remembered the look on my parents' face when they busted Michael with scissors and four inches of my hair on the kitchen floor.

My head tilted back, and I let out the biggest laugh. For the first time in years, I wasn't the only one laughing. I couldn't stop.

"Look at her," Jesse said, gripping my mom's arm. "She's smiling, and beautiful as ever."

Mom stared at me. So did Dad, a grin on both of their faces.

"You've come back to us," Mom said.

"And you're more beautiful than when you were in college," Dad said.

A knot lodged in my throat. I grabbed the edge of the table to stop my hands from shaking. My freshman year in college was the happiest year of my life; I was on my own, living with my friends, doing drugs, and getting good grades. How could I be more beautiful now?

"After everything you've been though, your smile is as pure as ever," Jesse said. "It's nice to see. I hope it never leaves."

"You don't look like you've fought a battle," Dad said.

It was as though I'd asked my question out loud.

"You may have scars, but they have made you stronger," Mom added. She looked at my father and then back at me. "I've missed you, pumpkin."

I couldn't stop my lips from trembling or my voice from cracking. "I've missed you too, Mom."

"Come here, baby."

I didn't feel my chair move, my feet step on the ground, or the air swish across my face as I ran to her lap. But I felt her arms squeeze around me, her hair tickling the sides of my face, and her eyes drip tears on my shoulders. I heard her tell me she loved me. I said it back. Then I took a deep breath and released it slowly as though it were the first time air had ever touched my lungs.

* * *

Asher and I went for a walk after dinner. I'd eaten more than I had in weeks, maybe months, and my stomach needed to digest. As it was close to ten, the bars were blasting music through their open doors and the sidewalk was full. The restaurant was downtown, and I hadn't been here since I'd worked for Mark. His bar was on the next block, as was the first hotel I'd lived in. As we got closer, I pointed out both.

"I'd like to meet Mark," Asher said.

"Right now?"

"Why not?"

I wasn't too excited about bringing Mark and Asher together, especially after Mark and I had almost kissed. Mark wouldn't tell Asher that, of course, and there was no reason for me to say anything to him. Our lips hadn't touched, and that's what mattered. But still, it was a little weird to introduce the two of them. I couldn't come up with an excuse; we were already here, and Asher knew I didn't have a problem going into bars.

Big Dan, the bouncer, was working the entrance, and we handed him our IDs. He returned Asher's and held onto mine, looking between the card and me. "Nicole?"

I smiled. "It's been a while."

"You look...*great*."

"So do you," I lied. Dan was well over six feet tall and close to four hundred pounds. Underneath, though, he was a big softie who drank milk from a straw during his breaks.

"Is Mark here?" I asked.

He nodded. "Check his office."

It was still too early for the place to be packed with college kids, but a crowd close to my age filled the high tops and the seats around the bar. Mark's office was at the end of the hallway. By the look on his face, I could tell he was surprised to see me. Maybe he was more shocked that I had showed up with another man. I'd already thanked him for the flowers, but I did again as I hugged him.

"What are you doing here?" he asked.

"We had dinner a few blocks away."

"Asher?" Mark asked, extending his hand.

Asher reached forward to shake. "Nice to meet you."

"I've heard a lot about you," Mark said.

Mark was trying to be friendly; I rarely spoke to him about Asher. His words seemed to work, though. Asher's expression softened, and he smiled.

"Nicole tells me you used to be in a band?" Asher said.

"Lead singer and bass guitar."

"Ska? Rock?"

Mark waved him over to his desk and typed something on the keyboard. Music started playing through the computer's speakers. They'd found something they had in common; although Asher had never been in a band, music was his thing. I never heard the same song twice at his place.

The five Diet Cokes I'd had at dinner finally kicked in, and I excused myself to use the bathroom. The guys nodded and went right back to listening. As I stepped into the hallway, I smiled inwardly. The two men in my life were bonding. There was never awkwardness when I brought up Mark's name, and Asher hadn't shown any jealousy when Mark sent me flowers. But I didn't want Asher to think I was hiding my relationship with Mark or keeping him to myself. It was just that Mark worked every night and a bar wasn't the right place for me to hang out; there hadn't been a good time for the two of them to meet. Or had there been? Had I wanted to keep those two relationships separate? I didn't know. It didn't matter anymore.

The bathroom was on the other side of the bar, and as I weaved around the center tables, I remembered doing the same years ago but being rocked out of my mind. I'd met Renee at Mark's bar, who introduced Eric and me to Que, our first drug dealer. Renee was addicted to coke, and after an all-night binge at her apartment, Eric and I were using as much as she was. When the three of us got short on cash, Eric and I went over to Que's to talk to him about doing runs, like a delivery service, for which he could pay us in coke. Instead, Que asked if we wanted to try some heroin. It was so much cheaper than coke, and it looked all professional with its perfect, wax-paper wrapping and stamped emblem.

While I hovered over the toilet, my eyes closed; the memory was so vivid. I was back in Que's bedroom, and he was holding a foil of heroin for me.

*   *   *

I could taste the sweet kid vitamins and bitter vinegar in the back of my throat. I felt it, slowly, at the tip of each limb, and then a rush to my head. It was nothing like coke. It was euphoric. A cloud of cotton swallowed me, and the sun wrapped its rays around my body like a blanket. My chin fell toward my chest, my back hunched forward, my body acted on its own, and my mind emptied. There was scenery behind my lids...aqua-colored water and powdery sand that extended for miles. I didn't know how long I was like that—asleep or awake or totally fucking out of it—but when I came back, Eric and Que were staring at me. I was never going back to coke. I wanted more heroin. And I wanted it now.

*   *   *

I flushed the toilet and walked over to the sink. I soaked my hands with water and pressed them against my face. The first time I'd tried heroin was an amazing memory I'd never forget. But the ones that followed were nightmares. Eric and Renee were dead. As far as I knew, Que was still in jail. I was the only one of our group who was living a normal life again. And despite how incredible I'd felt during that first high, I didn't miss it right now. I finally had my parents back, a man who cared about me, and friends who didn't want anything except my attention.

I opened the bathroom door and bumped into something hard. It took a second before I realized it was a person, and I stepped backward. The man's chest was eye level, and as I looked up, I opened my mouth to apologize. No words came out.

Roger? What the hell was Sada's boyfriend doing here?

"I told you, you better watch your back," he said. He moved a little to the side; Sada stood behind him. Her arms were crossed, a smirk on her face.

"This is crazy," I said, trying to slide past him. He wouldn't let me. Each time I attempted to get around him, he matched my steps.

"You started this. I'm going to end it," he said.

His hands clasped my throat, and he pushed me against the wall. He wasn't the same size as Big Dan, but he was close to it. No matter how much I tried to wiggle, his grip was too tight, and he dodged my hands as I clawed the air.

"Baby," he said, "you know what to do."

Sada got in my face. "Who's a stupid bitch now?" she asked, mocking the last words I'd said to her.

Her fist pounded my right eye and my left, and then black filled my vision.

* * *

Looking in the mirror the next morning, I realized no amount of makeup would cover the bruises under my eyes or the swelling. I'd lost my sunglasses during the move; besides, wearing them on an overcast fall day would look odd. The skin that bulged over my eye throbbed, matching the pain in my head. Suddenly the intercom in the kitchen buzzed loudly, which didn't help, notifying us that my parents were here.

Asher opened the front door, and I joined him in the kitchen. Mom was holding a wrapped gift in her arms, and Dad was carrying breakfast. Once they saw my face, they dropped their things on the counter and rushed over to me. Mom put her hands on my cheeks and lifted my head toward the light. "It's much worse than I thought, pumpkin."

"Cole, I think you should go to the hospital again," Dad said.

"There's nothing they can do."

"Who did this to you?" Dad asked.

When I'd called my parents early this morning, I had avoided answering that question. I didn't want to have to explain who Sada and Roger were or how Asher and I had ended up at a bar last night. I didn't think my parents would be too excited to hear that part. But I didn't want to lie and say I'd fallen down.

"I ran into someone from my past while we were walking home," I said. "Asher tried to protect me, but there were too many of them. I'm fine, I promise; I just don't look so pretty."

After I woke up in Mark's chair, he and Asher told me what had happened: Mark had rushed out of his office, thinking I'd been in the bathroom far too long. Mark found Roger holding me against the wall and Sada punching my chest. Asher wasn't too far behind, and he and Mark both jumped on Roger. I had begged them not to call the police—I didn't want any more reports with my name on them— but they were already on their way. Roger and Sada got arrested, we all gave statements, and I was taken to the hospital to get checked out.

"If you stay in this city, you're never going to be able to escape this kind of shit," Dad said.

"I can't leave yet, Dad. I have eight more months of probation."

"Sweetheart," he said, and pulled me into his arms. "I want to protect you, and I can't. You don't deserve this anymore."

"Asher is doing a good job at trying to protect me, Dad."

Mom joined our hug. "We're not going anywhere today."

My parents had offered to take me shopping, but she was right. I was in no shape to show my face around town.

"I'm going to make you some homemade chicken noodle soup, and Daddy will rent us some movies. How does that sound?"

I closed my eyes, letting them hold my weight. Nothing had ever sounded better.

CHAPTER
TWENTY-FIVE

Even though Nadal and Tyme had broken up, Asher and I were still going to the Cape for the weekend. I'd cleared it with my parole officer, and Al gave me the time off. I didn't know whether Asher had told his parents the truth or that he and Nadal were going alone, but I didn't ask. I didn't really care. There was spending money in my wallet, and my suitcase was by the front door. Once Asher swung by in the rental car, we'd be in the Cape in less than two hours, watching the sunset from the back porch of his parents' house with hot chocolate in our hands.

My cell phone rang; I reached for my suitcase, opened the front door, and answered it all at the same time.

"Nicole?"

I stopped in the doorway. I hadn't bothered to look at the caller ID. "Tiffany?"

"I need your help. I'm really sick." Her voice was pitchy and hoarse.

"I'll be right there."

"No, I'll come to you."

I gave her directions and walked back inside. She said she'd be here in ten minutes and hung up. If Tiffany was as sick as she said, could that mean she was dying? Could I even handle that?

I didn't have a choice, I realized. She needed me, and I had to be there for her.

I paced between the kitchen and bathroom, trying to picture what state she'd be in. I remembered what my grandmother looked like when she was dying. Weak and frail, no longer keeping food down, clumps of her hair missing, and her skin was dry and cracked. Would Tiffany look the same, and how much help would she need? Someone to bring her to doctor appointments, make sure she ate and took her meds? Or worse? I knew from how much care my grandmother had needed that it could be much worse. I wasn't really in a position to take care of someone all the time. I had work, meetings, and Asher. But Tiffany *had* been such a good friend to me.

The buzzer in the kitchen went off, and I bolted down the steps and opened the door. Tiffany was alone, a backpack over her shoulders, and a hat covering her eyes.

"Come inside," I said, through chattering teeth. "It's freezing out there." She was dressed in a thin cotton shirt and jeans.

"No, I have to go."

"But you just got here."

"Nope, got to go."

"I thought you needed my help?"

"I'll take some money and go, go, go."

The child was back, if it had ever left, and I knew her answers were only going to get more confusing. "Let me grab my jacket; I'll be right down."

"No, no, no." She shook her head a little too hard. "You're not coming with me."

"What do you need money for?"

"The pharmacy."

"For your meds?"

"Yes. Yes. Yes."

"The only way I'll give you money is if I go with you."

She skipped around in a circle, her arms waving in the air. After a few twirls, she stopped. "Let's GO!"

"Give me a second," I said. I called Asher on my way up the stairs and told him about Tiffany. He was just picking up the rental car. He told me to be careful and that he would meet me back at my apartment. I grabbed my purse and jacket and found Tiffany sitting Indian style in the middle of the sidewalk, pedestrians weaving around her.

I stood in front of her. "Are you ready?"

"We need to hurry, hurry," she said, crawling to her feet.

I had to double my pace to keep up with her. For someone so sick, she was moving pretty well and didn't appear to be winded.

"What kind of meds does the doctor have you on?"

Her bottom lip stuck out, pouting. "Lots."

"Tiffany, talk to me." I grabbed her arm, pulling her close. "You haven't spoken to me in weeks; why all of a sudden do you need my help now?"

Having her in my face, I noticed the dark circles under her eyes and open sores on her forehead and chin. "I don't have anyone else, Cole-y. I moved out of sober living. Too sick. I'm just too sick."

"Are you living with the professor?"

"His place, a few others."

"I thought..." It didn't matter that I'd thought they were in love. If their relationship were as serious as she had said, she would be living with him now and not carrying a bag like I had when I hadn't had a place to sleep. "Why aren't you in the hospital?"

"There's nothing they can do. I'm dying, dying, dying—how many times do I need to tell you that?"

I released her and followed a few steps behind, watching her scratch her arms and neck while her shoulders twitched. Even when her fingers weren't digging at her skin, they wouldn't stop moving—fixing her hat, pulling at her shirt, and adjusting the straps of her backpack. I was so focused on her that I didn't realize we had entered Northeastern's campus. This was where Tiffany was finishing her bachelor's degree, so she probably got a discount on healthcare and medications at the campus health center. What didn't make sense was why she was climbing the steps to one of the dorms.

"Where are you going?" I asked.

"I told you. I have to see the pharmacist."

"They live here?"

"Mm-hm," she said and smiled. "He's got the magic meds."

He was her pharmacist; Que, my first dealer, was my Jesus. I was so stupid. All the signs had been there, yet I'd always stood up for her and trusted her despite what everyone else had said. How could I have been so easily fooled? During the beginning of my addiction, I'd lied to Michael and my parents; based on their reactions, I knew they'd believed me. They didn't want to think someone they loved and cared about was on drugs. I'd thought the same about Tiffany, even if a part of me had known the truth all along.

"Do you even have a tumor or did you lie about that too?" I asked.

She touched the side of her head, moving her fingers around in circles. "I've got it; I've got it real bad. And it hurts. It hurts so much, Nicole. These meds are better than the doc's because they make me forget. Forget that I'm dying."

This was messy. Could I really blame her for wanting to block out the death sentence she had been given and the pain she felt? I probably would have relapsed too. But whatever her dealer was giving her was only going to kill her faster. She needed to be sober and appreciate the time she had left, spending it with the people who loved her—and that included me.

"What do you want from me?" I asked.

"Buy me drugs."

"You know I won't do that." I turned to get my cell phone out of my purse and she pounced on my back, wrapping her arms around my neck.

"You have to buy them," she whined. "Help me, Nicole-y, help me."

I pushed her arms off and held her face between my palms. "You want my help?"

"Yes. Yes. Yes."

There was only one way to get her back to my apartment, where I could keep her safe until I could get help for her. I didn't want to enable her addiction, but I didn't think I had a choice.

"If I buy you drugs, will you go to rehab?"

"Rehab?"

"Will you let Allison and Dr. Cohen come up with a plan for you? These drugs are going to kill you faster than anything else."

"OK. I promise. I'll even give you cross-ies," she said, sticking her pinkie in the air.

I couldn't believe I was going to a dealer's apartment, but she wasn't going alone.

CHAPTER
TWENTY-SIX

The two hundred dollars that had been in my wallet for our trip to the Cape was now on my coffee table in the form of three Oxys and a vial of bath salts. I'd never done bath salts—it wasn't popular when I was a junkie—but I'd heard a lot about it in rehab. Like meth, it caused severe behavior impairment and hallucination. Mixing it with a downer like Oxy, which was similar to heroin, explained her mood swings—her childlike behavior, rage, and gaunt figure. The tumor probably added to those symptoms. She was slowly deteriorating and was completely out of touch with reality.

With a miniature cheese grater, she turned one of the pills into a fine powder and separated it into lines. "Magic meds. Magic meds. Come to me. Come to me," she sang.

"I don't think you should watch this," Asher said. He stood next to me, only a few feet away from the coffee table.

"I can't lock myself in the bathroom every time she uses."

I'd been sober for 310 days; I could handle being around drugs. I'd proved that when I'd gone to visit the pharmacist. My past dealers had sold mostly coke, heroin, and meth, even though they pushed E pills and painkillers. But this guy had at least forty different types of pills, each brand filling a gallon-sized plastic bag, and he kept them in a trunk under his bed. If I'd wanted to chase the dragon, one of Tiffany's Oxys would already be up my nose. The fire from his mouth would be spreading through my veins, and I'd be riding his green, studded back while I nodded out. But I wasn't dreaming. I was staring at my friend, who licked her lips like a rabid dog. Her hands shook from hunger.

"You can lock yourself in the bathroom," he said. "That's why I'm here."

"I'll be fine; I only have to get through the next two days."

During our walk home from the dorm, I'd called Allison and told her about Tiffany. After checking with Dr. Cohen and administration, she said they'd have a bed available in two days. She also said that would give her enough time to consult with Tiffany's neurologist and primary physician, as well as Dr. Cohen, to come up with an appropriate treatment plan. I told Allison I would keep Tiffany at my apartment until she was admitted. "If she leaves or I kick her out, we'll never find her," I said.

"I'm not comfortable with that," Allison said. "You should not be around Tiffany while she's using."

"This is my choice. What happened to Sunshine isn't going to happen to Tiffany."

"I understand your reasoning," she said. "But Nicole, you're an addict."

"Asher is here, and he'll keep me strong."

"I still don't think it's a good idea. Tiffany was your mentor and sponsor, and this isn't going to be easy to watch."

Allison was right; it wasn't easy. Tiffany had a rolled-up dollar bill in her nose. She snorted the first line, the second, and then the eighty milligrams was gone. She leaned back against the couch, a grin slowly spreading over her face. As the pill took hold, her arms twitched and relaxed, her chin dropped to her chest. Her mouth opened, and lines of spit spread from her top teeth to the bottom ones.

Asher grabbed my hand and pulled me toward the back of the apartment.

"I can't leave her," I said as we climbed the stairs to the bedroom, but he didn't let go.

"She's not going anywhere."

"But—"

"I'm not letting you watch this." He led me over to the bed. "You've come way too far to have Tiffany fuck it all up."

"You're going to make me stay in my room for the next two days?"

"At least until her high wears off."

"That could be hours."

"Then I'll see you in a few hours." I heard his feet on the living room floor and the squeak of the leather when he sat down on the chair across from Tiffany.

The bedroom overlooked the living room. All I had to do was slide to the edge of the mattress to view the whole downstairs through the barred railing. But why would I want to do that? To make sure she didn't OD? Asher was there for that. So I could watch her high? My hands had tingled after she finished her first line. The sensation had shot to my arms and legs once she snorted the second. Asher was right.

I lay on the bed, but I couldn't sleep. I didn't have a TV or a radio in my room, and I couldn't afford a computer. Except for Tiffany's breathing, there was total silence. I knew I should go to a meeting, but if she woke up to Asher and not me, she might try to run. They'd met only once, and she had probably been fucked up at the time.

I hadn't heard *his* voice in a while. The dragon was back, loud and begging, clogging my mind. He missed the old Nicole, the one who sacrificed her body and morals to be with him. I rolled to my side and pulled a pillow over my open ear. It didn't help. His screaming was on the inside, and he demanded that I go downstairs, take one of Tiffany's pills, crush it with a hammer, and sniff every speck. He lived inside that powder, and his touch could rub all my spots at once. He could show me the beauty behind the sun, the depth of water, the soft petals of a flower tickling up my arms. His words would be my lullaby. My body would shudder for hours.

"Leave me the fuck alone." Tiffany's shout was followed by a slap.

I moved to the edge of the bed. She was hunched over the table opening the vial of bath salts. Asher stood next to her, running his fingers through his hair. I didn't know if he'd ever been around someone who was being controlled by their addiction. What I did know was that it would only get worse. If Tiffany used as much as I thought she did, withdrawal would hit her by tomorrow morning. I wasn't going to get her more drugs. Taking her back to the pharmacist was too risky. She could bolt in a second, and we'd never find her. Detox was a dirty stage, but I'd gotten through it more than once.

And that was exactly what I told her when she was throwing up the next morning. Asher and I hadn't slept. Even though she had passed out for a few hours, I couldn't take my eyes off the rising and falling of her chest. Asher was probably too worried about me to go to sleep. Maybe he was too horrified by what had occurred throughout the night to even consider going to bed. Tiffany had climbed on the kitchen counters, searching cabinets for red-eyed monsters who were supposed to deliver a message. Then she gave up on her hunt to claw at her arms, covering herself in blood, to rid her body of the flesh-eating bugs. It was her nails that caused her to bleed, but she didn't believe us.

She got up from the couch in a rush, and I ran to the door. "You're not leaving," I said, blocking her with my body. That didn't stop her from trying to get past me.

"I just need a taste." Strands of her hair still stuck to her wet lips, and her shirt was soaked with splatters of puke. "Get out of my fucking way!"

Asher moved behind her, picked her up, and carried her to the couch. She kicked her arms and legs the whole way, crying, "I just need a taste. A little one. Then I'll come right back."

"You only have to get through one more day, and then Dr. Cohen will give you some medicine to make you feel better," I said.

Allison had sent me a text, confirming Tiffany's admission for tomorrow. In her message, she said they were still working on a plan and that, due to the circumstances, the treatment would be aggressive and short term.

I sat next to Tiffany, and she put her head on my lap. "But it hurts, Nicole. It hurts so fucking bad."

"I know," I whispered, combing my fingers through her hair. "I know."

And I did know—at least the detox and addiction parts. I remembered going through withdrawal in Sunshine's hotel room without the help of any medicine. My stomach cramps were like a combination of food poisoning and PMS. I tried to sleep, but when I closed my eyes, my head would spin. Sweat dripped down my forehead and cheeks. Then I'd shake from the chills. It was as though the heroin gods were moving the thermostat from right to left every few minutes. I would have done anything to take that pain away; I would have killed for a hit. But I wasn't dying from cancer. Tiffany's situation was so much worse than mine.

She crawled off the couch but moved only a few feet before falling flat. She screamed when her face thumped against the wood floor, stabbing her nails into the ground. She tried to pull herself up; she didn't have the strength. Instead, she scraped her fingers back and forth and cried out in pain. Asher put a wet washcloth on the back of her neck, and she flung it at him. She asked for water, and he handed her a plastic bottle. She dropped it on the way to her mouth and licked the puddle on the floor.

I stared at Asher, but I couldn't get his attention. He leaned against the counter, and it looked like that was the only thing keeping him standing. His face was filled with emotion. Overcoming his own demons had made him strong, but this was different. This was a lot to deal with, even for me, and I had witnessed some fucked-up things in my life. But we still had twenty-four hours to get through; we were only at the beginning stages of her withdrawal.

* * *

"N-Nicole," Tiffany screamed through chattering teeth, "I n-need a t-taste."

She was on the floor, her head in my lap. Drool had left wet spots on my jeans, and hers were wet from when she had peed, refusing to let us change her clothes. I looked at the clock on the microwave. "Twenty more hours."

"I can't fucking wait that long."

I rocked back and forth, hoping the movement would ease her. She began to gag and threw up on my stomach. Asher rushed over with a towel and sat down to take my place while I got in the shower. Despite the humming of the water, I could hear her screams. I curled up in the corner of the tub, letting the stream beat over my legs, and covered my ears with my hands. The rocking didn't soothe me either.

I thought back to all the times I had spoken to Allison during my monthly call-ins and when she had asked how things were going. I'd never told her about Tiffany because I thought it wasn't my news to tell. Maybe I should have. The drugs might have caused her tumor to grow even faster. And maybe her withdrawal would have been less intense if we had stopped her using earlier on. Maybe she could have stayed in sober living while getting treated by an outpatient program instead of having to check in.

*   *   *

Asher ordered pizza for dinner, but neither of us touched our slices. We gripped our mugs of coffee, willing it to keep us awake, and clasped fingers under the table. Tiffany had finally fallen asleep, but I knew it wouldn't last long; her churning stomach, the pounding in her bones, or the drips of sweat that felt like knives swiping her skin would wake her up.

The bags under Asher's eyes matched Tiffany's. I was sure mine did too. The caffeine had stopped working hours ago, and we had thirteen more to go. When Tiffany stirred in her sleep, we both jumped. Had I dozed off for a minute? I didn't know. My head was fuzzy, and my eyes were too tired for my vision to be sharp.

Her breathing was loud and grunt-like, the pain seeping into her sleepy state. Arms jerked and hit the couch, legs kicked against the floor. She popped up, eyes wide and mouth open, and slid to the ground. Asher's hand tensed, and I squeezed his fingers. She moved on all fours and landed in front of me, wrapping herself around my knees. Her face rested on my shin. I rubbed the back of her head, my fingers shaking from her sobs.

*   *   *

My panhandling cup sat empty because the people passing by wouldn't spare any change. They didn't understand how fucking dope sick I was. None of the drug dealers on the streets of Roxbury would let me pay them with my pussy. The soup kitchen had run out of food for breakfast. And lunch. The only thing that held my attention was the clock outside the bank, the minute hand showing it was almost time to trick.

My clothes were covered in filth from sleeping in the park. I tucked the bottom of my T-shirt under my bra to show off my caved-in stomach, but even that didn't help how I looked. My face was dirty. My hair was greasy and tangled, and I had nothing to tie it back with.

A car pulled up and rolled down the window. "You want a full, baby?" I asked.

I was the only one left on the block. All the other girls had been hired already, which meant I could charge whatever I wanted. And without competition, he'd have to hire me or rub one off on his own.

"Just get in," he said.

It was too dark to see his face, but his looks didn't matter. I'd let a he-she fuck my ass if that meant I could buy a few bags to last me until morning.

I pushed the McDonald's bags on the floor and slid in. The scent of sour milk filled my nose, and I dry heaved. My stomach was too empty for anything to come out. As we drove under a streetlight, I glanced toward him. Randomly spaced long hairs poked out of his chin and neck, bug-like eyes bulged out of his head, long fingernails gripped my leg, and his belly was so big the steering wheel created a cave between his rolls. I gagged again.

He pulled into an alley and pushed his seat back. As he faced me, his chins rippled from the movement. He breathed through his nose; it sounded like a whistle, it was so full. "Take your shoes off."

I did as I was told.

His mouth opened, and a giant bubble of spit formed between his top and bottom teeth. "Give me."

"Let's talk money first."

He placed two twenty-dollar bills in my hand.

"One more," I said, then tucked all three in my bra.

I dropped my heels on his palms, and his mouth went straight for my toes. I hadn't showered in weeks. Maybe months. The stench from my sneakers was almost as strong as the milk. His mouth, overloaded with spit, bobbed on my big toe and then on the second toe before he let my feet fall to his lap.

He poked his dick out of the open zipper. "Jerk me off." I reached with my hands, but he stopped me. "I want it between your wet toes," he said. "And if they get dry, spit on them."

* * *

"Nicole! Get in here!"

My eyes shot open, my mind disoriented and stomach turning from my gruesome dream. I was resting on top of the kitchen table, the slice of pizza inches from my face. My legs were numb from Tiffany using them as a pillow. Had I fallen asleep? I sat up carefully so I wouldn't wake her. But as I looked down, she wasn't on the floor.

I bolted from the chair and followed Asher's voice. I stopped in the doorway of the bathroom. An empty bottle of aspirin was in the sink along with an uncapped bottle of cough syrup. Asher was leaning into the bathtub, holding her limp body.

"Call 9-1-1," he shouted.

He threw his phone at me, and I dialed with shaky fingers. When the call was answered, I told the operator about the aspirin and cough syrup and gave him my address.

"Turn her on her side," I said, repeating the operator's directions. "Open her mouth, and if nothing comes out, stick your fingers down her throat."

Her mouth was empty. Her face didn't move even when Asher gagged her.

"Is she breathing?" I asked.

"Barely."

I hung up after the operator told me to unlock the downstairs door. There was a bag of phonebooks by the mailboxes that I stuck in the doorway to hold the door open, and then I rejoined Asher. He was sitting on the edge of the tub, holding Tiffany's head up.

"Where did she get all this?" I asked, picking up both bottles.

"They must have been in my bag from when I was sick last week."

"Didn't I tell you to hide all your stuff?"

Tylenol was the only medication I had, along with the kitchen knives and my razor, and I'd locked them all in the trunk of Asher's rental car.

"I put my bag under your bed."

I couldn't blame him for this. As far as I knew, Asher had never been around anything like this. He hadn't known Tiffany would search his bag, and now that didn't matter. The most important thing was getting her to the hospital. Her skin turned bluer every second. When I put my fingers under her nose, I could hardly feel any air passing by.

I heard the sound of feet and moved into the hallway. "She's in here," I yelled.

The paramedics forced us out of the bathroom so they would have enough room to work. Asher and I stood in the hallway, his arms wrapped around me. When he started to say something, I quieted him and tried to listen to the paramedics. After all the times I'd been in the hospital, medical language should be something I understood. But none of the numbers they were saying back and forth told me anything about her condition.

The stretcher wouldn't fit in the bathroom, so the paramedics carried her to the hallway, secured her under the straps, and brought her down the stairs. Once we got outside, they told us which hospital they were taking her to, and Asher hailed a taxi. When I told him we should take the rental car to save time, he said it was six blocks away and there wasn't much parking at the hospital.

Once we got in the cab, he banged his head against the back of the seat. "Ten more fucking hours, and she would have been in rehab."

I reached for his hand and kissed his fingers. He'd been through a lot in the last two days, and it was all for me. "When you're going through withdrawal, every minute feels like an hour."

"Do you think she was trying to kill herself?"

If Tiffany had wanted to score, she would have left my apartment and gone out on the streets, or she would have taken only the cough syrup. A bottle of Robitussin, after you stopped puking— it tore up your stomach—would make you trip like acid. But the bottle of aspirin confirmed her real intentions.

"I think so."

"But she saw how well you're doing—"

"I don't think her withdrawal symptoms were the only reason she did it. She was sober for three years; she knew exactly what it would take to get there again. She also knew the tumor was eventually going to kill her…" I didn't want to think she had succeeded in taking her life. Although her breaths were shallow, she was still breathing; after they pumped her stomach, she would be fine. She couldn't have been in that bathtub for more than fifteen minutes. But the more I thought about it, the more I realized how wrong I was. The last time I had looked at the clock, there were thirteen hours left. That meant I'd slept for almost three.

I knew how it worked when someone was taken to the hospital. The nurses wouldn't let you in farther than the desk, and you sat in the waiting room until someone came out to speak with you. I'd done just that when Sunshine had overdosed and after Michael was shot—and now again, when the paramedics wheeled Tiffany in. Asher got me a cup of water from the bubbler, and I pretended to watch TV. During the taxi ride, I'd called the rehab center and told Allison what had happened. After three sets of commercials, she arrived at the emergency room. She was dressed in her counselor uniform: a white lab coat with her name pinned on the pocket and some type of pants that weren't jeans.

The first thing she said was, "This isn't your fault." Then she hugged me and introduced herself to Asher.

"I shouldn't have fallen asleep."

"I shouldn't have either," Asher said.

"That can happen, you two, especially after being up all night," Allison said.

"But I was supposed to watch her."

"You did your best," Allison said. "You both did."

"My best wasn't good enough."

"Nicole—"

"I'm sick of this place." I moved out of my chair and stood in front of them. "I've been here way too many times and seen too many people die. When is it going to stop?"

"Dying is part of life," Allison said.

"But the people I've lost didn't deserve to die."

"No one does, Nicole."

A doctor wearing blue scrubs and a white lab coat walked toward us. There were two expressions doctors wore when they came out to the waiting room: survived and dead. I'd witnessed both looks, and I knew Tiffany's fate even before he said the word.

My friend was gone.

CHAPTER
TWENTY-SEVEN

My call-ins with Allison had ended once I'd moved out of sober living, but after Tiffany died, we started talking a few times per week. She thought I needed the extra counseling. I did, especially after Tiffany's cause of death was ruled as aspirin toxicity. Addicts knew which drugs could get them high, and aspirin wasn't one of them. Allison agreed that Tiffany had taken the aspirin to commit suicide, but we didn't tell the police or the hospital that; we didn't want suicide to appear on her record.

I couldn't find Professor Allen's number in Tiffany's cell phone, so Allison and I went to Northeastern to notify him in person. Allison didn't think it was something I should do alone. When we stopped by campus billing and admissions, we learned that Professor Allen was in jail. He had been caught dealing coke to an undercover cop. We also discovered that Tiffany had dropped her classes a few months ago, around the same time Professor Allen had been arrested. The timeline made sense. For the last several months, her behavior had gotten much worse. That was the difference between coke and bath salts. Coke had kept her awake all night so she could study; bath salts made her psychotic. And the whole thing was disturbing. I hadn't missed all the relapse signs; I'd just chosen to ignore them.

A few days after our trip to the university, Allison called and asked if I would come to the rehab center. They kept updated records on all their employees, even those who no longer worked there. I figured Allison wanted to document Tiffany's behavior—how she treated the roommates and me, where the pharmacist lived, and the drugs she took—and she'd probably want me to sign my statement.

When I arrived, Dr. Cohen was in Allison's office. He stood and hugged me. "Three hundred and forty-five days sober. We couldn't be more proud."

I felt my face turn red. The last time he'd said those words to me was at the graduation ceremony; they had meant a lot then and meant even more now. But Dr. Cohen treated too many patients to keep track of their sobriety. He must have checked my records. I wondered why.

"Dr. Cohen and I have an offer we'd like to present to you," Allison said. There was a folder on her desk, and she slid it over to me.

Inside was a brochure from the University of Massachusetts explaining its online Addictions Counselor Education Program Certificate. The program consisted of five courses, pre-practicum, and practicum experience.

"You think this program will help with my sobriety?" I asked.

"Well, yes, but that's not the reason we'd like you to enroll," Dr. Cohen said. "Allison was impressed with the way you handled Tiffany and your friend Sunshine. The program will prep you for your certification, and eventually we'd like you to consider getting your bachelor's, even your master's."

"I'm not sure I understand," I said. "Why do you want me to get certified?"

"What the doctor left out," Allison said, winking at Dr. Cohen, "is that we would like to offer you a job. As you may know, we require one year of sobriety for our entry-level positions. We don't want to start you at entry level. We'd like you to work with our patients, which requires a minimum of an addiction certification."

"You're offering me a job?"

"We'll cover the cost of your schooling," Dr. Cohen said. "We'll even lend you a laptop if you don't have one, as long as you sign a contract with the center, guaranteeing five years of employment once you've finished the certificate."

And they were going to pay for my certification? With my criminal record, I hadn't expected an employer to offer me anything above minimum wage. Al gave me a few dollars more than that plus overtime. I didn't think he'd be my boss forever, but I hadn't expected to be a part of the professional class either.

"You'd make an incredible addition to our team, Nicole. Our patients would be extremely fortunate to have someone like you as their mentor, especially with your commitment to the Steps and your background."

The next sheet of paper Allison slid over was the contract. It was three pages long and written in legal language. Before I agreed to anything, I wanted to talk to my parents and Asher and show them the contract. I knew what they would probably say, but I needed time to decide whether this was what I wanted.

"Can I have some time to think about it?" I asked.

"Of course," they both said.

"Take a week to look it over, and call me if you have any questions," Dr. Cohen said. "The salary and benefits are outlined in the contract, as are the requirements of the course."

"Why don't we meet again the same time next week to discuss your decision?" Allison asked.

I thanked both of them, and while I waited for the commuter rail, I went over my options. There weren't many. Al's café was perfect for when I'd gotten out of rehab, but I didn't have a future there. I'd gone to the University of Maine to become a teacher, but with a felony on my record, I wasn't able to teach. Allison was right; I had more than enough experience with addiction, and mentoring addicts was considered teaching. They even offered to pay for my advanced degrees, and I could become a certified counselor, if that was the angle I wanted to take. In the meantime, I'd continue working at the café so I could afford my rent and take online courses at night after my NA meetings. That was a lot of work, and it would take time away from Asher, but I could do it. I was going to have a career.

Asher's shoes and computer case were by the door, indicating he was home. Shortly after Tiffany's death, Asher's landlord had terminated his lease and put the apartment up for sale. Nadal was staying with friends until he found a place, and Asher moved in with me. We hadn't discussed whether the arrangement would be permanent, but he had slept over every night before he had moved in anyway, so other than having all his stuff here, it wasn't much different.

He was in bed, with his laptop on his lap and headphones in his ears. I sat next to him, cuddling into his side.

"Did you have a good day at work?" he asked.

"I have some news."

He closed his laptop and rolled to his side to face me. I told him about my meeting with Dr. Cohen and Allison, and everything they had offered.

"I have to look over the contract; your parents should too, but I think this could be the perfect opportunity for you."

"Me too."

"So you're going to take the job?"

I nodded and smiled. "As long as the contract looks good, I think it will."

He pulled me against his chest and kissed the top of my head. "We've both had great days. You're not the only one with news."

"What's going on?"

He moved over and crossed his legs. "Do you remember how, when we left Jesse's apartment, I said you had saved me and that when the time was right, I would show you?"

"I remember." I couldn't forget. I'd asked him about it several times, and he always repeated those same lines to me.

"I told you that I'd written several novel-length pieces in the past, but none of them were good enough to submit. I was focusing on the wrong genre, and my work lacked a personal touch." He pulled my hands into his lap. "What you don't know is that I started this book when I met you, and since you've been in my life, my writing has completely changed. You, Nicole, were my inspiration."

He got up from the bed and returned with a notebook. He handed it to me. Inside were hundreds of sheets of paper, three-hole–punched and bound.

"This is the final draft. The last set of edits got approved this morning, and my editor thinks he can start submitting it next week."

"Asher, this is amazing." I flipped through the pile; his hard work covered each of the pages. I knew how much time he'd dedicated to this book, the miles he'd jogged when he was stuck on a scene, and the pad of paper he kept in his back pocket for when a thought came to him. His dream was coming true. So was mine.

"I want you to read it," he said.

"Right now?"

"Soon, because it can't be submitted until you've given me your approval."

I looked up at him, my eyes warm. "Why do you need *my* approval?" I asked, giving him the biggest smile.

He didn't smile back. His expression was more serious than it had ever been. "You'll see once you start reading."

CHAPTER
TWENTY-EIGHT

I wasn't really a reader. I had checked out books from the prison library because there wasn't much to do behind bars. Those stories had taken me to a world where my brother hadn't gotten killed, my parents didn't resent me, and heroin hadn't owned me. I had hoped Asher's would do the same. But after the first page, that hope was shattered. I didn't need to read any further to know where the story was going. I did, though, the pressure building in my stomach as I turned each page. I skipped the sections that were too hard to read, and when I got to the end, I slammed the notebook shut. My feet moved so fast down the stairs that I almost tripped, and I stopped when I reached the coffee table. I didn't dare sit next to him.

"You're done already?"

Two hours had passed since Asher left me in the bedroom. It was a quick read, but I'd skimmed most of it.

"I didn't really need to read it, did I? I think I know the story pretty well."

"So what do you think? Did I capture all of it?" His serious expression was still there, but there was a smile hidden between his lips.

"I think you're a fucking asshole."

"What? Why?"

"Get out of my house."

He stood and tried to reach for my hand, but I slapped it away and took a few steps back.

"I don't understand," he said. His voice had changed. It was shaky, and his weight shifted between his feet.

"That's exactly it. You don't understand! You thought writing the story of my life, retelling every moment I've been trying to forget, and sharing it with the entire fucking world would be OK."

"I thought you'd be honored."

"Honored?"

"You know, that you were my muse. That you inspired me."

I took some deep breaths to drain the blood from my face and gripped the railing of the stairs. I didn't trust my hands. "I should be honored that you wrote about how much heroin I injected, about all the men I fucked for dope money, and how I got my brother killed?"

"Nicole—"

"I was nothing more to you than a research project."

"Nicole—"

"That's why you got close to me, so I would tell you all the details of my past. So you could make money off my pain. So you..."

"You have it all wrong."

"You even described the rape. Both of them."

I could barely read the part about how Nikki, the main character, got raped by her drug dealer. I couldn't relive Richard throwing Nikki on his bed—his touch, his force, holding his dead girlfriend's hand while he fucked *me* dry.

He rushed over to me, and I darted into the kitchen, grabbed my keys and purse, and opened the front door. "I trusted you," I said. I kept my back to him. I couldn't look at his lying eyes.

"You still can. Let me explain."

I ran down the stairs and out the front door. He was behind me, shouting my name, and caught up to me at the end of the block. His fingers went to my waist, but I pushed him off. "Don't ever fucking touch me again."

He put his hands up in the air. "You can't leave, Cole. Not like this."

"I have nothing to say to you, and I don't think I ever will."

"I thought your story could make a difference. That it could help people. I only want to do this if you feel good about it. I didn't want this to tear us apart."

I knew what Asher had given up for me. He had deferred graduate school, continued to date me when his parents didn't approve, jeopardized his relationship with Nadal. But I couldn't help how I felt. He had betrayed me, and that wasn't a scar that could be healed.

"It's too late for that." I turned my back and walked away. He didn't follow me, and I didn't hear another sound come out of him.

Asher had described so perfectly what it felt like to be on heroin—the prick of the needle, the rush, and the nod—and for most of the book, I was high. I felt a flush of shame, and suddenly again, the words filling my head weren't Asher's but rather the voice of my addiction. I hadn't forgotten about Dr. Cohen's job offer or the 345 days I'd been sober. I just didn't care. Asher's sequel wasn't going to be about recovery. It would tell how a trigger had caused me to cave.

I got on the train and held onto the edge of the seat. The hunger that pulsed in my veins turned my palms sweaty. My feet tapped on the floor. The need was stronger than I was, and it was begging to be fed.

Eight more stops and I'd be in Roxbury.

I had twenty dollars in my wallet, which was enough for four bags. I didn't have a syringe, but I didn't want to waste time going to the needle exchange. Snorting the powder would do just fine, and it would get me nice and rocked because I hadn't used in so long.

I still had three more stops to go, but I could already feel the warmth spreading through my blood…how my thoughts would liquefy and run from my brain…the beautiful dreams that would appear behind my lids while I nodded out. The train shook as it slowed down, and the vibration was similar to what I'd be feeling in each muscle.

As I stepped off the platform, my phone rang, and Jesse's name appeared on the screen. Asher must have called him. He was probably worried I was going to relapse and thought Jesse could talk me out of it. I hit the ignore button and kept walking.

Jesse called again. A third and fourth time. Didn't he realize after the first call that I wasn't going to pick up? That nothing he could say would change my mind? That heroin's voice was so much louder than his, and Asher's, and…

Michael.

I stopped in the crosswalk. The train station was a block behind me, and I was only three streets away from where the dealers hung out. I was so close, but my feet wouldn't move, and something forced me to close my eyes. I learned it wasn't something; it was some*one*, and he was standing before me in the darkness behind my closed lids. Michael reminded me of everything I was about to give up—how hard I'd worked and what was waiting for me in the future. I fought back. I told him I didn't care; the urge was too powerful for me to fight. I didn't want to turn into a junkie again; I just wanted a taste. He didn't need to tell me that wasn't possible—I already knew that—but he did anyway. He said the second that dope hit my bloodstream, I'd be right back where I was before I'd gotten cleaned up. This time, I might even be on his side of the tracks.

I opened my eyes and pulled out my phone. I couldn't call my sponsor—she was dead, and I hadn't found anyone to replace her yet. I dialed the only other person whose face I wanted to see.

"Are you OK?" Mark asked. I never called him this late.

"No, I'm not."

"Where are you? I'll come get you."

"The train station in Roxbury. You *know* the one."

"Find a store and go inside, and don't leave until I get there."

I hung up and did as I was told. There was a store a few blocks away, and I waited inside by the window, close to the register. The store clerk gave me a once over, but his eyes didn't leave my face.

"I'm just waiting for someone," I said.

He nodded. "A girl like you shouldn't be around here. Not alone." He didn't have any teeth and sucked on his lips between words.

He was right; a girl like me shouldn't be in this section of town. Not anymore.

"I got off at the wrong stop," I said.

"I bet you won't do that again."

"No, I won't."

When Mark pulled up, I ran out the door and straight into his arms. He lifted me up and squeezed so tight that I didn't want anyone else's arms around me. His protection felt good. It filled me the way that heroin had.

"I'm so glad you called," he said.

I buried my face in his neck. The softness of his shirt rubbing against my chin and his hot skin gave me the comfort I needed. His fingers holding the back of my head only made that feeling stronger.

"Me too," I said.

He put me in the passenger seat, making sure I was strapped in before closing the door. He held my hand while he drove, and I told him everything that had happened with Asher and what had led me to Roxbury.

"You're so strong, Nicole, I hope tonight has made you realize that."

I squeezed his fingers. "It has."

Mark never would have done this to me. No one who cared about me would have—especially not someone with whom I'd shared everything: my scars, pain, and memories. I didn't understand Asher's motives or reasoning. And he didn't understand my addiction or me. The trust was gone—and that meant our relationship was too.

"How can I make this better? What can I do to help?"

"You're doing it right now."

He tucked a stray lock of hair behind my ear. A tingle shot into my stomach when his finger brushed over my cheek. The sweaty palms were back, but now it wasn't because I was desperate for a hit. Heroin hadn't left my mind; it was just that something stronger grew inside me.

Mark parked outside his townhouse and opened the car door for me, leading me up the front steps. I shivered from the breeze and he put his arm around me, instantly warming me. It was dark inside his house; he turned on the lamp by the couch, filling the room with an orange glow. Oddly, it matched the smell of the room. The scent reminded me of Halloween and the pumpkin spice candles my mom used to light.

He kneeled in front of the stereo, his jeans tightening on his ass, and turned on some music. It wasn't too loud, but the bass thumped, similar to what was played during raves. If I were on E, the beat would be massaging each of my muscles. That wasn't happening, but something else was—a tingling that moved in the same pace as the rhythm.

"Hungry?"

I shook my head.

"Let me get you something to drink."

I followed him into the kitchen and watched his fingers lift two mugs out of the cabinet and fill them with coffee from the automatic dispenser. He dumped a little cream and two spoonfuls of sugar into mine. I hadn't told him how I took my coffee; he remembered from the last time I was here. He gave me the mug, but my eyes didn't leave his fingers. They were long, thin, and masculine, and his nails were trimmed and rounded. They would look good on my body, holding my breast, because his hand was about the size of my bra cup.

He went into the freezer and took out a pint of ice cream and two spoons, setting them between us. The few silver hairs in his scruff sparkled under the kitchen light, making him look distinguished and professional. Age was attractive. While working the track, I'd learned that the younger men were usually selfish and inexperienced. Mark had showed me he wasn't either of those things.

"You know you want some," he said with a mouthful.

The ice cream was chocolate, with swirls of marshmallow and caramel. I reached in and our spoons touched.

"You first," he said, pulling out.

I brought the spoon up to my mouth, and he watched my lips cover it and my tongue lick the ice cream off, observed the way I swirled it around in my mouth before I swallowed. His mouth opened slightly for just a second and then closed. There was some chocolate on my bottom lip, and I sucked it until it was gone. My eyes never left his.

I took another spoonful, and because his was still in the ice cream, our fingers touched. A shiver ran up my arms, down my chest, and past my stomach. My eyes closed, and I took a deep breath. When they opened, they landed on his lips. They were full and soft, and I could feel them on my neck.

An urge had taken over, and only Mark could fill it. I'd felt the attraction when I'd gone to his bar opening. Maybe even before. Had I been fighting this because of Asher's connection with my brother? I didn't know. What I did know was how sexy Mark's smile had been when he listened to music with Asher in his office, how he always showed up whenever I needed to be saved, how safe I felt when his arms were around me.

He put the ice cream back in the freezer and the spoons in the sink. He walked toward me; I was directly in his path, but he stopped a foot away. His hands clenched at his sides as though he were trying to keep them from reaching out. I leaned against the wall and slightly spread my legs.

He took a step closer, sending me a whiff of his scent. It was woodsy with a hint of musk. My back arched and my head moved down so the side of my neck was exposed.

His breathing deepened.

My eyes were the best feature on my face, and I knew how to use them. How to open them just enough that only the deep, ocean blue showed. How to slowly blink, revealing the length and thickness of my lashes. Mark's gaze became even more intense, and his hands slammed into the wall behind me. His head dipped, and his lips hovered in front of mine.

I didn't want to take. I wanted to be taken. But I knew Mark too well; he wasn't going to take without my permission. He needed to hear the words because of what had happened between us in the hallway of his bar when I'd been high. But I wasn't ready for words just yet.

I pressed my fingers into his stomach and climbed my way up to his hair, grabbing a handful and pushing him against me. Because I was being so aggressive, I thought his lips would tear into mine. But he was gentle, opening his mouth, his tongue gliding in and out. I could taste the sweetness of the chocolate and marshmallow. I wanted more.

The way his shirt lay on his chest showed the tightness of his muscles. There were too many buttons to undo. I held both sides of the collar and pulled; his shirt busted open as each of the buttons dropped to the floor. Underneath was a white T-shirt, and I began to yank it over his head. He stopped me. He grabbed my hands and held them in place.

"Is something wrong?" I asked.

He took a deep breath. "I can't do this. Not tonight."

My face turned red. The ice cream sloshed around in my stomach. Mark was rejecting me? Now? After giving me a taste of his lips?

I pulled my fingers out of his hand and moved around him.

He blocked me from the side. "Nicole, listen to me." He held my cheeks with his palms. "I care about you so much."

I shook his hands off. "Just not in *that* way."

"That's not true. I want you. But tonight, I just want to hold you." He pulled me into his chest and pressed his lips against the top of my head.

He just wanted to hold me? No one had ever said that to me before.

My breathing slowed, and my body relaxed. He wasn't rejecting me because he didn't want to have sex with me. He wanted to comfort me and be there for me the way I needed him to be. Mark was amazing.

CHAPTER
TWENTY-NINE

I woke to lips on the back of my neck and hands curled around my stomach. The scent coming from behind me wasn't Asher's. It was toothpaste, mixed with a hint of cologne and sleep. The sheets and blanket wrapped around me weren't mine. Suddenly, memories from last night came rushing back, and I rolled over. Mark's face met me.

His thumb brushed a piece of hair behind my ear, and his palm cupped my cheek. "Good morning."

I opened my mouth to respond, but my words were stuck. His hands were powerful. A shiver ran up my chest, and I stopped the moan from coming out of my lips.

"Do you want some breakfast?"

I nodded, and he got out of bed. He was wearing basketball shorts and a T-shirt but changed into jeans and a V-neck.

I waited for him to leave the room before I got out of bed. Mark had given me a pair of boxers, and I'd worn my tank top to sleep in. My jeans and sweater were folded on a shelf in his closet. That wasn't the way I had left them last night. I put on my clothes and went into the bathroom, noting that yesterday's mascara and liner were smudged under my lower lids. I washed my face and swished around some mouthwash.

The scent of coffee hit me as soon as I got to the bottom of the stairs. He handed me a mug when I walked into the kitchen and placed a bowl of fruit in front of me as I sat at the bar. The pineapple made my mouth pucker.

"Did you sleep well?" he asked.

"Your bed is really comfortable."

He smiled. "That's the only reason you slept well?"

"Maybe," I said, returning the smile.

He flipped the pancakes one last time. Then he moved around the island and set the plate in front of me. "I hope you like blueberry?"

I didn't take my eyes off his lips. "I do."

I squirted a little syrup over the top and handed the bottle to Mark. He wasn't looking at the bottle; he was staring at me. My body was responding, but I didn't want him to know that. After last night, I didn't want him to think I was begging for his touch, so I filled my mouth with a bite of pancake. He hadn't picked up his fork and was still holding the syrup. He hadn't sat down yet. I took a sip of orange juice. "Aren't you hungry?"

He nodded.

"Are you going to eat?"

A smile came to his lips. "I want to."

I shifted in my chair to face him, and he pressed his thighs against my knees. He hadn't wanted to have sex last night, and I understood why. But it was morning. There was no reason to wait. "I want you," I said between breaths.

He lifted me off the chair, holding me against the wall, and I wrapped my legs around him. There was tenderness in his movements, but his teeth were hungry. They bit my lip and nibbled down my neck. My sweater stopped him from going any further, and his hands were cradling my weight.

I couldn't reach past his waist. My fingers wanted so much more of him. So did my lips. "Mark," I said softly in his ear. "I need all of you."

He carried me through the kitchen, and I threw off my sweater as we got to the steps. I unhooked my bra at the top of the landing, and once we were in his room, he tossed me on his bed. I went straight for his belt, but he grabbed my wrists and held them over my head. His mouth devoured my nipples, his teeth tugging and biting. I tried to wiggle out from his grip, but he was too strong. I liked that.

He tore my jeans off with his other hand—my panties too—and his lips went to my stomach. He marked me with his mouth, biting small sections of my skin. As he moved lower, my begging for his tongue got even louder. The harder he bit, the more I wanted him.

When he got to my waist, he released my wrists, and I steered his face into me. Though his hands were soft, he held me with force, and his tongue showed even less resistance. There was nothing amateur about Mark's movements. He knew the spot that needed to be licked, just the right number of fingers to fill me, and how to do both at the same time.

My hands clenched the back of his head, pulling him closer. My legs closed, and he pushed them apart. I had lost control of my movements the second Mark's mouth had touched me, responding with moans and jerks, but now I could no longer manage what was happening inside. His tongue moved faster, flicking over me. Other than the parts he licked and fingered, everything else was numb.

A spark began to build in my back, warmth shooting into my stomach and exploding, making my whole body sensitive. I tried to wiggle away, but he followed. And his tongue didn't leave my spot. He licked around the edges, holding me open with his fingers, and then slowly began to suck. I tried to move again, but he wouldn't let me. I reached for him, and he drove my hands away. I screamed out, and his mouth tightened. I tilted my head back, and the mirrored tiles on the ceiling showed Mark's head buried between my legs, my stomach caving inward with each breath and shuddering as another orgasm rippled through me.

I heard the buckle of his belt hit the floor, and the mattress indented. His hands wrapped around my thighs; he yanked me against him. I screamed as he entered, squeezing the back of his knees from the strength he used. His first strokes were gentle, but as I got used to his size, I asked for more. The pain turned to pleasure. His hands moved around my body, covering every inch of my skin.

He lifted my legs in the air, placing my heels on his chest. I pushed my toes into his hard muscles, and he gripped my ankles, kissing the tops of my feet. That was when he whispered my name. I heard it once, twice, getting louder each time; then he flipped me on my stomach. Spreading his body over my back, his mouth went to my ears, my neck, my shoulders. His teeth bit; his lips sucked. His fingers were on my clit, rubbing at the same speed he stroked. The blanket was the only thing within reach, and I grasped it with all the strength I had left.

My mind was empty; the most intense sensation was filling my body, and my vision blurred. The blanket was the only reminder of reality; no man had ever brought me to the edge this fast or this many times, and even squeezing my nails into my palms couldn't stop me from plowing through it.

I didn't need to tell him what he'd done again; my shouts told him everything he needed to hear. His moaning was just as loud as my wetness dripped over him. He held the tops of my hands, his lips went to my earlobe, and he told me exactly how good it felt until he collapsed on top of me.

I couldn't move. I had nothing left, but I didn't have to. Mark pulled back the blanket and sheet, placed me under both, and pulled me onto his chest. I looked up again at the mirrored tiles, my hair spread out over his pillow, a bump in the blanket where my legs curled around his. He kissed my forehead. It all looked so right. It felt right. And my eyes closed.

*   *   *

I couldn't remember where I had thrown my sweater or bra, so I dressed in a button-down I found in his closet and went into the bathroom.

"My shirt looks nice on you," he said. His fingers grabbed my ass as I washed my hands.

I rubbed my nose against the collar. "It smells just like you."

His nose went to my neck. Then his lips did. "It doesn't taste as good as you." He took my fingers and led me over to the shower, slowly unbuttoning the shirt. My fingers glided over his stomach, pulled the waist of his boxers, and let them drop to the floor.

He placed me, naked, under the hot stream. The water sprayed from the main head and side jets that were built into the wall, and they massaged my shoulders and back. Mark's hands were covered in soapy bubbles, and he caressed them over me, stopping just below my chest.

His eyes met mine. "I want to be your new memory."

His words slammed into me as though I'd been sleepwalking and had fallen down the stairs. I searched his pupils, really looking at them for the first time.

"Give in to me, Nicole." His hands moved to my face, and he leaned down so his lips were inches away. "Relive with me who you always wanted to be."

I took his lip between mine, giving him a taste of what I could do with my tongue before it licked the rest of his body.

* * *

Mark told me he'd call Al and get me out of my evening shift, but I couldn't leave Al shorthanded just because I didn't want to leave Mark's bed; plus I needed the money. I did let him drive me home, and I kissed him before I got out of his car.

"I'll see you tonight?" he asked, before I shut the door.

I smiled. "Yes, you will, and I can't wait."

"I don't want you to take the train, so I'll pick you up after your shift."

"How do you think I'm going to get to work?" If he was worried about me relapsing, there were ways to get to Roxbury other than the train. I'd been triggered to use before, and I'd probably be tempted again. Mark couldn't protect me every second.

"I just want to pick you up. Is there something wrong with that?" He laughed a little and winked.

"I'll see you at midnight."

Mark didn't drive away until I got inside. As I put my keys in my purse, I noticed my cell phone. There were over twenty missed calls—all from Jesse and Asher—and two voicemails.

I stood by the mailboxes and listened to Jesse's message, telling me he'd talked to Asher and was worried about me. He asked me to call him.

The second one was from Asher. "Cole, I feel sick that you're in pain and that I caused it. I hope you're somewhere safe. I hope...I hope you're not doing anything to harm yourself. If I was the reason you relapsed...I love you. Please come home to me."

Asher was probably upstairs waiting for me. He wanted me to come home to him. And he loved me? We hadn't said those words yet. There were times when we'd looked in each other's eyes and said, "love." We hadn't questioned that aspect of our relationship because that one word had been enough.

I was dressed in Mark's button-down. I smelled like him—his cologne on the collar of the shirt, his shampoo in my hair, his saliva all over my body.

What had I done?

Even though the top of the shirt was unbuttoned, I yanked the collar away from my throat and pushed my way back outside. I needed air. There was a bench on the next block and I took a seat, curling my knees into my chest.

What was happening to me?

My pulse throbbed in my veins, and I could feel my heart pounding under my fingers. I took a few deep breaths, trying to slow everything down so I could piece it all together.

I'd almost given up sobriety last night.

Asher hadn't even explained his side. I hadn't let him. But I wasn't sure he deserved a chance to explain. Was I sure I had cheated on him? I'd told him I had nothing to say and that I didn't think I ever would. Was that considered a breakup?

Michael's voice had stopped me from becoming a junkie again.

Then I ran straight into Mark's arms.

There had been a need screaming inside me, and I wanted Mark's dick to fill it. Sex had been the only thing on my mind after I'd gotten to his apartment. Just like heroin had been on my mind when I left Asher. Was I subbing one addiction for another?

My phone rang, and I looked at the caller ID.

"I'm OK," I said into the phone.

"You don't sound OK," Jesse said.

"I'm better now."

My body was still shaking, but Jesse didn't need to know that. He needed to know I hadn't relapsed, nothing more.

"Where are you?" he asked.

"A block away from my apartment."

"Why haven't you gone inside?"

"I don't know…"

"Come over. We'll talk."

Michael had been the person I'd gone to when I was younger. He always had the answers and knew the right things to say. Jesse had shown me how much he was like Michael; I knew I could count on his advice. But he was Asher's brother.

"I can't. It's about Asher, and I don't want to get you involved."

"I want the best for you, too, Cole. I can put Asher aside and help you through this."

I didn't have anyone else. And I didn't have to tell him everything. I asked him for his address; the last time I'd been to his apartment was a bit fuzzy. Then I said I'd be there in a few minutes.

During the short train ride to his place, I didn't rehearse what I was going to say. I didn't know what to say; my thoughts were all jumbled together, and nothing made sense. Asher and Mark. Whom did I care for the most? Who was better for my sobriety? I wasn't sure whether either of them was right for me. Maybe what I needed was to be alone. By the time I started making a list, I was already at the lobby door. Jesse must have called down to let the doorman know I was coming because he greeted me by name and led me to the elevator.

Jesse was waiting for me in the entryway of his apartment and hugged me as soon as I stepped off the elevator. "What happened to you last night?"

I pulled away and looked into his eyes. They were so similar to Michael's eyes—honest and nurturing. How truthful could I be? Asher was still his brother no matter how much he wanted to help me.

"Can we sit?" I asked.

He took my hand, and we moved over to the couch. I snuggled into the corner, pulling one of the pillows onto my lap. Jesse's legs touched mine. After several seconds of silence, I told him about getting on the train to Roxbury.

"So you didn't use?" he asked.

I shook my head.

He let out a deep breath. "Where did you go?"

His eyes moved to my shirt. Jesse knew it wasn't Asher's; Asher didn't really wear button-downs, and he didn't own anything baby blue.

"I went to a dark place, but Michael's voice stopped me before I got too far."

"That's not what I was asking."

"I know."

"We'll get back to that." He covered my fingers with his. "Are you upset because you heard Michael's voice?"

I shook my head. "I hear his voice all the time. I see him when I close my eyes."

"Then what is it, Cole? Are you questioning your feelings for Asher?"

"I don't know how I feel."

"Have you ever been in love?"

There were only three men I could have even considered loving. Dustin had taken me out of rehab and kept me fucked up on his drugs. I had used his dick and his connection to heroin; I just didn't realize it at the time. That wasn't love. Asher and I had started off slowly and became friends before we'd had sex. But he was Jesse's brother, and that never left my head. Mark and I had known each other for years. Before last night and this morning, I hadn't wanted anything from him other than his friendship.

Was that true? At the aquarium, I had wanted his lips—and probably more than that. Had I simply fallen in love with sweetness and care because I'd never been treated that way by a man before? Did I really love either Mark or Asher?

"Maybe," I said.

"You can feel love in every part of your body. It's not just a sexual connection, although there's that too. Your feelings for him will completely consume you. You'll know it, and you'll never doubt it."

"Asher's saved me from some bad situations."

"You want to feel protected because of what happened to you in college."

Jesse was talking about the rape. And he was right. The feeling of being protected had been more important to me than love. The two men I'd dated while I was a junkie, Raul and Dustin, were in gangs. They were tough, covered in tattoos and battle marks, probably carried a gun—and nothing had happened to me while I was with them. Asher and Mark weren't as rugged, but they kept me safe. I had given all of them my body. Suddenly Mark's words echoed in my head, "Give in to me, Nicole. Relive with me who you wanted to be."

"After you dropped out of college, you turned to drugs," Jesse went on. "Heroin helped you with your pain, and I understand that. But was Asher giving you the protection you didn't have that night?"

"I think so."

"You deserve to know love."

Mark had told me that right after my lips had left his mouth. He said it again while we drank our coffee in bed. Was Mark trying to say I had given him my body but not my heart?

"I told Asher everything. I haven't lied to him once, and I trusted him."

"I don't doubt that, but don't confuse trust with love."

"Asher led me to you," I said.

"And now?"

"I finally have all the answers I need about Michael."

"Is that why you didn't give Asher a chance to explain last night? Because you never loved him in the first place?"

My eyes moved to my hands. Jesse deserved to hear the truth, but when I looked back into his eyes, I couldn't give it to him. Things were clearer, but the resolution still wasn't obvious. Did I love Asher, or was he filling something that I was missing?

"Asher was never the man you were after. It was Michael. You wanted your brother back, and Asher gave you a taste of him." He paused and searched my eyes. "You deserve to know love, and if you and my brother never have that, that's OK. You will know when it's right."

CHAPTER THIRTY

Asher was sitting on the couch when I got home. The news was on the TV, and his cell phone was in his lap. Before I even had my keys on the hook, he stood and was at the door. His hands were on the counter and the wall, blocking me so I couldn't duck underneath. When I stopped moving, his fingers went to my cheeks, and he stared into my eyes. "You're not high..."

"Are you fucking kidding me? That's what you have to say to me?"

I should have cared that he was worried about me. He was watching the news, which he never did, to see if my name appeared on the screen, and holding his cell in case I called. But I didn't care. The only thing I felt bad about was having sex with Mark. I should have waited until after Asher and I had talked because, from the way he was acting so far, he didn't think our relationship was over. Was it? He had destroyed my trust, but I wasn't any better. Were we even now? I didn't know if that even mattered. I didn't know much of anything.

"I'm—"

"No, I'm not, and I didn't use," I snapped.

"I never would have forgiven myself if you had."

Michael would make sure that never happened, but Asher didn't need to know that. I didn't think my brother's voice was ever going to disappear, especially when I got in one of those situations in which I needed some reasoning.

"I shouldn't have let you leave." His hands dropped from my face and reached for my waist. "Come here, I need to—"

"We need to talk." I slid past him and moved over to the couch, waiting for him to take the seat across from me. "I know I didn't give you a chance to explain last night, but I won't apologize for that. I don't think I need to."

"You were angry," he said. "I can understand why. I should have told you about the book instead of throwing it at you when it was completed. That wasn't fair, and I'm sorry."

From his expression, I could tell he had a lot of questions: where I'd spent the night, why I was wearing a man's shirt, and how I'd stopped myself from using. But I had questions of my own.

"Why did you write my story?"

"There are so many families who don't understand why their children are addicts. Your story could teach them about the power of your disease. Your struggles could give them some clarity."

"Isn't that up to me? Not you?"

"That's why I changed the names of the characters. It's your voice with my twist."

Asher's main character was named Nikki, and her best friend was Aaron, instead of Eric. I wouldn't count that as a major change because everything else he covered was almost identical. The melodramatic moments he threw in were probably his way of filling in the gaps on the parts he didn't know. And the book left out the things I had never told him, like how one of the squatters who lived at my dealer's house tried to kidnap me when he bailed me out of jail, or how Dustin had killed my old roommate, Renee, and most of Que's gang members because one of them had beaten me up. I hadn't talked about those things even during my therapy sessions at rehab. I wanted to forget I had ever been involved with those people.

"You said you needed my approval for the book? Why? Aren't you going to send it to publishers anyway?"

"My editor wants you to sign a legal document; technically, I can't send it out without your permission."

"So I won't sue?"

"It's an adaptation of your story. So yes, it's for legal purposes."

It sounded as though an attorney were answering these questions, not the man I'd been dating for the last six months.

"You're unbelievable."

"You used to say that when I was inside you."

"Now it has a different meaning." I got off the couch and walked up the stairs to my bedroom. I grabbed my backpack from the floor in my closet. When I turned around, Asher was behind me.

"I know this is hard for you to understand, but I wrote this book to make a difference, to—"

"I don't care what your reasoning is." I took my black pants out of the hamper and stuffed them in the backpack. "If you wanted to make a difference, you should have started with me instead of going behind my back."

"I was wrong."

"You had no right to put my secrets out there. Do you know what it feels like to know people are going to read about Richard raping me and my brother getting shot by the pimp I worked for?"

"Nicole—"

"Don't you see how this looks? Like the only reason you got close to me was to air my pain?"

"I know how it looks. I promise you that wasn't my intention."

"What was your intention?"

He combed his fingers through his hair and stopped when he reached the ends, pulling the strands with his fists bunched. "I was doing what Michael would have wanted; I was watching over you, but I didn't know my feelings for you were going to grow."

"What about your parents? You're just going to ignore their feelings?"

"My parents will learn to accept you."

"When? They can't see past the pain I've caused your family. They don't want us together, and I can't blame them. I wouldn't want my son with me either."

My phone rang from the kitchen, and I ran downstairs to answer it. Melissa, my attorney, was on the other end. She told me the district attorney had contacted her and that I was being subpoenaed to testify in Dustin's appeal. The court date was in six months, and she wanted me to come to her office a week beforehand so I could review my statement and prep for my testimony.

"There's no way around this?"

"Unless you want to go back to jail for failing to appear in court, you don't have a choice."

I told her I'd call her to set up an appointment and hung up. I wrapped my arms around the counter, my heart too heavy to carry. Dustin was expecting me to disappear. What if I didn't?

"Are you OK?" Asher asked.

"Dustin's court date was set."

"Who was that on the phone?"

"My attorney," I said.

"The same one you used when you took the plea?"

"Yes, the 'Megan' in your book." I pushed off the counter and moved toward the stairs. I had to get out of this apartment and away from Asher's questions. Work would keep my mind busy for the next eight hours, and I could deal with Asher and Dustin when I got out.

"How did she get your cell phone number? Have you been in contact with her?"

I threw my white button-down and some clean panties and a bra in my bag, but Asher stopped me at the top of the stairs. He blocked me from going any farther. Suddenly, I remembered that Mark was picking me up from work. How would I explain that to Asher?

"Will you talk to me?" he pleaded.

"What do you want to know? Yes, I've been in contact with Melissa. I went to her office after Dustin's messenger came to the café."

"Dustin's messenger? What are you taking about?"

He didn't know anything about Dustin's messenger paying me a visit because I'd never told him. Mark had been at the café at the time, and he had gone with me to Melissa's office. Mark was the one who asked whether I'd heard from Melissa and whether the state had subpoenaed me. It was Mark I spoke to about the things going on in my present. Asher was the one I spoke to about things in my past. The past I was trying to forget.

"Cole?"

Jesse had told me not to confuse trust with love. But was that what I had done? I was comfortable with Asher; I could be myself and not hide my scars. That wasn't love; it was trust. Asher's protection had initially replaced the hole Michael had left. But now, with Jesse in my life, he was the one who filled that space. Plus, things with Asher had changed. We didn't have as much sex. We didn't talk like we had in the beginning; Asher had all the information he needed to know. And what he had done with that information had shattered the trust I had in him. He wasn't the one I thought about when I was at work, in bed, or staring into emptiness.

Asher didn't want new memories. He didn't want me to give in to him. If he had, he would have asked for my heart. He asked for my past instead. He didn't care who I'd always wanted to be; if he had, he wouldn't have trumped my news with his own. He was looking for a muse, and he found one. I was looking for clarity, for how to transition out of rehab and find my place in life, and for answers about how my brother had found me the night he'd been killed. Asher gave me those answers.

"Nicole, are you just going to ignore me?"

Michael had led me to Asher, but it wasn't for the reason I'd thought. Michael trusted Asher and Jesse, and he knew they would watch over me and keep me protected. I was never supposed to fall in love with Asher. He wasn't the reason I smiled, although his friendship, what he had done for me, and what I had accomplished because of his support had set me on my way.

Mark was the reason I smiled. His touch and his words filled me. He had given me everything I needed, and he was finally asking for something in return. He didn't want only my body; he wanted all of me. He wanted me to have the future I'd always dreamed of, and he wanted to be a part of that.

"I can't be with you," I said.

"Is this about the book? I won't have it published. I'll tell my editor—"

"This has nothing to do with your book. I'll sign whatever papers you need me to sign."

"Then what is it? You don't love me?"

"Can you look me in the eyes and honestly say you love me? I know you care about me, as I do about you. But Asher, do you really love me?"

His expression gave me the answer I needed.

CHAPTER

THIRTY-ONE

I sat to the left of the podium, waiting for my name to be called. I'd never heard this part of the ceremony before. Last time I'd spent most of it in the bathroom, throwing up my breakfast and then counting my steps to the rec room and shaking with anxiety as I walked down the aisle. The addicts were telling their stories, and all I could do was nod my head. Some were only ninety days sober and just graduating rehab; others were further along like me. But I had things in common with all of them: causing my family pain, selling my body for dope, overdosing, and watching my friends die. Addiction was like a big game of fill-in-the-blank; if you changed the names, faces, and our drugs of choice, almost everything else was the same.

Dr. Cohen called me to the podium. I didn't have a hard time breathing as I made my way over this time, and my breakfast was not threatening to make its way back up. There were so many faces smiling at me. My parents sat a few rows back, Jesse was next to my mom, Mark was on the other side of my dad...even Al and Jami, from work, had come to celebrate. I hadn't prepared a speech. I didn't need to.

I gripped the podium to make myself a little taller. Even with heels on, I barely topped the edge. "My name is Nicole Brown," I said. Jesse winked at me, and I couldn't help but grin. "And today I'm three hundred and sixty-eight days sober. Nine months ago, when I graduated from rehab, I didn't know what lay ahead for me…if I'd give in to my addiction again, if I'd lose more people I love." I glanced over at Allison, and she nodded. She knew I was referring to Sunshine and Tiffany, friends I thought about every day. I hadn't been able to stop their addiction from killing them. "I now know what it takes to stay clean—the voices I have to ignore and the ones I need to listen to. For the first time, I know what lies ahead and where I'm going. I'll always be a recovering heroin addict, but heroin no longer owns me."

After a round of applause, I stepped off the platform. As I passed Dr. Cohen, he reached for my arm and pulled me back to the podium.

"As most of you know, we award our patients with chips when they reach ninety days and one year of sobriety. This year, we're adding something else."

Allison joined us and stood at my other side.

"We've decided to recognize one of our graduates who has not only shown an exceptional level of dedication to the twelve-step program but has also supported and mentored addicts, assisting in their sobriety while maintaining a clean lifestyle."

Allison pulled out a long, black velvet box. She smiled at me as she opened it, flashing it in front of me before holding it up for the audience to see.

"Nicole is the recipient of this honor," Dr. Cohen said. "And I'm proud to announce that she's recently enrolled at the University of Massachusetts to obtain a certificate in Addiction Studies. Once she's completed the courses, she will be working here full-time." He turned toward me but kept his mouth close to the microphone. "I'm honored, Nicole, to have you as part of our team. In celebration of your hire, we'd like you to have this."

Allison removed the gold chain with a matching coin, engraved with the one-year emblem, and clasped it around my neck. I held the coin, warming the metal with my fingers. As I glanced up, my mother was crying. My father was clapping. Jesse had his arm around my mom and was pounding my father's arm with his other hand. Mark was on his feet, applauding.

My gaze wandered to the back of the room, where Asher stood in the doorway. I had helped him move his stuff into Jesse's apartment, and we still checked in through texts. He had been really upset that I'd hooked up with Mark; I didn't blame him. Only a month had passed since we'd broken up, and we weren't ready to hang out as friends yet. He tilted his head, and I smiled back before he turned around and disappeared.

I stepped off the platform as Dr. Cohen ended the ceremony and invited everyone to the cafeteria for brunch. My family and I had other plans. Mark had cooked lunch for all of us, and we were going back to his apartment. I joined them in the hallway, wrapping my arms around each of them and thanking them for coming. After a long moment, I had to pull away; it didn't seem like they wanted me to let go. And that made me happy. I kissed Mark last, just a soft peck on the lips, while my parents watched. Then we all went out to the parking lot. Jesse and my parents got into Mark's car, with Al and Jami following.

During the drive, Jesse told us about his new boyfriend. He was an environmental attorney who lived in his building.

"When do we get to meet him?" I asked.

"It's still new," Jesse said. "I'm not ready for him to meet the family yet."

When he said the word *family*, Jesse looked at my parents and me. Jesse was becoming my Michael. He would never be blood, and he could never take my brother's place, but he now was the closest thing I would ever have to a sibling. I didn't think a new boyfriend in his life would change that. We had all experienced something together, and even though that event was something we all wished we could forget, it had bonded us.

Mark's hand fell in my lap, and I wrapped my fingers around it. I couldn't stop my face from beaming. My parents' voices were upbeat, and the only tears shed today were of happiness. Al knew of my plans to leave the café once I finished all my courses, and he supported my decision. He had said the coffee shop was just a starting point, that I was destined to move on to something better.

Asher's latest text said a publisher was interested in his novel and he was signing their contract in the next few days. I knew my story would help families understand addiction, but I wasn't excited that my past would be out there for everyone to read. My parents hadn't seemed surprised when I told them we'd broken up. Dad said they'd had a feeling our relationship was based on my desire to have a piece of Michael in my life...but they weren't pleased when I told them about Asher's book. Once I explained Asher's reasoning, they understood. Nonetheless, they weren't happy about it.

My parents had heard a lot about Mark—I'd been bringing his name up since he'd gotten me a job at Al's—so they acted as though they already knew him when they finally met. They didn't think I was ready for a relationship, despite having a year of sobriety behind me, but they seemed to really like Mark. They appreciated his knowledge on addiction and the way he supported me. They weren't thrilled that he was the owner of two bars, but they were impressed with his success. As long as his work didn't interfere with my sobriety, they approved.

So many times, I had questioned whether I would make it to the one-year ceremony. Triggers had caused urges, and they had been strong, pulling my darkness to the surface. I hadn't known whether my parents would ever forgive me or if my questions about Michael would ever be answered. Ten months ago I had graduated from rehab and moved into sober living. That wasn't a long time, but over that period so much had been resolved. I had a job waiting for me once I finished my online courses. I spent my nights in Mark's bed. My breakup with Asher hadn't affected my relationship with Jesse. Jesse and I spoke at least once a week, and Mark and I had dinner with him every Sunday.

I turned around again, looking at each of the faces of my family. Jesse was sitting between my parents—a seat Michael should have been filling. But my brother was still here, floating above the car, in a cloud, or as one of the stars in the sky. Last night, after I'd closed my eyes, he'd said he was so proud of his baby sister. Then he vanished. We were all moving on, and we were finally smiling.

CHAPTER
THIRTY - TWO

I had written Henry, Claire's son, a few times since I'd gotten out of prison. One of the rules of being on probation was that we weren't allowed to visit inmates. But I had finished my year and a half just last week, and my parole officer signed off on my release papers, reinstating my visitation rights. It was a good thing the approval process hadn't taken too long; Henry had called yesterday and asked me to visit. He was in the infirmary and didn't sound well. I told him I'd be by in the morning.

If it weren't for Henry, I would never set foot in the South Bay House of Corrections again. I had lived on the top floor; he was only four floors beneath me, but I never got to see him. Men and women didn't have yard together or eat at the same times. Still, there had been a tiny bit of comfort knowing he was so close, that I had someone with me on the inside. We'd sent each other kites—letters passed between prisoners that were considered illegal contraband—and I'd filled him in on what had happened before I'd gotten arrested—Michael's death and how the cops had busted Dustin and me. He also kept track of my progress as I completed the addiction program in jail. What I left out of the kites was I had relapsed shortly after completing the program.

I never asked how drugs got smuggled in past security; I just knew they were available. I worked in the prison laundry room, and my earnings went straight to powder. My parents added money to my account so that I could buy toiletries and food, and I traded those canteen credits for pills. When I ran out of money, I hooked up with the dealers. The women who sold drugs were butch, not fem like me; the only thing they were missing was a dick. They looked and acted so much like men that when I closed my eyes, their rough hands and firm tongues felt like those of any guy I'd been with.

It was hard to feel normal in prison. I stared at steel bars until I fell asleep. When I got in trouble, I was caged like an animal, locked in the Special Housing Unit for twenty-three hours a day. But for the few minutes I snuck into the stairwell or in the linen closet to get eaten out by a dealer, I was in control. Getting off and feeling loved gave me the tiniest sense of normal. I would forget about the slop I'd eaten for lunch, the cries from the neighboring cells that kept me awake, and the blood that had covered me when Michael had been shot. Those few moments were as intense as getting high, and they came with the same side effects: realizing I was still in prison after I rejoined general population from the SHU, going through withdrawal when I entered my cell, thinking about my next orgasm when there weren't any women around me.

Before prison, I'd been with only one woman, Casey, who had worked with Eric at the club; we were together when I was on shrooms. In the past, I had found women beautiful, but they didn't have that spicy smell and rough edge like guys did, and those were the things that had turned me on. But something about Casey was safe. We had hooked up not too long after I was raped in college, and a woman felt safer than a man. I didn't think she'd hurt me, and she didn't.

The women in jail didn't hurt me either, at least not emotionally. I hurt them. Like my celly, Devry, with whom I cuddled at night until I requested a new roommate because she gave me a black eye. She wanted to be the only girl I made out with. She wanted all of me. But she served a purpose: soothing me with her words when I was too scared to close my eyes, or an orgasm when I couldn't fall asleep. Most women turned into lesbians when they came to prison. I didn't even consider myself bi; I pretended they were men, and knew I would never do it again once I got out. I couldn't promise what Devry was asking. I was going to kiss others during yard time, let the guards touch me while I showered, and have sex with the dealers. There were hundreds of female inmates, and most of them gossiped. I could have lied to Devry, but eventually she would have heard the truth.

Other than Devry, Big Nan was the one I had hooked up with the most. She told me she liked the clingy type, so I followed her around during yard and sat next to her at chow. I'd sneak into her cell while her roommate was on lookout, and she'd go down on me. I'd leave with an orgasm and two pills under my tongue. If we didn't have a chance to be alone, I'd touch myself and let her lick my fingers, the pills dropping from her mouth into my hand. But she wanted more from me, too. She wanted my tongue and for me to be her girl. As much as I wanted the sexual and mental highs she gave me, I had limits. I wasn't going to commit to any woman, and tasting one wasn't an option either. I put it off as long as I could, but it didn't take long until Big Nan cut me off.

*　*　*

Now, as I walked back through the metal detector at the prison's entrance, the two-and-a-half years I'd spent inside all came rushing back again. The orgasms, the tightness of my cell, the cries that echoed at night, and the nightmares that would wake me in a cold sweat. With Henry being in the infirmary, the guards probably wouldn't let me spend too much time with him, so I could catch the morning NA meeting. I was still attending meetings; I'd found a group near Mark's place because I went to his house every afternoon after work.

I showed my ID and filled out the necessary registration forms. I had a copy of my approval letter, and they scanned it into their system. A guard escorted me upstairs and stayed by the door while a nurse brought me to Henry's bed. The infirmary looked just like a hospital but with shackles bolted into the walls above the beds, and the sick were wearing prison uniforms. Henry was by the far wall, near the only window, and I sat next to him. The nurse woke him up to let him know I was here.

His eyes opened slowly, his cracked lips parted. "You look so beautiful."

The last time I'd visited him, I was fucked up on dope. He'd given me Claire's gold band to wear and told me to put it on when I got sober. I'd stuck the ring in my pocket. At that time, I was dating Dustin, living in some nasty motel in Dorchester, and barely showering. I had probably looked worse than Henry did now.

I covered his hand with mine. The sunlight poured in through the window and shined on my fingers. The glimmer caught his attention, and he glanced down.

"You're wearing the ring."

"I have been for a while." I pulled out the necklace that was buried under my shirt and showed him the gold chip. "I'm fifteen months, clean and sober."

I tried to remember the last time I'd written to Henry; it was when I'd just moved into sober living and gotten a cell phone. Too much time had passed. He should have known I was over a year sober and had moved into my own place. He definitely should have known I was wearing Claire's ring; I guess I had left that out of the letter.

"You're happy," he said.

He didn't phrase it like a question. So much had changed in my life that I couldn't stop myself from smiling, and he could see that. My time in prison had been rough, but I'd deserved it—and even though those memories weren't good ones, I was a better person for the time I'd served. Being with him only reminded me of what I'd gained.

I told him about the online courses I was taking, how I had completed three out of the five, and I would be starting at the rehab center as soon as I was done. I talked about Mark, how I'd be moving into his townhouse once my lease was up, and about my relationship with Jesse and my parents. Henry appeared weak and his face barely moved, but there was a light in his eyes as I spoke. More light than I'd ever seen when visiting him in jail.

"Are you feeling any better?" I asked. "Enough to move down to general population? My visitation rights have been reinstated, so I can come see you once a week."

"No, I'm not getting better."

I didn't know how old Henry was, but he looked weathered and exhausted. Whenever one of the inmates got sick, the virus spread quickly throughout the cellblock. The only people who usually stayed in the infirmary were those recovering from stab wounds or self-inflicted cutting. They didn't have enough beds to keep everyone who was sick. Henry must have been really ill.

"Did you catch something from your celly?"

"No, dear. I have pancreatic cancer."

"You have what?"

"I got sick a few months ago, and now look at me; I'm just lying here, waiting to die in this bed."

"You're dying?"

He did look skinnier, but I'd figured the flu could do that to you. The flu didn't usually cause dark circles under your eyes and a grayish tint to your skin, though. I should have known better. What I did know was that with medicine and will, you could fight certain types of cancer. Not the kind Tiffany had.

"Pancreatic cancer isn't treatable?" I asked.

I didn't need an answer. I could tell by his voice that he didn't have the strength to fight it even if there was medicine that would help.

"I wanted you to come here so I could say good-bye," he said.

"Good-bye?"

"The doctor says I only have a week or two left."

A knot formed in the back of my throat and my eyes filled with tears. I should have written more. I should have begged my parole officer to grant me permission to visit the jail. Henry shouldn't be in here dying alone. Claire had been my best friend; she would be so disappointed in me for abandoning him.

"No, I'm coming back every day."

"Nicole, I'm only going to get worse."

"I don't care—"

"I don't want you to see me like that. I want you to remember me like I was when you visited me with my mom."

I wiped the corners of my eyes and poured myself a cup of water from the pitcher by his bed. He didn't need to see my tears; that wasn't why he'd asked me to come here. I remembered that when I'd visited him with Claire, he'd said he didn't know anyone but her and me on the outside. I would be the last familiar face he'd see before he died. I had to be strong for him.

"I see her sometimes," he said. "Late at night when the medicine makes me tired. She's not in my dreams. She's here with me."

"I'm sure she's trying to keep you safe."

Knowing Claire, that was exactly what she was doing. She had tried to do the same for me.

"I miss her."

"I do, too," I whispered.

The guard came over and said I had only a few minutes left. I didn't know how to say good-bye, not to someone I'd never see again.

"The nurse has your phone number," Henry said. "She'll call you when I pass."

I'd lost so many friends over the years, but their deaths were sudden and unexpected; they didn't have time to plan. The more I looked at Henry and his frail body, the more I realized I would choose the unknown over wasting away in a hospital bed. He could feel death approaching. I couldn't imagine how horrific that must be.

"Are you sure I can't come back?" I asked.

He shook his head; I could tell the movement caused him pain.

The infirmary wasn't like a hospital, where you could pick your meals and watch TV in bed. He ate what they served, and there wasn't even a radio. He had no rights, but he had one last wish. I would grant him that.

"Is there anything you want me to tell her?" he asked.

While I was in prison, I'd thought about Claire a lot and what I would have said if I'd had a few minutes to talk to her before she died in the hotel fire. Back then, I couldn't promise her I'd get clean because I was too deep into my addiction...and an apology wasn't worth shit.

"Tell her I love her and think about her every day."

"She knows that."

"Tell her again." I smiled. "And make sure she knows I'm wearing her ring, and I don't plan to ever take it off."

"She'll be happy to hear that. So am I."

I gave his hand a final squeeze and stood, bending down to kiss his forehead. "Good-bye, my sweet Henry." I turned around and joined the guard in the hallway before Henry could respond. I didn't want to hear him say good-bye. It was hard enough having those words come out of my own mouth.

Outside the elevator, a man was mopping the floor. The back of his bald head was covered with tattoos of spiderwebs and skulls. There was also an inked teardrop under his eye. He looked so much like Que. Que had a big family, and all the men had similar looks. But none of them had the same tattoos, and Que's had stood out in my mind.

As the guard pushed the down button, the prisoner turned toward us. My breath caught in my lungs. It *was* Que.

"Checking on your boy D?" he asked.

"He's not my boy," I said.

He glanced at the guard and then back at me. "What, my lady's killer was too much for you?"

So he did know Dustin had killed Renee, which meant that he knew the situation had involved me. It would be easy for Que to piece it all together; there was no other explanation for Renee's death. Que's gang wouldn't have killed her. They gave her free drugs and let her hang out at their house...and she wouldn't have associated with Dustin if it hadn't been for me.

"I had nothing to do with it," I said. "That was all D."

"She was your friend, boo. You got some real b's to be doing that to a friend."

The guard must have felt the tension in Que's tone because he moved between us.

"Wasn't just my lady, though. Michael's up there too. How does that feel, boo? Feel good knowing he's up there because of you?"

"This is your only warning," the guard said. "Shut your mouth. Now."

When the elevator door opened, the guard put his hand on my back and guided me inside.

"I'll see you one day, Nicole, and you can explain it to me then. That's right; we'll have a nice little chat about my lady."

From what I could remember, Que's sentence was pretty long. He wasn't getting out anytime soon, but once he did, he wouldn't come to me for answers. Anything he wanted to know was right here in this prison; Dustin and his gang were somewhere in here too.

The sun was higher in the sky, but the temperature was still cool. There was a crisp smell in the air, and a dusting of snow covered the ground even though spring was just a few weeks away. I zipped up my jacket, trying to find some warmth. My bones still shivered. It wasn't from the breeze.

Near the sidewalk, a taxi was parked down the street with its lights on. I raised my hand, and the cab pulled up to the curb.

"Where are you going, ma'am?" the driver asked as I got in the backseat.

I gave him the address to Mark's apartment and reached inside my purse to get my cell phone. There was a text from Mark, and just as I started reading it, the other door to the backseat opened and someone climbed in.

"Excuse me," I said. "This is my taxi—"

The locks clicked and the driver turned around. "I told you I'd see you again, Nicole."

Martin, the last messenger Dustin had sent, was in the driver's seat. Ignoring the man sitting next to me, I turned toward the door, reached for the handle, and yanked, but it wouldn't open. The window wouldn't smash when I banged my elbow against the glass. As I began to scream, the man beside me put his hand over my face. But it wasn't his skin that rubbed against my lips; it was a piece of cloth. His other arm reached across my body, pinned my arms down, and pulled me against his chest. I tried to kick my legs. I couldn't. My mind began to cloud and my lungs tightened.

Everything turned black.

CHAPTER
THIRTY-THREE

My head felt heavy and sore. The back of my neck throbbed. My chin pressed into my chest; I lifted it, slowly opening my eyes. I expected it to be bright, making my sensitive pupils hurt even more. But the overhead light was off, and the small window by the ceiling was covered in tinfoil, only letting in a crack of sunlight. There was hardly anything around me: a cement floor and walls and a set of stairs. I was in a basement, and it smelled like one.

Where the hell did they bring me?

I was in a chair in the middle of the room, my hands bound behind my back, my ankles shackled to the wooden legs. The ropes he'd bound me with were just tight enough to keep me in place, but they were also wrapped in cloth so they didn't burn or bite my skin. My jacket and purse were gone; I was dressed in my cotton long-sleeve, with spots of drool on the front and soaked jeans. The scent of urine rose from my pants.

The basement door opened and the overhead light turned on. As the footsteps got louder, so did the creaky stairs until the man from the backseat stood before me. He was average height, with blond shaggy hair, blue eyes, and a scar above his lip. His arms were crossed, and he shifted his weight back and forth as I looked him over. I hadn't had enough time to really study him in the car, but I thought he had looked familiar. Even though it had been a while since I'd seen him, I never forgot a face. I especially never forgot someone's eyes.

"Coke-head Cale," I said.

When Dustin had introduced me to his friends, he'd told me mini-stories about each person so I'd remember their names. Out of all the squatters who stayed at our dealer's house and ran drugs with Dustin, I had interacted with Cale the least.

"I thought you would have forgotten."

I didn't forget any of the names I had turned in to the police, but I wasn't going to say that. I couldn't freak out either. If I hoped to get him to untie my wrists and ankles, I had to stay calm.

I looked toward the stairs. "Where's Martin?"

"He doesn't do house calls. Only deliveries."

"When did you get out of prison?"

"Couple months ago," he said, wiping his nose on his sleeve.

"You're using again?"

"Aren't you?"

"I got clean a while ago, but you already know that, don't you?"

He grinned as though he were proud of himself. "You know, someone like *you* should really change their name."

I had flashbacks of how Dustin had somehow gotten my phone number and called me not too long after I'd moved into sober living. He sent his first messenger after me, then a second messenger, and now Cale. Maybe Cale was right. I could be easily found.

"Are we alone, or did the rest of the gang get out too?"

"Just me...for now."

Dustin's trial was in three days. I'd already met with Melissa and the district attorney, and they had prepped me for the questions I'd be asked. None of my answers were going to help Dustin. That was why I was here. He wanted to make sure I wouldn't show up to court.

"How long do you plan on keeping me here?"

He smiled again, but this time the grin was devious. "If you're a good girl, I'll let you go after the trial."

Cale was going to let me go? Didn't he know that as soon as I got out of here, I'd tell the police he had kidnapped me? Ratting him out was the only way I'd get out of all the trouble I'd be in for skipping court.

"Where are you going?" I asked as he moved to the stairs.

"You're hungry, aren't you?"

"Starving." I couldn't remember the last time I had eaten.

Dustin was fucking crazy, but I'd known exactly what I was getting involved with when I'd first started dating him. I knew he ran dope from Boston to various hubs throughout New England and New York. Because of the amount of heroin he was pushing, I had to know he was dealing with some hardcore gangsters. He paid for the motel we lived in and gave me money for food and as much smack as I could shoot. Back then, that was all that mattered to me, but this was where it had gotten me. In some shitty-ass basement, unable to move, with a crackhead for a guard.

Mark knew me better than anyone, but that didn't mean he wouldn't eventually think the worst. He'd probably start searching for me soon, if he hadn't been already, checking the streets to see if I was slumped over in some doorway or alley with heroin flowing through my veins. Even if he got the police involved, they wouldn't be able to find me; Dustin would make sure of that. Cale had probably gotten rid of my cell phone so the cops couldn't track the signal. I wondered if Mark had called my parents and Jesse. My poor parents; they had been through enough.

The question my father had asked me when I'd graduated from rehab—"With everything that's happened here, do you really think Boston is the right place for you?"—had never left my head. The words always seemed to echo whenever my past became my present. My name wasn't the only thing that needed to be changed. Boston wasn't the right place for me anymore. I was trying to start over and live as though my addiction had never existed, as though I hadn't ratted out an entire ring of people now out to get me. I was off probation and halfway through my online courses. If I spoke to the rehab center and explained my situation, they would understand why I had to get out of here. I didn't know where I would go, but I knew Bangor wasn't the right place for me either. Too many lies had been spread about me, especially after Eric died, and it would be impossible to change my reputation there. I needed to go to a place where no one knew my name. Mark was the only thing holding me back. He couldn't leave the business he'd started. But I couldn't stay.

The basement door opened and Cale appeared in front of me, wearing the same grin as before. His hands were behind his back.

"Are you going to feed me? Or will you let me feed myself?"

"I brought you something better than food." His hands moved to the front. He was holding a syringe. It was full. And I knew the liquid inside the chamber was heroin.

I shook my head. "I don't want it."

But I did.

But did I really want to get high? I could feel the weight of my one-year chip pressing down on my throat. There were multiple voices in my head; some told me I'd been sober for far too long to ruin it now, and others reminded me how strong I was. The voice of my addiction said dope would turn this basement into a cloud of warmth. But in my heart I knew that regardless of how damp this room was, I didn't need heroin. I needed to wait out the next few days and get the hell out of here.

"It doesn't matter what you want; Dustin wants you to have it. It's his gift to you, and when he gets out, you'll be his gift."

"You don't have to get me high; I'll give Dustin whatever he wants."

He shook his head. "This is Dustin's plan and I can't change it."

"Plan? What plan?"

To get me addicted and needing dope? I doubted the street pushers in Roxbury would sell to me after my mug shot had been plastered all over the news. That was probably what Dustin was hoping for, and that I'd come running right back into his arms, relying on him like I had before.

"Enough questions." He pulled off his belt and took a few steps closer.

"No! No, you can't do this to me. I'll do whatever you want; just keep that shit away from me." My voice got louder with each word.

His lips moved into the biggest smile. "Dustin wants the old Nicole we all remember, the one who needed him for survival."

"He can have me back. I'm his. Forever. But I don't need heroin to be with him. You've reminded me how much I miss him. I do need Dustin. I-I need him, Cale, and I love him."

I tried to pull my wrists out of the rope, but the cloth only rubbed against my skin. I rocked in the chair to tip it over, hoping the fall would break the wooden legs in pieces. "Please, don't," I screamed. "Don't do this to me. I'm begging you! Don't stick that fucking needle in my arm. I'll do anything!"

He didn't respond.

Snot ran from my nose, tears dripped into my mouth, and my sobs convulsed through my body. "Did you hear me? Cale, you need to fucking listen to me. I said I'll do anything!"

He moved behind my back, the chamber of the syringe between his lips.

I closed my eyes, preparing myself for what was about to come, and a memory hit me. A while ago, when I'd lived with Sunshine, the city had shut down from an ice storm and we were stuck inside her hotel room with only a few bags of heroin. We split the bags between us, knowing they wouldn't get us high but would stop us from getting dope sick. We watched the TV, waiting for the weatherman to tell us the storm had cleared and the trains were running again. That didn't happen; the storm was scheduled to last a few days. Sunshine told me what to expect from withdrawal, and that's exactly what happened.

I felt worse now than when I had hugged Sunshine's toilet for two days straight. The high was driving toward me, and I knew what was ahead. How loud I was going to scream for the needle once I started to come down. The beautiful silence of the nod.

No matter how much I squirmed in my chair, shouted for him to stop, or tried to pry my hands out of the rope's hold, Cale wouldn't listen. He slapped my arm, and fresh, untapped veins popped up through my skin. There was a prick when the tip of the needle entered and a slight burn as he emptied the chamber. What came next was warmth. Tingles. Melting. The chair was a waterbed, rippling beneath me. It was fucking amazing.

My chin dropped to my chest. The rope tickled my wrists and ankles. The gray cement walls that surrounded me began to swirl like a tornado, mixing in blue and pink and yellow, and my lids closed. Behind my eyes was the most magical land, lit by a serum of happiness. There was buzzing in my ears. Little bees danced around my lobes, and porcupines stuck me with their quills. The pricking stimulated my sensitive skin. The buzzing was soothing. I was inside the most stunning nightmare, and I was the star.

* * *

Addicts never forget the first time they got high. I remembered each of the drugs I'd tried before heroin and how rocked I'd gotten when I had smoked and snorted them. But the highest I'd ever been was the first time I mainlined. The dragon had injected its claws, making me crave its fiery breath, and I had been chasing that high ever since. But it never happened again, no matter how much dope I shot. The only way to ever feel that intensity was to take a break and then come back. I couldn't shoot heroin in prison because I didn't have access to needles, so it had been about four years since I'd mainlined dope. Cale had just given me a taste, and I was right back to the first time I had shot up. I was chasing the dragon. Again. I didn't know how long I'd nodded out for. Maybe hours. Maybe a day. I wanted more. Now.

"Callllle," I shouted.

The basement was pitch black. There wasn't even any light coming in through the crack in the window. My yelling vibrated against the walls, and it got louder as I continued to scream. My wrists pulled at the rope. Everything was hurting again—my ankles from the ropes, my neck from my chin pressing into my chest, my stomach from not eating.

The door opened and the light turned on. I counted his steps; it took him twelve, and then another eight until he was in front of me.

"I need more."

His eyes bulged out of their sockets, but not because he was surprised. He was on something a lot stronger than coke. Something like meth. I wanted to feel that. I wanted to be high.

"I knew you'd fall in love again," he said.

"I want it. Now."

He told me to give him a few minutes, and he laughed as he climbed the stairs. My feet tapped the concrete. My fingers intertwined and twisted each knuckle until they cracked. My mouth watered for its flavor, the bitterness that filled the back of my tongue when the smack hit my bloodstream. I stopped fidgeting and listened to every noise above me. The ceiling creaked. The faucet turned on. He was getting the dope ready, heating the powder, dropping in the cotton ball, and filling the chamber.

His footsteps got louder; when he appeared, the syringe was in his hands.

"Stick me." My tone matched the one I'd used just a few nights earlier, when Mark's tongue had left my clit and I'd begged him to fuck me.

There was a buildup in my stomach, the same type I had when an orgasm was coming on, but this was more intense. Not just between my legs—this was a need that took over my entire body. It owned me. It branded my thoughts. It marked my emotions.

He moved behind me, and the needle glided into my vein. In addition to the high that shuddered through me, it was as though the four-year break had never happened. The needle and I were still best friends. The dope was still my savior. There was a brief pause while he pulled back on the chamber, and what followed was the most angelic sparkle.

* * *

I woke up on the floor, curled in a ball, my arms wrapped around my knees. Cale sat not too far away, leaning against the wall and watching me.

"Don't do anything stupid," he said.

I remembered him untying my hands and ankles and bringing me to the bathroom after I threw up all over myself. The high had been too strong. So had the next one, and the one after that. My body wasn't used to junk. It would be soon. Then I'd be able to handle the high...until my stomach started revolting from shooting up too much. Then I'd be back to throwing up a few times a day the way I had before I'd gotten arrested.

There was a musky smell in the basement, and the floor was like ice. I was wearing Cale's clothes, and I'd only eaten toast and eggs in between the shots he gave me. I didn't know what time it was. I didn't even know how long I'd been down here.

"What's the date?" I asked.

Cale looked at his watch. "April fourteenth."

Dustin's court date was tomorrow. I'd been with Cale for two nights, and today was my birthday. I was twenty-nine years old.

"Is it afternoon?"

"It's eight in the morning," he said.

"I need another shot."

He had everything he needed in his pocket: the syringe he'd been using on me, a water bottle, a bundle of dope, a spoon, and a lighter.

"It's my birthday," I said. "Give me a good one."

I watched him cook up the mixture, and I stuck my arm out. Cale wasn't very good at finding a vein, and a tiny scab had formed in the crook behind my elbow next to the scar where the doctor had lanced the cyst. It almost seemed that nothing had changed, except that one bag of dope got me high. I remembered being sober, but smack turned those memories into a lullaby...one that made me close my eyes and drift off into a nod.

Warmth, like a fuzzy blanket, cuddled my body as soon as he pulled out the rig. The cool cement felt like a steel breeze. There was a pain in my neck, and it wasn't because my chin had fallen toward my chest or that I had slept on the ground. It was from the necklace that was bound around my skin. I clasped the chain with my fingers and pulled. I moved my arm out over my body, and just before I rested it on the floor, I emptied my fingers. The gold clunked onto the concrete, sending a ringing sound throughout the room. My neck was finally free. My nails dug into the cement, holding on while the high took me toward its peak. And my eyes closed.

I heard Cale move back to the wall, sliding down until his ass hit the ground. "Don't you dare try to leave, or I'll tie you up again."

"I'm not going anywhere," I whispered.

CHAPTER
THIRTY-FOUR

Hours blurred together. Time existed, but I didn't care to keep track of it. It didn't matter whether the basement was light or dark, cold or warm, whether I threw up on myself or made it to the bathroom in time. Heroin filled me. It was my dream maker. It had become my everything. Again.

Again was a word often used by addicts. Cale would shoot me up again as soon as the high wore off. I had forgotten what it felt like to be sober again. I didn't have to sell my body, dig through the trash to find a receipt to return items for cash, or go to my dealer's house. Cale cooked me food if I was hungry, carried me to the bathtub when I got sick on myself, even let me wear his clothes. This setup was actually kind of perfect.

Before the basement, relapse had always haunted me. If I'd had a bad day or was triggered by something from my past, my mind would go to heroin. Except for when I'd taken the train to Roxbury and called Mark, though, I hadn't taken it further than just thoughts. I had fought against my addiction, and I'd always won. But Cale hadn't given me a choice; he had taken away my freedom. Did I hate him for that? Heroin was putting a smile on my face. I guess the answer was no.

I had watched a TV show on sex slaves, how traffickers kidnapped young girls and got them addicted to heroin before they sold them on the black market. What Cale had done wasn't much different. Dustin was my buyer, and instead of my body, I was giving him my soul. But aside from sex slaves, how many people were actually taken against their will, tied to a chair, and forced to have dope shot into their body? This was one of the consequences of my addiction.

There were always repercussions from addiction. Some got HIV or Hep C from sharing needles; some developed health problems because drugs had ruined their bodies. There were girls, like me, who caused a miscarriage because they injected too much. Then there were those who died either from accidental overdose or as an indirect result, like Sunshine getting beaten to death and left in a garbage can.

This was the side of addiction that all addicts feared when they got sober—the side never mentioned during rehab, in counseling, or in any of the addiction books we were given to read. We were told to change our lifestyle, to stop hanging out with our old crowd, and to find friends who were clean. But when you owed a dealer money, stole drugs from the wrong people, or took a plea and put an entire gang behind bars, there were consequences. I had thought my punishment for being involved with Dustin and trafficking heroin was the two-and-a-half years I'd spent in jail. But that was only the state's punishment. Now I was serving Dustin's sentence.

I was in deep, and every time I opened my eyes and met Cale's stare, I was reminded of how much I needed him. How the sound of his footsteps made me forget about all the progress I'd made in sober living. How watching the powder melt in the spoon trumped the high I'd once gotten from sobriety.

"Are you hungry?" Cale yelled from upstairs.

"A little," I tried to shout, but it wasn't loud at all. My throat was sore. Everything hurt because the high was wearing off.

He handed me a cup of ramen noodles. I didn't bother to dump in the packet of seasoning. I just needed something in my stomach; I didn't care how it tasted. He sat next to me while I ate. We hadn't spoken a whole lot to each other—mostly because I was in a constant nod—but I was comfortable with him. He hadn't tried to fuck me. He took good care of me, and there wasn't much he hadn't seen; he cleaned up my puke and sat outside the bathroom while I took a shit.

"The trial is in twelve hours," he said.

I slurped up a noodle and twirled more around the fork.

"That means your boy will be here soon."

I met Cale's eyes. The only thing to stop him from giving me another shot would be if I said the wrong thing.

"I can't wait to see him."

"Good girl."

I finished the noodles and drank the cloudy water from the bottom of the cup. Once I set it on the ground, I pulled up my sleeve.

"I have enough for only one more shot. While I go and re-up, I'm going to tie you to the chair."

I shrugged.

He lifted me in the air and placed me on the chair, binding my wrists and ankles. While he went upstairs to cook up the dope, I tapped my heels against the cement. I stabbed the pad of each finger with my thumbnail, counting to ten forward and backward.

The floor was thin. I could hear his movements in the kitchen, water dribbling from the sink, and the click of his butane lighter. Then his phone when it rang.

"Everything set for tomorrow?" Cale asked.

I normally tried to keep my brain busy while Cale prepared my shot. I wouldn't just fidget when I got impatient; a wave of anger would spread through my body. But there was something about Cale's phone call that caught my attention. Dustin's trial was tomorrow, and I had a strange feeling Cale was talking to him.

"She thinks I'm letting her go after the trial," he said and paused. "I know you want to be the one to do it." Another pause. "Yes, I'll take care of it if you don't get out." He let out a long sigh. "Accidental overdose—I know the plan." Pause. "No, I can handle it."

My whole body began to shake. Blood rushed to my face, and my skin broke out in a layer of sweat.

Cale had never planned on letting me go. He just wanted me to think that so I'd cooperate, and the heroin was to keep me sedated and quiet. Or maybe Dustin wanted me high and in a nod so I wouldn't fight him while he fucked me one last time. It didn't matter. Unless I escaped, one of them was going to kill me. He would continue to inject me with smack until it caused my heart to stop beating. I had fresh track marks on my arms; the cloth around my wrists and ankles prevented the rope from burning my skin. One of them would probably dump me in an alley, and the police would never suspect a thing. I would be just another junkie who had shot too much, and my criminal record would back that up.

My eyes connected with Cale's as soon as he got to the bottom of the stairs. A syringe was in his hand. A frown was on his face. Based on his expression, the phone call had bothered him. His tone hadn't been convincing; it didn't sound like Cale could handle what he had promised.

He moved behind me and slapped my arm, waiting for a vein to pop. "Sorry I took so long."

I didn't want him to know I'd overheard his conversation. If I acted clueless, maybe he would let me out of these ropes. Then I could find a way out. My chances weren't good, but I had to try.

"Hurry up," I said. "I want it."

The needle pierced my skin.

My chin dropped.

"You be good while I'm gone," he said as he climbed the stairs.

* * *

Cale set me on the floor in the basement and sat next to me. He had let me take a shower and change my clothes because I had thrown up on myself again. But this time it wasn't that the heroin made me sick; I had gagged myself with my tongue. I needed a reason for him to untie me.

While I was in the shower, I repeated in my head everything I had heard during that phone call. Yet my body craved another shot. My veins ached for the stabbing of a needle. I had fallen in love again. Although I'd been sober just days ago, it felt like years. My addiction was pulling me into the darkness; a force equally as strong was telling me I would die if I didn't get out of the basement. And I was questioning what to do even though the answer should have been obvious. I wanted more heroin.

Standing under the spray, my hair snarly from Cale's cheap shampoo and my skin waxy from his soap, I was startled by Michael's voice...reminding me of everything I had. I hadn't forgotten; I was just putting something else first. But Michael was right—I didn't want the life of a junkie.

I wanted to live.

I didn't know what would happen if the state's lead witness didn't show up, didn't know whether the judge would delay the trial. It didn't matter. I had to get out of here as quickly as I could.

In front of Cale were two fresh needles still in their packages, several bundles of dope, a water bottle, a cotton ball, two spoons, and a lighter. He usually went upstairs and locked the door while he got my shot ready.

"Why do you have two needles?" I asked.

"My dealer only had heroin. He was out of everything else."

"That's a problem?"

"I've never used H."

Most addicts would sub one drug for another. We didn't get nervous about trying a drug we hadn't used before, especially when we were into the hard stuff like smack or meth—and Cale was. Sure, we all had a favorite drug, but that didn't stop us from using others; getting high was the ultimate goal. Cale was weak.

There was weakness in his voice when he had been on the phone, and it showed on his face when he came downstairs. He was much bigger and stronger than I was; I wouldn't be able to outrun him or tie him up. Getting out of the basement would be too hard. But maybe I could get Mark to come here. The bulge in Cale's front pocket was shaped like a cell phone. He would feel my fingers if I tried to steal it, which meant I had to get him to take his pants off. So far he had proved he was loyal to Dustin. Maybe my mouth could change that.

"Have you ever fucked on E?" I asked.

He grinned. "There's nothing like it."

We were both leaning against the wall, but I turned toward him and uncrossed my legs. "You know that tingling feeling you get? The sparks that shoot through your whole body when you're on E?" I briefly touched my clit, rubbing two small circles with my head tilted back. Then I met his eyes. "That's what heroin is going to do to you." I placed my fingers on his knee, drawing small shapes with my nails. "Every muscle is going to react." I traveled up and stopped at the top of his thigh. "Your body is going to want to release. Your mind will want to follow the intensity."

His lips parted and his eyes widened.

"When I'm high, I crave for something in my mouth. Something to suck on, twirl my tongue around, and rub my lips against." I stuck one of my fingers up to my mouth and teased my lips with it. "My finger isn't big enough to fill my needs."

I reached for his hand and gripped it between mine.

"Nicole…" he said as I began to pull it toward my mouth.

"Do you know why Dustin was crazy about me?"

He shook his head.

"There's this thing I can do with my tongue…how I don't have a gag reflux…and how I suck the come out with just the inside of my lips."

"This is a bad idea."

I put the tip of his finger inside my mouth and swirled over and around his nail with my tongue. As I made eye contact, I dipped my head taking all of it in.

"Dustin will kill me if he finds out I've touched you."

"You don't have to touch me; I'll touch you. And we don't have to tell him."

His breathing got heavier. He stuck a second finger into my mouth.

"Let me swallow you." I got on my knees and bent my head toward his lap. Placing my tongue at the bottom of his zipper, I licked all the way up until I reached his button.

"Fuck," he moaned.

I did it again, never breaking eye contact, and when I got to the top, I bit my lip. "I need you in my mouth."

His stare hardened. So did his dick, and his hands moved to the zipper.

"No, baby, heroin first, and your pants need to come off. The zipper will tear up my mouth."

He opened the two bags and began to dump them onto each of the spoons.

"Just give me half a bag," I said.

"Only half?" He sounded surprised, but he continued to move quickly and gave me what I asked for.

"If I take too much, I'll throw up while I'm sucking your dick, and I don't think you want to clean up any more puke."

He shook his head.

When both syringes were ready, he took his pants off and placed them on the other side of him. As he sat back down, he adjusted his dick, and it poked out the waist of his boxers.

"Give me your arm," he said.

I got on my knees and pulled my sleeve back. I had been using for only three days, but I'd been using a lot, and the nod didn't set in like it did with a full bag. The rush was there, though, and it was intense. I licked my lips. "Hurry, baby, my mouth wants to suck on you."

The high definitely hit Cale. His eyes rolled back, and his chin dropped. A line of drool formed on his bottom lip and dribbled down his shirt. He was still hard, but that wasn't going to last for too much longer. Dustin had always gotten soft once the heroin really set in.

Just because he was in a nod didn't mean he couldn't hear what was going on around him or feel my touch. I had to at least try to get him off. I took a deep breath and pulled down the waist of his boxers. I had been here so many times before: a dick staring at me, waiting to be sucked for drug money. This was different, and Mark would understand that. This was hopefully going to save my life.

As my lips closed around him, I reached inside the pocket of his jeans. Plunging up and down, his dick getting softer with each stroke, I dialed. His leg twitched. I hit the button on the side of the phone to lower the volume so Cale wouldn't hear the phone ring or Mark answer. When Mark picked up, his voice was so faint I could barely make out what he was saying. I looked up; Cale's eyes didn't open.

I was down on my knees; my breasts dangled and hid the phone while I talked. I pressed my lips against his tip. "Cale, you feeling good? Do you want more or can I stop?"

A moan escaped from his lips.

I had to be careful what I said. Mark would recognize my voice and wouldn't hang up, but I didn't want Cale to snap awake because I said the wrong thing.

"Are you going to miss my mouth when *Dustin* gets out of prison?" I asked. "You know he'll come straight down to the *basement* and make me his again."

"You're his," he mumbled.

Because he wasn't hard anymore, I ran the pads of my fingers over his pubic hair and down his thighs. "I guess I am his because he *forced* me to skip court. If the police find me, they'll throw me in jail."

"The police won't know where to find you," he grumbled. "You're safe."

"That means I'll be with Dustin forever."

Now that Cale was more responsive and it was clear he wasn't going to get off, I sat up and moved over to the wall. Leaning against the cold cement, I placed the phone in the small space behind my lower back. But I didn't disconnect the call.

"You think Dustin will ever let me out of this basement?" I asked.

He scratched his arms. "Only if you're real nice to him."

"I hope he isn't mad or have plans to hurt me." My eyes got heavy and closed. "I don't want to die down here, Cale." I let my body relax into the high. I had probably said more than I should have, and now all I could do was wait. Wait for Cale or Dustin to kill me, or for Mark and the police to bust in.

CHAPTER
THIRTY-FIVE

A pair of hands reached underneath me, between my back and the cold concrete; my eyes opened as I was lifted into the air. A police officer kneeled in front of Cale, trying to wake him up. Two more were bagging the heroin, the syringes, and the rest of the paraphernalia. I didn't need to look to know I was in Mark's arms. I'd memorized his touch and smell. He held me differently than everyone else did. I nuzzled his neck.

"God, what the hell happened to you?"

Right before Cale had started to come down from his high, I'd disconnected the call and stuck the phone back in his jeans. Then he'd shot another bag of heroin in my arm and one in his. While I fell into the nod, I prayed that Mark had contacted the police and that they'd be able to trace my location...and that this would be the last time dope would ever enter my body. As much as I loved it, I wanted this to be my lullaby to addiction.

"I'll tell you everything on our way home," I said.

As Mark moved toward the stairs, one of the cops said, "You need to wait for the ambulance. She has to go to the hospital and get checked out, and then I need her for questioning."

"Can you wait just a little bit longer?" Mark asked me.

"As long as I'm with you, I can."

"You know I'm not going to leave your side."

Before Mark took me upstairs, I told the cops about the chair and ropes. They took pictures, bagged both, and documented them as evidence. Mark wouldn't set me on the couch; he held me in his arms and walked back and forth between the kitchen and living room.

It took only a few minutes for the paramedics to arrive. They brought in a stretcher, and Mark placed me on top. Cale was carried out on one too, and we were put in separate ambulances. Mark told me he'd call Melissa and meet me at the hospital. The paramedic shut the door and sat next to me, taking my vital signs. A tear dropped from the corner of my eye, and I caught it before it hit my chin. The paramedic handed me a napkin, but I had already wiped my fingers on my jeans. "Thank you," I whispered.

"Your heart rate is slow," he said. "When was the last time he injected you?"

"How did you know he injected me?"

"Dispatch said it was a kidnapping, so I just assumed. Addicts are in and out of this ambulance every day. You don't look like a junkie, and you surely don't act like one."

Whenever I'd been in the back of an ambulance or at the hospital, there had always been a hint of disgust on the person's face who treated me. Junkies didn't exactly have the best reputation; many carried diseases, and nonaddicts couldn't understand why we wouldn't just get sober and clean ourselves up. I had deserved those expressions in the past. But as I lay on this stretcher, with heroin pumping through my bloodstream, I felt relief that his look was full of sympathy. I wasn't that person anymore. And I wasn't ashamed that I was high.

As soon as we got to the ER, two nurses wheeled me to an exam room. They tried to shut the door on Mark, but I wouldn't let them. I said that if they didn't allow him to stay, I wouldn't give them permission to touch me. Mark moved over to my side and leaned against the wall while the nurses helped me change into a gown. My clothes were placed in a bag and handed off to the police officer waiting outside the door.

Once they got me comfortably on the bed and covered with blankets, a doctor came in. I didn't catch his name, but he said he would be performing an examination. He started with my back, running his gloved fingers over my shoulder blades and down my spine. My legs were next, then my stomach, and finally my neck and face.

"I don't see any signs of physical abuse," the doctor said to the nurse. She then wrote something down in a chart.

"He didn't hit me," I said.

"Do we need to perform a rape kit?"

"No."

The doctor gave the nurse a look, and she leaned down, close to my ear. "Would you rather everyone else step out of the room so we can discuss this in private?"

"He never touched me," I said, loud enough for everyone to hear. I took a deep breath. "But I touched him. My mouth...I put him in my mouth...it was the only way to get out of there."

The nurse put her hand on my shoulder. "We understand."

"To finish your exam, the nurse is going to take a blood and a urine specimen," the doctor said.

I shook my head against the pillow. "No more needles."

Mark kneeled at my side. "Nicole, they have to take your blood so they know how to treat you."

"Isn't there another way?" I asked.

"You're going to be sick, and I can help alleviate those symptoms, but all the medications have to be administered intravenously," the doctor said. "Ms. Brown, you've been through enough. You don't need the pain of withdrawal too."

The last time I had been in the hospital, the doctor had lectured me. He'd told me I was killing my body and that if I kept using heroin I would die. Now I was being treated like a victim. I guess I was.

The arm I'd always given Cale to stick was by my side, and I flipped it over. Mark's eyes got watery. Bruises spotted my forearm; a sore behind my elbow looked infected.

"Close your eyes," Mark said. His lips pressed against my forehead as the nurse stuck in the needle. It was thicker than the syringe Cale had used, and it hurt. Probably also because I knew the shot wasn't going to get me high.

When I opened my eyes, the nurse was holding a plastic cup and asked if I could fill it halfway. She held out her hand and, with Mark supporting my back, helped me off the bed and down the hall to the bathroom.

"Melissa will be here in a few hours," Mark said once I got settled back in bed. "She wants to be here when the cops question you."

I'd lost my sense of time as soon as I had been shoved in the basement, so I didn't know how many hours had passed since Cale had last shot me up. But it couldn't have been that long. My eyes were still so heavy, my head cloudy, and the tingling hadn't stopped.

"I'm so tired," I said.

A nurse was moving around the bed pushing buttons on different machines. An IV was in my hand, and I hadn't even felt her stick me again.

The last thing I heard was, "Get some sleep, baby," before my eyes closed.

* * *

The heart monitor and IV came with me as I was moved out of the ER and into a room on one of the other floors. The doctor wanted me to get some rest before I was questioned, so he told Melissa and the cops to hold off until tomorrow. He didn't think I was clear enough to process everything that had happened. He was right. The medicine they were pumping into me was strong, and the heroin was still in my body. I couldn't do much more than sleep.

Mark never left my side. The few times I stirred, he was either watching TV or napping beside me. Between his breathing, which soothed the jittery feeling in my chest, and the medication, I went right back to sleep. At one point, he told me that my parents had come by late in the afternoon but I'd slept through their visit. He said they looked so exhausted by nine o'clock, and since I still hadn't woken up, he sent them to his place to get some sleep.

I was still groggy the next morning when I woke up to a room full of people. My parents stood by the window; Mark was on my bed; a nurse was checking the monitors; and Melissa, two police officers, and a few others I didn't recognize were huddled around me. Mark and my parents were asked to leave, but Mark wouldn't go. He wanted to hear it all. He said the more he knew, the more he could help protect me in the future.

I told them everything, starting with Dustin's first messenger. I described his phone call to me from prison, Martin showing up at the café, the taxi I'd gotten into outside the jail, and the days I'd spent in the basement with Cale. They had questions. Lots of them. I did my best to answer each one despite the nausea and the pain rippling through my head. After about an hour, Melissa asked everyone to leave so I could get some rest. That was the last time I saw the police, Mark, or my parents for several days. To keep me from experiencing any withdrawal symptoms, the doctor kept me sedated. I slept for almost three days straight.

*   *   *

The night before I was scheduled to be discharged, my parents asked what my plans were for when I got out of the hospital.

"I'm going to take some time off from the café, finish my online classes, and move in with Mark. He's going to sublease my apartment." Mark and I had discussed my living arrangements that morning. He wanted to protect me as much as he could. I had been staying at his place every night anyway, so it made sense.

"You're not going to rehab?" Dad asked.

"I don't think I need it."

"I realize relapsing wasn't your choice—and the physical part of your addiction is gone—but you became addicted again," Mom said.

"I'm going to work the Steps," I said. "I'll attend NA meetings like I've been doing all along, and my doctor thinks I should start seeing a private therapist. Rehab isn't going to teach me anything I don't already know."

"But now that you've been reminded of what heroin feels like, you might be tempted to relapse on your own."

"I never forgot what heroin feels like. I never will, Mom. Rehab isn't going to improve my chances of staying clean. Dedication to the program and the fact that I want to be sober will."

My parents knew it wasn't my fault, and they weren't blaming me. They were just concerned—and they had reason to be. They were right; the physical addiction was gone, but the mental part of my disease was still very loud. It had been loud during the thirteen months I was clean, and it would always have a voice. It would take time to prove to my parents that I didn't need rehab, but time was something I had.

"Honey, we just want the best for you," Mom said.

"I know you do."

"I'm not going to let anything happen to your little girl," Mark said.

That made me smile, and despite how horrible this situation was, my parents smiled too.

A nurse carried a tray into my room and set it on the table next to me. My mom lifted the cover, revealing meat floating around in juice and mashed potatoes. It looked hard enough to break a window.

"How about some chicken nuggets and sweet-and-sour sauce from McDonalds?" Dad asked.

"You know that's my favorite," I said.

"That's why I asked," Dad said. "You mother and I could use some nonhospital food too."

They took Mark's order, and the two of them left the room. Mark lay next to me, and I rested my head on his chest.

"We're going to get through this," he said.

"I hope so."

CHAPTER
THIRTY-SIX

By the time the doctor signed my discharge papers, there were no traces of heroin in my blood. My head was clear, and I was back to sleeping normal hours. I left the hospital with my purse, my jacket, an outfit Mark had brought me, and a referral for a shrink. I had made an appointment, and I was scheduled to see the therapist in a few days.

Mark and Jesse had already taken care of moving everything to Mark's house. My clothes hung in his closet, my personal items in his bathroom, and Michael's stuff went back into storage. I wished Mark had more room at his place. But even though Michael's belongings were locked away, he was still in my head. His voice came out at night, after Mark was asleep, while I lay in bed looking for answers on what I should do. Now that I was living with Mark, I wasn't sure whether I should move out of Boston, but I'd created so many nightmares here that part of me felt that I needed a fresh start to go with my sober life.

What gave me some relief was knowing Dustin wouldn't be able to hurt me again. At least not for a while. Melissa told me his appeal had been denied. In Cale's statement to the DA and judge, he'd handed over his phone records, showing the incoming calls from Dustin, and detailed their plan to kidnap me. Cale also ratted out the dealer who sold him the drugs and Martin's true identity. Melissa said Dustin was being charged with conspiracy and a few other crimes. He had been placed in solitary confinement, with no access to phone or mail, and they were probably going to move him to a maximum-security prison. In exchange for his statement, Cale received a twelve-year sentence.

Melissa's news didn't stop Mark from being overprotective. He had a security system installed at the house, drove me to my NA meetings, and even canceled my cell phone and got me a new number under his plan. He hired a manager at the new bar so he didn't have to be there at night and went in only a few hours during the day. I went with him. It gave me a chance to get out of the apartment, and I could work on my online courses there. I had missed several assignments and was behind on the lectures, but in response to the note from my doctor, the professor extended the due dates so I could get caught up. Mark even waited a week to tell me about Henry's death. He obviously thought I couldn't handle the news, based on everything that had happened.

After I filled my therapist in on the last ten years of my life, Mark was the first person I discussed with her. He was more than just my boyfriend. He was my caretaker, bank, and bodyguard. I had become one of his responsibilities, and I didn't want that to ruin our relationship. My therapist explained how Mark might be feeling and that he could be blaming himself. Even though there was nothing he could have done to stop Cale, the fact remained that I'd been taken from him. He was powerless over the way I'd been treated and felt that he had failed as the protector of our family. If Mark upping the safety was his way of healing and proving he deserved that role, then I needed to accept that. I wasn't a burden; I was someone he cared about.

At the same time, I couldn't be screened in forever, and that was also something I discussed with my therapist. Was Boston the right place for me? She said I would figure that out in time. For now, I needed to work through the issues of having been taken against my will and becoming addicted to heroin again.

And I was doing just that, discussing my relapse during my NA meetings, practicing the Steps, and continuing to open up with my therapist. Mark tried to keep us busy so we wouldn't spend too much time at home. I thought he was trying to get my mind off things, and it worked; we had picnics in the park, went to the movies, took a duck tour of the city, visited museums, and even hiked the walking trails. Before the basement, we had started having Sunday night dinners with Jesse, and we kept that up. Cooper, his new boyfriend, joined us, and the four of us spent a few weekends in the Cape.

But as we entered fall, the college students returned. Everyone was back from summer vacation, and Mark hit his busy season. He had a computer system installed at the house so he could watch all the activity at both bars, and he spent a lot more time working in the guest room. I was finishing my final assignment for school, an exam that covered the different kinds of drugs, their side effects, and how to effectively treat addiction. Maybe it was my coursework or that I'd been reminded how amazing heroin was, but I found myself thinking about it more.

Boredom is one of the biggest triggers for addicts, and there was plenty of that. I never went anywhere without Mark; he took me where I needed to go and picked me up afterward. I didn't have a chance to fear what might be hiding because I was never alone in the dark. I couldn't keep living like this. I had to regain my independence; begin taking the train by myself again; and meet my old friends from sober living, Kathy and Ashley, for lunch or dinner or to go shopping downtown.

My therapist thought I'd made a lot of progress in the months she'd been treating me. She praised my practice of the Steps and the fact that I was staying sober. During one of our sessions, she asked me to write a letter to Cale and Dustin and tell them how they had made me feel. She didn't want me to send it; she just wanted me to read it out loud at our next session. I did. In the first few paragraphs, I described the fear I had felt when I'd woken up in the basement, not knowing what was going to happen to me, and how I was worried what my parents and boyfriend would think when they realized I was missing.

Cale injecting me for the first time was like a rape. I was helpless. I had screamed and begged him to keep the needle away from me, just as I'd yelled when Richard had dragged me over to his bed. The panic and anxiety that had run though my body were the same as when Richard ripped off my jeans and panties. The syringe was as rough as his dick.

"Can you forgive them?" my therapist asked once I finished reading.

"I forgave Richard, so I'll forgive them too."

She looked up from her notebook and set down her pen. "How are you going to do that?"

"The only way I know is to apply the Steps."

"Explain that to me."

"Step Five is admitting to God, to ourselves, and to other human beings the exact nature of our wrongs. I've processed their wrongdoings and how they affected me. As Step Six requires, I can accept their defects of character."

"Addiction caused their actions?"

"Selfishness, too. Dustin did what he thought would get him out of jail."

"That took a lot of work."

"I've had a lot of time to think about it."

"Have you thought about what you're going to do next?"

I had just completed my classes and told her that at the beginning of our meeting, yet I still hadn't come up with a plan. What I had thought about was Mark. He protected me and kept me safe, but that wasn't why he picked me up from all my appointments, why I never went anywhere alone, or why I didn't have a chance to fear what might be hiding in the dark. I was blaming him for taking away my freedom. But it wasn't Mark who had done that. It was me. I had asked him for all these things, and he fulfilled my demands.

"I need to stop being scared of my own shadow and start living again," I said.

"Your practicum in-field work is a perfect place to begin this process, gradually building that confidence again."

To receive my certificate, I needed to complete over three hundred hours of in-field work. That meant I had to go to the rehab center at least five days a week, my time had to be logged, and my work supervised. I had spoken to Allison only once since the basement to let her know I'd gotten a new cell phone number, but I hadn't told her what had happened. And there was no way she could know. The police had kept my name from being mentioned in the news. Because of Dustin's connections and the way our heroin bust had been all over the media, they didn't want to draw any more attention to me.

"I have to talk to Allison about it," I said. "By relapsing, I might have broken the contract, and there's a chance she won't want me to work there."

"When do you plan on speaking with her?"

"I'm meeting with her tomorrow."

Once the session was over, Mark took me out to lunch, and we discussed some of the things I had covered with my therapist. He agreed; field practicum would be a good way to build back my confidence, and he didn't think my relapse should keep me from working there. I could only hope Allison felt the same way.

* * *

I took my jacket off, rolled up my sleeves, and fanned my face with my hand. Sweat soaked my armpits, and the more I spoke, the hotter I got. I'd finished telling Allison about the kidnapping and moved on to Mark, the NA meetings I attended every night, and the therapist I met with twice a week. Her mouth had dropped open and her eyes widened during my story. She never interrupted me, but once I stopped, several moments of silence passed and I couldn't get a read from her. That was, until she grabbed a tissue out of the box and dabbed the corners of her lids.

"This isn't very professional of me, but I'm going to say it anyway." She took a deep breath and reached for another tissue. She handed one to me. I didn't need it. "I've met thousands of addicts over the course of my career. None of them has experienced even the smallest percentage of what you've gone through, let alone survived to share their tale. Nicole, you continue to prove how much of a fighter you really are."

Mark had called me a survivor when we'd visited the aquarium, and that wasn't the only time he'd said it. Asher had written a novel about everything I'd gone through. Allison told me I was a fighter. It wasn't that I didn't hear what they were saying, or even that I disagreed. I just couldn't take all the credit. If it weren't for the three of them, I wouldn't be alive. Their support, along with that of Michael, Jesse, and my parents, made me stronger.

I didn't know how to thank someone who had mentored me through rehab, reiterated the Steps when I needed to hear them most, and given me confidence when I doubted my ability to stay clean. Sometimes words weren't important. I had to show Allison how much of a fighter I really was. And I would do that if she let me keep my job. I couldn't wait any longer.

"Have I ruined my chance of working here?"

"How long have you been sober now?"

"Five months. I know that isn't much time, but—"

"Will you still meet with your therapist and attend NA meetings?"

"Of course I will."

She smiled. "Then the job is still yours if you want it."

The knot that had been building in the back of my throat began to loosen. I reached for the tissue.

"When would you like to start?"

I told her I was going to Maine the following weekend for my dad's retirement party and asked if I could start on Monday. That gave me over a week to buy some extra work clothes and meet with my professor for the exit interview. The school had to get in touch with Allison and send her paperwork so that my hours could be documented and logged.

"Monday is perfect," she said.

I met Mark in the parking lot. He was on the phone when I got in the car, but he hung up as soon as I shut the door.

"You still have a job, don't you?" he asked.

I used the tissue to wipe my eyes. "As long as I keep going to NA and therapy."

"I told you, baby. She couldn't blame you for what happened; it wasn't your fault."

"Just hug me." I didn't even need to say those words. Mark's arms were already wrapped around me.

*   *   *

The next morning while Mark and I drank coffee, his phone rang. It was Jesse, asking if he and Asher could come over. I hadn't seen Asher since he'd appeared in the doorway at my one-year sobriety ceremony. Mark said he'd visited me in the hospital, but I didn't remember. He'd sent me a text once I was discharged, and one every week to hear how I was doing.

They must have been in our neighborhood because the doorbell chimed only a few minutes after Mark hung up. I met them in the living room and gave Jesse a kiss. Asher was behind him, fidgeting with his hands, and his feet stayed planted. I closed the gap and hugged him. There was no reason for there to be any awkwardness; Asher and I had been through a lot together, and over nine months had passed since we'd broken up. I got a whiff of his scent, sunbaked sand, and some of those memories flashed through my head. He really was a good guy; Mark was just better for me.

We all went into the kitchen and took seats at the table while Mark made them some coffee. Asher and Jesse kept looking at each other. Jesse grinned, but Asher had a more serious expression. No one said anything.

"What's going on?" I asked as Mark sat down.

"Asher has a surprise for you," Jesse said. Asher's mouth had opened; Jesse's words came out first. "I tagged along because I have to see your face when he shows it to you."

Asher unzipped his jacket and pulled out a manila envelope from the inner pocket. He slid it over to me. "Look inside."

I tore off the top and my hand reached in. It was Asher's novel. On the front was the profile of a young girl; knotted hair covered most of her face, her sneakers were filthy, and her clothes had holes. A train track ran though the bottom; on one side were graffiti, litter, broken bottles, and syringe caps. On the other side were trees. The top of the picture was the skyline of Boston. The girl was me. I was on the wrong side of the track. And if the cover had shown her arms, it would have revealed scars of track marks. If she had been inside the city, she would have been working the track. This cover summed up my past. It showed everything I had survived, and Boston was where it all had happened.

My eyes met Asher's.

"Flip to the first page," he said.

Two sentences were typed under the word Dedication: *"It's not a mess, Cole. It's a beautiful mess."*

I remembered the first time he had said that to me. It was the day after I'd found out Jesse was his brother, and we had gone for a walk. He'd told me he wasn't scared of what he knew about me, and when I called my past a mess, he said it was a beautiful mess. And any time I had said that since, he always corrected me.

"This is just a mock-up. My publisher can change the cover and—"

"No, it fits my story perfectly."

"Are you sure?"

I put my hand on his and squeezed his fingers. "I'm sure."

My cell rang, and I glanced around the room, trying to find where I had left it.

"It's next to the fridge," Mark said.

It was Allison. "Is everything OK?" I asked, moving into the living room for privacy.

"I've been thinking about you since you left my office, and I came up with an idea. But first I want to ask—what's keeping you in Boston? Is it this job? Because if I were you, I'd want a fresh start."

Her question surprised me. Allison was my boss, and I didn't want to say the wrong thing. I didn't want to lie, either; I hadn't prepared an answer.

"The job is part of it, of course. I don't want to lose this opportunity because I think it's something I'd be good at. Then there's Mark. His business is here, and he can't move away. But even if I did want to leave, I don't have a place to go."

"What if you did have a place to go? Would that change your mind?"

"It might."

"We have a sister facility in Fort Lauderdale, Florida, and they're looking to hire a housemother for a new sober living apartment. It would be free room and board, a salary, and benefits. The contract would stay the same. During the day, you would work your hours at the rehab center, and they'd hire you full-time after you receive your certificate."

"Do they know about my relapse?" Such a position required at least two years of sobriety. Even if the basement hadn't happened, I still wasn't close to that.

"I've explained everything to them, and they're willing to make an exception. They think you'd be an incredible mentor to their patients, and I agree."

"Can I think about it?"

"Absolutely," she said. "Given the recent events, I don't want you to feel stuck. You need to choose what's best for you, and having options will allow you to do that."

"How much time do I have to decide?"

"They're opening the apartment in about a month, so I'd say a week or two. We can discuss it when you come in, if you want."

I told her I'd see her on Monday and thanked her before she hung up. I set the phone down and glanced through the living room door at the faces around the kitchen table. No matter where I lived, Jesse would always be in my life. He had become part of my family. Asher would always be a text message away, but our friendship would never be more than that. Mark was the only thing keeping me here. We had talked about marriage and kids, and those were things we both wanted. We couldn't have that if I moved to Florida. And it wasn't fair to ask him to give up everything he had built in Boston.

I knew what would happen between us if I took the job, yet something inside me was telling me to do it. It wasn't because I didn't care about Mark or that my feelings weren't genuine. It wasn't because I'd repaired things with my parents and Bangor was only a four-hour drive from them.

The book lay in the middle of the table and caught my attention. Most of my past was written on those pages, and everywhere I went in the city, I was reminded of those days. There had been consequences for every decision I'd made. I'd served those punishments, and Allison had rewarded me. I couldn't escape the memories of the track. But I could leave those triggers behind.

CHAPTER

THIRTY-SEVEN

Mark pulled into my parents' driveway and put the car in park. Jesse was the first to get out, and Mark met him at the trunk. Since we'd gotten off at my parents' exit, things had been pretty quiet. I had turned down the music, and the conversation I'd been having with Jesse sort of died off. They unloaded our bags; Mark opened my door.

"I'll meet you inside," I said.

The look he gave me told me he knew I needed a minute alone, and he pecked my lips. Jesse squeezed my shoulder, and they walked up to the front door. Mark must have said something to my mom because she closed the door behind them.

I hadn't been to my parents' house since I'd moved to Boston nine-and-a-half years ago. I'd visited Bangor once during those years to go to Eric's funeral. I'd stayed only one night, and that short time had been one fucked-up trip. I'd gotten drilled and mocked by my old high school friends, I shot up in the park with Renee, and I got into a fight with my parents at Eric's service. I deserved all that. I was sick and high, living with my dealer, and letting him screw me so I could get free dope. I was in a better place now, but that didn't make this trip any easier.

Their house looked the same: white siding that was a little aged, blue shutters that Dad had painted over the summer, a brick box on the roof for the fireplace that was never used. Dark orange and red fall flowers were planted next to the row of shrubs. The first two windows on the main floor looked into the kitchen. Jesse and Mark sat at the table, and Mom handed them something to drink. There were three windows on the second floor; the one on the left was my parents' bedroom, the middle one the bathroom, and the last was Michael's room.

The driver's side opened and Mom got in. She placed a bottle of water on my lap and put her arm around me. "Thanks for coming, pumpkin; it means so much to Daddy and me."

I took off my seatbelt and moved closer, resting my head against her chest. "This is a lot."

"I know, baby, but you need this. We all need this."

This trip wasn't just for my dad's retirement party. It was also about visiting Eric's parents and his grave. Michael's grave as well. I'd been putting it off since I'd gotten off probation. I wasn't ready to see where he had been put to rest. But because of Allison's offer, whichever one I chose, I didn't know when I'd have the time off to come here again.

"I offered the boys lunch, but they want to wait for you," she said. "Why don't you come inside and have some of the hot clam chowder I made. Then you can get unpacked and take a nice, long bath before the party tonight."

She kissed me on the forehead, and I followed her up the path to the front door. The furniture in the entryway and living room hadn't changed: Nana's old couches that my mom had reupholstered, and a cabinet where they used to keep all our school projects.

Dad stood from the table, and I walked into his arms. "We're so happy you're here, baby."

I squeezed even tighter.

Mom moved over to the stovetop and began to scoop chowder into three bowls.

"None for me, thanks," I said.

"You're not hungry, Cole?" Mom asked.

I shook my head. "I think I'm going to take a nap. I'll eat when I wake up."

She nodded, and I knew she understood. Before any food hit my stomach, there was something I needed to do.

"I'll come check on you after I eat," Mark said.

Jesse winked at me, and I walked up the stairs. The first door at the top was the bathroom. Mom had placed three hand towels next to the sinks, three toothbrushes in their plastic wrapping, mini-bottles of mouthwash and floss. She had always done that whenever guests stayed at our house. Without looking in Michael's bedroom, I stepped into mine. She had redone everything: replaced the pink carpeting with a medium blue and painted the walls a light yellow. My posters, pictures, and framed certificates were gone, and canvases of flowers hung instead. The only piece of furniture that had stayed was my old bed, but a yellow-and-blue comforter took the place of my pink-and-black one.

I took a deep breath, closed my eyes, and backed up into the hallway. My fingers clasped the doorframe, and I leaned against the wood. Michael's room had been completely redone too. Once, it had been painted red and navy, the colors of the Boston Red Sox, and his comforter and drapes were tiled with their logo. Now the paint and decorations matched those of my room, and all his furniture was gone.

The window seat was filled with pillows, but when Michael and I were young, he had built an army of figurines on that ledge. Once in a while, he'd let me clear off the seat, and we'd peg water balloons at the neighborhood kids. At the far end of his room was a door that led to the attic. We used to play up there on the weekends—set up a tent and camp out, pretending it was our own apartment. We'd even cooked on a little oven that I'd gotten for Christmas one year.

When Dad would get home from work, we used to hide behind Michael's pants and surprise him as he opened the door. We did it every night for a whole year. We had so much fun covering ourselves with his clothes and trying not to laugh and give away our hideout.

"It's changed a lot, hasn't it?" Dad asked from behind me. I moved over so he could stand next to me in the doorway.

"There's nothing left of him."

That was, except for a few framed pictures on the dresser. There was one of the two of us at his college graduation and another of him and my parents.

"Your mother thought it would be easier that way. He's in all our hearts, Cole, and that's the most important place for him to be."

"I hear him, Dad, all the time. His voice has helped me get out of some dark places."

"He talks to me, too." He rested his arms around my neck, and I leaned into him. "I'm glad he's here to help you. We're so proud of you, baby, and we're excited for all the things you have coming up."

I hadn't told anyone about Florida. I didn't want to be influenced. I wanted the decision to be my own, and I had to make it soon; I was supposed to meet with Allison in three days. My parents were really happy when I went back to school and finished my courses after the basement. They said this career was the best thing for me.

"You're going to make a difference in a lot of people's lives," Dad had said.

"I hope so."

I took a final look around Michael's room before my dad closed the door.

*   *   *

I lay in my old bed, Mark sleeping next to me, and I counted the popcorn on the ceiling. The streetlamp shone through the blinds and off the mirrored doors of the closet. The light wasn't keeping me awake; neither was my father's snoring, which I could hear through the wall. My body was tired, but I couldn't shut my brain off.

Dad's retirement party had lasted until midnight, and I'd eaten more there than I had in the past week. He had worked at the *Bangor Daily News* for over forty years, and they threw him a really nice celebration, with catered food and champagne. It was a relief to have the attention off me, for someone else in my family to be recognized in a ceremony. I had expected nasty glares from Dad's coworkers; everyone in town knew about Michael's death and my arrest. What I didn't expect were hugs and words of congratulations on my sobriety; I got plenty of that. Some people even shared stories with me about their kids and other family members in Acadia Hospital for addiction. Weed had always been big in Bangor, but the harder drugs had moved in and were doing damage. I listened and gave the best advice I could. Besides staying strong, not enabling, and joining a support group, there wasn't anything they could do. It was up to the addict. I was proof of that.

Mom had gotten rid of the TV in my room, and I couldn't take all the quiet. When I was a kid and had a hard time sleeping, I'd wake Michael up and we'd go down to the basement. There was something about that room that always gave me comfort. It was cozy, the blanket Mom had knitted was snug, and we got every channel on the big-screen TV. Sleep wasn't coming anytime soon, so I gently climbed out of bed and tiptoed down the stairs. Apparently, I wasn't the only one who couldn't sleep. Jesse sat at the table holding a mug of tea.

"Take a seat," he said. "I'll make you a cup."

When we had gotten back from the party, Mom had offered to make up a bed on the couch downstairs so Jesse didn't have to sleep in Michael's room. Jesse had said he would be fine. Clearly, he wasn't.

He handed me a mug and sat down next to me. "Feel like talking about it?"

"Not really; do you?"

He shook his head. Neither of us could wait for this trip to be over, I thought.

"Something else is bothering you," he said. "You've been a little off since Asher showed you the book cover."

Jesse was right, but it wasn't the book cover that was bothering me. It was what had happened right after—the phone call. Even though something was telling me to take the job in Florida, I couldn't make a decision. I didn't know what was best for me. But maybe he would. Michael had always given me good advice, and he and Jesse were so much alike. I told him everything about the meeting I'd had with Allison and our phone conversation the next day.

"I think you should go," he said.

"Just like that?"

"I know why you've stayed in Boston for this long, but you have to get out. Besides Mark, Asher, and me, nothing good has happened to you there."

"But what about Mark?"

"I'm not telling you to give up your relationship. I think Mark is perfect for you, but you can't stay because of him."

"I would stay for both of you."

He smiled and brushed a piece of hair behind my ear. "You're not going to lose me; you know that. As for Mark, he knows your past is holding on to you, preventing you from being the woman we both know you can be."

I took a sip of the tea. The knot in my throat was making it hard to swallow, so I swished it around in my mouth.

"Allison is offering a place for you to stay, a salary, and benefits, and you're going to have a counseling job once you're done with your hours. You're getting everything you want, Cole."

"Everything except Mark."

"Who says you can't have him too?"

"He's not going to leave Boston."

"Maybe not now, but that doesn't mean he won't leave in the future. Have you asked him?"

I shook my head. "I haven't told anyone but you. I planned on telling him this weekend, but I have to get through today first."

He stuck out his hand, and I grabbed it. "It's time you do something for *you*."

* * *

The five of us got out of my dad's car and followed the sidewalk behind the line of trees. Past the entrance, there were more trees scattered throughout the grass and a light blanket of leaves on the ground. I shivered from the breeze and pulled my jacket tighter. I'd had a sweater on this morning, but changed into a button-down; then I put on a cotton long-sleeve. I couldn't decide what to wear, and everyone had been waiting for me downstairs. This wasn't Michael's funeral, but I'd been in jail for the real one; it was his funeral to me.

The sidewalk jetted out to the smaller sections of grass and ran through the middle, over the short hills. We were far enough from the road that there wasn't any noise. The eerie silence was a reminder of exactly where I was. My parents' pace began to slow after the second hill, and they stopped at the edge of the grass. We stood in front of the private patch with just one grave along the side. My parents had told me they'd purchased the entire lot and were going to be buried next to Michael. His tombstone was oval and white, his name and the years he'd been alive written at the top. "Loving son and brother," was written just below.

Mom replaced the flowers in front of the stone with the ones she was carrying and pressed her lips against his name. My father did the same before they joined hands and moved behind us. Jesse set his flowers next to theirs and patted the stone with the tips of his fingers. He didn't say anything out loud. He didn't need to; I could practically hear his words. He closed his eyes and rested his forehead on the top of the headstone, motionless for a few minutes.

I released Mark's hand when it was my turn. I had heard it was disrespectful to walk on the dead, and none of the others had stepped on the grass in front of Michael's tombstone. I didn't, but I sat on it. I didn't trust my knees; I wanted to be as close to him as I could. Six feet of dirt and a wooden box separated us, but I still felt him. A warmth spread through me and clouded around me, almost like heroin. I still shivered, but it wasn't from the breeze.

Like Jesse, I spoke to Michael in my head and apologized for taking so long to visit. He didn't respond. It was odd; this was the only place where I didn't hear his voice. I didn't tell him what was going on in my life, the decision that lay ahead of me, or how long I'd been sober. He already knew all that. So did Eric, which was why at his gravesite I told him only how much I missed him. I made both of them a promise. It was one I would keep.

* * *

As soon as we got home, I told Mark I was going to take his car to Eric's parents' house. I had planned on going this evening; now I just wanted to get it over with. Mark offered to drive me, and when I refused, he insisted. He said it had been an emotional morning and he would feel more comfortable if he drove.

Eric's parents lived only about two miles from mine. Before we turned sixteen and got our license, we used to ride our bikes to each other's houses. He had a pool, and we'd spent summer breaks floating on a raft in his backyard; he would crash at my house at night because we had air conditioning. We were carefree kids. Then we found drugs, and all that changed.

I hadn't spoken to Eric's parents since the day he had overdosed. I should have called them and asked if I could come over. But judging by the look his mother gave me when she opened the door, they would have hung up on me.

"What the hell are you doing here?" she asked.

"I came to visit…and…" I needed to get my thoughts straight. I hadn't prepared what I was going to say. "You deserve an explanation."

"What makes you think I want one? From you?"

Had I really thought his parents were going to greet me with a hug? Did I expect to hear acceptance in their voices and feel comfort in their touch?

"I'm sorry for the way I treated you when I told you Eric had died, and for bolting from his funeral. There are a lot of things I wish I could change from those years."

"Like noticing my son was turning blue and calling 9-1-1 sooner?"

"I wasn't there—"

"The hell you weren't. You're nothing but a fucking liar. You did nothing to help him because you were just as strung out."

I was just as strung out and did nothing to help him, but I hadn't been there when he'd overdosed. Eric's mom needed someone to blame, and that person was me. If making me the murderer gave her peace, then I would give her that.

Eric's addiction had killed him. Not the needles he used, the brand of dope he shot, or the fact that Renee had waited to call 9-1-1. His mom knew that. One day she'd be able to admit it out loud.

I straightened my back and looked her in the eyes. I had to live for the both of us, and I needed to show her that. "I'm sorry for the pain I've caused your family."

A tear dripped from her lid. Her hands shook and grabbed the doorframe. She didn't say anything, but her head nodded just slightly. "Get out of here."

I turned and walked down the steps to the car. She watched as I sat down and put on my seatbelt; then her stare shifted to Mark. So many nights she had stood in the doorway and watched Eric and me drive away. I knew she was wishing her son were in the driver's seat. If that meant he would still be alive, then so did I.

CHAPTER
THIRTY-EIGHT

As I lay in bed that night, the conversation I'd had with Jesse replayed in my mind. Mark and I hadn't had much time alone since coming to Maine, but that was only part of the reason I hadn't told him I was moving to Florida. The other part was that I was scared of what he would say. I didn't want my news to be the end of our relationship, but how could it not be? Long distance wouldn't work. I couldn't take a weekend off every month to fly to Boston, and neither could Mark; Friday and Saturday were the busiest nights at the bar.

By keeping this from him, I was no better than Asher had been with me. Mark deserved more than that. I turned on the side lamp and shook him awake. "We need to talk."

Suddenly, the dinner I'd eaten wasn't setting well in my stomach. Blood rushed to my face, my hands shook, and my bottom lip dropped.

He rubbed the sleep out of his eyes. "Nicole, are you OK?"

"I should have told you before we came to Maine. I just didn't want to fuck everything up."

"What are you talking about?" He reached for my fingers. "Nothing you can say will fuck anything up."

"This will."

"You're starting to scare me."

I took a deep breath. It didn't help. "Mark, I'm moving to Florida."

He didn't release my hands as I told him about my meeting with

Allison and her phone call, but his expression changed. It became distant, and there was pain in his eyes.

"You're my best friend. I want to be with you forever," I said. "But I can't let my feelings for you stop me from doing what's best for me."

"Nic—"

"Boston is my past, and no matter what I do, I can't seem to escape it. It keeps haunting me. I don't think I'll be able to move on unless I get out of there."

"Baby—"

"That doesn't excuse what I did, though. I kept something from you that affects our future; I shouldn't have done that. I should have discussed it with you before I made a decision. I'm so sorry—"

"Will you give me a chance to talk, please?"

I nodded.

"I accept all of you. And if that means you need to leave the city, then I'm OK with that. Boston isn't the right place for you. I've known that since the day I heard you got out of jail."

"What are you saying?"

"I'm saying I support whatever decision you have to make."

"Does that mean this is the end of us?"

"Of course not. There is no end to us."

I threw my arms around his neck and buried my face in his skin. I couldn't change the way I'd handled things, but I could learn from it. Mark was a part of me, and he deserved a voice when it came to my decisions, especially one as big as this. Discussing my move with him earlier on wouldn't have made my trip to Maine any easier, but I would have felt less guilty lying next to him at night.

I wasn't going to ask him to move with me. At least not yet. He needed time to think about everything. Plus, I didn't want to put that kind of pressure on him. As long as this wasn't the end of us, I could handle whatever he decided. Even if that meant traveling back and forth as much as we could.

He pushed me back against the pillows and kissed me. A moan escaped his lips, and his hands traveled up my tank and around my breast.

"My parents are in the next room," I said.

"I'll try to be quiet."

"We should go into the closet." I pulled back the covers and climbed out of bed, opening the door to the walk-in.

"The closet? Is that where you took your high school boyfriends?"

I laughed. Then winked.

*   *   *

Mark had planned something for our last day in Bangor, but he wouldn't tell me what it was. He just said to dress warmly. When I met him downstairs, he had my jacket and a cooler in his hands. I kissed my parents and Jesse, and they smiled as Mark escorted me to the front door. When he pulled out of the driveway, I asked why the others weren't coming too.

He turned on the music and his fingers went to my thigh. "Your dad has a meeting, and your mom is taking Jesse shopping. I thought we could use some time away from the house."

"I agree."

I was an easy person to surprise except when it came to Bangor because I knew the area so well. Mark didn't stay in town, though. He drove through Brewer and onto Route 1A. There was only one place this road led to that was even worth visiting, and that was Bar Harbor.

Mark didn't pull in to the village or by the harbor like I'd expected. He turned onto Route 3 to Mount Desert Island and into Acadia National Park to drive up Cadillac Mountain. The only traveling I'd ever done was when Michael and I still lived at home. My parents took us to the Caribbean, Disney World, and Vermont, but the top of this mountain was the most beautiful place I'd ever been.

Mark carried the cooler and a blanket, and we found a flat surface in the middle of the mountain. He covered the rock and unpacked the lunch he'd made: ham and cheese sandwiches, a bag of chips, and two cans of Coke. Because it was chilly and tourist season was over, we had the mountaintop mostly to ourselves. The sun peeked through the clouds, the rays reflecting off the ocean.

"This is amazing," I said.

Throughout the week leading up to this trip, my anxiety had been intense. I wasn't sure how I'd feel when I got to my parents' house after being away for so long; the emotions of going into Michael's room, the way my dad's coworkers would treat me at the party, and whether my brother's grave might affect me in ways I hadn't expected. The cemetery was the closure I needed, but it had left me raw. Another sleepless night followed. My body was worn out from Mark, but my head swarmed with thoughts from my past—why I'd been in jail during Michael's funeral and what had led me there. It was the same thing that put him in the ground. Being here cleared all that. It gave me a chance to breathe.

"Since you described this mountain, I've always wanted to come. I'm glad my first time is with you."

I smirked. "At least I could be your first for something." I took a bite of my sandwich and noticed he hadn't touched his. "Aren't you going to eat?"

"Come with me," he said. He stuck out his hand for me to grab. "Let's make it two firsts."

I didn't know what he meant, but I let him guide me down the rocks. We stopped at the edge of one of the peaks. There was a canopy of trees below us, and the leaves were almost every color of the rainbow. The dark water looked endless, and tiny islands popped up through its surface. Mark stood behind me, his hands on my stomach, and I tasted the salty air. It reminded me of when my parents had taken Michael and me to Bar Harbor every summer. We'd sit outside by the water, eating steamers, lobsters, and whoopie pies. We'd laugh throughout the whole meal—one of us always spilled the butter on our first dip, and it would land on our lap. Mom learned to bring a change of clothes for each of us.

Mark pressed his lips against my ear. "I love you."

Whenever he said those words, it felt like the first time all over again. My stomach tingled, and there was a flutter in my chest.

"I love you, too."

"You were made for me."

I smiled and closed my eyes, relaxing against his body. I could feel his heart beating through my jacket.

There had been only a few times in my life when I'd wanted to stop time from moving forward. This was one of them. The conversation about whether Mark was going to move to Florida needed to happen, and I was dreading it. But I didn't want to think about that. I wanted to take in my surroundings, Mark's breath, his words...and let them simmer for a moment.

But I couldn't.

"Have you thought about our conversation last night?" I asked.

"I've thought about it."

"And?"

"Are you asking me to move with you?"

I turned, then, and put my hands on his cheeks. "Mark, will you move to Florida with me?"

"Before I answer that," he said, "Nicole, you make me a better man. You've shown me what it feels like to be loved, and you've accepted me unconditionally." He took my hands off his face, moved to my side, and kneeled down on the rock. "I've wanted to do this since the day you chose me; I was just waiting for the right time. I think that time is now." He reached inside his jacket and pulled out a black box. He opened it. And there was a diamond ring inside. "Will you marry me?"

My eyes blurred from the tears. The tingling in my stomach and the fluttering in my chest returned. My feet felt unsteady on the jagged ledge. There was no hesitation. I knew exactly what I wanted.

"Yes, of course. Of course I'll marry you!"

He slid the ring on my finger and lifted me into the air. My smile was as wide as his, and it landed on his lips. My fingers gripped his hair, pulling him even closer. My legs wrapped around his waist and squeezed. We kissed all the way back to the blanket.

"I think I can breathe now," he said after he set me down. He picked up his sandwich and took a bite.

"You're really going to give up everything to come with me?" I asked.

"I asked you to marry me. That means I accept all of you. If I need to move to Florida to be with you, then that's what I'm going to do."

I looked down at the ring. It was a square diamond set in platinum, and little diamonds ran all the way around the band. Cadillac Mountain was beautiful, but it didn't compare to this ring. I spread my fingers apart and held my hand in the air. I blinked. Each time I opened my eyes, it was still there. It wasn't going to disappear. All those nights I had lain in my prison bed, this was what I had dreamed of—marriage and a family of my own. It was finally coming true.

I climbed into his lap and wrapped my arms around his neck. I'd already told him how much I loved him right before he proposed. But I told him again. And again.

* * *

Three weeks later, Mark pulled into Logan Airport and parked at the departures entrance. Everything I owned was in the two suitcases that he lifted out of the trunk. It was hard to believe that less than a month ago we had been in Maine. We had stayed an extra day to celebrate our engagement with my family, and once we got back to Boston, I'd accepted Allison's offer.

In the days that followed, Mark and I spent every possible moment together, planning the next six months. We both decided I should be a housemother in sober living instead of getting an apartment; neither of us liked the idea of me living alone. Mark was going to get his house ready to sell and would set up a more reliable computer system that would allow him to work from Florida. He wanted to keep the bars for as long as he could, they were doing so well, and he even mentioned opening one down south. We looked online at houses near the rehab center that we could buy after his sold, and we talked about what furniture—his and Michael's—we would move to our new place.

I stood on the sidewalk next to my bags and put my hands on his shoulders. "I'll see you in a month?"

"Twenty-eight days, babe. It will go by so fast."

"I don't know about that. Once-a-month visits don't seem like enough."

"You won't be able to forget me, not after what I did to you this morning."

I smiled and leaned into his lips. We'd done so much talking over the past few weeks; I knew exactly how he felt about our future and how many hours it would be until I was in his arms again. What

I wanted now was a kiss that would keep me going for another twenty-eight days. And he gave me just that.

"I don't want to miss my flight," I said. His lips made me hungry for him again. If I didn't leave now, I never would.

I gave him one more kiss, told him I loved him, and rolled my bags into the airport. I didn't look back. I didn't need to see his face, the fingers he would wave, or the love in his eyes. I'd memorized all of it. Just like when the plane looped around the city, I knew exactly what was below. Boston was a city I'd never forget. It was tattooed on my foot, it was my past, and it was where I'd found my first love. Heroin. I couldn't take any of it back, and I accepted that. But what had happened in this city wasn't going to define the person I would become.

I didn't know if I'd return, if I'd ever again walk through the streets of the North End, Back Bay, South End, Roxbury, or Dorchester and point out to my kids all the places where my memories were born. Some things didn't need to be revisited. But if they were, I could prove how far I'd come.

Just before I closed the window shade and leaned back into my airplane seat, I took it all in...the skyscrapers, the park, the harbor, and the heroin...and I said the word I'd always feared. It was permanent. But I was all right with that.

Good-bye, Boston.

CHAPTER
THIRTY-NINE

My last patient closed the door on his way out of my office. This had been his twelfth session, and I hadn't cracked him yet. He didn't believe he had an addiction; he thought he could stop using meth anytime he wanted. His wife had filed for divorce and moved their kids into her mother's house. The drug had already cost him his family and almost his life. During a five-day binge, he had wrapped his car around a palm tree, and the judge had given him the choice of jail or rehab. I'd worked with enough addicts to know which ones were committed to the program and who would relapse right after graduation. He hadn't reached his rock bottom; sadly, death would probably come first.

I charted several paragraphs of notes, detailing our last one-on-one, and shut down my computer. My ankles were throbbing, and I lifted one to rub. I had stayed off my feet for most of the day, but the humidity was making them swell even more. As I massaged my calf, the wedding picture on my desk reminded me that I had to pick up dinner. Grouper? Steak? I couldn't recall what Mark had said he wanted to grill. These long nights and lack of sleep were making me forgetful. Thankfully, I had only a month to go until my master's degree was complete.

With my briefcase looped over my shoulder and keys in hand, I locked the door and went into the lobby. Pat, who was working behind the desk, handed me tomorrow's schedule. "Did you hear about Santos?" he asked.

I reviewed my appointments and shook my head.

"He was released last week. Something about good behavior; can you imagine?"

"I wish he would have shown that good behavior in here."

Santos was one of my first patients after I was hired full-time. He was addicted to bath salts and was in a psychosis at the time of his admission. He refused to wear clothes—they harbored nests of bugs, he said—and he threatened our staff. He was later transferred to another facility, but he made quite the scene in the lobby before his departure. He broke a framed painting and tried to slash his wrists with the glass.

"I'll see you in the morning," Pat said.

The grocery store was only a few blocks away, and I found a parking spot near the front. It was in the nineties outside, but inside it was at least fifteen degrees cooler. That was the problem with Florida summers: a layer of sweat covered your body as soon as you stepped into the sun, yet you dressed in winter clothes so you wouldn't freeze from the air conditioning. I filled the basket with three sweet potatoes and a head of broccoli and then stood between the fish and meat cases. The thought of grouper's flaky consistency made me want to gag. I asked the butcher to cut me three pounds of fillet. After he handed me the wrapped meat, I moved to the checkout line.

The cashier swiped the steak across the scanner. Then she looked at my belly and smiled. "When are you due?"

I dug my fingers into my back, trying to relieve some of the pain. "Three weeks."

"Not soon enough, right?"

"Exactly! The little one doesn't know the difference between day and night, and neither does my bladder."

"Is this your first?"

I nodded. "How about you?"

I normally didn't ask a stranger if she was pregnant. But the cashier was petite, except for her stomach, and she had that glow.

"My fourth—and my last," she said. "Do you know what you're having?"

"We wanted to wait. We like surprises."

She laughed. "Oh, you're in for a surprise, all right."

"That's what I hear."

I thanked her as she handed me my receipt, and I waddled back to my car. The traffic was heavy along the beach. August was when Europeans took their holiday, and for the entire month, the town was packed with tourists. I didn't mind, though. The sun shined down on the dark water, and teal waves splashed along the sand. Parents were making sandcastles with their kids. In a year or two, Mark and I would be doing the same. That was, if I could take the weekends off; work was getting busier. The rehab center was adding on a new wing to house more patients and was acquiring six more apartments for the sober living program. I managed and counseled the housemothers, and the results of the drug tests—from the residents *and* the housemothers—were sent to me. Drug testing was a procedure I had implemented soon after getting hired. I wasn't going to let a situation like Tiffany's happen again. My graduates needed a sober mentor; if the housemothers didn't test clean, they were removed from the apartment and offered another chance at rehab.

I drove past the spot on the beach where just three years ago, Mark and I had exchanged our vows. It was an intimate ceremony, officiated by a justice of the peace, and only our closest friends and family attended. Al served as Mark's best man, and Jesse was my man of honor. Diem's daughter was our flower girl. Since leaving sober living, Diem had stayed clean and gotten married. Shortly after her daughter was born, she got divorced, moved to our coast, and opened a clothing boutique. We lived minutes from each other and were best friends.

The morning after the wedding reception, Mark and I flew to the Bahamas and spent a week there. When we got back, I found out I was pregnant. That was the first of three miscarriages. We stopped trying after that; the pain became too much for us—especially for Mark. He was so hopeful every time I got pregnant, and the letdown destroyed him. Six months ago the doctor confirmed the pregnancy tests I'd taken at home. We didn't have any expectations, and this turned out to be the one.

As I grabbed the groceries out of the trunk, the sun shone down on my fingers, and Claire's band sparkled. I hadn't taken it off since the morning I'd graduated rehab over five years ago. It was a little too tight, but I insisted on wearing it. My ankles weren't the only things that had swelled from this pregnancy. I was thirty-three years old, was happily married, had a career and an almost complete master's degree, and would be a mother in a month. But sometimes I needed to be reminded of where I came from. Claire's ring did that for me. It brought back memories of my time on the streets—of how the high had never been enough, of all the people I'd lost to my addiction.

I set the groceries on the counter and walked through the family room, stopping in the doorway of the nursery. I was always the first one home from work, and for the few minutes I had alone, that was where I spent my time. It had taken us months to finish it. We hired an artist to paint an animal mural on the wall, assembled the furniture, and chose neutral colors. The chocolate furniture was a bit masculine, but that was because I was secretly hoping I was having a boy. Our real estate agent's name was Michael, and she was the first female I'd met with that name. If we had a daughter, she would be Michael too.

I heard footsteps on the tile and closed my eyes, waiting for Mark's arms to wrap around my belly. They didn't. They touched the base of my neck, and I took a deep breath, trying to inhale his scent.

"I told you I'd see you one day."

My eyes shot open. It wasn't Mark's voice; it was deeper, with an accent. Panic blasted through me as I tried to place his voice. My knees became weak, my stomach churned.

"Que?"

His fingers dug into my throat, and he stabbed something into the side of my neck. "Surprised that I found you?"

"Please don't hurt me," I begged. "My husband will be home any second—"

"He won't be here for another fifteen minutes."

How did he know that? Did he have someone following Mark?

"I'll give you anything you want; just don't hurt me."

"Shut up!"

Tears streaked down my face; I could taste the mascara on my lips. I was too big to try to escape his hold. But even if I weren't eight months pregnant, I wouldn't have been able to escape the gun he was driving into my neck.

In school, I was trained to handle hostile situations, but nothing could have prepared me for this. Still, I knew that if I could keep him talking, I would have a better chance of surviving.

"You don't know anything about me, what I do for others, how I coordinate rescue missions to get addicts—like Renee and I had been—off the streets and into rehab...and how I can help you."

"I told you to shut up!" He pushed the gun even harder against my skin. "Don't you dare mention her name."

I cried out in pain. "I have a baby inside me—"

"You think I care about your baby? You didn't give a fuck about my baby when you had Renee killed, did you?"

"Of course I cared about your child. I love children—"

"Renee was my baby's mama, and you fucking took her from me."

"I didn't have anything to do with it. It was all Dustin, I swear. Renee set me up and got me in trouble with your cousin, and when Dustin found out, he flipped. He went to find her—that's when he killed her. I wasn't even there—"

"It's too late for explanations," he said and laughed. "You took my family away from me, and now I'm going to take yours."

The last thing I heard was the gunshot. My tears weren't caused by my blurred vision. It was the animal mural, the baby mobile, and the crib passing by my eyes. I hit the carpet.

My mind drifted to Mark, hoping desperately he wouldn't be killed when he came through our front door, and to our baby, praying the little one wouldn't die with me. I hadn't been able to escape my past, but the years I'd had since making the right choices were the best I'd ever had...with my mind finally free to see the love that was always waiting for me. Mark and my baby were my true loves. Not heroin. Dope had led me straight into the darkness...left me with scars. Now it was singing me a lullaby.

Pain seared my muscles. Something came out of my lips. And finally, there was nothing but darkness.

EPILOGUE

I had waited years for this moment, and now that it was here, my stomach was in knots. Mommy-D—that's what I called Diem, the only mother I had ever known—had taken my angel pendant out of my hand and pinned it to my shirt when we'd left the hotel this morning. I'd squeezed it for good luck as we passed through the metal detector at the prison's entrance, and I held it now as I waited outside the double doors. The pin was warm from my touch and seemed to calm my stomach. Dad and Mommy-D had given it to me on my eighth birthday; it symbolized my mother's constant presence with me, and I knew she was here today.

My dad sat next to me. Two months had passed since our trip to Hawaii, and he was still tan. So was my husband, because he had skin just like my dad. My tan never lasted more than a few weeks—I had Mom's complexion—and Mommy-D and my sister covered up so they wouldn't freckle. The trip had been for my parents' anniversary, a date we celebrated every year as a family. It was our time for remembrance of all good things: how Mom was still deeply embedded in our hearts, how strong we all were, and how much love there was now between Dad and Mommy-D.

A woman opened the double doors and asked us to come in. We sat across from her and two men dressed in suits. They introduced themselves, spreading some papers out in front of them, but I forgot the first two names as quickly as they said them. I remembered Jocelyn—her name was the same as that of the first patient I had ever treated at the rehab center. I'd found her during one of our community outreach programs and had stopped her from overdosing on heroin. She later became a housemother at one of our sober living facilities, and in a few months I would be attending her wedding.

The three of them glanced over the paperwork; when they were done, they signaled the guard at the far wall. The door creaked as it opened. For several seconds, feet shuffled against the concrete floor and steel rattled as the chains rubbed together, and then Que appeared.

Jocelyn pointed to the end of the table. "Please place Mr. Sanchez right there."

I knew I would have to look Que in the eyes, at some point, and remind him of what he had done to my mother, to my family. I wasn't ready to do that yet, so I stared at my father. Dad's jaw was clamped shut; the bones in his cheeks moved as he ground his teeth and glared at him. Twenty-five years had passed since Mom's death, and we were all in a good place—my husband and I had just closed on a townhouse, Dad volunteered every Sunday at the rehab center, and he and Mommy-D were looking at beautiful houses in Arizona where they'd retire soon—but Que triggered memories that brought out emotions in us.

"Ms. Nicole Conrad," Jocelyn said, "is there anything you would like to say to the prisoner?"

I took a few deep breaths, stood, and turned toward him. I didn't want him to know how badly he'd hurt me by taking the mother I'd never known, so I pushed back my shoulders and stared right at him. He had aged quite a bit from the pictures I'd seen in the newspaper clippings, but there was still evil in his eyes and no remorse in his expression.

His gaze penetrated my face...only for a few moments, and then he looked away. Maybe he was surprised that I had been named after my mother, or turned off by how much I looked like her.

He knew the story. I was going to remind him anyway. "You almost killed me; it's a miracle I'm still alive. The first bullet missed, and the second grazed just above me. I wish I could say the same for my mother, but she died when the doctors tried to remove the bullets. I spent the first three months of my life in the NICU. If she hadn't been so far along in her pregnancy, you would have murdered us both." My father grabbed my fingers and squeezed. "You've been in jail for twenty-five years, and that isn't nearly enough time. I've met people whose life my mother touched for good. What you are is a murderer, drug dealer, and gang member. And even worse, you cut down those who chose to break away from the evil you introduced them to. You deserve to spend the rest of your life in here. And as you waste away, I hope you're haunted by my mother's face, a good woman you shot in cold blood, and by all the addicts who died from the drugs you sold them."

I turned my back to him and looked into the eyes of the parole board. "Do you want a man like him living near your children? Shopping at the same stores as your wives or husbands? Because this isn't his first heinous crime, and you can tell by his face that he isn't sorry for what he's done. I beg of you, please, don't grant him parole."

I sat down, and before my father released my hand, he pulled it up to his mouth and kissed my knuckles.

"Mr. Mark Lucido, would you like to address Mr. Sanchez?"

My father remained seated, his fingers clinging to the armrest. He probably didn't trust himself to stand. I didn't blame him; Dad wasn't a violent person, but Que had murdered my mother. Dad had been unable to protect us, and I knew the emotions from that horrific period of his life were resurfacing as he viewed this perpetrator of such evil.

Dad cleared his throat and turned toward him. "Nicole wasn't just my best friend and the woman I loved. She was my breath. My home. My everything. You took her from me and shattered my reason for being. If my daughter hadn't survived, I don't know if I would have either.

"Do you know the woman my wife turned out to be? The amazing person she became? She didn't have an easy life, but she used her past to make a difference. She dedicated all her time to changing lives and giving addicts hope. And she didn't deserve to die—not my baby—and you didn't have the right to play God. You selfish son-of-a-bitch, you took my angel from me; I hope, God I hope, they don't have mercy on your soul."

I lifted his hand off the armrest, wrapped my fingers around it, and pulled it up to my lips, kissing his skin the way he had done to mine. I couldn't remember the last time my father had been this stirred up. There was always happiness in his voice whenever he talked about Mom, especially when he would tell me about her pregnancy—the peanut-butter and pickle sandwiches she had eaten every day and the early morning walks they would take on the beach because her ankles would swell up at night. Mom was his first love; they had moved to Florida because she wanted a fresh start, and being here probably reminded him of that. As he learned, regardless of where they lived or how hard she tried, she couldn't completely escape her past.

Diem had been my mother's best friend; after the shooting, she'd helped with everything. She arranged the funeral, took care of my dad and me, even ran Dad's bar when he couldn't bring himself to go to work. They grieved together, they eased each other's pain, they told me stories about my mom, and eventually they fell in love. That was partly because of me. When I was three, Dad sold the bar and house in Florida and we moved back to Boston. He wanted to be closer to Uncle Al, Uncle Jesse, and Nana and Papa so they could help raise me. But I asked for Diem every day. I cried for her daughter, Shay—my soul-sister. Diem came for a visit, and she never left.

"Mr. Que Sanchez, is there anything you would like to say?" Jocelyn asked.

Que's eyes darted between my father's and mine. He opened his mouth, but no words came out. He shook his head. Nothing.

Jocelyn asked us to wait in the hallway while they discussed the case. Que was removed as well. I leaned against the wall next to Dad. I wanted to say something—anything that would break the silence—but I didn't have any words. At least not yet.

Jocelyn stuck her head out the door and asked us to come back in. We took our seats, and Que was shackled into his chair. The paperwork was piled in front of her, and next to the stack were two stamps. She chose the one closest to her and pressed it onto the top sheet. She removed it, "DENIED" stamped in red capital letters.

"After careful consideration," she said and paused, "we've come to a unanimous decision. Mr. Que Sanchez, your request for parole has been denied."

Que didn't make eye contact with my father or me. His expression didn't change. And when the guard lifted him out of the chair, he turned his back and shuffled out of the room.

My father wrapped his arms around me, and I squeezed as hard as I could. My tears fell onto his collar, and I used my sleeve to wipe my eyes.

"I can't wait to tell your mom," Dad whispered.

We had agreed to make one stop before the four of us headed back home to Boston. The beach close to our old house was where my family had scattered Mom's ashes, and we wanted to visit her again. When I was younger, Dad and Mommy-D would take me to the beaches near Boston. As we swam and made castles, they would always tell me that a piece of my mom was in the water and in every grain of sand. But Mom wasn't just on the beaches. She was in the air and sprinkled across the sun. She was in Dad's heart and in Diem's touch. She was in me.

"Neither can I," I whispered back. "Neither can I."

T H E   E N D

MORE GREAT READS FROM BOOKTROPE

Sweet Song, by **Terry Persun** (Historical Fiction) This tale of a mixed race man passing as white in post-Civil War America speaks from the heart about where we've come from and who we are.

Ouroboros by **Christopher Turkel** (Science Fiction) In a dystopian future, Thomas the assassin is about to face the job of his career -- and his life.

Billy Purgatory: I Am the Devil Bird by **Jesse James Freeman** (Young Adult Fantasy) A sweet talkin', bad ass skateboarder battles devil birds, time zombies and vampires while pursuing Anastasia, the girl of his dreams (and they aren't all nightmares). Funny and compelling.

Deception Creek, by **Terry Persun** (Coming of Age Novel) Secrets from the past overtake a man who never knew his father. Will old wrongs destroy him or will he rebuild his life?

The Printer's Devil by **Chico Kidd** (Historical Fantasy) a demon summoned long ago by a heartbroken lover in Cromwellian England, now reawakened by a curious scholarly researcher. Who will pay the price?

… and many more!

Sample our books at:
www.booktrope.com

Learn more about our new approach to publishing at:
www.booktropepublishing.com

Made in the USA
Lexington, KY
12 March 2013